I0735379

The Rector's Wedding

The Rector's Wedding

ELENA GRAF

PURPLE HAND PRESS

Purple Hand Press
www.purplehandpress.com
© 2022 by Elena Graf

This is a work of fiction. Names, characters, places and incidents are the product of the author's imagination or used fictitiously, and any resemblance to actual persons, living or dead, businesses, institutions, companies, events, or locales is entirely coincidental.

Trade Paperback Edition
ISBN-13 978-1-953195-16-6
Kindle Edition
ISBN-13 978-1-953195-17-3
ePub Edition
ISBN-13 978-1-953195-18-0

Cover photo © creativecommonsstockphotos | Stock Free Images, used under Creative Commons (CC0) public domain license.
Editor: Elaine Mattern

07.20.2022

To Sheila

PART I

LENT

1

Lucy Bartlett watched the early morning joggers pound Central Park's winding paths. The late winter colors of the landscape below were dark and dull. The naked trees were gray. The roadways had been treated with salt and looked like the ashes Liz raked out of the wood stove in the morning. Here and there, a few patches of sooty snow relieved the bleak scene.

The view from the sixteenth floor of the Plaza Hotel was certainly different from the one Lucy usually saw in the morning. The blaze of brilliant colors in the sky made it worth getting up early. Even on cloudy days, the ocean was mysterious and beautiful.

Lucy loved living in Maine, but traveling the world as an opera singer had left her with cosmopolitan tastes. She'd missed New York's round-the-clock energy, its avant-garde restaurants, and the music, especially the music. Tomorrow night, they would hear one of her favorite operas, Verdi's *Don Carlos* at the Met. She could hardly wait, although it occasionally saddened her to sit in the opera house she'd once called her musical home, but only because it hadn't been her choice to leave.

"Taking in the view?" asked Liz, slipping on her jacket. She looked elegant in a stylish suit and high heels, so different from her usual casual appearance. She stood beside Lucy at the window. "Not much to see at this time of year. The city in winter looks so desolate."

"Manhattan has its own beauty." Lucy gazed at the orange reflection of the rising sun on the windows of the buildings surrounding the park. "I'm glad we're staying the weekend."

"I reserved this room for our honeymoon. The view from here isn't as good as when I proposed."

Lucy nudged Liz with her hip. "*I* proposed."

"I gave you the ring. You said the words."

"So, let's say that we proposed to each other."

"I like my version better," insisted Liz.

"Of course, you do, because it fits your narrative about yourself."

Liz frowned, looking unsure what to think about that statement, but Lucy had no intention of explaining it on such a busy morning. She took a teardrop-shaped, leather case out of her bag.

"Here. I could use your help. I can't keep my hands from shaking."

"That's hard to believe. You're always so confident." Liz located the latch and snapped open the box. She studied the collection of white clerical collars and the gold and silver studs neatly arranged in compartments. "Linen, because it's a formal occasion. Right?"

"One of the biggest days of my life. I wasn't even this nervous before my Met debut."

"That's probably because you didn't have time to think about it. An understudy might hope to step into a starring role and become a big success, but who actually lives the dream?"

"People say I've lived a charmed life. God always shows me the way."

Liz pointedly cleared her throat. She had limited patience for God talk. She fished in the collar box and chose the studs she'd given Lucy as a birthday gift. They were solid gold, shipped at great expense from England. Liz had ordered three pairs to justify paying the exorbitant postage.

Lucy's mind drifted back to that perfect summer evening. Maggie had made an extravagant dinner and baked a fancy cake. They'd ended up drinking too much wine and singing Broadway duets in full voice. Good thing Liz had no close neighbors.

Another time. Another life. Before Erika. Before the dark winter.

"I'm surprised you haven't lost these yet," said Liz in a mildly scolding tone, separating the back from the stud. Lucy had to admit the little dig was deserved. She usually took off her collar the minute she went off duty, which meant she lost her collar pins almost as often as she lost earring backs. Sometimes, the errant jewelry turned up under the bed or in the washing machine. But Lucy always carefully replaced the gold studs in their holder because they were from Liz.

Liz studied the mechanics of the collar trying to figure out how it attached. Lucy decided not to interfere, trusting Liz's uncanny ability to assemble and disassemble things in her mind. "The front stud goes in first. Right?" Liz asked.

"Yes, through the hole in the inner band. Then through here." Lucy pointed to the double buttonholes in the collar of her black blouse.

"You must really be nervous. Don't you do this every day?" Liz asked, inserting the stud.

"Yes, but it's not every day I defend my doctoral dissertation, which we both know will be controversial."

"Sex and religion are a volatile mix. But you've got your mentor there to support you, and your own cheering section. Tom is coming, and Emily. And you really know your stuff. You'll be fine." Liz got the front of the collar fastened and went around to the back. Lucy was wearing her red hair up today, so it should be easy for Liz to find the buttonhole where the collar fastened in the back. "There, that should do it," said Liz with satisfaction.

Lucy felt the warm press of lips on her neck. She closed her eyes to savor the delicious sensation. "Sweetheart, that feels really good, but we don't have time now."

"I know, but I couldn't resist. I love your freckles." Liz handed back the collar box.

"Thank you again for ironing the linen collars. You do it perfectly, just like Erika."

"It's that Teutonic attention to detail. My grandmother taught me how to iron. I practiced on my father's shirts. I even had to iron his cotton boxers. But don't get used to it. I only did it for you because it's a special occasion."

"Liz, I know some people take advantage of you. But I don't love you for what you can do for me. I love you for being you."

Liz still looked skeptical, so Lucy took Liz's face in her hands and pulled her down into a kiss. She kept it brief to avoid smearing her lipstick. When their lips parted, Liz's blue eyes looked dreamy. She leaned down, obviously hoping for more, but Lucy held her back by the shoulders. "When we're alone later, I promise to kiss you until you beg me to stop." She glanced suggestively at Liz's crotch and raised an auburn brow.

"You know I'll hold you to that promise." Liz picked up Lucy's black suit jacket and carefully brushed off the shoulders. She held it up so Lucy could slip her arms into the sleeves. "Ready?" Liz slung the strap of Lucy's laptop case over her shoulder. "Onward, Christian soldiers!" It was one of Lucy's least favorite hymns, but the tune inserted itself into her mind and continued playing annoyingly while they waited for the elevator.

After the elevator door shut, Liz reached out for Lucy's hand. "You know how you always try to bless me whenever we get into an elevator? Today, I feel I should bless you."

"Well, you can. I might be ordained, but that doesn't necessarily make my blessings count more than yours. Blessings are a wish for God to grant someone grace. Of course, God gives us grace without being asked, but it feels good for us humans to think we have influence."

"Spoken like a true theologian." Liz turned to engage Lucy's eyes. "But what if I don't believe in God?"

Lucy moved closer. "Liz, you don't have to pretend with me anymore," she said in a whisper.

"Pretend what?"

"About being an atheist. I know your secret."

"No, you don't. Even I don't know what I believe."

Lucy patted Liz's arm. "You're a smart person. You'll figure it out."

The elevator door opened onto the lobby. "Do you mind if we take a cab uptown?" Liz asked. "That way, we won't have to wait for the valet, and I won't have to worry about finding parking."

Lucy made a little bow. "I put myself in your capable hands, Dr. Stolz."

When they went outside, there was a taxi waiting in the queue. Liz gave the driver the address of the seminary. When he made the turn to go through Central Park, she glowered into his rear-view mirror. Lucy knew what she was thinking. The Henry Hudson Parkway would have been faster.

"Don't worry. We have plenty of time," she said, as much to soothe her own nerves as to reassure Liz, who pulled back her sleeve to look at her watch. When she wore the gold Cartier that Yale had given her on her retirement with hiking clothes, it seemed out of place. At least today it went with her outfit.

Lucy hummed softly while the cab made its way uptown. Music always relaxed her. Fortunately, the traffic was light, and they were making good time.

"It's a shame Erika's not here," said Liz. "She put you up to this adventure. She would have been so proud of you today."

Lucy sighed and embraced Erika in her mind, feeling that little ache she always felt when she thought of her. She blinked away the tears that started to form. Today was a day for joy and triumph, not sadness.

"I'm sure Erika will be sitting right beside you," said Lucy.

"Of course, she will, and we'll discuss the quality of your arguments."

"And find them lacking, I'm sure."

"No, you've learned to stay on point. Just answer the question, and only the question. Like when we were testifying in the adoption hearing for Brenda and Cherie. Remember what Melissa said. Don't elaborate unless specifically asked to. Otherwise, you'll be tempted to go off on one of your tangents."

"Any other unsolicited advice, Dr. Stolz?" asked Lucy, pinching Liz's thigh.

"No, I think that's enough. I don't want to erode your confidence."

"Nice of you to think of it now, after the damage is done." Lucy smiled to take the sting out of the criticism.

"Do you want me to pull right up to the front door?" asked the cabbie as they approached the campus.

"You can let us off across the street instead of making a U-turn," Liz replied.

Hastings Hall came into view. "I always feel strange coming here," said Lucy, admiring the elaborate tower, "as if I don't really belong. Like I'm an imposter."

"For years after I became chief of surgery at Yale, I felt the same. Girls aren't supposed to do what we do, or at least not when we were growing up."

"It took so long to get my divinity degree, I thought I'd never be ordained. I couldn't go full time because I was still trying to revive my career. I was overseas too much and had to drop courses, sometimes in the middle of the semester. Susan took notes for me, but it wasn't enough. In those days, you had to show up for class."

"Susan. I wonder how she's doing. Have you heard from her?"

"Yes, we talked on the phone the other day. She said she's tired of the long winters in South Dakota and wants to come back to New England."

Liz's left brow went up slightly. She was skeptical. Probably she didn't approve, but she wouldn't say it outright. "How do you feel about her coming back?"

"I want her to be happy and fulfill her God-given potential, and she's been working hard to get herself together. She's been faithfully attending AA meetings, and she's been in therapy to reconcile her sexual identity with her beliefs. She says she's changed."

Lucy saw the frank worry in Liz's blue eyes. "She made a lot of trouble for you last summer. She tried to break us up. Are you sure you want her around?"

"No, but I don't think she poses as much danger as you seem to think." Lucy turned away to avoid Liz's steady gaze. "She congratulated me when I told her we were engaged."

"That's what she's supposed to say, but did she really mean it?"

"I don't know, but I don't want to talk about it now. I'm anxious enough."

Liz opened her mouth to speak but thought better of it. "Okay. We can talk about it later."

Lucy didn't want to talk about it later or any time. The subject of Susan was controversial, no matter how much Liz pretended to be understanding.

The driver pulled up to the curb, and Liz dropped her credit card into the little tilting drawer in the partition.

After the taxi drove off, Lucy said, "You don't have to pay for everything."

"I know, but I'm used to it."

"That's because you always beat me to it. I'm not Maggie, and I'm not into role play."

"If you say so," said Liz with a shrug.

"I'm not kidding. We're equals in this relationship or nothing." She gave Liz a stern look for emphasis.

When they entered Hastings Hall, Lucy felt the same feeling of awe as the first time she'd accompanied Susan on a campus visit. The echo in the rotunda still sounded like booming notes in the voice of God.

Apparently, Liz was impressed too. "Do you know where we're going?" she asked in a reverential whisper.

"Yes. It's in one of the big conference rooms. Follow me." Lucy realized Liz was still carrying her laptop bag. "Give me that," she said, tugging on the strap. "People will think you're my porter."

"Well, it's true," said Liz, but she handed over the bag. Their footsteps on the highly polished floors echoed against the neo-Gothic walls as they headed down the hall. Lucy knew she was in the right place when she saw a knot of men in black suits and clerical collars gathered outside the door. She recognized them as the examiners and her advisor, Jerry Spangler.

"Do you want me to disappear while you schmooze with the enemy?" Liz asked, eyeing them with a frown.

"No, of course not. I'm going to introduce you as my fiancée."

Lucy watched Liz slip into what she'd come to recognize as her professional persona. Unfortunately, that, combined with her exceptional height, could make her seem forbidding. When they approached, the men stopped talking and stared at Liz.

"Good morning, gentlemen," Lucy said with a brilliant smile. She saw it instantly mirrored on their faces.

"Good morning, Rev. Bartlett," replied Professor Hernandez, the chief examiner. Liz liked to call him "the Grand Inquisitor," and his strong Spanish accent made the irreverent name even more apt. He'd been a

Catholic priest in South America, but he'd left the priesthood to marry a nun. Although his writings showed a wholehearted commitment to "liberation theology," he was conservative on doctrine related to sexuality. Lucy dreaded the questions he might ask.

"We are very much looking forward to discussing your paper," he said, reaching for Lucy's hand. "It is so unusual to have a dissertation that has already been accepted by a publisher. Does this mean we cannot make any recommendations?"

"My editor and I are still working through the manuscript. So, yes, you can recommend changes. I look forward to hearing your suggestions."

Out of the corner of her eye, Lucy saw Liz nod in approval at her diplomatic response.

Professor Spangler came forward and reached out his hand to Liz. "Dr. Stolz, how nice to see you again. Lucy, do you mind if I introduce your fiancée to my colleagues or would you like to do the honors?"

Lucy recognized the offer to lead her through this academic gauntlet. "Thank you, Jerry. Please go ahead."

"Gentlemen, meet Lucy's intended, formerly head of surgery at Yale New Haven, Dr. Elizabeth Stolz. Dr. Stolz now runs a family practice in the Maine town where Lucy is rector."

"I have heard of you, Dr. Stolz," said Dr. Hernandez, coming forward. Did you not give a presentation here on compassionate choices for the dying?"

"Years ago. I was on a panel while I was teaching at NYU. I'm an advocate for death with dignity. We have a law in Maine protecting that right now."

"Yes, but there are many aspects to consider on this subject. It's not as simple as some people think."

"Nothing is as simple as people think," said Liz, raising her chin. Lucy was mildly anxious that Hernandez would presume to lecture her, which could be dangerous. Liz was especially knowledgeable about bioethics and could quote primary sources from memory. With the spotlight focused away from her, Lucy saw an opportunity to escape from the examiners. She managed to catch Liz's eye before she ducked into the conference room.

At the front table sat the one female examiner on the panel. Professor Lewis was a distinguished black theologian, who had also written a book on the theology of sex. Although it had been meticulously documented, it had remained obscure and mostly unread. Lucy was delighted when she'd discovered it in her research. Not surprisingly, Professor Lewis was sitting alone while the men gossiped outside. She nodded when Lucy offered a discreet wave on her way to the candidate's table. Lucy knew she was on her side because they'd corresponded but guessed that as one of the examiners, Professor Lewis needed to maintain her distance.

As Lucy turned, she ran headlong into an extremely tall, red-headed woman.

"Mom," said Emily, clamping Lucy into an awkward, mechanical hug. Lucy had no doubt that it was sincerely meant, but her daughter was on the spectrum and didn't do affection well.

"Hello, sweetheart," said Lucy, squeezing her tight. "Thanks so much for coming."

"Are you kidding? I wouldn't miss this for anything. And I expect you to show up when I defend my thesis." Emily grinned an authentic, emotionally felt grin. Since she'd been studying at Yale and practicing social behavior, she was getting much better at expressing emotion.

"That's a promise," said Lucy. "But I don't understand your theorem, so I'll probably just sit there and smile."

"That's okay. That's what mothers are supposed to do. But I'll explain it to you ahead of time, so you don't feel stupid."

"Thanks. Between you and Liz, I always feel stupid."

Emily frowned. "You're not stupid, Mom. You're smart in a different way."

"Thanks, sweetie. I needed to hear that today."

"Are you nervous?"

"Yes."

"Don't be. I know you'll do great. I really liked your paper, even if I didn't understand it all. Denise explained some things. That helped."

Lucy saw Tom waving from the back. "Are you sitting with Father Tom?"

"Yes. We were waiting for you and Aunt Liz to get here."

"Can you stay the night?" Lucy asked hopefully. "There's an extra bed in our suite."

"I can stay for dinner, but I need to get the last train back to New Haven. I have a class tomorrow." Emily looked over her mother's head toward the examiners' table. "Mom, it looks like they're getting started. I'd better get back to my seat. Good luck. I love you." Emily enfolded her in another suffocating hug. Fortunately, she didn't crush her collar.

Lucy watched the tall redhead retreat to the back of the room. She turned around and saw the examiners taking their seats at the front table. On her way to sit with Tom and Emily, Liz stopped to give Lucy's shoulder an encouraging squeeze. "Your dissertation is brilliant. You are well-prepared, and you've got this," she whispered into her ear. When her warm breath moved away, Lucy felt a chill. She closed her eyes and sent a quick plea to heaven.

***

Tom Simmons stroked his meticulously manicured white beard. "About time you got here," he said, his blue eyes merry as Liz sat down beside him.

"Lucy thought arriving early would make her look too anxious," explained Liz. "How long have you been here?"

"Oh, not long. I drove because I didn't have time to play around with trains and risk being late."

"Who's holding down the fort?"

"Our new deacon. The assistant priest at St. Anne's is on call in case Reshma gets into trouble."

"So, I guess that means you have to get back tonight."

"Unfortunately, I do."

"How about dinner?"

"Maybe if we eat early and I can take a nap this afternoon. It's a long drive back to Maine."

"Lucy says they closed the guest rooms here during the pandemic, but we have an extra room in our suite. We'll be gone all afternoon. Take a nap while we're at the Neue Galerie. Grab some lunch in the hotel coffee shop and charge it to my room."

"I'm sure that suite in the Plaza is already costing you a fortune."

"Oh, it is, but I figure I should start spending my money. Can't take it with me."

Tom grinned. "You could leave it to me."

Liz smacked his knee. "Fat chance. You have plenty of money. Besides, you have a multi-millionaire boyfriend. When are you going to make it official?"

"We're looking at this fall. I don't want to upstage my boss, never mind you. You'd never forgive me. Which reminds me. I have something to tell you later. Don't let me forget."

A loud thump made Liz flinch—Professor Hernandez was testing the microphone. "Could everyone please take your seats? We are about to begin." The volume of conversation in the room gradually subsided until there was silence. "Thank you," he said. His accent gave his voice an exotic quality. "Welcome to the thesis defense of *Divine Eros: Rediscovering Human Sexuality as a Mirror of God's Love* by the Rev. Lucille Bartlett. The author will have five minutes to summarize her arguments to provide the context for our discussion. Please hold your questions for Rev. Bartlett until the end. We will announce when the floor is open." He nodded in Lucy's direction. "Rev. Bartlett, you may begin."

On her way to the podium, Lucy glanced toward the back where her "cheerleaders" sat. Liz gave her an exaggerated, double thumbs up.

"Good morning, everyone, and thank you for coming today. Many people have asked me why I chose to write my dissertation about sex. Obviously, it's a controversial subject. People have widely differing opinions about what is normal and permissible, and what is not. Faith traditions have had a lot to say on sexual morality, not all of it positive or helpful, especially not where women are concerned. Yet our sexuality is part of God's creation and touches all our lives. It is how all of us came to be. One of the reasons I chose to explore this subject is my personal experience of sexual violence. In my former career, I was raped by a colleague I trusted." There was a murmur in the crowd. Lucy paused to let the gravity of her words sink in.

Liz glanced at Emily to see her reaction. Whatever she was thinking didn't show on her face, but Liz was glad that Lucy had finally told her daughter about the circumstances of her conception.

"This incident could have ruined my sexual relationships forever," Lucy continued, "but God had other plans. In an unconventional sexual relationship, one that was forbidden by the Church at the time, I recovered from my trauma and found my self-esteem again. Through love and intimacy, I was healed and inspired to become a priest. That's my story, but all the best stories come from experience. And mine was to experience God's love through human love. Consequently, I was inspired to give careful thought to why religion has often regarded sex and its expression so negatively. This dissertation is the result of that exploration.

"First, I examine how Greek philosophy and apocalyptic expectations influenced the early Church. The Greek idealists held that spirit was superior to our physical nature. The first generation of Christians expected Jesus to return in their lifetime, so they had no use for sex or procreation. Unfortunately, contempt for sexuality and women persisted, along with unrealistic expectations of virtue and purity. To this day, it causes great harm. In my book, I offer a platform on which to build a new attitude toward Christian sexual ethics, one that honors established norms but interprets them in a compassionate and positive way. As an Episcopalian, I use reason and science along with scripture and tradition to support my arguments. I hope you will find them convincing." Lucy nodded in the direction of the examiners. "Thank you."

Liz was tempted to jump up and clap as Lucy headed back to her seat. "She did well," Tom whispered into Liz's ear. "A perfect introduction. Short and sweet, but she hit all her main points."

Professor Hernandez smiled at Lucy. "Thank you for such a succinct summary, Rev. Bartlett. We will allow your mentor, Professor Spangler, the honor of asking the first question."

Liz wondered if Spangler, who was obviously fond of Lucy, would lob her a softball question, but he didn't. "Rev. Bartlett, you discuss Jesus as a sexual being, an idea that has become part of public imagination since speculative fiction like *The DaVinci Code* created a pseudo-historical context for it. Why do you raise this when there is no scriptural mention of Jesus being married or having a sexual relationship?"

"That's a good question. There is no mention in canonically accepted scripture, but there are hints in the Gnostic Gospels and other early Christian documents. However, the main argument for it would be anthropological. It would be considered odd for a Jewish man in the first century C.E. not to be married. In that culture, it was considered a duty to take a wife. According to the Gospels, Jesus was intent on fulfilling the law, so he would have been unlikely to reject such a deeply embedded cultural norm."

"Score one for mom," Emily murmured.

"Rev. Bartlett, you adhere closely to Professor Spangler's materialism in your chapter on the body," said Dr. Lewis. "Can you explain how his work has influenced you?"

Liz tensed, knowing that Lucy had confided in Dr. Lewis that Spangler had warned her to distance herself from his work to avoid an accusation of plagiarism. When Lucy cleared her throat to buy time, the microphone unnaturally magnified the sound.

"I think calling Professor Spangler's theories 'materialism' is a narrow reading of his theology. Professor Spangler never denies the existence of the spiritual realm, but sees it as being fused with the physical world. He points out that the central ritual of our worship is the consecration of earthly food into the body and blood of Christ. The Eucharist anchors the

Christian religious experience squarely in the physical world. I agree with that point of view."

"Rev. Bartlett, on the subject of the Eucharist," Hernandez began, "you say that physical love between committed persons is sacred and liken it to Holy Communion. Obviously, you mean this as a metaphor, but can you explain?"

Liz could see how tense Lucy was in the way she held her shoulders. This was one of the most controversial sections of her book. "In my faith tradition, we don't consider matrimony a sacrament, but others do. I think it is not the ceremony blessing the union that should be a sacrament, but the spiritual and physical love expressed between the partners. The giving of the body during sex is a mirror of Christ giving his body to merge with ours in Communion. The physical bread and wine literally become part of us and sanctify our bodies. In likening sex to Communion, I am speaking metaphorically, but also pointing to something mystical."

"So, sex is always sacred?"

"No, certainly not. People have sex for many reasons—they are consumed by lust, or they want to conceive a child. Maybe they're tense or bored. Some sexual acts like rape, sexual abuse, or sex trafficking for exploitation, are the opposite of sacred, which is why they are considered sinful and, in many cases, criminal."

Tom leaned over to whisper into Liz's ear. "She's Teflon. Did you prep her?"

"Only minimally. Lucy knows her material inside out, and she's a smart woman. Hopefully, this experience will give her more confidence in her intelligence." Someone in the front row turned around and glared at them for talking.

The next examiner was a small, elderly man. "Rev. Bartlett, you spend an entire chapter on St. Paul, especially his negative views on women and sexuality. As a trained therapist yourself, were you ever tempted to psychoanalyze him as some of his critics have?"

Lucy laughed softly. "Of course, I was tempted. Some people say Paul suffered from Geschwind syndrome. Paul does hit many of the marks of frontal lobe epilepsy, but that would amount to diagnosing someone who lived two millennia ago on few facts. Because he had such a profound influence on early Christianity, his misogyny and anti-sex attitudes have found a permanent home in Christian thinking. While I acknowledge Paul's contributions to our tradition, it's my duty to see faith through twenty-first-century eyes."

"Well said!" murmured Tom.

Most of the pointed questions came in the beginning. Lucy skillfully parried them. As Liz had anticipated, the longest discussion was about sex outside of marriage. It got bogged down in what Liz considered theological minutiae. To Lucy's face, she would have plainly called it bullshit.

Lucy remained calm and patiently answered the examiners' questions. After two hours, they ran out of things to ask. Professor Hernandez asked if any of the examiners had suggestions for revision, but they all shook their heads. "And now, I will ask each of the examiners to vote on whether or not to pass this dissertation. Professor Spangler, as Rev. Bartlett's advisor, you may go first."

"Pass," said Spangler.

Hernandez went down the row, first to his right and then to his left. Every vote was to pass. Finally, it was the chief examiner's turn to cast the deciding vote. "Pass. Congratulations, Rev. Bartlett. Your dissertation is accepted by this committee in partial fulfillment of the requirements for the degree of Doctor of Philosophy. We wish you every success with its publication. Now, are there any questions from the audience?"

A young man in the front row raised his hand. "May we applaud now?"

Professor Hernandez laughed. "Yes, of course."

Emily jumped to her feet and clapped enthusiastically. Liz and Tom got up too. After the applause died down, there were a few curious questions. Finally, Hernandez ended the session by thanking the examiners and the audience. "And special thanks to Rev. Bartlett for writing such a thought-provoking dissertation."

Well-wishers instantly crowded Lucy, offering their congratulations.

"Let's give her a chance to mingle and meet her in the hall," Liz suggested, and Tom agreed it would be a good idea.

Emily excused herself to use the ladies' room. While they were waiting, Liz located the card to access her hotel room and gave it to Tom. "I hope the bed in the spare room is as comfortable as the one we're sleeping on."

"Thanks, but I'm so tired I could sleep standing up. I had to get up ridiculously early to make it here in time."

"Before you go, you wanted me to remind you to tell me something."

"Oh, right," said Tom, his smile instantly fading. "Two matters of importance. One is happy news. Jeff bought a condo in Key West. The idea is that we will winter there after we get married."

"Lucky you," said Liz, frowning. "But doesn't that mean you'll need to resign as associate rector?"

Tom sighed and glanced away. "Yes, and I hate to leave Lucy in the lurch, but church attendance falls dramatically in the winter. Now that Lucy has Reshma to help her, I don't feel quite as bad about leaving for a few months. I'll be back in Hobbs by April, in plenty of time to help with the summer chapel. I'm hoping the vestry will agree to keeping me on as a part-time priest. Honestly, that was really all I was looking for when I moved to Maine."

"Tom, you've been a tremendous help to Lucy, especially after Erika's death. I'm sure she'll understand, but why are you telling me about it instead of talking to her?"

"I wanted to run it by you first. Maybe you can think of a good time to break the news. I didn't want to cause her more stress while she was preparing for her thesis defense."

"That was considerate. But there's never a good time with Lucy. She always has something going on."

"So it seems, but there's something else that's more problematic." He paused to scrutinize Liz's face. "Susan Gedney called the other day to ask if the curate's studio she occupied last summer is still available."

"What?" asked Liz, unable to stop herself from looking shocked.

"I know. It's pretty bold, especially presuming that she'd be welcome after all the trouble she caused."

"What did you tell her?"

"The truth. That the curate's studios are being used by our music director and our new deacon, and I'm living in the rector's apartment. I told her I would do what I could to help find her a place to stay."

"Why? We all went out of our way for her. Lucy tried to involve her in ministry, gave her a place to stay. When we found out she's an alcoholic, I pulled strings to get her into rehab. Brenda and Lucy personally escorted her to the airport for extradition."

Tom assumed a patient expression. "Lucy cares for Susan. Helping her is a kindness to both of them."

Liz scowled, but she knew Tom was right. "What do you propose?"

"Well, we could play musical homes. I could move in with Jeff, which would leave the rector's apartment vacant. Or Lucy could let Susan stay in the beach house."

"That won't work. She doesn't want any official moves until the wedding. Besides, Sam wants to start work on turning Lucy's garage into an apartment. A tenant will only be in the way."

Tom grinned. "You have lots of space, Liz. You could always invite her to stay with you."

Liz made big eyes to show her opposition to the suggestion. Tom laughed heartily. "I didn't think that idea would appeal to you."

"I wonder what Lucy will think about all this," said Liz, speaking her thoughts aloud.

"Me too. That's why I didn't make any promises."

Lucy came into the hall, looking for them. Liz swept her up into a hug. "Congratulations! You were brilliant!"

Lucy was all smiles from the adulation. "Did I seem nervous? I was."

"Not a bit," Liz replied. "You looked cool and confident. You absolutely killed it."

"Congratulations, dear." Tom bent to hug Lucy.

"Thanks, Tom, for being my most sympathetic critic. You anticipated their questions perfectly." She looked around. "Where's Emily?"

"Potty break," Liz explained. "She'll be right back, and we can go to lunch. Luce, I invited Tom to join us for dinner, but he says he needs a nap before driving back to Maine. I offered him the extra room in our suite. If Emily decides to stay, they can make up the bed again."

People were streaming into the hall. Professor Spangler came out and waved to Lucy to return to the conference room. After she left, Liz said near Tom's ear: "I'd hold off on making any moves before talking to Lucy. I'd be surprised if she'd be happy to have Susan that close to home."

"Me too, but I didn't dare to presume. It's a tricky situation for me."

"For all of us," Liz said. She spotted Emily searching for them in the crowd and waved to her.

❋❋❋

Emily seemed unusually quiet at dinner. While Liz and Tom did a postmortem on the thesis defense, Lucy kept an eye on her daughter. Emily's upbringing in the strict, religious home of her adoptive parents had deprived her brilliant mind of stimulation. For that reason, her attention would usually be riveted on any intellectual conversation, but not tonight.

Liz was mocking Hernandez as "the Grand Inquisitor." "You know he's a character in the opera we're seeing tomorrow night," she said. "That scene between him and King Phillip is one of the most dramatic in the entire repertoire. Too bad it is seldom sung by basses of equal talent."

The comment got Lucy's attention because Liz was a fanatical opera fan and always had strong opinions. Usually, Emily would have something to contribute when the topic turned to music, but Lucy saw that she had completely left the conversation.

After dinner, Liz offered to walk Tom to the parking garage. Emily looked even more distant than before. "What's bothering you sweetie?" Lucy finally asked.

It took a long time for Emily to formulate her words. "I don't know why, but I didn't expect you to talk about the rape today."

Lucy moved her hand closer to Emily's, but let it rest on the table. Emily didn't always like to be touched. "I'm sorry, Emily. Did mentioning the rape upset you?"

"Not exactly, but I haven't thought much about it since we had that big talk."

"That's understandable. Who likes to think about such a sad subject?" Lucy took Emily's hand but held it lightly to make the affection less threatening. "Tell me what you were thinking."

"I was wondering if it hurt."

"You mean the act itself? Have you had sex with a man?"

Emily shook her head. "I would have told you, Mom." Lucy wasn't sure that was true. Lacking the usual filters, Emily occasionally blurted out details of her life that most people kept private. Other things she kept to herself until she was finished processing them.

"Intercourse isn't usually painful," said Lucy gently increasing the pressure on Emily's hand, "but if a woman isn't receptive and aroused, it can be, especially if the man is aggressive."

"Was he?"

"Are you sure you want an honest answer?"

"Yes, Mom. I need to know." Emily's blue eyes implored earnestly.

"Yes, it hurt, but not only physically. I was attacked by someone I trusted. Everyone noticed the bruises, but no one said a word. I felt like a ghost."

Emily's eyes began to fill. "Oh, Mom, I'm so sorry. Why didn't you report him?"

"I did. Afterward, he claimed it was consensual, and I was lying to get back at him. He was powerful at the Met. The management brushed off my complaints."

"You should have gone to the police."

"I know. I tried to work inside the Met organization to avoid a scandal, and only to prevent it from happening to other women. That's when I discovered it already had. By that time, it was too late to involve the police."

Emily looked thoughtful. "I used to be sad that he died before I could meet him. Now, I don't think I missed anything."

"Like most people, he was a mixture of good and bad. In the beginning, he was very kind to me, which is why I thought we were friends. I didn't suspect he was only being helpful so he could get me into bed."

"That was really shitty."

"Yes, it was."

Lucy studied Emily's young face. Most of the time, it was like looking in the mirror. Emily's face was covered with pale freckles. Their delicate features were the same, but Lucy could also see Emily's likeness to Alex. "You have his height…and his blue eyes."

Emily frowned. "Is it ever hard to look at me because I look like him?"

"Oh, no, darling, never!" said Lucy, gripping her daughter's hand more tightly. "You resemble me too."

"Everyone says how alike we look. I'm glad, because you're beautiful."

"And so are you." Lucy felt Emily's hand squirm in hers, so she let it go.

"Did you give me up for adoption because I came from the rape?"

"Oh, no, sweetheart! I had to work. I couldn't go back to the Met because I was blacklisted. I had to go overseas and travel for engagements. I couldn't drag an infant all over the world. I wanted you to be well taken care of and loved."

"The Cunninghams did take good care of me. I'll give them that. I think they did love me."

"Do you miss them?" Lucy asked, gently probing.

"Sometimes. When I was little, they were the only parents I knew. Except for them wanting me to quit school and become a house cleaner, I would have stayed with them."

"Would you like to see them again?"

Emily frowned as she considered the idea. "Maybe. Let me think about that."

"Emily, it was very hard to give you up. After I held you and looked into your eyes, I never wanted to let you go, but I thought I was doing the right thing."

"Are you sure you didn't want to get rid of me because of the rape?"

The question cut deep, but Lucy knew that even a moment's hesitation would cause more doubt. "I am absolutely sure. I didn't want Alex to know about you because he was so controlling. He would have insisted on being involved, and I couldn't have that."

"I'm sorry I was so much trouble, Mom."

"Oh, baby. You weren't trouble. You were a beautiful child, and I so much wanted to keep you, but I had to make some quick decisions. Are you angry that I gave you away?"

Emily shook her head. "No, I'm sad, but I think I understand."

"Oh, sweetie, this is exactly why I didn't tell you sooner. I never want you to doubt yourself. You had nothing to do with your conception. You were a beautiful, innocent child, and I am so grateful to have you in my life." Lucy's heart hurt for her daughter as she watched her try to process her feelings with her limited emotional tools. She debated for a long moment before she said, "There's something I haven't told you. It will prove that I chose you out of love, even though I gave you up for adoption."

Emily deliberately focused on Lucy's eyes to show she was paying attention. Because of her Asperger's, it took an act of will for her to make direct eye contact. Lucy could see how uneasy she was and almost changed her mind. She decided to risk it because they were being so truthful. "When I found out I was pregnant, I was going to have an abortion." Emily's eyes grew large. "At the time, it seemed to be the simplest, quickest solution, but when I got to the clinic, I just couldn't go through with it. You were my child, not an inconvenience to be dealt with quickly. While I carried you inside me, I began to love you. I sang to you every morning and every night."

Tears formed in Emily's eyes. "Maybe that's why I love music."

"Maybe," Lucy agreed. She looked up and saw Liz walking through the dining room. The rest of this conversation would have to wait.

When Liz arrived at the table, she put her hand on Emily's shoulder. Lucy was surprised her daughter didn't flinch away as she sometimes did, but Emily seemed comfortable with Liz. "Em, we should get you a cab to Penn Station. What time is your train?"

"The nine-sixteen will get me to New Haven around eleven."

"So, we can't convince you to stay the night? I can call the desk to have housekeeping make up the bed in the spare room."

"Thanks, Aunt Liz, but I can't miss this class. He's my thesis advisor."

Liz glanced at her watch. "How about I ride with you to the station and give your mother some downtime? She's had a long day."

Emily studied her mother. "You do look tired, Mom."

"Oh, but I want to have your company as long as I can."

"I know, but the semester will be over before you know it, and I'll be coming home to help with the wedding."

Lucy beamed with pleasure. "Does that mean you'll be spending the summer in Maine?"

"If it's all right with you and Aunt Liz."

"You know you're always welcome," said Liz, helping Emily into her coat.

Lucy got up to hug Emily goodbye. "You be careful when you get to New Haven."

"I have a friend coming to pick me up at the station. I'll be okay." Emily bent stiffly to allow her mother to kiss her.

Watching Liz leave with Emily, Lucy felt torn between accompanying them and some much needed privacy. She'd been "on" since they'd arrived at the seminary that morning. She was grateful that Liz, who could sometimes be insensitive, had intuited her need for some time alone.

The grand-luxe suite had been tidied in their absence. The bed in the ancillary bedroom had been changed and remade since Tom had left. Lucy imagined Emily sleeping there and sighed. The king-sized bed in the main bedroom had been turned down. On the bedside table was a plate of premium dark chocolates, one of the small amenities that were costing Liz so much money.

Lucy unwound the colorful scarf she had worn all day to cover her collar. She didn't want to take it off and spoil it after all of Liz's hard work or—God forbid—lose one of the precious, gold collar studs. The collar was still as pristine as when she had put it on that morning, so Lucy returned it to the case to wear on another occasion.

While her bath in the enormous bathroom filled, Lucy put her feet up and ate a tablet of dark chocolate. It tasted so good she couldn't resist eating all the others. Despite the delicious dinner, she felt depleted of energy. Now, the sugar jolt jangled her nerves. She hoped the hot bath would relax her. The bathtub had spa jets, but she was too tired to figure out how to turn them on. She settled into the steaming water and closed her eyes.

This day that she'd so dreaded and eagerly anticipated was finally behind her. In a few months, she would be addressed as "Reverend Doctor Lucille Bartlett." The idea gave her a little thrill—she, who had once been a star of the Metropolitan Opera and was now the rector of her own church! Why did the title mean so much, especially compared to her other accomplishments?

She suddenly remembered her father praising her for getting the highest grade in math class. Her mother had scoffed and advised her not to show up the boys with her smarts. After that, Lucy lost interest in math. She now regretted the self-effacing white lie she'd told Emily. She did know something about math and could follow some of the complex conversations between her daughter and her father-in-law, famous mathematician Stefan Bultmann.

Despite the noise of the hot water dribbling into the tub, Lucy heard the suite door open and close again. Liz was back. She knocked on the bathroom door. "It's just me."

"You can come in."

Liz opened the door a crack. "Don't you look comfy?"

"I am. When I heard the knock, I was hoping it was a sexy woman coming to share my bath."

Liz grinned and looked over her shoulder. "Should I leave and give you privacy? Maybe she'll show up."

"No, get undressed and join me."

"Okay, but you may need to let out some water to make room for me."

Lucy admired Liz's naked body as she descended into the water. Her skin sagged here and there, but her muscles were still clearly defined. Her breasts were full but firm. For a woman in her mid-sixties, she was in excellent condition. For all its objective appeal, this aging body belonged to the woman Lucy loved, so its minor imperfections didn't matter.

"You could turn on the jets," Liz suggested.

"I couldn't find the switch, and I've never really enjoyed rushing water pounding on me."

"I know what you mean. That's why I never installed a hot tub. Plus, a spa can be a breeding ground for bacteria unless it's scrupulously maintained."

Lucy studied Liz's frowning face. "Don't you ever take a break from being a doctor?"

"Sure. But not often. I block it out when I eat or drink bad stuff, like that single malt scotch you hate so much. Do you ever take a break from being a priest?"

"I try to have a personal life—some space I reserve for myself."

Liz's frown grew more pronounced.

"What? Don't you believe me?"

"No, I was just thinking it could get harder for you to have a personal life."

Lucy sat up and stared. "Why?"

"Well, Tom shared some information with me today. Maybe I should wait for him to tell you."

"Liz, now you're worrying me. Come on. Tell me what he said."

Liz shrugged and moved closer to Lucy until their bare thighs touched. She reached for Lucy's hand. "Jeff bought a condo in Key West. After they get married, they're going to be snowbirds and spend their winters there."

Lucy was too practiced as a therapist to show overt surprise, but she was hurt that Tom hadn't come to her first. She took a moment to digest the news before she said, "I'll miss Tom, but I wish him every happiness."

"He'll be back by April. He's hoping you'll keep him on as a part-time priest to manage the summer chapel."

"That's up to the vestry."

"I know, but you have a lot of say in the matter." Liz stared at the surface of the water. "There's something else."

"What?"

"Susan Gedney called Tom to ask about the curate's studio she occupied last summer."

Unintentionally, Lucy's mouth gaped a little. "That's incredible. Our deacon is in that apartment."

"Yes, I know. Tom offered to move in with Jeff to leave the rector's apartment vacant. He had other suggestions, including having her move in with us."

"No! Absolutely not."

Liz smiled. Obviously, that was what she'd wanted to hear. "I know you hate triangulation, but that's the story."

"Of course, I wish Tom had come to me first."

Liz nodded. "And I probably should have kept my mouth shut."

"No, we shouldn't be keeping secrets from one other," said Lucy, distracted by trying to absorb the news. Tom leaving for Florida would have more impact, but Susan's presumption was galling. With effort, Lucy concealed her irritation. Liz already resented Susan and needed no encouragement. "If Susan needs a base of operations while she interviews for new positions," said Lucy, "I'll ask around. Another parish may have room for her, but she's not coming to mine."

Liz slid down in the hot water until it was up to her chin. "Glad you're not tempted to get sucked into her drama." Liz picked up Lucy's hand and inspected her fingers. "Your fingertips are like prunes. How long have you been in the water?"

"Since I came up to the room. I guess I should get out." Lucy hauled herself out of the tub. She wrapped herself in one of the luxurious bath sheets and headed into the powder room while Liz finished washing.

Lucy put on one of her favorite lace nightgowns and got into bed. Although she desperately tried to stay awake, she began to doze.

"No, you don't," said Liz, getting into bed naked. She slipped Lucy's nightgown off her shoulder and began to tease her nipple with her tongue.

"Oh, Liz, it's been such a busy day. I'm not sure I have the energy."

"This morning you promised to kiss me until I begged you to stop."

"I did, didn't I?"

Liz leaned on her elbow and grinned. "Since you've had a hard day, you can be my pillow princess tonight. You won't have to do a thing. I'll take care of you." Liz's lips enclosed Lucy's nipple. Her hand crept up her nightgown, lightly grazing the inside of her thigh along the way.

"You're bad," said Lucy with a sigh. Liz's touch was arousing her.

"That's why I'm marrying a priest," said Liz, raising her head. "For redemption."

"You don't need to be redeemed. God loves you just the way you are… and so do I."

"That's good because I'm not changing."

"That's what you think," replied Lucy, smiling. She didn't resist when Liz gently nudged her legs apart with her knee and lowered her weight on her body.

2

The sound of the blade scraping against the pavement reminded Sam to raise the plow. She'd forgotten that Lucy's driveway had a hump in the middle for the rain to run off. All the beach houses had poor drainage. Now that global warming was making the storms fiercer, the catch basins were often overwhelmed, especially in melt season.

Sam had considered skipping this plow. Lucy and Liz weren't getting back until Sunday night, so there was no rush. The March sun was often strong enough to melt a light snowfall, but it was supposed to get cold. If Sam didn't plow, the freeze-melt cycle could leave the driveway treacherous.

After Sam pulled the snow back from the garage, she hopped out and shoveled the walkway. She didn't spread salt. It just killed the little bit of grass in front of the porch and ate up the asphalt. Exposing the dark surface would help melt whatever snow remained.

When Sam had finished shoveling, she sat in the idling truck and looked over Lucy's garage. Building an apartment to create a beach getaway for Lucy and Liz was a relatively simple project. The structure had good bones and a solid foundation. Basically, all Sam needed to do was raise the roof and add another story. That was common in this beach community, where everyone was craning for a view of the ocean. Sam envisioned what used to be called a widow's walk off the front of the third story. Considering that Lucy had recently lost her wife, calling it a balcony would probably be a better idea.

Lucy had asked if there was any way to preserve the second story as it was. The practice room had been Erika's last gift to her wife before she died. Containing the powerful voice of a Metropolitan Opera soprano hadn't been easy, but Sam had researched lightweight soundproofing materials and figured out a way. Liz had helped with the construction to save Erika money. They'd celebrated Christmas in October so that Erika could present her gift, which was fortunate because she died right before the holidays.

Given all the sentimental investment in the space, Sam had been designing the expansion around it.

These local architectural commissions kept that part of her mind active. They were insignificant compared to designing award-winning high rises, but they presented their own interesting challenges. Working within small spaces and small budgets forced Sam to be more creative, and she could experiment with the latest building materials. Now that the renovation of Liz's medical building was mostly complete, Sam was itching to start a new project. She always got twitchy when she wasn't building something.

Visualizing Lucy's beach retreat had been a welcome distraction, but Sam knew she should get over to Olivia's place. The members of the "Thirsty Thursdays" crowd had been looking in on Olivia since she'd had a heart attack on Thanksgiving Day. With Liz and Lucy away, it was Sam's turn to be on duty. Guilt over dumping Olivia a few months before made Sam feel she should shoulder a bigger share of the load. Lucy's response was blunt: "Sam, if you were only hanging around for the sex, and the costs outweighed the benefits, you were right to leave."

"But I wouldn't have left, except she kept pressuring me for more than I was willing to give," Sam had said.

"Then you should have spoken up sooner."

"She never heard me. It was easier to ignore her bossiness until I couldn't stand it. Instead, I'd deliberately do the opposite thing, hoping she'd get the idea."

"You know what that's called, right?"

"Passive aggression?"

"Bingo." Although Lucy was always kind, she seldom minced words.

Sam banished the unpleasant conversation from her mind and headed to Gull Island. On the way, she decided she should call Olivia to warn her. She was a control freak, who didn't like surprises, and things between them were different now.

"I was hoping I'd hear from you," said Olivia's crisp voice through the Bluetooth speaker. "My snowplow didn't show up."

"I told you not to hire one of those commercial guys. They always clear the parking lots before private driveways."

"I would have preferred to hire you," replied Olivia impatiently.

"I'm not for hire. I don't charge my friends."

"I know. What do I need to do to become your friend?"

Sam rolled her eyes. *Try being less pushy*, she thought. "I'm on my way over."

"I appreciate the warning. I need to put on my face."

That phrase had always annoyed Sam. Her mother used to say it, as if her face didn't exist without makeup.

"Olivia, I've seen you every which way. I don't care what you look like." Sam realized too late that her attempt at reassurance had come out wrong.

"Thanks," replied Olivia in a tart voice.

Sam was tempted to tell Olivia to shovel herself out, but the woman was just stubborn enough to try. Sam didn't want her to drop dead because they'd had a snit. She took a deep breath to cool her temper. Lucy always said that kindness was the best antidote to anger.

"Is there anything you need from the store?" Sam asked in her most patient tone. "I can swing by the Foodmart on my way."

"I could use cream for coffee and a loaf of that high-protein whole-wheat bread. You know the brand I like."

"You got it. I'll be there in about ten minutes."

When Sam got to the IGA, she regretted offering to pick up groceries. The parking lot was jammed with people stopping for coffee and breakfast sandwiches before heading to work. She thought of heading to the big grocery store in the mall, but that meant backtracking. She grabbed what she needed off the shelves and took her place in the long checkout line.

"Hey, Sam," said a familiar voice. She looked around and saw Brenda Harrison in her police uniform, standing behind her.

"Busting shoplifters?" asked Sam. "I was tempted to slip out with my purchases when I saw the line."

Brenda laughed. "One of my officers has a birthday today. I came in to pick up some donuts. The line at Congdon's was even longer. You can tell the snowbirds are back."

"They're early this year."

"The weather has been terrible down South, and we've had a mild winter. Although I was surprised to see the snow this morning."

"Yeah, me too. I'm heading over to Olivia's to plow. She needed some cream and bread."

Brenda eyed the bread as if it were tainted. "I wonder if she'd do the same for you if the situation were reversed."

"Well, I'm the one who left the relationship. I'm sure she's still steamed over that."

"But here you are, playing Girl Scout."

Sam made a face. "I was never a Girl Scout. Thought they were silly. I might have been a Boy Scout if they would have let me."

"They let girls join the Boy Scouts now."

"Doesn't surprise me, especially with all the lawsuits for pedophilia, and those Christian Right loonies starting their own Scouting organizations. I'm sure the Boy Scouts need all the recruits they can get."

"Keith wants to become a Cub Scout, but Megan has no interest whatsoever. Thank God. Like we need more places to drag the kids," Brenda said, shaking her head. "I gotta go, Sam. Nice to see you. Have a good day." She gave Sam a friendly pat on the back.

"Say hi to Cherie for me," Sam called after her.

The shopping trip Sam had planned for ten-minutes became half an hour. When she finally returned to her truck with her few purchases, she was cranky about wasting so much time for so little.

She plowed the driveway and shoveled the walk before she rang the bell. Although Olivia could have let her in with her phone app, she appeared at the door all made-up and smiling. She appeared to be the picture of health. Looking at her, no one would ever guess she'd had a heart attack.

"You're looking good," said Sam cheerfully.

"You say that like you're surprised."

"Not really," replied Sam, uneasy that they were getting off on the wrong foot. "You always look good." That was the right thing to say. Olivia smiled, obviously pleased.

"Thank you. And thank you for plowing me out."

"Olivia, three inches isn't much snow." Sam wiped her feet on the doormat. "Your fancy BMW would have gotten through it with no problem."

"As if I have any place to go…now that they've forced me to take leave from the town manager's job."

"Well, Liz says you can go back to work next month. I'm sure the people in the town hall can't wait."

Olivia put her hands on her hips. "Samantha, I have an extremely sensitive sarcasm meter. Of course, I know they hate me, but I'm bored out of my mind." Olivia reached for the grocery bag, but Sam held it out of reach.

"No, you don't. I've got it."

"I'm not an invalid. How much do I owe you?"

"Nothing," said Sam. "Comes with the plowing service."

"Well, come in. I put on a fresh pot of coffee. I'll make you some toast now that I have bread." Sam shrugged off her parka and hung it on the coat tree. "And take off your boots," Olivia called as she headed to the kitchen.

"Think I'm not smart enough to figure that out?" muttered Sam under her breath. She was tempted to put her coat back on and walk out the door. *Don't let her get to you*, said a little voice in her head. *You came to help her. Have a cup of coffee with her and go.* Sam forced a smile to her lips as she entered the kitchen.

"I'll make you some eggs," Olivia said, putting a skillet on the six-burner Aga.

"Thanks, Olivia. I'll just take coffee. I'll pick up something on the way."

"You plowed my driveway and won't take any money. Making you breakfast is the least I can do." Olivia's deafness to her protests felt too much like when they were dating. She never seemed to hear a word Sam said, although her hearing was acute. She rolled over dissent like a bulldozer. That's when Sam would go silent and let her do whatever she wanted.

At the memory, Sam squirmed in her chair. She told herself that Olivia was lonely, and staying a few minutes longer was a kindness. Besides, the smell of the bacon frying was making her hungry. At least, she would get a tasty meal out of the deal. Olivia was an excellent cook.

"What have you been doing with yourself now that you're not seeing Amy Hsu anymore?" asked Olivia, cracking eggs into the skillet.

Sam sat down at the kitchen table. "I've been busy. I've mostly finished Liz's project, and I'm making sketches for that apartment over Lucy's garage."

"That was smart of her to make an apartment in the garage. She can always rent it for extra income."

"Was that your recommendation as her financial advisor?"

"No, she came up with it on her own. Lucy is extremely shrewd when it comes to money, but, like every attractive woman, she's had to fend off negative assumptions about her intelligence. That's probably why she wants a Ph.D. after her name. Did you hear how her dissertation defense went?"

"She passed with flying colors."

"Of course, she did. Maybe now she'll be accepted in your elite society of brainiacs."

"Olivia, why are you so damned crabby this morning?"

"Well, let's see." Olivia began buttering her toast with some nasty looking faux butter made with olive oil. She'd always preferred fancy, imported butter, so this must be part of some special diet because of her heart condition. "I'm tired of being cooped up here alone. I'm bored out of my mind. And I'm horny." She peered intently at Sam.

"Don't look at me," Sam said, drawing back in feigned alarm. "I'm only here as your friend."

"How about friends with benefits?"

Sam deadpanned and stared at her, which made Olivia laugh.

"I like you too much, Samantha, to use you like that. Besides, I'm not sure Dr. Hsu would agree that I'm healthy enough for sex."

"Are you serious?"

"Would I kid about something like that?"

Sam had fond memories of Olivia's voracious libido, and it saddened her to think that it had been involuntarily tamed. She bit into her toast and reflected as she chewed. "That's a shame. Can't anything be done about it?"

Olivia shrugged. "Amy thinks I can recover if I give it time. She's fine-tuning my meds to make sure. She's a good doctor. I like her…as a person too."

"Are you interested in her?"

"I can't make good on the offer, so I haven't pursued it. We'll see."

"Hmm," replied Sam in a thoughtful tone. "I hope you get better. You really like sex."

"I do."

"So do I."

"Well, don't change your mind about Amy. She's in my sights."

Sam considered Olivia's warning with a frown. Olivia always got what she wanted. Not that Sam was interested in dating Amy again, especially now that Maggie was in the picture. But that was none of Olivia's business.

✳✳✳

Maggie folded a lace bra into her carry-on bag. She was so glad to get rid of the thick, ugly mastectomy bras, and just in time. She wanted to look especially attractive for Sam this weekend, expecting that they would finally make love. The dear woman had been so patient, never pushing while Maggie recovered from the double mastectomy. Sam was attentive, but she never hovered. Her inquiries about her health were interested but not invasive. Sam had clear boundaries and didn't cross into other people's territory unless invited. Maggie approved.

Zipping the suitcase closed, she wondered if this affair would go any-where. Sam was basically a loner and not likely to invite Maggie to cohabit any time soon. That suited Maggie. After being married to Liz for seven years and the contentious end of their relationship, she wasn't eager to live with someone again. Besides, moving out would deprive her daughter of childcare when she desperately needed it.

The chime clock in the hall struck three. At first, the sound of it had annoyed Maggie because she'd purchased it for the Hobbs house shortly after marrying Liz. Her new wife had definite ideas about interior design, which mostly meant less is more. Liz had allowed her previous lover to do some of the decorating. Little by little, Maggie had tried to remove Jenny's influence, but Liz wouldn't let her touch the L. L. Bean moose quilt in the "North Woods room" or the nautical accents in the "seashore room." Her office was strictly off limits.

Otherwise, Liz was reasonably tolerant. She occasionally grumbled about the rocks, shells, and knickknacks Maggie scattered around the house, but she never banned them. Maggie had needed these small personal touches, both to assert her presence and stake out her territory. After she'd moved her things out, Liz's home had returned to its former spartan appearance. Maggie felt like her existence had been erased.

What had she expected? Liz was in her late-fifties and had an established household when they'd reconnected. Although Maggie's Greenwich Village apartment was tiny, most of its contents had remained in storage over Liz's workshop. Maggie had to be content with superficial accents, probably the best she could hope for when two middle-aged women merged their households.

Middle aged? Who am I kidding? I was sixty when Liz and I got back together. Unless I live to be well past a hundred, I'm not middle aged. Since genetic testing had confirmed that Maggie carried the BRCA2 gene, any predictions about her longevity ended with a question mark. For that reason, she should probably stop ruminating over the past and embrace the future. *And why am I thinking about Liz anyway?*

But the thought of her ex-wife reminded her to stow the little jar of lubricant in her toiletry bag. Maggie's current doctor of record needed to break into Liz's prescription records to figure out what she'd prescribed for Maggie's vaginal dryness. Menopause made it bad enough, but the tamoxifen, meant to keep her breast cancer at bay, made it worse.

When she'd had sex with that young man, it was painful. Apart from being dry, she was tight because it had been years since she'd had a penis inside her. She'd only slept with him because she knew nothing would hurt Liz more. When she told Liz about the affair, it had, as expected, resurrected all the anger and insecurity from the past. During their college relationship, Maggie had been one of the popular girls on campus and continued to date men. Nothing made Liz crazier than the thought of Maggie sleeping with a man.

Maggie was sorry now that she'd ever said anything about Brad, but when Liz started talking about trying again, Maggie had felt it necessary to underscore that the marriage was over. If she'd handled it differently, they might have parted as friends. If only…. She was sorry about so many other things, including letting Liz get away with flirting with Lucy. But everyone, even she, had thought it was harmless.

The clock chimed again: quarter past the hour. Time to walk down to the end of the road to meet the girls' school bus. Along with sharing the expenses, cooking, and helping the girls with their homework, this chore was one of the many ways Maggie supported her daughter. The girls were getting older now and would soon be able to fend for themselves for the few hours before and after school. Maggie was glad because their independence would free her from this daily burden.

She hated thinking that way. She loved her granddaughters, but she missed being able to come and go as she pleased. She especially missed adult company. Most nights, Alina came home exhausted by her job as a news producer at the local TV station, and Maggie hated to engage her in even essential conversation.

Despite the date on the calendar, it was brisk outside, so Maggie pulled up her hood and warmed her hands in her pockets as she waited for the girls' bus. When it pulled up, the driver, a woman about Maggie's age, waved to her as she opened the door for the children. The girls were lucky to have the same driver since school started. So many had quit during the pandemic.

Katrina reached up for a kiss from her grandmother. Nicki pulled at Maggie's parka to indicate she wanted a kiss too.

"It's Friday, so I made a special treat for your snack this afternoon," Maggie told the girls, taking their hands.

"What kind of treat?" asked Katrina.

Maggie looked at each of their faces in turn, delaying the answer to build anticipation. "Cupcakes!" Predictably, the girls cheered and did a little happy dance. Guilt over leaving them for a few days had inspired the little surprise, although she felt bad that her daughter would have to deal with the sugar high.

"Did you make roses on the cupcakes?" Katrina asked, skipping along beside her grandmother.

"No, I made pansies and violets because in just a few weeks, it will be spring!"

"That's good. I like purple," Nicki declared, which made Maggie smile, remembering how her own adopted daughters had once loved violet in all its many hues.

After the girls unbundled from their winter coats and stowed their cartoon character backpacks, Maggie ushered them into the kitchen. They sat at the breakfast bar to enjoy their cupcakes. Each had her own strategy to approach the iced decorations. Katrina removed the paper from the bottom and ate the cake, saving the rich icing flower for last. Nicki slowly and sensually licked the icing off the top, which left her tongue purple. She only ate half the cake and left a pile of crumbs in the fluted paper cup.

Maggie had just finished cleaning up after their snack when her phone rang.

"Hi, Sam."

"Hey, I've been busy today between plowing and real work. I'm going to pick up sushi for us tonight."

Maggie's mind began to scan Jacques Pepin's recipes for some quick comfort food she could prepare instead. Her mouth began to water at his go-to, fast-cooking chicken, spatchcocked and covered with mustard sauce. "Sam, you don't need to get take out. I can cook something for us."

"I know you can, Maggie, but you're always doing the cooking, which makes me wonder if you don't like mine."

"Oh, Sam, you know that's not true!"

"Well, you say you like it, so I suppose I should take you at your word. But you're my guest and shouldn't have to cook. Besides, I'm craving some good sushi." Put that way, Maggie couldn't refuse.

"Okay. Sushi sounds great. Alina should be home by five-thirty at the latest, and then I'll head down to Hobbs. Can't wait to see you."

"I have a few things to finish up, and then I'll be home."

"Are you still working on Liz's office?"

"Yes, but that's mostly done. I've hired subs to do the finish work. I was over at Lucy's measuring for materials."

The sound of Lucy's name made Maggie bristle. The intense physical reaction took her by surprise. She'd thought she'd forgiven the woman she used to call her best friend, but Lucy had stolen her spouse. Maggie knew that was an exaggeration. Lucy hadn't stolen Liz. She'd gone willingly.

Sam picked up on the reason for the extended silence. "Maggie, you have to let that shit go. They're engaged, and it's time for everyone to move on."

"I know, but it's hard when you've been publicly humiliated."

"Your friends know what really happened, and we love you, so stop owning shame you don't deserve. People break up all the time."

"But Liz and I have known each other for almost fifty years. I was sure this time it was forever."

"I'm sure Lucy thought the same when she married Erika, but sometimes, the universe has other plans."

But that doesn't mean I have to like them. Maggie wasn't going to continue the conversation because she knew Sam was right. Saying anything more would only sound catty. "Have you heard from Liz? How did Lucy's dissertation defense go?"

"She passed."

"Of course, she did." Maggie, who had spent years in academia, didn't say that it had been a foregone conclusion, a mere public formality. Instead, she said in a neutral tone, "It's unusual to fail a defense unless the candidate doesn't address the suggestions of the committee beforehand." Maggie felt proud of herself for putting aside her jealousy and sounding both objective and authoritative. That always gave her pleasure, especially when she wanted to say something bitchy. She hoped Sam had noticed, but she changed the subject.

"So, spicy salmon roll and a scallion yellow-tail roll for you. Plus, seaweed salad and miso soup with extra tofu."

"You remembered!" exclaimed Maggie with delight.

"I don't have the phenomenal memory that Liz has, but I do remember certain things, especially if I think they're important."

Maggie was pleased that Sam considered her preferences in sushi important. Maybe this relationship had possibilities.

***

Sam had just grabbed a bag of wood pellets, when her ear caught the sound of a car coming down the driveway. She pressed the button to raise the garage door and saw the familiar Subaru pull into the gravel parking area. Maggie waved through the window before she got out of the car and opened the hatch.

"Come in this way," called Sam, "Leave your bags. I'll bring them in as soon as I get the pellets inside."

"I can manage," Maggie called back, taking out two bags—more than Sam would expect anyone to need for a weekend visit. Maggie never traveled light. "I'm no longer an invalid who needs to be waited on hand and foot," she said as she rolled a large suitcase into the garage.

"No, just a high maintenance woman who enjoys it." Sam stashed the pellet bag near the door. She'd come back for it later.

Maggie stretched a little to kiss Sam, who was tempted to prolong it, but it was chilly standing in the open garage.

"Come inside," said Sam, wrestling away the handle of Maggie's bag.

"I think you like high maintenance women," said Maggie. "Olivia fits that description."

"Yes, she does. So does my mother. She's the one who trained me how to treat the ladies."

"Well, she taught you well. I approve."

Sam tapped the button to close the garage door. "I wasn't expecting you so soon."

"Alina came home on time for a change, so I was able to leave."

"Did the girlies pout when you left?"

"They always do. I felt so guilty for leaving them."

"They'll appreciate you more when you come home. And you're entitled to have a life."

"I do, but they're not old enough to understand. To them, I'm just Grandma."

"Well, to me, you're much more." Sam put down Maggie's bag outside the door of the guest room, where she usually slept. She felt Maggie watching her. "There's no message in that except to say I don't want you to feel any pressure," she said with a shrug. "You can sleep wherever you want and just use this room to store your stuff."

"Let's see what happens," Maggie said with a quick, anxious smile

Sam gave her a half hug. "Come into the kitchen. I was hoping our soup would still be warm enough to eat, but we probably should heat it up a little." In the kitchen, Sam divided the soup into two bowls and put them in the microwave to heat. "I know you hate microwaves, but they come in handy."

"I admit that I'm a culinary snob, but they're perfectly fine for heating up things." Soon, they were slurping salty miso soup. "Some things are just better from restaurants," said Maggie.

"Thanks for agreeing to my lazy way of providing dinner tonight."

"You're not lazy, Sam. Just busy. You have a company to run and work to do. I'm jealous. I wish I had something to do besides being a full-time grandma."

"You talked about going back to teaching."

"The University of New England contacted me about teaching some classes next term. Maybe I should consider it."

Sam pushed aside her soup bowl and opened the containers of sushi. "I know you have your favorites, but I'm happy to share. Do you mind eating out of containers? I know you prefer a formally set table."

"I do, because it's important to maintain social standards." Maggie studied Sam's face. "It's ironic to be telling you this. You're a trust-fund baby from old money, and I came from an Irish Catholic family just one college degree up from working class."

Sam shrugged. "That's probably why you feel it's necessary to maintain social standards whereas I don't give a flying fuck."

"Please, Sam. I don't like that word."

"Forgot. Sorry."

"The truth is, I don't mind eating out of containers, especially when I'm on cleanup." Maggie winked, which made Sam smile.

"Want to watch a movie tonight?" Sam asked, dipping a piece of rainbow roll into the wasabi-infused soy sauce. "The new version of *West Side Story* just came back to HBO-Max."

"I've been putting off seeing it. I have a soft spot in my heart for the original version. I can't imagine how Spielberg could have improved on it."

"But would you be willing to see if he did?" asked Sam, congratulating herself for being cagy. "I really want to watch *Dune*, but I know you're not a sci-fi fan."

"Who says?"

"Who do you think?"

"Well, Liz doesn't know everything about me. I read *Dune* back in high school and loved it. It's a brilliant allegory, where the spice is a metaphor for oil. But you knew that."

Sam crossed her arms on her chest, defensive because she hadn't known. She couldn't decide how she felt about Maggie knowing more about her favorite sci-fi franchise than she did. "That's interesting," she said neutrally.

"*Dune* is up for a slew of academy awards. I'll watch it over *West Side Story*, if you don't mind."

Sam tried to force the skeptical look off her face. "Are you sure you're not just giving in to please me?"

"No, I'm done with doing things to please others. That's how I was brought up—to be the good little girl who behaves according to expectations to get approval. No more." Maggie shook her head. "I'm going to be seventy soon. About time I start being truthful about what I want."

"Well, good for you, Maggie Fitzgerald. You go, girl!" Sam said, offering a fist bump. Maggie stared at her hand at first, looking unsure. Finally, she returned it.

"Thank you. I'm going to need encouragement. It's not going to be easy."

Sam was a fast eater and quickly demolished all the sushi she'd ordered for herself. She was still hungry, so she went looking for more in Maggie's container. Despite her love of cooking, Maggie ate sparingly.

Cleaning up the kitchen took only a few minutes. They shortly found themselves in the living room, where they took their usual positions on the sofa while Sam set up the movie. When Maggie had first started spending weekends at Sam's, she'd sat snugged up against the far side of the couch. Over time, they'd moved a little closer. Now, they sat close enough for their thighs to touch. Sometimes, Maggie leaned against Sam's shoulder. The last time she'd stayed at Sam's place, they'd held hands.

Adjusting to the possibility of a romantic relationship was taking time. When they'd first met, Maggie was engaged to Liz. After the divorce, Sam had kept her distance. Their community was too small and interwoven to take sides. Maggie was still recovering from the double mastectomy when they'd first admitted there was an attraction, but her lack of strength and limited range of motion had prevented them from exploring it. Now, the long habit of keeping their hands off one another was proving hard to break.

Sam raised the remote to start the movie but felt Maggie's hand weighing on her arm.

"Hold off on the movie. I want to talk to you first."

A feather of anxiety tickled the back of Sam's neck. She braced herself, hoping Maggie wasn't going to say how much she valued their friendship, but there could never be anything more. Sam had heard that line many times from women. Unlike Liz, who could be smooth and assertive to the point of being aggressive, Sam was shy. She literally stuttered trying to express her interest in a woman. That's why, despite her butch appearance, her partners had to make the first move.

"I think I know where you would like this relationship to go," Maggie said.

Sam held her breath before asking, "You do?"

"Yes, I think you'd like to take the next step. I'm sorry my…condition… hasn't allowed it. I believe sex should be a mutual thing."

"So you explained, and I understand. But I don't want you to think that's all I want from you."

Maggie smiled sadly. "Oh, Sam, after all these years, why would I think such a thing? I know you. I love you for your kindness and your patience. I just hope it hasn't been too hard waiting."

Sam felt herself blushing and faced forward. "Don't worry. I know how to take care of myself."

Maggie chuckled softly. "I bet you do. And I'm sure you know how to take care of a woman too. Thank you for being so patient. If you don't mind…I would really like you to put your arm around me." She slid over on the couch. Her warmth felt good and sexy, and a delicious tension gathered between Sam's legs. Maybe it really would happen tonight.

Sam grinned for the first half hour of the movie, especially when Maggie gently stroked her thigh. The battle scene with its violent explosions broke the mood. Sam hit the pause button for a break from the noise of weapon fire and explosions. "I'll make some popcorn."

"Good idea."

Sam returned shortly and balanced a large bowl on their thighs.

"I think I've figured out why I don't enjoy space operas," Maggie said, reaching for a handful of popcorn. "They're so loud."

"That's part of the fun. In the theater, you can feel those explosions vibrating against your chest.

"It can also make you deaf."

"Not really. The decibel level isn't high enough, and it's short-term exposure." Sam knew what she was talking about. She taught construction classes for women and regularly lectured on hearing safety. She hoped Maggie wouldn't think she sounded pedantic.

"I'm glad we're watching it here," said Maggie. "I still worry about the virus. And if we went to the theater, the popcorn would cost five times as much, and we wouldn't be able to sit this close."

The movie grew progressively more exciting as it wound to its conclusion. The brief silences were punctuated by the sound of crunching popcorn, but the end was unsatisfying because this installment was only part one. "I hate waiting for the next movie in a series," Sam grumbled as she switched off the TV.

"Me too," Maggie agreed.

They looked at one another, wondering what to do next.

✳✳✳

"Do you need help cleaning up the kitchen?" Maggie asked, slipping back into the polite rituals she'd been taught since girlhood.

"No, it's only the popcorn bowl. I can manage that. You do what you need to do."

"Okay," said Maggie and headed to the guest room to get ready for bed. After she undressed, she stood at the vanity in the bathroom, debating whether to take off her makeup. She decided that removing it would spoil the romance of making love for the first time. Afterwards, she could slip out of bed and take off her eyeliner and mascara.

In the mirror, she studied the scars beneath her breasts. They looked less angry and grew fainter every day. Her surgeon had assured her that eventually they would be nearly undetectable. Maggie touched her nipples. They had some sensation, a little more as time passed, but she doubted she would ever feel the same degree of pleasure as before the surgery. Her doctor had advised her to be patient. That's what she was supposed to say, but Liz, who was an expert on breast surgery, had warned that full sensitivity might never return.

Maggie had brought along a revealing lace nightgown, hoping to please Sam, who had a good eye for design in any form. After Maggie pulled the beautiful nightgown over her head, she gazed at her reflection. Anyone else would see her as glamorous, but when she looked at herself, she only saw an aging actress whose beauty was quickly fading. *That only means there's no time to waste.*

She threw the coordinating negligee over her nightgown and headed down the hall. She found Sam sitting in bed, scanning her tablet. She was topless, but her breasts were modestly covered by the covers drawn up to her armpits.

"Hello there! I was hoping you'd join me, but I didn't expect it."

Maggie smiled nervously. "I see you're already naked. Should I undress or would you like to do it?"

Sam considered the request. "You, please."

Maggie draped the negligee over the arm of a chair. As an actress, she knew how to make undressing seem dramatic and sexy, but Sam didn't deserve a cheap show. Maggie shyly pulled the nightgown over her head. "Don't look at me like that, Sam. You've seen me naked before…when we skinny dipped in your pond."

"But we were just having fun. It's different tonight. You look…" Sam was obviously struggling to find the right word. "… radiant."

Maggie smiled. "Every woman looks radiant through the eyes of her lover." She approached the bedside. "Please don't notice the scars. They'll fade."

"I've seen your scars, Maggie. But I'm not looking at them now. All I see is a beautiful woman who takes my breath away."

Maggie wanted to weep at the kindness of those words. A tear finally escaped when Sam enfolded her in her arms.

3

"New haircut?" Liz asked the counter waitress at the Hobbs Diner. After watching for months as the unnatural shade of vivid red grew out, Liz was relieved to see the last remnants finally gone. As a doctor, she was practiced in controlling her face, but it was hard not to stare at Paula's buzz cut.

"Oh, doc, I know it's short, but I couldn't stand it anymore."

"Why did you decide to stop dyeing it?"

"After my sister died, I read that hair dye is a cancer risk."

The thought of all the misinformation on the internet made Liz sigh. "Modern hair dyes aren't really dangerous, but coloring your hair can be messy and expensive."

"You got that right." Paula eyed Liz. "How would you know? You've had gray hair since I first laid eyes on you."

"It used to be chestnut brown, like Sam McKinnon's. When it started to gray, I dyed it for a while. I had a bunch of smart ass young doctors to keep in line. I didn't want them thinking I was old. When I left Yale, I couldn't wait to grow it out. Now, gray hair is the big fashion. Even young women want to be gray. Go figure."

Paula shook her head. "Everything is inside out." She glanced toward the back of the dining room. "Chief Harrison is already parked at your table. Got here early today."

As Liz headed to the back dining room, her feet knew to adjust to where the floor became uneven and to avoid the bent-up piece of linoleum. Despite the Hobbs Diner's shabby appearance, it was a Maine landmark, nationally known as a tourist destination.

Brenda was sitting by the window, scanning her phone. "Hey," she said, not looking up.

"Some urgent police business?" asked Liz, swinging into the bench seat.

"An accident on 95. The troopers have it covered."

"Don't you ever take a break?"

"No, do you?"

Liz laughed. "No, I guess I don't."

Lois, the morning waitress, came over to pour Liz's coffee. "I'll put in your order right away, Doc."

When she was out of earshot, Liz said, "I see Paula finally got rid of her red hair. It looked ridiculous, but now she's practically bald. She should have just had her hair stripped. They do it all the time."

"That costs a lot, Liz. A diner waitress doesn't have that kind of money." Brenda slipped her phone into her pocket. "I've considered letting mine grow out, but Cherie says I'm too young to go gray. Besides, I don't want the young officers to start thinking I'm old."

"Funny. I just explained to Paula that's why I used to color my hair. Had to keep the young Turks in line." Liz tried to picture Brenda with gray hair, finding it difficult because she'd always known her as a blonde. She'd gotten a little peek when Brenda was depressed over her COVID heart troubles and let her roots show. "Cherie's right. You're too young to go gray. What color is your natural hair?"

"I think it was brown. I've been dyeing it so long I don't even remember."

Liz nodded. "It's funny how ideas we have about ourselves get stuck." Lois delivered the plates containing their usual order—fried eggs over easy, bacon, and whole wheat toast. "How long have we been eating this breakfast, Brenda?"

"Years."

"We should change it up once in a while," said Liz, biting into a piece of toast.

"You keep saying that, but we never do."

"When I was first seeing Maggie, I once ordered the lobster Benedict. Paula was so shocked she nearly poured my coffee into my lap."

Brenda chuckled softly. "I'm sure nothing you do would shock Paula. She's seen everything. How was your trip to New York?"

"Great. We're going back in May for Lucy's graduation, and then we're spending a week there for our honeymoon."

"You used to live there. Why not go somewhere new?"

"When Lucy was an opera singer, she flew all over the world. So did I for medical conferences. There aren't that many new places to go. We considered Acadia, but it has significance with our former spouses and didn't feel right. We're both culture vultures. New York is just right."

"How many times did you go to the opera while you were down there?"

"Only twice. There are no performances on Sunday."

"Did Lucy make you wear a long dress?"

"Lucy doesn't make me do anything. She's not like Maggie. I wore a long dress one night, a tux-inspired pants suit the next. She has all these wonderful gowns left over from singing concerts. They're from that era when it was very chic to show a lot of cleavage. Yum," said Liz, smiling.

Brenda stabbed a piece of bacon. "You see her naked boobs all the time."

"I know, but that little suggestive peek is sooo sexy."

"I miss sex," said Brenda with a sigh. "I'm hoping when the kids are more settled, we'll have time for it again."

"Brenda, we've had this conversation. You need to make time for it. I'm telling you as your doctor and your friend. Sex is good for you. Gets your heart pumping. Your juices flowing. The stimulation is even good for your brain."

"What am I supposed to do? Set an alarm and wake up in the middle of the night when the kids are asleep?"

"If you have to."

"You don't understand. It's exhausting having young children in the house."

"Oh, I know. When my grandnieces and grandnephews come to visit, it takes a week to recover."

"But you can send them home with their parents. Keith and Megan are ours now, and their parents are dead, so we can't send them back."

Liz studied Brenda's face and saw how worn it was. There were creases around her mouth that she hadn't noticed before. The lines in her forehead had deepened. Liz looked again, this time through her physician's eyes, looking for signs that Brenda's long-COVID heart problems had returned. "I know it wasn't your idea to adopt the kids, but you jumped on board fast. Was it because Cherie wanted kids so much?"

"Partly, but now, I love them like they're my own flesh and blood. That doesn't mean they don't wear me out sometimes."

"I'm sure. There's a reason people have kids when they're young. By the time people get to be our age—I should say, your age, since you're younger—they don't have the energy to run after small children. You need to figure out how to pace yourself."

"Tell that to the kids!" Brenda sat back against the booth and sighed.

"Maybe you need a little vacation from them."

"Right. Like that's going to happen."

Liz mopped the last of the egg on her plate with her toast. "Obviously, you can't jump on a plane and fly away to Paris, but you could have a 'stay-cation' without the kids."

Brenda eyed Liz. "I know that look, Liz Stolz. What are you up to?"

Liz smiled. "Something you might like. Maybe Lucy and I can watch Keith and Megan to give you a few nights alone with Cherie."

"Don't you need to ask Lucy about this?"

"Of course, I'll ask her, but I'm sure she'll be fine about it. You know how much she loves kids." Liz looked up from her plate. "She always says she's trying to make up for missing Emily's childhood, but I think she just likes kids. She gave up the idea of being a mother when her opera career began to take off. Her mother was on the cusp of becoming a successful opera singer when she became pregnant with Lucy. She was an oops. Lucy's parents were Catholic, and they practiced the rhythm method. Like they thought that would really work! Lucy's mother quit singing professionally. She became a high school music teacher and gave private voice lessons on the side."

"Is that how Lucy learned to sing?" said Brenda, pushing the last of the home fries around her plate.

"It is. Her mother trained her from very young. She made her practice every day for hours."

"And Lucy made it to the Met, but she had to quit too."

"Once she decided to go against the male establishment at the Met and report her rapist, that was the end of her career. If she'd kept her mouth shut, like so many other women, and ignored the assault, she'd still be singing now."

"That totally sucks."

"Yes, it does."

Brenda grinned. "Is this the kind of stuff you talk about after sex?" Liz knew she was just trying to lighten the mood, and she couldn't blame her for expecting an answer. Liz had always talked freely about her sex life, but her usual bravado didn't feel right when it came to what she and Lucy did in bed. "Our intimacy is 'sacred,'" Lucy often said, and Liz was finally beginning to understand. Making love with Lucy was something special that Liz felt should be kept private. She offered Brenda a quick smile, so that she wouldn't feel that she'd intruded. "Among other things…" she said vaguely.

Brenda looked surprised but she got the message and changed the subject. "Okay, Liz, I accept your offer to take the kids for the weekend, pending Lucy's approval. I just don't want you spoiling them. I finally got them to stay out of our bed. Then Megan started crawling in with Keith."

"I know you were trying to impress the CFS inspector by giving Megan her own room, but why not let them sleep in the same room for a while? You won't even have to do much rearranging. I have an extra twin bed frame and mattress in my barn."

"Thanks. I'll swing by and pick it up this weekend."

Liz patted Brenda's hand. "Give them time. Losing both parents to domestic violence is a huge trauma. A few months with you isn't going to heal it."

Brenda scrunched up her face in frustration. "We're doing the best we can!"

"And doing a great job," said Liz, realizing her friend needed encouragement, not criticism.

Lois appeared to refill their coffee cups, but Brenda covered hers with her hand. "Thanks, Lois, but I need to get going. Departmental training today."

Lois brandished the coffee carafe. "You keep those troops in line, Chief!"

Brenda laughed amiably. "I keep trying."

Lois flipped through the pages of her order pad, ripped off one, and put it next to Liz's plate because she almost always paid the bill.

"I have to go," said Brenda. "But I'll talk to Cherie about your idea when I get home."

"I'm heading to the office now," Liz said, finding her credit card in her wallet. "Okay if I mention it to her?"

"Sure, if you want to. Thanks for breakfast."

"Don't mention it."

Liz smiled as she watched Brenda head to the front door, feeling pleased that she'd done something to lighten a friend's load. Now, she only needed to convince Lucy that keeping the Harrison kids for the weekend was a good idea.

❋❋❋

Lucy got up from her desk chair and sat down beside Tom in one of the visitors' chairs. "Tom, I'm not angry that you shared your plans with Liz before telling me. I know you two go back a long way."

Tom hung his head like a guilty boy. "When I told her, I didn't expect her to be the messenger."

"I know, but we're a couple, and you didn't tell her not to share it with me, so of course, she did."

"I'm sorry."

Lucy patted his arm. "Stop it. I won't have you feeling bad about this. We're all friends, even if, technically, I'm your boss."

"I know that hasn't been easy for you, Lucy."

"Especially since you had so much more experience than I did when you first came. And you're a man, so people automatically look to you to make the decisions. That was really annoying in the beginning."

"But you asserted yourself appropriately, and now they all know who's boss." Tom's warm smile indicated that he entirely approved.

"I am grateful for our friendship, and so glad we met, even if the reason was sad."

Tom sighed. "Erika's mother was failing, and it was her time. There was another Episcopal church nearby. If you hadn't chosen Trinity, we might never have met. I never would have had the opportunity to rekindle my friendship with Erika and Liz."

"In the beginning, I was a little jealous of your relationship with them." Lucy stared at her feet. "The three of you could talk philosophy. Inside jokes were zinging around, and I felt left out while you all laughed."

Tom leaned forward to see Lucy's face. "Oh, Lucy. I'm sorry. I never knew. We certainly didn't do it to be mean or to leave you out."

"I know. It's what you had in common, and it was a way of relating that went back a long time."

"Why didn't you say anything?"

Lucy shrugged. "Before Erika encouraged me to go back for my doctorate, I felt insecure. I barely muddled through my divinity degree."

"So, you just smiled and pretended to be amused while we carried on?"

"That's what women do, isn't it?"

Tom let out his breath in a long, steady stream. "A shame, but true. Thanks for sharing this, Lucy. A lesson learned."

Lucy patted Tom's hand. "So, tell me about your plans with Jeff. Since the bishop offered to officiate at our wedding, I'm sure he'll offer to do yours too."

Tom rolled his eyes. "Which is exactly what Jeff and I are hoping to avoid! We don't want all that pomp and circumstance and Bishop Greene making himself the center of our nuptials. Like many gay men, he adores theatricality and loves to be the lead actor in his own productions. No thanks. Jeff and I have other plans."

"If I can help in any way, let me know what I can do."

"You can help by coming to my wedding. Bring Liz and look as gorgeous as you always do."

"Ah, I'm beginning to get the picture. When your plans come together, I hope you'll share them with me."

"Oh, I'll tell you right now, Lucy. I've asked the present rector at Trinity to officiate at our wedding. Holding it in my old parish will allow me to invite old friends and new. It's not that far from Maine that it will burden anyone. It will also be a public coming out to my former parish. The ceremony will be modest, but we'll have a big reception. We're scouting a venue to host it, hopefully on the shoreline. My friends can't wait to meet you. Some of them are your biggest fans."

"How do they even know about me?"

Tom leaned forward and looked Lucy in the eye. "From your opera days, my dear. You know how much gay men love opera. Forgive me for being presumptuous, but I'm hoping you'll be inspired to sing, like you did for Brenda and Cherie at their wedding."

There was a knock at the door. Lucy glanced at her watch. "That will be Reshma. She's giving the homily at my Sunday service. I promised to critique it before she got in too deep."

"Good idea."

"She's come along nicely. You've done a good job with her, Tom."

"Thank you, Lucy. I made her my project, but she's yours too. When she's ordained, we'll both be proud of the young priest we helped form. And I refuse to believe that kind of pride is a sin." Tom leaned on his knees to get to his feet. "Thank you for being understanding about telling Liz before talking to you."

Lucy went to her desk to print out the draft of Reshma's sermon. She scanned it quickly to review her notes, thinking how glad she was to have someone else preaching on this Gospel. Not that it wasn't fertile ground for a lesson, but it had so many messages to choose from. An unskilled preacher would be tempted to address them all, which was exactly what Reshma had done.

The young woman gazed at her cautiously, trying to gauge Lucy's mood. "Are you ready for me, Mother Lucy?"

"Come on in," Lucy said, enthusiastically waving. She instantly saw her smile mirrored in the deacon's face, which just glowed. Reshma was a natural beauty with flawless dark skin. Being attractive could help in her future ministry, but as Lucy had learned, beauty could be a mixed blessing. People were often so busy admiring her, they failed to hear what she had to say. That's when Lucy told a story to help her divert attention from herself to the lesson she was trying to teach.

Reshma was already a natural storyteller and needed only a little encouragement to incorporate her experiences into her preaching. Her narrative was compelling. As a child, she'd been brought as a refugee from Africa with nothing, not even warm clothes for the Maine winters. Two churches had joined forces to sponsor her education at an Episcopal boarding school, but she'd earned scholarships to college and divinity school on her own merit.

Lucy pointed to a nearby chair, a bit worn, like most of the rectory furniture. "Why don't you pull that over and sit next to me, so we can look at this together?"

Reshma dragged the chair next to the desk. She sat down and struck an attentive pose, but her rigid posture betrayed her anxiety.

"Relax, Reshma. You have a great start here. The only problem is, you have too many starts and not enough endings."

Reshma sighed. "I was afraid of that. It's a short text, but there was so much going on: the Pharisees warning Jesus. He tells them thanks, but I'm too busy doing God's work. Next, we have this wonderful, motherly image of a broody hen gathering her chicks to keep them safe. I didn't even know where to begin."

Lucy laughed softly. "An embarrassment of riches. But from what you wrote, it sounds like the motherly hen really spoke to you."

"My mother raised chickens and sold the extra eggs for money when we lived in Sudan. I often felt guilty removing the warm egg from under a hen. I felt like I was stealing from the poor creature, and you have to be quick, or she'll peck you."

"You're describing a vivid experience many people haven't had. The tactile feel of reaching under the chicken. The still warm egg. The protectiveness of the hen. And you associate the chickens with your mother. You've got lots of raw material there. But choose one road to go down and develop the lesson from there. I'd probably leave out the part about being pecked."

Reshma gave her a brilliant smile. "You often talk about God as Mother," she said. "I think that's where I wanted to go."

"I talk about the female aspect of God as an antidote to the vengeful, capricious male deity of the Old Testament. I often struggle with that part of scripture. The motherly gentleness of Jesus and his wish to care for his people, even the nasty Pharisees, is a powerful image."

"I don't know if I feel brave enough to go there. This is only my third sermon here, and these people don't really know me yet. I'm young, and I'm black. I don't even look like them."

"I once heard a panel discussion among some of the first women ordained in our Church. They talked about how hard it was because they looked different from the priests that people were used to seeing. Now, there are so many of us, no one thinks twice about it. Maine is almost ninety-five percent white, so I understand why you feel you stick out in the crowd, but remember, our presiding bishop is black." Lucy reached over and patted Reshma's hand. "Have the courage to be authentic, and the rest will come. No matter how nervous you are, don't doubt yourself, or you'll signal you should be doubted."

Reshma smiled and nodded. In addition to being beautiful, she was whip smart and got the point of the little lesson instantly.

"Let's see if we can figure out how to rein in some of your many good ideas," said Lucy in an encouraging voice. "You also developed the theme of Jesus telling the Pharisees that he's too busy to worry about Herod and his threats."

"Oh," confessed Reshma in a whisper, "I borrowed that from one of the Gospel commentaries in Father Tom's office."

"That's okay. Sometimes, it helps to find inspiration in what scholars have written. Often, I learn a new point of view I never would have thought of on my own."

"Makes sense," Reshma agreed.

"Look, I'm going to give this back to you and ask you to focus your thoughts and show it to me again. You have good ideas here. Just too many to fit into a fifteen-minute sermon, and I don't recommend you go longer. People's minds start to wander." Lucy saw how discouraged the young deacon looked. "You've got this, Reshma. Let me tell you a little secret." Lucy glanced around like she was checking to see if they had privacy, then spoke in a conspiratorial tone. "Before Dr. Stolz showed me how to edit myself, my sermons were all over the place. I used to tell myself that it was the inspiration of the Spirit, but most of the time it was just me rambling. You'll get there. You already know to go to Tom's library for help. And you're always welcome to use mine. And we're both here to help you."

While Lucy had been speaking, the deacon's despondent expression vanished, replaced by a look of determination. "I think I know where to go now. I feel lucky to have two bonafide theologians to mentor me. How lucky is that?"

"A good sermon has less to do with theology and more to do with connecting with your listeners. It's the same with singing. Technique is great but touching the heart is what matters."

Reshma looked thoughtful. "I think I'll go with the hen image. It reminds me of my mother. I really miss her. I know many women priests reject being called 'Mother.' When I address you as Mother, it's out of respect but also affection. You really have been like a mother to me—pushing me steadily but gently, picking me up when I fall, encouraging me to do better when I screw up, which is often."

Lucy swallowed hard to avoid getting teary. She could hear the most horrific confessions and never get emotional, but moments like this broke her. "Thank you, Reshma, but that's what teachers are supposed to do."

"Maybe you'll get a seminary job, now that you're getting your doctorate."

Lucy laughed. "You think I don't have enough to do?"

Reshma's dark eyes grew wide with concern. "Oh no, Mother Lucy. I never meant to imply that."

"I know you didn't," said Lucy, patting Reshma's hand. "I'm just feeling overwhelmed at the moment."

"Which is why I won't take up more of your time," Reshma said, getting up. At the door, she turned around and said, "Thank you, Mother Lucy. I'll come back when I have it sorted out."

After the deacon left, Lucy closed her eyes to center herself. Her energy was at a low ebb. She hadn't slept well the night before because Liz was still having nightmares brought on by her counseling sessions with Tom. They were winding to a close, but the decades-old pain being dredged up still found its way into Liz's dreams.

Lucy didn't need Liz's fitful sleep to keep her awake. The photos of the war in Ukraine stayed with her long after the news broadcast ended. When she closed her eyes to sleep, she couldn't dismiss the images of the shattered maternity hospitals with pregnant women wheeled out covered by dust and debris. Sometimes, as Liz slept beside her, Lucy silently wept into her pillow.

The little break was refreshing. Lucy opened her eyes. Reshma was her last formal meeting of the day. There was still enough daylight for a quick walk on the beach. This weekend, the clocks would be set forward. Just the thought made Lucy smile.

She neatened her desk. Just as she was about to leave the office her phone rang. *Ignore it*, a little voice in her head said. *Even you deserve to take a break. If it's important church business, it will be bounced over to Tom.* Unconsciously, Lucy had been counting the rings, but the phone kept ringing, so this was a personal call.

When Lucy saw Susan's name come across her screen, her hope of a quick walk on the beach dissolved. "Hello, Susan," she said into the phone as she opened the office door with her shoulder.

"Lucy! I'm sorry if I interrupted anything."

"No, I'm free now. I just finished critiquing my deacon's sermon."

"Tom mentioned you were training a transitional deacon. How are you finding it? I hope it's not just adding to your other burdens."

"Well, yes, of course it is, but I'm enjoying it. I didn't realize how much I like to teach."

"That doesn't surprise me. You may not have formal training in education, but you're patient and explain things in ways ordinary people can understand. You may even find yourself recruited for seminary work after you get your degree."

"Ugh. No, thanks. I already have enough on my plate. And the bishop hinted at some new duties once I finish school." Lucy waved to Jodi, the church admin on the way to the door. "You sound good, Susan. What's going on?"

"I'm so excited. I just signed the lease for a winter rental I can afford."

"A winter rental? But it's March," observed Lucy, walking through the parking lot. "Winter's almost over."

"I know. But I can have this place until the middle of June. Hopefully, by then I'll know where my job will be, and I can find something permanent."

Lucy clicked open the doors to her car. "That sounds good. Where is it?"

"A few blocks away from your beach house."

Lucy stopped short but managed to avoid blurting out the obscene word that popped into her mind. She unlocked her car and started the engine, which transferred the call to Bluetooth. "That's a nice location. You're lucky."

"Yes, I am. The previous tenant had to leave abruptly because of a family illness. I'm guessing COVID. Since I'll be living so close, we can take walks on the beach together." The last thing Lucy wanted Susan to know was that she was living with Liz instead of down the street. Never mind what Liz would say about Lucy taking beach walks with her ex.

"Are you at your new place now?" Lucy asked, backing out of her parking space.

"I am. Just moving my things in. Not much. Fortunately, the place is furnished. Since you're free, maybe you could come over and see it. I'll make you a cup of Earl Grey. I bought some because I know you like it." Lucy had long since lost her taste for tea, partly because of its association with Susan. During Lucy's long and difficult discernment, Susan would often prepare a cup of strong tea with lots of sugar to fortify her. What began as comfort sometimes led to a session in the bedroom. Lucy hoped Susan didn't expect to replicate that result.

Watching for a break in traffic to make the turn on to Route 1, Lucy tried to think of an excuse to justify turning down Susan's invitation. Needing a restorative walk on the beach didn't seem good enough.

"You're welcome to stay for dinner if you want to," Susan added in a hopeful voice.

"Thanks, but I think Liz expects me for dinner."

"Oh, so you're living with her?"

"Not officially," said Lucy, irritated that she felt forced to explain her situation. "I'll tell you about it when I see you."

"So, you're coming over?"

"Yes, if you tell me where to go," said Lucy with a sigh. She was annoyed with herself that she'd given in so easily, but she forced herself to concentrate on remembering the address. When she heard it, she knew exactly where it was on the street that ran parallel to Ocean Road. It faced a part of the salt marsh that tended to flood, so it was considered a less desirable location than where Erika had bought her house. Lucy hoped the place wasn't a dump. No matter what had transpired between them, she would always care for the woman who had brought her out, restored her sense of well-being, and inspired her to become a priest.

Lucy easily found the old house. She was relieved to see that it was in good repair, although it hadn't been raised to be compliant with the new flood map. That probably meant the landlord didn't live there and the building was solely used for rentals. Lucy began to worry again when she discovered the apartment was on the ground floor. There were puddles in the low-lying areas near the door, and flood season was just getting started. A moldy smell emanated from the tiny apartment when Susan opened the door. Involuntarily, Lucy wrinkled her nose.

"That bad?" Susan asked, looking surprised. "I've been burning candles to get rid of it."

Lucy shrugged. "Most of these homes by the water have a damp smell unless they're aired out regularly. Candles help."

Susan opened the door wider. "Come in, Lucy. It's good to see you."

Lucy merely nodded. Her training as a therapist had taught her to avoid responses simply because they were expected, so she didn't automatically say, "You too." She stepped into the dark place and cautiously looked around. The furniture was worn but in good condition. The kitchen appliances looked nearly new. Lucy was especially relieved to see how clean the place was.

"Welcome to my new home," said Susan with a little bow and a theatrical sweep of her hand. "You look great, Lucy."

Before she responded, Lucy studied Susan's face. It was the sort of gentle face one might expect of a former nun and elementary school teacher. The openness in Susan's blue eyes belied the Catholic dogmatism that Susan had tried to reject in turning to the Episcopal Church and yet couldn't quite leave behind. The rigidity and doubt about her sexuality had tortured her during her relationship with Lucy. Alcohol was the only way she could release herself long enough to embrace it. Back then, Lucy had been so needy that she'd failed to see the warning signs.

There were new lines in Susan's forehead since she'd left last summer, escorted to her plane by Chief Harrison to face charges in South Dakota. Lucy's quick assessment of Susan finally coalesced into a guarded smile. "You look much better than the last time I saw you."

"It's amazing what giving up booze does for the body. I've lost some weight too."

"I can see."

"But you've filled out a little."

Lucy felt her cheeks warm. She gained some weight, and some of it had settled in her rear. "Liz is a good cook," she said casually.

"You must eat there a lot."

Lucy shrugged, unwilling to confirm a statement that was so obviously probing.

"I found a kettle and scrubbed it thoroughly. I'll put on some water for tea."

"If you have coffee, I'd prefer it," Lucy said.

Lucy watched Susan's face as she revised her plan. She could be rigid, so adjusting to an unexpected change wasn't easy for her. "Sure," she finally said and gestured to a chair at the small table. "Have a seat while I get it ready."

Lucy watched Susan move around the unfamiliar kitchen trying to navigate what would ordinarily be a simple task. Lucy found herself folding her arms on her chest but scolded herself for the closed gesture and forced herself to relax.

"I'm surprised you came back to Hobbs," she said to Susan's back while she measured off the coffee into the filter.

"Why?"

"I guess I would have expected you to go someplace where you could make a fresh start."

"I don't really have anywhere else to go. Since my mother and sister have passed, I no longer have ties to Massachusetts. I have no other family. At least here, I know you." Lucy felt the weight of the statement pressing down on her like a stone. "Does everyone in Hobbs know why I left?" Susan asked.

"Tom and Liz know, and Brenda, of course."

"Thank you for keeping it to yourself."

"Of course I would. Besides being bound by professional confidence, I care about you."

Susan paused pouring water into the coffee maker and set down the pitcher. The statement had moved her. She finally resumed preparing the coffee and leaned against the counter, waiting for it to brew. "I wrote to Courtney Barnes about teaching jobs at Hobbs Elementary. She says they're hurting for teachers and gave me information about how to apply for a job."

"I thought you were worried about the DUIs and the hit and run coming up on a background check."

Susan's gaze shifted to the floor. "I don't have to worry about that now."

Lucy instantly had an uneasy feeling. "Why not?"

"My bishop talked to the judge and had my record expunged in exchange for community service."

Lucy's mouth gaped a little.

"Don't look so surprised, Lucy. I confessed my sins, repented, and did penance. The judge is a religious man and was convinced to forgive me."

"Because you're a priest?"

Susan glanced away. "I'm sure that had something to do with it."

"But isn't that as hypocritical as the Catholic Church reassigning pedophile priests?"

"No, Lucy," Susan said sharply. "It's not the same. I didn't molest children. I had an accident while I was drinking."

"You left the scene. An old woman was hurt."

"She recovered and declined to press charges."

"Was she coerced?" Lucy asked.

"She wasn't hurt that badly," said Susan in an irritated tone. "She's just one of those old-fashioned types who don't like to make a big thing of something." Susan studied Lucy's face. "You're judging me without knowing the whole story."

Lucy examined her feelings to see if Susan's observation had merit, but she couldn't determine exactly how she felt. "I don't approve of how your record was cleared, but I'm happy you can go on with your life."

"Lucy, I paid my debt. I went to rehab. I've been attending my AA meetings. I tutored kids in Math, and I cleaned bathrooms in the homeless shelter all winter. I've done everything I can to make amends for what I did. Have some compassion. I'm a sinner like everyone. Sometimes, I fail."

"I'm sorry, Susan. I want the best for you. But I hope you learned your lesson."

"Oh, believe me. I have." Susan poured two mugs of coffee and brought them to the table. "I'm sure you would prefer a glass of wine, but for obvious reasons, I can't offer you one."

"Coffee's fine. I can have wine when I get home."

"You mean Liz's house," said Susan, her eyes focused on her coffee cup as she stirred cream into it. "I'm sure she won't like having me back."

"You know, Susan, you make a lot of assumptions, but you can understand why Liz might not like having you around. You kept pushing to get back together with me after I told you I wasn't interested."

"You're right. I owe Liz an apology. It's one of the amends I intend to make while I'm here."

"So, you don't intend to stay?" Lucy felt the tension in her body finally relax.

"It depends on where I can find a church that will have me. I've applied to congregations all over northern New England—Maine, New Hampshire, Vermont. Massachusetts too."

"Good idea to spread a wide net."

"I don't really care where I land as long as it's an active congregation with traditional worship. But I'm not going back to South Dakota. I'm a New Englander and here's where I belong. Of course, I'd love to stay in Hobbs, but now that you and Tom have a deacon, you don't need more help."

Lucy was glad to hear Susan had figured that out on her own, but she made a mental note to ask Tom not to reveal his plans to reduce his duties. She felt guilty thinking such a thing, but she knew that Susan's presence in Hobbs would make many people uncomfortable. It would drive Liz crazy. When Brenda had discovered Susan was wanted by the police in another state, she had been the soul of compassion, but she would be watching Susan like a hawk.

***

When the news broadcast cut to commercial, Liz got up to head to the kitchen. As usual, she'd assembled her dinner ingredients on the counter, ready to start cooking the moment Lucy walked in the door. The vegetables would certainly keep, but the shrimp needed to go back into the refrigerator. After Liz put the food away, she picked up her phone to see if there were any messages. A moment later, the garage door opened, and Lucy came in.

"What kept you so long?" Liz asked, bending to give her a kiss.

"I'm sorry, honey. I was going to call on the way, but it was easier just to get into the car and come home." Lucy put her bags on one of the counter stools and reached up her arms. "Hugs. I need hugs!"

"Did you have a late appointment? A pastoral visit?"

"No. Neither one. Susan Gedney called. She's taken a winter rental near the beach house and wanted me to see the place."

Liz released her and took a step back. "What? She's here? In Hobbs?" Liz realized she sounded like she was stuttering. "She has a lot of nerve to come back here."

Lucy pulled her close again. "Calm down, Liz. It's only temporary. Now, hug me. I really need it."

Lucy's breasts felt soft and warm against her as she tucked into Liz's body. She hung on longer than Liz expected, which gave her an inkling of how difficult her day had been. She willed her to feel the love communicated by the hug.

"Go up and change into comfy clothes," Liz murmured into Lucy's hair. "Go on. I'll get dinner started."

"Thank you for taking such good care of me," said Lucy, finally releasing her. She smiled and raised her face for a kiss.

After Lucy left, Liz took the food out of the refrigerator again. It was a quick meal and ready to serve by the time Lucy returned, wearing a yoga outfit and her fuzzy slippers.

"Do you think my butt is getting too big?" she asked, turning around. "I wouldn't necessarily ask another woman, but I know you'll be truthful."

Liz looked up from dishing out pasta to admire Lucy's firm buttocks. They formed a perfect inverted heart. "No, I think your butt is fine. Not too big and not too small. Just right."

Lucy mimed wiping her forehead in exaggerated relief. "That's good. Susan made a crack about me 'filling out.'"

"Susan is a jealous bitch who needs to shut her fucking mouth," Liz snapped. "And I don't want to hear about her while I eat. It will spoil my appetite."

Lucy gave her a sharp look, but otherwise didn't respond. Instead, she turned her attention to her plate, expertly winding the spaghetti onto her fork with her spoon. "This looks good. Is it one of your *New York Times* weeknight specials?"

"It is. It's called Spaghetti Shrimp Piccata."

Lucy tasted it and smiled as she chewed. "I love the brininess of the capers and the sweetness of the peas," she said after she swallowed. "You can make this for me again."

Liz made a little bow. "As you wish, Madame Bartlett."

Lucy laughed. "I love pasta, but the carbs."

"That's garbage. Pasta, properly prepared, has carbs, but it's high in protein." That seemed to please Lucy. Across the table, her green eyes smiled. "Apart from she who shall be unnamed, how did your day go?" asked Liz.

"I'm just glad it's Friday, and I have a day off before services. Reshma is preaching at my service, so no sermon prep. I could get used to that. How about you?"

"I had breakfast with Brenda this morning."

"That's right. You changed your day because of Cherie's new schedule. How is Brenda?"

"I think she's overwhelmed by the kids. I told her we would babysit them one weekend to give them a break."

Lucy stared at her. "Liz, you know I'd love to help them, but I can't possibly do it until after Easter. Between now and then, it's going to be crazy busy."

"I should have thought of that," said Liz.

"I'm sorry I can't do it sooner. I've sensed that Brenda is overwhelmed by the kids. Cherie looks tired too. I hope they're getting enough rest."

"Me too," said Liz, forking pasta into her mouth. The dish was tasty. She decided to add it to her already extensive recipe collection.

After dinner, Liz picked up the plates. "Why don't you go upstairs to watch the news?" They'd started using the guest TV room on the second floor because Lucy had complained about feeling dwarfed in Liz's huge media room. "Unfortunately, all the news has been bad today."

Lucy sighed. "But it's important to be informed."

Before she headed upstairs to join Lucy, Liz poured herself a glass of single malt scotch. She made herself comfortable on the futon, and Lucy snuggled against her.

"You were right. The news is all bad, especially this war. Women and children are fleeing and leaving their men behind. They showed a woman trying to give birth in a subway station. It's horrible!"

"It makes me so angry to see what this bully is doing. I admire the Ukrainian women fighting for their country. I may be a left eye, right-handed shooter, but I'm a dead shot. I have all the equipment, the weapons, the ammo. I'm thinking of volunteering."

"What?" Lucy sat up and stared at her. "You've got to be kidding."

"I'm not kidding. I want to go, but I'm too old. I'm sure they won't take a gray-haired woman in her sixties, although I've seen some photos of grandmas with AK-47s."

"But you don't have any military training."

"I could volunteer for Doctors Without Borders. My hands are still steady enough to do battlefield surgery."

"You're serious." Lucy's green eyes grew wider. "Liz, that's incredibly brave but totally insane. Remember you're still practicing medicine because there's a shortage of doctors in Maine. We need you right here in Hobbs. If you want to be a hero, open your checkbook and write a big check to Doctors Without Borders, but stay home and take care of business," Lucy said firmly.

"You mean I can't run away and join the foreign legion?"

"No, you can't."

"You can't stop me," said Liz, bristling. She hated to be told what to do.

"No, but I can try to talk sense into you. I know you're a passionate woman, but you have responsibilities. And I'm one of them."

Liz rolled her eyes.

"Elizabeth Stolz, don't you dare! I've taken enough crap from people today, and I'm not taking it from you!"

To avoid Lucy's stern gaze, Liz slouched down on the futon and silently complained about being forced to abandon her fantasy of fighting in Ukraine. Lucy picked up Liz's arm and draped it around her. One of Lucy's best qualities was that she never held a grudge.

4

Maggie focused on Denise's face to avoid staring at her hands and wrists. Apart from her height and her outsized joints, the new music director looked like any other woman.

Curious, Maggie had read up on her career, which was how she'd discovered that Denise Chantal had once been Dennis Chantal, an up-and-coming countertenor. Since she'd transitioned, Denise had been fighting with her record company to expunge her "dead name" from previously released albums. So far, the management had been uncooperative. Ironically, her past success ensured that her former gender would continue to haunt her.

The industry gossip gave Maggie no pleasure. As a card-carrying member of the ACLU, Maggie supported trans rights on principle. Viscerally, she found the physical aspects more difficult to accept. It helped that Denise was attractive and made a completely convincing woman.

Obviously aware of the intense scrutiny, Denise eyed Maggie with a little frown. "Thanks for coming down here today, Dr. Fitzgerald."

"Please, Denise, using my academic title is so formal. I'm not teaching right now. Plus, it makes me feel old." Maggie didn't need any reminders that she was probably old enough to be the woman's mother, maybe even her grandmother, although she doubted Denise could be that young. She'd finished graduate school and launched her singing career. Simple arithmetic told Maggie she was probably in her late twenties. Her smooth skin glowed with youthful health. Maggie wondered if taking female hormones also kept her complexion fresh.

Denise sat back and folded her arms on her chest. "Sorry, *Maggie.* I was trying to be respectful."

"And you were." Maggie smiled, attempting to ease the palpable hostility between them. "Denise, we seem to have gotten off on the wrong foot. Meeting with your predecessor can't be easy. I'm guessing you only agreed to do it because Lucy pushed you."

Denise's blue eyes flashed fire. "Lucy never pushes me," she corrected in a brittle voice. "That's not how she works. She makes suggestions. I usually follow them because she's the rector. If we disagree, which is seldom, we talk about it."

Maggie sighed. Obviously, her attempt at empathy had fallen flat.

"Thanks for sending your music plans from past years," said Denise, her tone still cold, "but I'm trying to raise the bar in this parish. Hearing the same old music is not very inspiring. Popular hymns have been so overused they've become trite."

"Maybe so, but people can sing them *because* they're familiar. When I was music director, Lucy always reminded me that liturgical music should encourage participation. Otherwise, the service is just a performance."

Denise's face became rigid. It was clear that she was barely restraining herself from stating the obvious. *She* was now the music director, and *she* called the shots. Maggie wondered how to convince her that she wasn't a threat.

"I'm sorry, Denise," she said in a conciliatory tone. "It's clear that you are in charge now. My point is that people like to sing in church, especially because COVID prevented it for so long. Don't get me wrong. I get bored with the same old hymns too, but liturgical music is part of worship. We should encourage people to participate, no matter how good the choir is or the other talent in the parish. Look at Lucy. She was an opera star, but she never sings in full voice during a service. She sings as a member of the congregation."

Denise folded her arms on her chest. Having been an acting coach and theater director for decades, Maggie knew exactly what that body language meant. This conversation was going nowhere.

"Okay, Denise. I only came today because Lucy thought I could help. If you're not interested in my suggestions, I have other things to do." Maggie got up and began to collect the sheet music and hymnals she'd brought.

"Please don't go, Maggie," said Denise, looking worried. No doubt she was wondering how to explain to her boss that Maggie had walked out of their meeting "Please. You've come all the way from Scarborough. The truth is, I haven't gotten far in my planning. I've barely sketched out the music for Palm Sunday and Holy Week, and I haven't even touched Easter. I can use your help."

Maggie sat down again and took a moment to revise her strategy. "Denise, I'm guessing because you'd studied sacred music at Yale that you'd prefer more classical material."

"How did you know?"

"I looked up your background. I hope you don't mind."

Denise looked flattered at first, then alarmed. "So you know that I was once a countertenor?"

"Yes, and a very good one apparently. You're a talented musician and very knowledgeable about music." Maggie watched Denise's bubble of hostility slowly deflate. Obviously, the positive reinforcement was working. "You can throw in some classical pieces along with traditional hymns," Maggie continued. "I've heard that the choir has really improved under your direction."

Denise looked pleased. "That's only because for months and months they couldn't sing in church. We were only practicing for ourselves, so I gave them increasingly difficult pieces to sing."

"I hope they maintained their distance. According to my ex-wife, singing in close quarters does spread COVID, so we still need to be careful."

"I won't allow any unvaccinated singers to join the choir," said Denise briskly.

"That's a good precaution, but not foolproof."

"How is it going down here?" asked a cheerful voice from the stairwell. Lucy stepped into the room and offered one of her solar flare smiles. She stopped to study their faces. "Are you making progress?"

Maggie wondered how long Lucy had been standing in the stairwell before she'd announced her presence. Obviously, she'd come down to check on them.

"I was just explaining to Dr. Fitzgerald..." Denise began to say.

Maggie glared at her.

"I mean, I was explaining to Maggie how we kept the choir safe during the pandemic, and how glad we are that it's over."

"As much as we'd like to think so, the pandemic is not over," Lucy reminded gently. "We still need to be careful."

Maggie could see that Denise didn't like being corrected. She quickly changed the subject. "We've been discussing how to choose traditional hymns, so the congregation can be more active."

"I'm a big believer in congregational singing," said Lucy, pulling out a chair from the table and sitting down. "It's the most joyful form of worship, and we most certainly need joy with this war going on. Everyone really missed communal singing during the pandemic. We should have as much of it as possible." Denise did not look pleased to hear Lucy confirm Maggie's point of view. "I can suggest a few of my personal favorites," Lucy volunteered. The steely look returned to Denise's eyes. "But I'm sure you've already made a list."

"No, we haven't gotten that far," said Denise, throwing shade in Maggie's direction. "Although Maggie kindly provided her Lenten and Holy Week plans from past years."

Apparently feeling the chill in air, Lucy studied each of them in turn. "I came down to ask Maggie to join me for coffee after your meeting, but I'm happy to stay and facilitate. You understand, Maggie, that Denise has the last word of the music program. She's in charge now."

"I completely understand," Maggie said in her most gracious tone. She felt like adding, *I'm only here because YOU thought it would be a good idea,* but it would be inappropriate to confront Lucy in Denise's presence.

"Maggie, why don't you come up with a list of traditional hymns you think the congregation would like to sing and send it to Denise? I'll do the same. Then we'll all get together and plan the liturgies."

"Excellent idea, Mother Lucy. I'll make a list too." With her boss present, Denise was suddenly much more cooperative.

"Good," replied Lucy. "With all the musical talent in this room, we should have an amazing Easter season."

"Maggie, do you sing in the choir in your new parish?" asked Denise. It seemed like polite interest, but her blue eyes peered into hers.

Maggie glanced anxiously at Lucy, who might be disappointed to know the truth. Even so, Maggie wouldn't think of lying to her face. "I haven't had time to investigate the local parish. The house needed some work, and I have two young granddaughters. I homeschooled them while the schools were shut down." The excuses sounded entirely plausible. In fact, Maggie wasn't interested in finding a new parish. The real reason she'd joined the Episcopal Church, despite being raised Catholic, was her friendship with Lucy. No church experience would be the same without her warm smile, inspiring sermons, and welcoming attitude.

"Well, I think we have a plan," said Denise, obviously trying to end the meeting. "After you both send me your suggestions, I'll compile them, and we can meet again." She turned to Maggie. "If you'll excuse us, I need a few minutes with Mother Lucy."

Lucy folded her hands on the table and sat forward. "Is this something we can't discuss in front of Maggie? She was part of this parish for years and knows all our dirty secrets."

Denise glanced furtively at Maggie. "I'd hoped to share the news privately, but since Maggie already knows my story, there's no reason she can't hear this too. The Boston Symphony is performing *The Resurrection Symphony*, and I've been invited to audition!" Denise's silent clapping under her chin conveyed a hint of her joy. "Lucy has been my voice teacher since I came to Hobbs," Denise explained for Maggie's benefit. "I couldn't afford one, so she volunteered to coach me. She's helping me learn to sound like a natural alto. It's the only way I can restart my singing career as a woman." Among all the challenges Denise might face, Maggie had never considered this one. She felt a sudden surge of compassion for her.

"Lucy's a great teacher." Maggie agreed. "She was coaching me for a while…before I moved away." That was all Maggie was willing to admit about why the voice lessons had abruptly stopped.

Lucy reached out for Denise's hand. "That's wonderful news! Tell me more."

"The assistant program director at BSO is a good friend. He mentioned to the conductor that you've been training me. Turns out he's one of your biggest fans."

"If trading on my name gets you the part, I won't complain," said Lucy, glancing at Maggie.

"I'm afraid it's more than that," said Denise, staring at the pile of sheet music on the table. "This is how it went down. I was having a few beers with Mike, my friend who works at BSO. I told him how you've helped me adjust my register breaks. He asked me if you'd kept up your voice, and I could honestly say that you had because I'd heard you sing. I should have known something was up. I could see the wheels in his brain turning. I never expected anything to come of it. This morning I got a phone call from the maestro himself, asking if I'd like to audition. What could I say, but yes? And forgive me, Mother Lucy, but I volunteered you."

"Volunteered me for what?"

"To audition with me."

"What?" The color instantly drained from Lucy's face. "You're joking."

"Please forgive me! I was so excited to get the call. I thought I'd never get the chance to sing professionally again, and here was Estefan Morales on the phone personally inviting me to audition. He kept raving about you and your wonderful voice and how he would love to hear you sing again. I knew right away that you were the real reason for the invitation, but that didn't matter. This is the big break I've been waiting for, so when he asked if I would bring you along, I told him I would. I'm sorry. I should have asked first."

While Denise had been speaking, Lucy's cheeks had mostly regained their normal color. Being a redhead, she was always a little pale, so it was hard to tell. "Denise, I haven't performed in years."

"That's not really true, Lucy," Maggie said, playing devil's advocate. "We gave those shows at the Webhanet Playhouse."

"But that was a benefit for a summer stock theater. This is the BSO! Yes, I do practice every day, but not like when I sang professionally."

"Maybe not, but your voice is still wonderful," said Denise. "When I hear you sing, you are Lucille Bartlett, star of the Metropolitan Opera."

"A long time ago."

"Not that long ago. I know because I looked it up. And I know you've sung this part before."

Lucy looked uncomfortable being confronted, but she said, "I have. In London, and Berlin. The summer festival at Aix."

"And at Tanglewood under Seiji Ozawa," said Denise, glowing with admiration. "I've watched the YouTube. You were fabulous. I bet you know the part cold."

"I don't know about that. I'd have to practice. It's not like singing a full-length opera, but the *Mahler Two* has interesting challenges." Lucy's green eyes grew wide. "Oh, Denise. I don't know if I am up for this."

"Lucy, don't be modest," Maggie said. "Maybe it's been a while, but I know, and you know, you still have the pipes." Denise nodded, looking pleased to have Maggie on her side.

"Please, Lucy," Denise said, clasping her hands prayerfully. "I've been waiting desperately for this chance. It could launch my career as Denise Chantal, which means I can finally appear on the stage as myself…in my *true* body."

Looking confused and desperate, Lucy turned to Maggie.

"Why don't you think about it overnight and get back to Denise in the morning?" Maggie suggested gently.

"Yes, of course. That's a good idea." Lucy released her breath in a long sigh. "Denise, you know I support you. I'll do my best to help you in any way I can, but this is so unexpected!"

"I understand, but please, I beg you, if you can see your way to doing this, I would be so grateful."

Maggie could see that Lucy was struggling to keep her composure. "Denise, why don't you let me and Lucy get that coffee she promised?" She looked directly into Denise's eyes, silently communicating that she would take it from here.

"You're right, Maggie. That's a good idea." Denise got up and collected her papers and headed to her office.

After she left, Lucy still looked dazed. Maggie gave her a few moments before asking, "You do still want to go out for coffee?"

Lucy focused on Maggie's face. "Yes, of course. Want to drive together?"

"Let's each take our own cars. I'm going to Sam's afterwards, and that's in the other direction."

Lucy's auburn brow went up slightly. "Hmm. You'll have to tell me more about that."

"I will…when we're having coffee, although you look like you could use something stronger."

Lucy glanced at her watch. "It's too early for alcohol. I'll meet you at Awakened Brews."

As Maggie headed up Route 1, she tried to figure out how she felt about Lucy's big break. For years, Maggie had been trying to make a comeback, acting in local theater, performing in summer stock, even auditioning for cold calls. Meanwhile, Lucy had made absolutely no effort, and an opportunity fell into her lap. It was hard not to be jealous.

The parking lot at Awakened Brews was empty. That meant they would have privacy for their conversation. Maggie pulled into a space right in front. When she got out of the car, the little chill in the air convinced her to wait inside the café. A few minutes later, Lucy came through the door. She went directly to the counter and placed their order.

"It's nice having a friend who knows exactly how you like your coffee," Maggie said when Lucy came to the table.

"We've been coming here since we met. Everything was so new then. Maggie, I don't know what I would have done without you showing me around town and introducing me to people."

"I was glad to be of help. I enjoyed it too."

Lucy's eyes were full of affection. "Maggie, I miss our friendship. I really do."

Maggie carefully considered her words before she spoke. "I do too, but it will take time to rebuild it, and it won't be the same."

"We're not the same people, so why would it be? So much has happened since I was a clueless, new rector. We've both changed. But I'm glad you're willing to give our friendship another try, because I'm going to really need a friend."

"Why? What's going on besides this surprise audition?"

"Well, I expect my book to cause a big stir. Sex always makes religious types lose their minds. Tom told me he's stepping back from his role as associate rector, and—as if I needed more drama—my ex is back in town."

Maggie was curious. Sam had mentioned something about the return of Lucy's ex but had given few details. Maybe she didn't know any more.

"She caused some real trouble when she was here last summer."

"Glad I missed it," said Maggie casually.

"Me too. It was not a good look for either of us." Maggie waited for Lucy to say more, but she didn't. Clearly, she was distracted. "Oh, Maggie, what should I do? I don't have time to get my voice in shape. Besides all the additional services because it's Lent, I'm finishing up my coursework and dealing with the final edits on my book."

"It's just an audition, Lucy, not the performance. Congratulations on passing your thesis defense, by the way. I'm sorry. I got distracted by the conversation with Denise and forgot to tell you. How did it go?"

"The committee grilled me harder than I expected. The people I least expected to hold my feet to the fire really burned me."

"That's usually the way. It's an inside out way of avoiding favoritism. I sat on many dissertation committees when I was teaching at NYU. It's not as easy as you might think."

"I'm just glad it's all behind me. After I turn in my last two papers, I'm done!" The idea of completion obviously pleased Lucy, but an instant later, she looked sad and desperate. "What should I do? I don't want to let Denise down, but I never imagined performing professionally again. During those years after Alex had me blacklisted at the Met, I would have killed for an opportunity like this!"

"That's how it works. The same with relationships. When you're looking for a partner, there's none in sight. Call off the search, and people are beating down your door."

The barista brought their coffee and an oversized blueberry muffin split down the middle. "Sorry for the wait," she said. "It just came out of the oven."

"I should have ordered two muffins," Lucy said in an apologetic tone, after the waitress walked away, "but we always used to split one."

"Half is fine. I don't need more sugar or carbs."

"Me neither," Lucy said, making a face. "My ass is getting big."

"Lucy, you look great. You lost too much weight after Erika died."

The distraught look returned to Lucy's face. "Maggie, if I don't help Denise, she might not get another chance. She's so talented. She should be doing more than being a church music director."

"Then do this one gig as a personal favor. You'll get to wear one of your pretty gowns and hear the applause one last time. It might be fun."

"Oh, it will be fun. I get a rush just thinking about it."

"And if you do this performance, it doesn't mean you have to give up your day job. You seem to really like being a priest."

"I do, but I also enjoyed being a singer, and sometimes, I miss it. It's what I was trained to do. And I was good at it."

"Yes, you were and still are. I wish I had half your talent."

Lucy gave her a long, thoughtful look. "Thank you, Maggie. That's very generous."

"Now that I'm in a relationship, I feel less deprived, so I can afford to be generous."

"So, it's a relationship? That's wonderful! Congratulations," Lucy said with genuine enthusiasm. "Tell me more."

Maggie smiled a little catlike smile. "I'm afraid to say anything and jinx it. It's not what I expected. And that's the best part of all."

***

Sam drove down the driveway of the Jimson Pond house and saw Maggie's Subaru parked in front of the barn. A smile instantly bloomed on her face. She imagined the glamorous woman, a thick white braid trailing down her back, busily preparing a delicious supper in her kitchen. Sam had yearned for such perfect domesticity her entire life. She'd internalized the cultural values of middle-class Americana from watching TV. Her family life couldn't be more different.

Her mother had a black housekeeper to cook and clean and keep an eye on baby Samantha. The only time her mother ever cooked was when the housekeeper was off on alternative weekends. Like clockwork, her mother became crabby and overwhelmed until the housekeeper returned. Domestic help became hard to find as black women began claiming their civil rights. Keeping up the house overwhelmed her mother. Sam was identified as the problem, and her parents sent her off to boarding school.

Some people thought boarding school was a place to learn manners and upper crust ways. In fact, the students were barely supervised and devised their own social system. In Sam's all-girls school, the popular girls clawed at each other for dominance and formed their followers into gangs. None of them ever picked Sam with her boyish ways and the big brain that put them all to shame. The contempt she'd later felt from her mother's junior league friends only hardened her fear and loathing of females of a certain class.

If choosing to study architecture at Princeton was asserting her independence, spending a few years in Italy to learn the methods of master tilers was an act of defiance. When she came home from Rome, she apprenticed to a carpenter, shocking her parents. She didn't understand why they were so upset. The brainy guys in her circle were doing the same—casting off their parents' expectations that they become captains of industry and joining the trades instead. But either way, girls weren't supposed to do such things.

After her little mental tour of the past, Sam finally turned off the truck engine. She rubbed her hands together to gauge their dryness. Even though she wore gloves, her skin got sandpapery from the mortar. It was always worse in the winter. Sam rifled through the console of the truck looking for the jar of industrial-strength hand cream she kept there. Maggie was soft and still fragile from the divorce. Sam didn't want to touch her with anything rough.

She took her dirty clothes out of the rear compartment and threw them into the washing machine before she went into the kitchen.

"What a nice surprise," Sam said. "I didn't expect you."

"I wanted it to be a surprise. That's why I didn't call first. I hope you hadn't planned anything special for dinner."

"I was going to defrost some venison stew I made last month. I'm sure whatever you're making will be tastier."

"You'll just have to wait and see," said Maggie with a mysterious smile. Hands wet from chopping vegetables, she raised her face for a kiss. "I heard your truck come in, but then I didn't see you. Is everything all right?" she asked anxiously.

Sam nodded. "I was thinking. I'm not used to having someone wait for me at home, so I didn't even consider you might be worried. Sorry."

"Don't apologize. I don't expect you to change your life for me."

"You already have," said Sam and gave Maggie a gentle kiss. She straightened, so she could dig deep into her pocket. "Here. I went for a walk at lunchtime and picked these up for you." She opened her hand and revealed two colorful, heart-shaped pebbles worn smooth by the ocean.

"Oh, they're beautiful! Thank you. Liz always..." Maggie looked up into Sam's face with a mournful expression. "I'm sorry...I didn't mean to..."

Sam smiled sadly. "It's okay. Liz is the reason I know you like heart stones. She'd always pick them up for you when we walked on the beach. She'd say, 'Oh, Maggie would really like this one,' and explain what rock it was and the minerals in it. Liz knows so much about everything."

"She does," Maggie said wistfully. She put the pebbles on the windowsill. "I hope you don't mind me putting them there temporarily."

"Not at all."

"I have a whole jar of them at home. Liz still brought them to me even after things got bad between us." Maggie shook her head as if dismissing the thought.

"Well, now you have more." Sam smiled to dispel the heaviness. "What smells so damn good?"

"Asian short ribs. I thought we could use some comfort food, and I love to make braised meats in cool weather. Soon summer will be here, and it will get too warm to heat up the kitchen."

"You could use a slow cooker." Maggie wrinkled her nose, and Sam laughed. "Like microwaves, they do come in handy."

"Food tastes better when it's cooked properly. And with grocery prices through the roof, I refuse to waste it."

Sam went to the refrigerator to take out a beer. "Did you find the wine I bought for you?"

Maggie pointed to the glass of red wine on the counter. "Thank you for thinking of me."

"Of course, I think of you," Sam said, flipping the cap off her beer. "I might have been up to my elbows in thin-set when you were meeting with Denise, but I was thinking of you. How did it go?"

Maggie wiped her hands dry and took off her apron. "Let's go into the living room, and I'll tell you about it."

Sam added wood pellets to the stove while she waited for Maggie. Although the day had been warm, the pond outside her back door could make the house feel damp and chilly.

Maggie finally came in and sat down on the sofa with her glass of wine. "The meeting with Denise was intense. She's really threatened by me," she said as Sam settled beside her. "I tried my best to make her comfortable, but she resisted. Thank God, Lucy showed up. Her presence instantly lowered the temperature."

"Lucy is good at that."

"Afterward, Lucy and I went to Awakened Brews for some girl talk."

Sam put her arm around Maggie and pulled her closer. "That's nice. I'm glad you're friends again."

"We're getting there. She might have a new gig. Denise was invited to audition for a Boston Symphony concert. They want Lucy to sing with her."

"Wow."

"Yes, wow." Maggie took a sip of wine. "I hate to be jealous, but I worked so hard to make a comeback. She does nothing, and gets an important gig."

"Don't hold it against her. It's just luck, not divine intervention. Your time will come. You should get involved with the Webhanet Playhouse again. Maybe put feelers out to your friends in New York."

"You wouldn't mind if I went back to the stage?"

"Hell, no. You're so talented. I'd love to see you perform again."

Maggie snuggled closer. "Tell me you're not too good to be true."

Sam laughed softly. "If you're asking if I'm just being on good behavior because we're dating, I can tell you I'm not acting any way special. I hope you know that by now. We've been friends for a long time."

"But I never really knew you."

"That's because Liz was always overshadowing me with that surgeon's charisma of hers."

"No, I don't think that's why. In fact, when I met up with Liz again, I didn't even think of her as a surgeon until I got cancer. At first, she was like the seventeen-year-old kid I first met in college. She fell into the role of adoring worshiper and had me on a pedestal…that is, when she wasn't still hating me for dumping her forty years before."

"She had your complete attention. That's why you didn't notice me. I was just hanging around…her junior sidekick."

"I did notice you, Sam, but you were so quiet. You never let me know who you are. Now, I can finally see you."

Sam took her arm back and slouched down on the sofa. "I hope you still like what you see."

"Oh, Sam, I like you more every day. In fact, I'm getting a little past just liking you."

"Don't tell me that." Sam anxiously took a long pull on her beer.

"Why? Will it scare you away?"

"Maybe. I don't like pressure or being crowded."

Maggie moved to the other side of the couch. "Is that better?"

Sam laughed and slid over to be closer. "It's not a matter of physical space. I was enjoying my relationship with Olivia, if you could call it that. If she hadn't kept pushing me, we might still be together."

"Is there a possibility you'll get back together?" Maggie asked cautiously.

"Hell no. She's way too much for me to handle."

"And I'm not?"

Sam gave her a skeptical side-eye. "You may be. I'm not sure yet."

Maggie leaned her chin on her hand. "Interesting. Tell me why you think I might be too much to handle."

"I'm not very good at psychological talk."

"Try."

Sam suddenly felt fidgety. "I need a snack. I bet there are some peanuts in the cabinet," she said, catapulting herself up from her seat. "I'll bring out the wine." In the kitchen, she found the jar of peanuts and grabbed the open bottle of merlot.

"Thank you, Sam," Maggie said as she refilled her glass. "You're so kind."

"See? That's part of the problem! You're always complimenting me!"

"Why shouldn't I compliment you? You are kind, one of the kindest people I know. I was really low after the surgery. If you hadn't taken care of me, kidnapped me so I'd get a break from the kids…taken me out on drives, I don't know what I would have done. That's when I realized you were more than a friend. I was delighted to find out you felt the same."

Sam stared at her feet. "I still can't believe you even looked at me," she murmured. After admitting it, she wanted to hide. Instead, she slouched deeper into the sofa.

"Why?" asked Maggie, looking mystified.

"You're so beautiful and sexy."

"Me? Sexy. A gray-haired woman who's almost seventy? With fake boobs? Foobs, they call them. That's supposed to be cute, I guess. Who are we kidding, Sam? I'm an old wreck."

"No, you're a gorgeous, sexy woman," Sam whispered. "I'm not sure I'm worthy of you."

Maggie's eyes began to glisten. "Sam, stop it! Of course, you are. You're beautiful and sexy too, never mind brilliant. Maybe I'm not worthy of you! It's my rotten luck to be attracted to geniuses, people who make me feel stupid."

"You're not stupid, Maggie. Hell, you were a college professor for years."

"See, Sam? Everyone has insecurities, including me." Maggie reached over and pulled on Sam's arm. "Do you mind sitting a little closer? I like feeling your warmth."

Sam raised her arm and let Maggie snuggle against her. "Thank you for surprising me tonight. I like having you here."

5

The knock on the open door was followed by a hesitant question. "Do you have a few minutes to talk?"

Liz looked up from her computer screen to see who was standing in her doorway. The face and attractive figure were backlit, but the honeyed Louisiana accent instantly identified her physician's assistant, Cherie Harrison. Liz closed her laptop and gestured to a visitors' chair. "What's up?"

After Cherie sat down, Liz gave her a quick critical assessment. Despite her perpetual tan, a gift of her biracial heritage, she was pale.

"You look exhausted," Liz observed.

"I admit I'm tired, but we're finally getting into a routine with the kids, so it's getting better. It's Brenda I'm worried about, that's why I'm here, speaking as her wife, not your PA."

"Go on. I listen to people in all their incarnations." Liz sat up to show she was paying attention.

"She's been having shortness of breath again. I want her to come in to see you, but she says she's fine. When I push, she says you're too busy, and she doesn't want to bother you."

"Well, you know how stubborn she is. She's into that tough-cop stoicism." While Liz considered the situation, she gazed at the ceiling. During the renovation, Sam had replaced the ugly recessed lighting with the latest ceiling panels. It had made a significant improvement. "Are you worried her long-COVID heart problems have returned? She's tolerating the meds well. All her recent tests have been normal."

"You don't live with her. Honestly, I'm not sure the symptoms ever completely went away."

"If that's the case, Amy should examine her."

"You don't understand. I can't get her to come near Hobbs Family Practice except to pick me up when my car is in the shop."

"Have you examined her?"

"She won't let me. She says, 'you're my wife, not my doc' and pushes me away. She swears she's perfectly fine, but I can hear her panting when she walks up the stairs."

"I know she's been trying to get back in shape. Is she spending more time at the gym? I just read an article recommending that COVID heart patients shouldn't jump right back into a strenuous exercise program. They should build up gradually."

"She's been at the gym a lot. She's trying to get rid of that little belly, but I think she's also trying to escape the kids. They're wearing her out."

Liz released a long sigh. "I wish I could make good on the offer to take them for a weekend, but Lucy says it's too busy until after Easter."

"And she's right to push back. She's holding services morning, noon, and night. She works way too hard. Don't you worry about her wearing herself out?"

"Of course, I do, but she's as stubborn as I am and doesn't always listen to me. I just try to take care of her as best I can and play the dutiful pastor's wife."

Cherie chuckled. "I know you try, but being a church lady doesn't come easily to you, does it?"

This was one of the times Liz regretted the informality she'd introduced in the office. When she was head of surgery at Yale, she would never let a PA talk to her like that. "I'm doing the best I can," she muttered.

Cherie reached across the desk to pat Liz's hand. "Keep up the good work. Lucy needs you now, and I'm sure she appreciates all you do for her."

"But I wish I could do something for you and Brenda. I can take the kids on Saturdays to give you and Brenda a chance to catch up on your chores."

"You have your own chores too, and that's Lucy's only day off."

Liz scanned her mind for a solution. "When is your Aunt Simone moving up from Louisiana?"

Cherie sighed. "She's getting her house ready to sell, but she doesn't have much money to make the repairs. Brenda and I have been sending her some, but it's not enough."

"You should get in touch with Habitat for Humanity. They don't just build houses. They do repairs for seniors like your aunt. I've volunteered with them, and they do everything from replacing windows to patching a roof."

"Hmm. Good idea. Hadn't thought of that. But I suspect Aunt Simone is dragging her feet. She's lived in that house since she got married, which was the year I was born…almost fifty years ago. It's her nest, the place where she hatched her chicks."

"I'm sure it's hard to leave a place where she's lived most of her life," said Liz, "but I've talked to her. She wants to be near family as she ages. She says she gets along better with you than her own kids."

"Well, you know how it is with boys. They want to take care of their mama, but their wives come first. You've heard the old saying, 'a daughter's your daughter for the rest of your life, your son is your son until he takes a wife.'"

"Not always. My youngest brother took care of my mother until she died. Not very well, I might add."

"When Aunt Simone comes it will be easier, but we can't count on her getting here any time soon. I'll be amazed to see her before fall, and then she still might be reluctant. She found our winter shocking."

"I'm sure she did, coming from a warm place like Louisiana. I hope the change is not too hard on her."

"Brenda is thinking about building an apartment over the garage for her."

"Well, I did that, and my mother never used it. It was expensive. Are you sure you can afford it?" Liz asked.

"No. We'd have to take a second mortgage."

"Just what you need—an additional financial burden and more stress on Brenda. You could put in an application in that new senior project near the mall. If your aunt is interested, you'll want to get her on the waiting list as soon as you can. With the housing shortage, it could take months, even years for a place to become available."

"What if a place opens up right away?"

"Then you move her up here and encourage her to sell the house 'as is.' With this overheated housing market, most buyers are in a bidding war. She should probably cash out before the mortgage rates rise, and they certainly will. What's the market like where she lives?"

"It's a mostly black suburb where professionals live. Her husband was a lawyer. He made a good living. Unfortunately, Aunt Simone couldn't keep up the place after he died."

"How about this? Give me the address. I'll have some time tonight while Lucy is doing her evening prayer service. I'll check out the local Habitat for Humanity and see what services they offer seniors."

"Won't Lucy miss you in the Zoom meeting?"

Liz spoke in a confidential tone. "Don't tell, but I turn off the video feed and half-listen while I do other things. And what can Lucy say? I'm doing a good deed."

Cherie laughed and shook her head. "Oh, Liz, don't ever change. You're one of a kind." She looked at her watch. "I should let you get back to work. I saw you have Olivia Enright next on your schedule."

"She's always early, so she's probably out there waiting. Send her down, please. On the way, give Amy a heads up that I might need her for a consult for a few minutes."

"Will do, Liz, but we haven't decided what to do about Brenda."

"Don't worry. I'll handle it. I'll tell her I need to examine her for my vaccine study. Brenda has an overdeveloped sense of civic responsibility. She'll report for duty, no questions asked. You watch." Liz raised a finger.

"You have us all figured out, don't you?"

"Not quite. Occasionally, people surprise me."

"Hmm. I'll have to work on that." Cherie got up. "I'll bring in Ms. Enright."

"Make sure she gets on the scale. She's lost too much weight since that heart attack. I want to keep an eye on it."

A short time later, Liz heard Olivia's distinctive voice in the hall. She was adamantly protesting the need to be weighed. Eventually, Cherie's gentle urging prevailed.

"One eighteen. That's still down ten pounds from your normal weight, Ms. Enright."

"Oh, Cherie, will you please stop with the formality? Call me Olivia!"

"I'm sorry, but it's what we're taught."

"Well, all right then," Olivia said irritably. "Do I need to get undressed?"

"Just to the waist. Dr. Stolz and Dr. Hsu will listen to your heart. Maybe they'll want to do a quick ultrasound. Let me ask."

Liz got up and went into the hall. Olivia, as always, was perfectly coiffed and wore a stylish, but classy outfit. She appeared to be the epitome of old money even though the reality was completely opposite.

"Hello, Liz," said Olivia. "Thanks for rescuing me from Cherie. She's very sweet, but she can be a tyrant!"

"You should be flattered, Olivia. Usually, PAs don't check a patient's vitals. It's something the medical assistants do. I'm guessing Cherie is only doing it because she likes you." Liz winked at Cherie.

"Thank you, Cherie," said Olivia. "I'm glad *someone* likes me."

"More people would like you if you didn't scare the hell out of them," said Liz.

"So do you," Olivia snapped. She looked Liz up and down. "You're all dressed up today. What's the occasion?"

"Lucy and I are heading up to Portland this afternoon to meet with her bishop. Part of our prenuptial counseling."

"Well, then, let's make it quick. You can't be late for the bishop!"

"Come with me, Ms. Enright," said Cherie, guiding her by the shoulder into an examination room.

"Liz!" called an elegantly dressed Asian woman, heading in her direction. "Cherie said you wanted me to have a look at Olivia Enright." Liz pointed down the hall, and Amy followed her into her office. Liz carefully closed the door.

"Olivia respects your opinion because you're a specialist. I'm still not sure she's ready to go back to work full time. But I'll defer to you."

Amy's perfectly arched black brow rose slightly. "Pushing the responsibility off on me? You think she'll be more receptive because she likes me?"

"She likes me too, but she *likes* you."

"I don't know about that," said Amy, her dark eyes glancing away.

"Oh, I do. Trust me on this, Amy. It's your business, but Olivia is a handful."

"Don't worry. It's my policy to avoid personal involvement with my patients."

"Technically, she's my patient, but when you live in a small town like Hobbs, it's hard not to be involved, at least socially."

Amy gave her a wary look. "I never realized practicing family medicine could be so complicated."

"Just you wait," said Liz, nodding. "We're all just getting acquainted. Just tell Olivia the truth, based on your professional opinion, but don't let her boss you around. She will try to get the upper hand."

Amy smiled. "There's no need to warn me about Olivia. Remember. I've seen her in action. I will give my professional opinion based on the facts, nothing else."

"Good," said Liz decisively. "I'm glad we understand one another."

Cherie poked her head through the door of Liz's office. "Doctors, your patient is ready for you."

Olivia, hugging herself to keep her johnny gown closed, frowned as they came in. "Joining forces, I see. Is there an extra charge for this?"

"It's part of an office visit, so no extra charge," said Liz.

"I just want to make sure. I don't want to get one of those surprise bills…doctors sticking their heads in the door, asking how you are, and then charging for nothing. I don't want my insurance rates to go up."

Liz managed to stop herself from rolling her eyes. Olivia had super-platinum health insurance. She was one of the richest people in Hobbs. Why would she worry about a minor charge to her account? "Don't worry,

Liv. We don't do piecemeal medicine here. We work as a team, and you get the benefit of Amy's expertise in cardiology."

Olivia smiled unctuously. "Amy, will you please explain to Dr. Stolz that I am fit for duty?"

"I'm glad to hear you feel better, Olivia, but that doesn't mean your heart is ready for you to go back to work."

"Whose side are you on?" demanded Olivia.

"The side of your health," replied Amy in a calm voice.

She inserted the earpieces of her stethoscope. Liz sat on the doctor's stool, watching her listen to Olivia's chest. Her attractive face was perfectly composed. She closed her eyes to help her focus. Finally, she took off the stethoscope and draped it around her neck. "Your heart sounds strong, but it's still beating too fast. I'd like to do a quick ultrasound to see what's going on."

Liz watched while Amy trailed the probe across Olivia's chest. Her tachycardia was not excessive but enough to cause concern.

"Well?" asked Olivia.

Amy nodded while she composed her thoughts. "Your heart is still working too hard. I know it's not what you wanted to hear, but I recommend another few weeks at home. I'll look at your meds, but I'd rather you continue to recover at home before I increase your dosages."

"But Amy, I've been away from my job for months. I don't trust those selectmen. They've been in power too long. The town has gone to hell in my absence!"

Liz laughed. "Liv, Hobbs moves too slowly to go to hell in just a few months."

"Please, Amy," Olivia begged. "I'm going insane sitting at home." Amy looked to Liz for support.

"Well, maybe you can go in a few days a week to start," said Liz. Olivia's face brightened. Amy's became stony. "But Amy is the expert. She has the last word."

Amy's face grew harder. Obviously, she didn't appreciate being made the bad guy, or Liz's easy capitulation after urging her to be firm. Amy quickly resumed a neutral expression. "Why don't you sit out this week?" she said diplomatically. "Next week, go in part-time as Liz suggests. One day, the first week. Two days, the second. Build up gradually. The point is to avoid taxing your heart with stress. Ease your way back into your duties."

"That sounds reasonable," Olivia agreed. "Thank you, Amy. Good advice."

Amy looked pleased that her compromise had been accepted so easily. "Unless you have any questions for me, I'd think we're done here. You can get dressed now." She turned to leave.

"Amy, there is one thing you could do for me," said Olivia.

"What's that?" asked Amy, turning around.

"You could join me for dinner this week."

Liz unsuccessfully tried to hide a grin. "Sorry, but I have to pick up my better half. I'll leave you two to set up your date."

❊❊❊

Lucy felt a pulse on her smartwatch and saw that Liz had sent her a message: *On my way.* Lucy breathed a sigh of relief. They couldn't be late for their last prenuptial meeting. Liz had already gotten on the bishop's wrong side by rescheduling it twice.

Lucy had dealt with some powerful people in her life: world famous conductors, general managers of the world's greatest opera companies, and fellow singers with superstar status. That never fazed her, but meeting with her bishop always gave her butterflies. The handsome, openly gay man had never been anything but kind and supportive of her ministry. He'd been especially, if sometimes annoyingly, attentive after Erika had died. Despite what seemed like an intrusion when all she wanted to do was roll up in a ball, she never resented it. At times, he was charming beyond belief, but she never doubted his sincerity. She'd finally figured out that nothing Bishop Greene did caused her discomfort. It was her issue.

As a singer, Lucy felt confident, even when debuting a new work. Like an athlete preparing for a big competition, she'd trained constantly to become a star. Her mother was determined that Lucy would succeed where she hadn't. As a result, Lucy could perform under the most grueling circumstances, even during a loud thunderstorm that briefly turned off the lights in the theater.

But the confidence Lucy felt about her opera career had never translated to her priesthood. She'd come to it late, studied for it sporadically, and only practiced for the role as required for her ordination. Subconsciously, she'd always hoped she could revive her singing career. She'd hoped that being blacklisted at the Met by the old boys' club and the whisper campaign started by her rapist, a powerful music producer, hadn't sunk her reputation forever.

She'd made a fortune while she was an opera star. Although some of it had been bilked by a dishonest agent, she could have survived on low-profile engagements, hiding in small European opera houses. At some point, she'd had to acknowledge her career was over. That's when she finally began preparing for ordination in earnest. Only she knew that becoming a priest was less of a vocation than an admission of defeat.

Watching Liz's Audi race into the rectory parking lot, Lucy wondered what her fiancée would think if she knew about her doubts—Liz, who never missed an opportunity to slam the Church for its hypocrisy.

The Audi pulled right up to the door. "Thanks for the text," said Lucy, getting into the passenger seat. "I was beginning to worry you'd forgotten."

"I'm sorry, but my appointment with Olivia ran long. I'm trying to keep Amy out of her clutches."

"Oh, Liz, you make it sound so dramatic."

"Now that Olivia is feeling better, she's getting frisky. She invited Amy to dinner."

"And you're worried Amy can't handle herself?"

"You know how Olivia is. What she wants, she gets."

"Liz, it's their business."

Liz leaned closer to the steering wheel to get a better view as she tried to pull onto Route 1. Now that the weather had improved, more snowbirds were returning, and the roads were busier. "I don't care who people date, but Amy told me how damaged she was by her marriage to that nut-case neurosurgeon. She sounds like a classic narcissist, and you know I don't throw psychological terms around lightly."

"But, Liz, it's not your job to protect people from making bad choices. Amy strikes me as an intelligent woman. Let her figure it out." Liz slammed on the accelerator to squeeze into the small break in traffic, throwing Lucy back in her seat. "Take it easy," Lucy urged. "We have plenty of time. I told you to come fifteen minutes early so we can get there on time."

"What?" Liz turned to give her dirty look. "Nice of you to tell me now."

"I know how much you hate to meet with the bishop, so I plan ahead."

"Lucy, I always keep my word."

"When you can. Sometimes, it's not your choice. You have an emergency. You get stuck with a patient." Lucy reached out to pat Liz's thigh, hoping to mollify her. "I know you have the best intentions."

"Well, not always," Liz replied in a grumpy voice.

Lucy hummed until Liz switched on the sound system to open a Bluetooth connection.

"Go on," said Liz. "Sing. It will make you feel better."

"Not sure about that. I'm still anxious about this Boston Symphony audition. I need to get back to Denise about whether I'm going."

"Oh, don't try to kid me, Lucy. Of course, you're going. Why wouldn't you go?"

Lucy studied Liz's profile, debating whether to share her concerns. "If I tell you something, do you promise not to bring it up later?"

"You know that's not how I work. Maggie used to save up information only to slam me with it when she was angry. I hate that." Liz glanced at Lucy. "So, what's the big secret?"

"I'm afraid if I get the part and do this concert, I'll make a fool of myself. I haven't performed professionally in years. I know the critics will compare my voice to when I was in my prime. All singers' voices change with age, especially women's voices after menopause. And finally, and this is the biggie, I'm afraid I'll really like singing again and want to go back to it."

Liz had listened with a thoughtful expression. She drove another mile before she spoke. "I can understand why any one of those reasons could make you reluctant. Let's dismiss number one. You are the ultimate professional, so you'd never make a fool of yourself. It's a very minor part, so you won't have big exposure. Of course, you'll be compared to when you were in your glory, but you'll also get lots of sympathy for coming out of retirement for this event. I don't know what to say about the last one. That *is* a biggie." Lucy had been smiling to herself while Liz had tackled her concerns logically and in the same order that she'd presented them.

"It's difficult to resist this tantalizing opportunity dangled in front of me."

"I understand. I often think about what could have been if I hadn't retired early from Yale and surgery."

"That's different. You made a big contribution to breast cancer care. I was just a performer."

"But you were a great performer. Your singing brought beauty and joy to many, including me."

"That's nice, but as a priest, I make a real difference in people's lives, just like you do as a doctor."

Liz nodded thoughtfully. "Do you have to tell the bishop you want to do this performance?"

"No, I don't have to ask his permission, but I will tell him out of courtesy."

"That's a good idea. Most bosses don't like big surprises." Lucy wanted to say that the bishop was only nominally her boss, but she knew Liz didn't really care about the subtleties of diocesan organization. "Do you mind if I stream a recording of *Mahler's Second Symphony*?" Liz asked. "When I was a kid, I listened to my recording of it so often the vinyl wore out."

The ride to Portland wasn't long, especially at the speed that Liz like to drive, so they had only gotten through the second movement of the symphony by the time they arrived. "Can we finish on the way back?" asked Liz, opening the car door.

"Sure," said Lucy, "but maybe you could turn down the volume a little."

"You're no fun."

"Hearing is important to a singer."

The bishop's assistant told them he was running a little behind and offered them coffee while they waited. Finally, he arrived, looking harried and full of apologies.

"My meeting ran long. So sorry to be late. I know you're both busy people!" He hugged Lucy and offered his hand to Liz. "Come in," he said, opening the door to his office. "Relax while I get myself together. This mask thing again!" he said, removing his.

"People are tired of them, and the CDC can't make up its mind," said Liz. "But the masks do keep people from dying."

"I know but trying to get consensus is so difficult," complained the bishop. "And the truth is, I'm sick of the masks myself."

"We all are," said Lucy with a sigh. "I'm guessing that at our next meeting, our vestry will vote to make them optional, and there's nothing I can do about it."

"Let's talk about something happier," said the bishop with a smile. "You both look great. How are you?"

Liz glanced at Lucy, looking for her to take the lead. She considered communication with the bishop her fiancée's domain.

"We've had a busy month since we last saw you," Lucy said.

"So, I've heard. Congratulations on passing your thesis defense. You're practically home free. Soon we must address you as Rev. Dr. Bartlett! And we'll be proud to do so, won't we, Dr. Stolz?"

"Bishop, you've been grilling us on our relationship for months. By now, I think you should be calling me Liz."

He chuckled. "Thank you, I will. And this is our last session. I'm sure you're happy about that. Are we still on track for a June wedding on..." He put on his reading glasses and opened his computer. There was an extended pause as he navigated to his calendar. "... the eleventh?"

"As far as I know, right, Liz?" Lucy glanced in her direction.

Liz shrugged. "Works for me. You two are in charge."

"Oh, Liz," scolded the bishop, "surely, you don't want to leave all the planning to Lucy. This is your wedding too."

"Honestly, we're both swamped. I've been thinking of hiring a wedding planner but haven't gotten around to it. Lucy still has to finish school, get her book published, and now she might be getting herself into yet another venture."

"Oh?" The bishop turned to Lucy and looked curious.

Lucy couldn't tell if Liz was encouraging her to say something about the BSO concert or had mentioned it casually, but it was a perfect segue. "I've been invited to audition to be a soloist with the Boston Symphony," she explained.

The bishop's face registered surprised delight. "How wonderful! Congratulations."

"Thank you. It's been a long time since I've been on a big stage, but it's an opportunity for our music director to reboot her career as a singer. One of her friends used me as bait to get her the audition. Not quite blackmail, but close."

"I think it's a wonderful opportunity for both of you. My only concern for you, Lucy, is your other duties. Lent and Easter are busy seasons. And now, Tom wants to go part time."

"He's talked to you already?"

"Yes. He's concerned about leaving you without support."

"That's kind of him, but he'll be back for the summer season. Attendance is low during the winter months. That's why we cut back to one service. Reshma should be ready for ordination soon. I'm more impressed with her every day. She's really grown in her ministry since she came to St. Margaret's."

"Thanks to you and Tom mentoring her so well. She can't say enough good things about you. Would you consider taking her on as an assistant priest?"

"In a heartbeat," replied Lucy.

"Good. That's what I was hoping to hear. I think she'll make a fine addition to your community. But who is this Susan Gedney who's applied for a priest's license in our diocese? She gave your name as a reference. Do you know her well?"

Liz sat forward aggressively and tightened her fists. Lucy had enough anxiety of her own without watching what Liz was doing. Instead, she focused on the bishop's handsome face. "Susan and I were at seminary together," she explained in a deliberately calm tone. "Later, we served as deacons in Boston."

"In her note to me, she seems to think you might take her on as a priest at St. Margaret's. I know you have that generous endowment from Ms. Enright, but can you really afford more than two priests?"

"No, of course not, and I don't know whatever gave her that idea. She mentioned applying for open positions in Maine and nearby states. I never suggested there was an opening at St. Margaret's."

"I hope Tom didn't tell her about his plans," Liz said under her breath.

"I asked him not to say anything," Lucy whispered back.

The bishop frowned, obviously disapproving of a sidebar conversation he couldn't hear.

"There's history," Lucy explained.

"Maybe you should share it with me?" he said, raising a brow.

"When Susan was here last summer, she was trying to escape the local police."

"What?" The bishop's blue eyes widened in surprise.

"She lost her driver's license after being caught driving while intoxicated. Then she ran a red light and injured an elderly woman. She fled the accident scene and came to Maine, hoping I would help her. She needed a place to live, so I let her move into one of the curate's studios. She told me she was unhappy in South Dakota and looking for a new church. Meanwhile, I put her to work helping me. I didn't know about the traffic violations until our police chief, Brenda Harrison, found them on a routine check after a traffic stop. I strongly encouraged Susan to go into rehab, but it was difficult to get her a placement until Liz got involved. Eventually, Susan agreed to return to police custody in her home state."

"This is very disturbing. So, she has no priest's license?"

"The charges in the hit-and-run were dropped. The local bishop allowed her to continue as a priest. He convinced the judge to give back her driver's license, which she needed to do her job."

The bishop continued to frown. "Lucy, your face tells me you don't approve."

"I don't approve of sweeping crimes under the rug because she's clergy. I care for Susan, and I'm glad she can make a fresh start, but the police chief and I worked hard to make sure there were appropriate consequences for her actions. Now, it seems she's gotten off without even a slap on the wrist. I'm not sure she's learned her lesson."

"But that's not for us to judge." The bishop studied Lucy's face. "You are one of the kindest people I know. If you are expressing these concerns, that tells me a lot."

"If I may," said Liz, "there's more to the story. While she was here, Susan did everything she could to break up our relationship."

"Why?"

Lucy could feel her face burning, but she couldn't lie to the bishop. "We were intimate partners in the seminary and when we were deacons in Boston. After she was ordained, she left for the Midwest and broke off all ties with me. When she showed up in Hobbs last summer, I hadn't heard from her for years."

"I know it just sounds like dyke drama," said Liz, "but someone needs to keep an eye on her before she really hurts someone."

"Unfortunately, lesbians aren't the only ones prone to drama," Bishop Greene said, gazing out the window. "Thank you for bringing this to my attention."

"Please don't dismiss Susan's request because of what we've shared," Lucy said, "but I can't recommend her without you knowing the backstory."

"But you would recommend her?"

Put off balance, Lucy weighed her words carefully, trying to figure out how to answer the question fairly. "Susan is a generous and compassionate person. Her ministry is focused on the needs of others. She aced homiletics and is a gifted preacher. Unfortunately, she has many ingrained prejudices. She treated our transgender music director like a leper. Her Roman Catholic upbringing left her with guilt about everything, including her sexuality. I watched her struggle to get past it, but it seems she just can't."

"Maybe one of your ministries is to help her keep trying," said Bishop Greene, but a frown continued to furrow his forehead. "Thank you for being candid. Let me think about the best way to handle this situation."

6

Sam decided against her favorite monochrome sneakers and rummaged around in the closet for more respectable shoes. She found a pair of casual mules and slipped them on. She ran a comb quickly through her hair. When she came into the kitchen, Maggie looked up from the newspaper and gave her a careful inspection.

"Sam, you have all those beautiful clothes from when you were working. Why don't you ever wear them?"

Sam's face began to burn. "You don't approve?"

"No, that's not what I said," Maggie said quickly.

"But you don't like the way I'm dressed," challenged Sam.

"We're going to church. You wear jeans every day. Do you have to wear them on Sunday too?"

"I'm comfortable in jeans. Other people wear them to church." Sam was annoyed that she had to defend herself, and Maggie hadn't even noticed the effort she'd made, including wearing what she would call "decent" shoes.

"People don't seem to have any respect for the Church anymore." Maggie released a long sigh.

"It has nothing to do with respect," Sam said in an angrier tone than she'd intended. "Haven't you seen Lucy's summer posts on Facebook? 'Come as you are. Our founder wore sandals'?"

Maggie compressed her lips in obvious disapproval. "I'm sure she thinks she's being clever. Maybe other people do too. It probably draws some of the summer people."

"Who wants to dress up for church when you're on vacation? Especially when it's hot."

"It's more informal at the outdoor chapel, so there, it makes sense."

"Where have you been, Maggie? Things are different now."

"Maybe they are, but it's important to have standards."

"You have standards. And you can go to church by yourself. I hated it when Olivia forced me to go."

"Don't you want to support Lucy?" asked Maggie.

"Lucy doesn't need my support. She does just fine by herself. You go support her if you want. I have other things to do."

Why waste time at church when I can get work done at Lucy's beach house? thought Sam. *Doesn't that count as supporting Lucy too?*

"I'm sorry," Maggie called after Sam as she headed back to the bedroom to put on her old jeans.

Sam stopped in the doorway. "No, you're not. You want me to dress up, so I don't embarrass you. You're all fixed up with your fancy clothes and makeup. You're embarrassed by what people will think when they see me with you."

"That's not true!"

"Sure, it is. If you want to wear femme clothes and makeup, go right ahead. I'm done with that shit!"

Sam closed the bedroom door with more force than necessary and then regretted losing her temper. A moment later, there was a soft knock at the door. "Can we talk?" asked a small, contrite voice.

"Go to church, Maggie, or you'll be late."

"Please?" begged Maggie through the door.

"Later. I don't want to talk about it now."

From the bedroom window, Sam watched Maggie walk down the path to the driveway. Her shoulders drooped slightly as she headed to her car. Sam had mixed feelings as the Subaru finally drove away. She felt embarrassed for melting down in front of Maggie, but she was done with women trying to reform her. Her mother couldn't do it, although she had certainly tried. Some of her partners too. When she'd worn a skirted suit for her first big interview, her lover had shared a mutual friend's catty remark that it was obvious that Sam was a lesbian, no matter what she wore. Sam had laughed it off, but in fact, the comment had cut her to the core.

After joining her first firm, she was grateful when the only other female architect had given her advice on how to dress for success without looking especially feminine. When an occasion called for a more formal look, like when she had to testify in court for Brenda and Cherie in their adoption case, she dusted off her old corporate suits. But Sam was done with the drag show, and if going to church meant dressing up, she'd rather stay home. And if Maggie didn't like it, too fucking bad!

Sam went out to the barn and grabbed a stack of lightweight, plastic drop cloths off the shelf. She spooled a couple of rolls of tape on her hand and threw them, along with a roll of 5 mil sheeting, onto the rear seat of her truck. Before the demolition of the old roof began, she wanted to put up plastic to protect the practice room in Lucy's garage. It was a boring chore but much more fun than sitting in a hard pew, listening to Lucy talk about Lent. Sam had never been into ashes and sackcloth.

When she arrived at Lucy's beach house, she was happy to see that the dumpster had been delivered. The demolition of the roof would create too much debris to haul away in her truck. With any luck, they could get all the framing done for the third story and new roof by the end of the week. Sam never liked to leave open framing during the rainy season, especially because she'd promised to preserve as much of Erika's renovation as possible. Tarps never really kept out all the moisture, especially when a high wind whipped up the ocean and sent salt spray across the barrier island.

Sam climbed the stairs and looked around the practice room, which showed little sign of use now that Lucy was living at Liz's place. She remembered how she'd worked with Liz to build it. That's when things had been good between them. Since Sam had been dating Maggie, Liz had been obviously distant. Gone were the breakfasts at Liz's table at the diner or beers in the evening on her boat. *What did I expect?* Sam thought sadly as she unrolled the sheet of plastic.

As she worked, she wondered if she should have gotten involved with her friend's ex-wife. It wasn't about the sex. Maggie was a tender and thoughtful lover, although not the kind of woman who set off fireworks in bed. Olivia had always been good at pyrotechnics, but that was the sum of the relationship, and she was tough, which made it easier to leave her. Maggie was still fragile from the divorce and the cancer coming back. Sam knew she couldn't just walk away from the relationship.

She'd gotten one wall done when she heard steps in the stairwell.

"Sam? You up there?" a familiar voice called. A moment later, Brenda stepped into the room. "Hey, I saw your truck out there. I can't believe you're working on Sunday."

"I needed something to take my mind off things."

"I know what you mean." Brenda looked around the room. "Getting ready for demolition?" she asked, as if the obvious needed to be stated.

"Yeah, hopefully, we'll get it done this week."

"Can I help you with the plastic?"

"If you hold it up while I tape, the job will go much faster."

Brenda moved into position and held up the next yard of sheeting. She knew enough about the process to hold it taut. "You playing hooky from church too?" Brenda asked.

"I had an argument with Maggie about what to wear, so I decided not to go."

"Maggie has definite ideas about how to dress, so I suppose she thinks you should too."

"Yeah, no. I don't let women tell me how to dress…not anymore."

"Good for you, I guess," said Brenda, but she sounded doubtful.

"How did you get out of going to church?" The tape screeched as Sam pulled it out.

"Cherie took the kids. I said I needed a break from them, and she understood."

"I can imagine. Before I bought the house on the pond, I used to stay at Liz's place. When her niece's kids were visiting, I'd use any excuse to get out of the house. Kids are a full-time job."

Brenda laughed. "Not quite, but they can wear you out if you let them."

"You need to carve out some downtime. Can't you get a sitter?"

"We could, I guess. But it can't be just anyone. Those kids were really traumatized when their parents got shot. They're clingy and won't let us out of their sight, especially Megan. She still cries when we drop her off at school. And Keith has started to get into a lot of mischief. Testing the boundaries, I guess."

"I don't know the first thing about kids, or I'd volunteer to watch them. At least, they know me."

"Thanks, Sam, but they are more than a handful. Liz volunteered to take them for the weekend, but she's so busy now that she's with Lucy. You know how it is when you're starting a new relationship." Brenda grinned in Sam's direction. "Can't keep your hands off one another."

Sam felt herself blushing. "It's not quite like that for me."

"Really? I've always thought Maggie was sexy."

"She is, but it doesn't always land us in bed…if you know what I mean." Sam felt Brenda's curious eyes on her. She could feel her expectation that she would reveal more. Ordinarily, she would talk openly with Brenda or Liz, but she didn't think Maggie would appreciate her talking about their sex life.

"Hmm. She's not still sore from the surgery?" Brenda ventured.

"No, she's all healed. But she's still shy about her body. I don't know what she's worried about. She looks great."

"Give her time to get adjusted is the only thing I can say."

"I hope she can," Sam replied in a quiet voice. "I don't know if I would have reconstruction if I lost my breasts."

"Really?" asked Brenda, pinning the plastic in the corner to turn to the other wall. "Why not?"

"My boobs annoy me. They're in the way when I have to crawl in a cabinet to reconnect plumbing. I don't need them for anything."

"Having them makes your clothes fit better. I like my breasts. I like that Cherie likes them too, and I love hers."

"Yes, I've seen you admiring them."

"That obvious, huh? I'll have to be more careful."

"At least, you're not like Liz. Her eyes are always focused on Lucy's boobs when she wears a low-cut top. I mean, she must see her naked when they're having sex. Does she have to ogle her in public too?"

Brenda chuckled. "She's been doing that since the day they met. I was always surprised that Maggie didn't smack the face off her."

"I don't think Maggie appreciated that behavior."

"She told you that?" Brenda asked with surprise.

"Think I'd tell you if she did?"

"Sure, you would. In the old days, we all told each other everything. Now, the only time I see Liz is when we have our regular breakfast at the diner, but that's to discuss town business. I know she's got the boat in the water. She told me she has a slew of chores to get it ready for the season, but I never see her down there."

"You spying on her?"

"No! I go by there when I take the cruiser out. It's a deal I made with the harbor master."

They were nearly around the room with the plastic now. "Maybe we should offer to help Liz get her spring tune-up done," Sam suggested. "I bet we could get some lobster rolls and beer out of the deal. I miss hanging out with the *tres amigas*."

"That's a good idea. Why don't you suggest it to her?" said Brenda.

Sam gave her a direct look. "I think it needs to be you. Since I've been seeing Maggie, Liz has been kind of standoffish."

Brenda's blond brows rose. "That's not like her. Maybe she's afraid things she says will get back to Maggie."

"She doesn't have to worry about that. She knows I never tell a soul what she tells me."

Brenda let out a big sigh. "Maybe she's jealous you're with Maggie now."

Sam glowered at her from under her eyebrows. "I'm not 'with' her, Brenda."

"But you're seeing her and sleeping with her. I would say you are 'with' her. Don't you think so?"

"I guess so, but I don't do commitment."

Brenda stood straight but didn't let go of the plastic she was holding to the wall. "Does Maggie know that?"

"She's known me for years. She should."

"Maybe you should talk about it to make sure."

Sam emitted a little groan at the thought, but she said, "That would probably be a good idea."

They finished taping the last section of wall. "That it?" Brenda asked.

Sam threw her a bag containing a plastic drop cloth. "We need to cover the furniture and other stuff to keep the dust out."

"Got it," said Brenda, ripping open the bag.

They finished covering everything and spread plastic on the rug. "That's the best we can do, I think," said Sam. "Let's get out of here."

"How about some coffee and pie at the diner?" asked Brenda with a grin.

"Sounds like a fantastic idea!"

✳✳✳✳

Maggie had a favorite parking spot from the days when she was an active member of St. Margaret's Church. The location was partially shaded by a tree. In the summertime, that meant the car was not unbearably hot when she emerged from services. Maggie eyed the SUV in her space. It wasn't new. Even she, who knew almost nothing about cars, could tell that, but it was in beautiful condition. The owner was probably an old lady, who only drove it to the supermarket and church. Wasn't that how car salesmen advertised used vehicles? "Only driven to church."

Liz had once explained that wasn't really a selling point. Gasoline engines needed to be run or the oil seals and other critical parts dried out. Maggie had always admired Liz for knowing such things and took comfort in her competence. She could always count on her to make sure the oil got changed on schedule and to reset the clock for daylight savings time. Now, she was basically on her own.

Maggie wondered if the old lady who'd taken her favorite spot knew she should go out more often. Maybe she had nowhere to go. Maybe she wasn't an older woman, but most people who attended St. Margaret's Church were gray-haired seniors. Since Lucy had come, her energy had drawn more young families. Then COVID hit, and no one could come to church. Maggie guessed many of the younger parishioners had fallen out of the habit.

It was easier to think about the car problems of old ladies and attendance at the church than the argument with Sam, who was even more prickly about what she wore than Liz. Sometimes, Liz took the idea of Hobbs Family Practice being her "retirement business" a little too far, but her clothes were expensive, high-performance outdoor wear, and she was always well-groomed. Sam was equally fastidious, but she preferred jeans for almost every occasion.

Maggie had been raised to dress up for church. Despite the lineup for the single bathroom in the modest Cape in which she had been raised, she was taught to make a special effort on Sundays. Pat Fitzgerald made sure her four children were clean and polished when they showed up for Mass. The boys always wore ties, and the girls wore hats. To this day, Maggie felt naked going bare-headed to church, but no one wore hats anymore.

A woman joined her on the walk to the side door. "Maggie, it's so good to see you back," she said, taking her arm. "We really missed you."

For a moment, Maggie struggled to remember the woman's name. She'd been experiencing more name-recall problems lately. Finally, it flashed into her mind. "Thank you, Julie. It's so nice to be back."

"I heard you'd moved to Scarborough."

"I have, but I miss St. Margaret's, and I'm often here on weekends, so I thought I'd come today."

"Oh, we'd love to have you back," said the woman with a warm smile. "We miss your singing."

"That's so kind of you to say."

The woman squeezed Maggie's arm before releasing it to turn to another parishioner coming from the parking lot. The exchange reminded Maggie that it wasn't only Lucy's friendship that had inclined her to join the Episcopal Church. The infectious friendliness of the membership, especially the women, was an even bigger draw. None of them seemed to mind that she was married to a woman. A miniature rainbow flag on the sign proclaimed that St. Margaret's was "an open and welcoming church." If anything, her status as Liz's wife, the doctor to many parishioners, had made her even more popular. Maggie had been invited to join the choir, the altar guild, the social justice committee, and the community outreach committee. She even became the head of the pie committee. She'd quickly become a regular "church lady."

It was an unfamiliar experience. The Catholic Church in which Maggie had grown up had few opportunities for socializing. The weekly Masses were filled to standing room only. Maggie would occasionally faint in the summer heat because the congregation was packed into the school auditorium like tinned fish. When she began singing folk masses in high school, her mother had become the church secretary, which gave Maggie a tighter bond with the priests, who were mostly old and inclined to drink too much. You could smell it on their breath in the confessional. In comparison, the Episcopal Church was like a bright dawn on a summer day.

Maggie entered the historic church, gazing affectionately at the beautiful carvings behind the altar. She recognized the usher as the head of the altar guild. She gave Maggie a hug before handing her the printed bulletin with today's service. "Welcome back, Maggie. We really missed you."

"Oh? I thought the new music director was very popular."

"Denise? Oh yes, we love her too, but you were one of us." Maggie hoped Jennifer was referring to her involvement in community activities and not that she was a cis-gender female—whatever that meant. Lately, Maggie felt like she was drowning in all the new terms. She resented that people expected everyone to know what they were talking about. Not being in the "know" left Maggie feeling shut out and old, which only underscored the need to get involved again.

Lucy broke away from a conversation she was having with a parishioner to greet Maggie. She gave her a full-body hug. "It's so good to have you here," Lucy whispered into Maggie's ear.

"Thank you. It's feels like coming home."

"No matter where you live, you'll always have a home here. People love you. And I do too."

The obvious sincerity of the statement and the vulnerability of the moment caused Maggie's eyes to fill. "Thank you," she murmured and finally let Lucy go. "By the way, you look wonderful in purple. I never thought of purple being a good color for redheads, but it really suits you."

"I hear it's the color of the season," quipped Lucy. Her green eyes danced with gentle mischief. "My best color is green, which is fortunate, because ordinary time is so long in the liturgical calendar." Lucy glanced around. "You're alone?"

Maggie shrugged. "Sam had things to do this morning." Lucy held her gaze until she confessed the truth. "We had an argument."

"Oh, no. I hope it wasn't serious."

"No, it was silly," said Maggie. "We were fighting over what to wear to church. I didn't mean anything by it, but Sam really took offense."

"Obviously, a sore point for her. Maybe you can talk about it and sort it out later."

"Oh, I hope so," Maggie said. "I'd hate to think I'd hurt her feelings. That wasn't my intention. But I should have known. Liz was always testy when I commented on what she wore."

"Mother Lucy!" someone called.

"Sorry, Maggie, but I have to go," Lucy apologized. "Maybe we can catch a minute later." She gave Maggie's shoulder a squeeze before she turned away.

Maggie headed to the front of the church. Like students in a classroom, churchgoers tended to stay away from the front rows. Just as her usual parking spot had been taken, her seat in her favorite pew was also occupied. She'd been displaced, and some would say it served her right after her long absence.

"Maggie!" someone called. Despite stiletto heels, the extremely tall woman was racing through the sacristy. She entered the pew in front of Maggie. "Oh, I'm so happy to see you here! Can you please, please help!"

Denise's sudden change of attitude from when they'd met to plan the Easter music schedule was unexpected to say the least.

"What can I do?" Maggie asked, modulating her voice to avoid any suggestion of sarcasm.

"Please join the choir, just this once. Now that masks are optional, everyone is coming down with colds. Three of my sopranos are out this morning. Otherwise, the treble section will be drowned out. There are plenty of cassocks and surplices in the robing room." Maggie glanced at her watch. "You don't have much time," Denise agreed. "Please, Maggie. Your voice could carry that section. I'd be so grateful."

Maggie was suspicious of Denise's sudden friendliness, but she knew that need can create strange allies. "I'll put on a choir robe."

"Quickly. The procession is lining up."

Maggie exited the pew on the other side to avoid the dour woman who had taken her seat. She hurried to put on a red cassock and surplice and ignored the heads that turned as she headed to the back of the church to join the choir. When she insinuated herself among the sopranos, she felt hands patting her shoulder and back. "Glad you're back," the tenor beside her whispered. He rolled his eyes in Denise's direction. Maggie wouldn't give him the satisfaction of following his gaze. People had probably said things behind her back when she was music director.

The huge pipe organ above them caused the stone floor to vibrate. The wall of sound was thrilling. The crucifer stepped off, and the procession was on its way. Behind her, Maggie could hear Lucy singing a little louder than usual, providing more support to the sopranos.

As Maggie passed a pew in the front, she felt eyes on her. She turned and saw Liz frowning. Well, she should have expected to see her there. She'd heard that Liz had become very devout since she'd been dating Lucy.

Lucy opened the service with the Collect for Purity, and the familiarity of the ritual flowed over Maggie. She loved the Episcopal worship, especially because it was so like the Roman Catholic Masses of her youth. Her mind wandered during the announcements, and she considered rejoining St. Margaret's choir.

When Lucy put the host into Maggie's hands at communion time, her green eyes looked directly into hers. Maggie assumed all priests were trained to give eye contact when distributing communion, but Lucy's expression was always so loving.

The choir sang as they processed out. As soon as the hymn was done, Denise found Maggie and scooped her up into a hug. "Thank you! Thank you! You have no idea how much I appreciate you pitching in at the last minute." The choir members crowded around them to say hello. Maggie felt like a student, who'd been out sick from school, being welcomed back by her classmates.

She noticed Liz, chatting with members of the congregation while Lucy stood in the back of the church to greet people. The crowd began to thin, so Maggie headed back to the clothing room to take off her surplice and cassock. People kept stopping her on the way to tell her how much they'd missed her. If she'd known she'd get such a warm reception, she would have returned months ago. But she'd thought everyone was whispering behind her back about her breakup with Liz. Maybe they had been gossiping about her, but why had she allowed her worry to drive her away from a community she loved?

The other choir members left the robing room. Maggie went to the cabinet to retrieve her purse. "I'm glad Denise was able to convince you to join the choir."

Maggie turned around to see Lucy pulling her chasuble over her head. She shook out her red hair and gathered it again into a big clip.

"Did you put her up to it?" Maggie asked.

"No, of course, not," said Lucy, untying the cord of her alb. "It was her idea. When she asked my opinion, I told her to go ahead."

"Thank you. It made me feel welcome."

"We're all glad to see you back."

"Would it be all right if I came more regularly?"

Lucy smiled one of those perfect smiles that could melt anyone into a puddle of affection. "I'd really like that."

"Maybe I could join the choir."

"I'm sure Denise would love to have you…as long as you two don't get into it about who's boss."

"Lucy? Are you almost ready to go?" Liz came into the robing room. She frowned. "Hello, Maggie." Her tone was cordial, if not especially warm.

Lucy slipped into her cardigan. "Maggie, why don't you come back to the house and have some brunch with us? I'm sure Liz won't mind."

Liz folded her arms on her chest and stared at the floor. Her body language said it all. And how could Maggie sit in that kitchen where she had cooked so many meals? In that house where she had lived for years as Liz's wife? It would be so hard to watch Lucy move easily in the place that had once been Maggie's domain.

"Thanks, but I think I'll head over to the pond and see what Sam is up to."

"Another time," said Lucy, glancing in Liz's direction with a disapproving frown.

Maggie headed out with them, calling good-byes behind her. She still found it hard to see them together. As much as she loved Lucy, she wondered if their friendship would ever be the same.

Before she started the car, she checked for text messages from Sam, but there were none. She didn't expect an apology, but she'd hoped for some word that things were okay between them. Maggie reminded herself that Sam wasn't the best communicator.

She took the backroads to Jimson Pond, imagining a pleasant lunch on the dock. She began to compose a menu of chicken salad made with leftovers from last night and crudités with a quick dip.

When she arrived at Sam's house, there was no sign of her. The truck was gone. Her chickens were wandering the yard in search of ticks and seeds. Maggie shooed them aside on her way to the house. She tried the doorknob but found the house locked tight. Maggie had a key, but she sensed she wasn't necessarily welcome. She checked the phone again. Still no message from Sam.

Maggie keyed one to her: *At the house. Planning lunch. Any idea when you'll be back?*

She sat on the porch rail while she waited for a response. After a few minutes, she realized she wasn't going to get one. She shoved down the pain and used her key to enter the house and get her bags.

7

"Thank you for driving," said Lucy, affectionately patting Denise's shoulder. "I'll give you money for gas."

"Don't worry. These hybrids are unbelievably efficient, but if you can get the next fill-up, I'd appreciate it. The price of gas is outrageous."

"It was high before this horrible war in Ukraine. I feel bad for low-income people who need to commute. Everything has become so expensive. With the price of food going up too, it must be hard to feed a family."

"I'll admit grocery shopping is a bigger challenge these days."

"Are you still sharing food expenses with Reshma?"

"I am. Lately, she's been researching her culinary heritage and cooking African recipes. We've invested in some expensive spices whose names I can't pronounce, but the dishes she prepares are delicious. It's so nice to come home to a home-cooked meal."

"She does most of the cooking?"

"Yes, but she's had to teach herself. She was away at that boarding school, so she couldn't learn to cook from her mother. Some of her early meals were…interesting, but I have to say I like this ethnic slant. The main dishes are either vegetarian or make the best use of small amounts of meat. Reshma has figured out how to make our food budget go far."

Lucy knew the dismally low salary that Denise earned as music director of St. Margaret's and gazed at her sympathetically. "I'm sorry we can't pay you more. You both work so hard."

Denise stole a quick glance at Lucy before returning her eyes to the road. "It was my choice to work for the church. I'm lucky to get work in my field. The people I work with are great. I get health insurance. I even get free housing in the rectory. What's not to love?"

"I'm sure you'd rather be performing."

"Of course. It's what I trained for my whole life. And if all goes well today, I might get the chance to restart my career in my new identity as a woman."

Lucy studied the side of Denise's face. The faint scars from the cosmetic work on her jaw were visible, but only on close inspection. "Would you quit your job at St. Margaret's if your singing career takes off?"

"Maybe, but not right away. You know how it is in the beginning. You can't live on the fees from engagements or royalties from recordings. You pay for your own health insurance, and that's gotten even more expensive. Right now, my job as your music director is perfect. I only hope you'll be flexible in allowing me to schedule gigs."

"Within reason. I don't want the vestry to accuse me of favoritism."

"Oh, God! Are they still keeping an eye on me?" She glanced guiltily in Lucy's direction. "Sorry about taking the Lord's name in vain."

Lucy shrugged. "Apologize to them, not me."

"I love that you use the plural pronoun."

"Why not? Theologically, it makes sense. Episcopalians believe in the doctrine of the Trinity, which means three persons in one God. In that case, they/them is more grammatically correct."

"Mother Lucy, you amaze me," said Denise.

"It's not original to me. I picked it up in one of my theology classes."

Denise smiled. "If I have to be away for a gig, I bet Maggie Fitzgerald would fill in for me."

"So, you two are getting along now?" Lucy replied casually.

"Yes, we are. Forgive the language, but I'm sorry I was such an asshole."

"I could see how working with someone older and more experienced could feel threatening. In the beginning, I felt that way about Father Tom. Now, I consider him one of my best friends."

Denise switched lanes to avoid the backup getting onto the bridge. "Did I ever tell you how much I hate driving in Boston?"

"I hated it too when I lived here. So many one-way streets. At least in New York, it makes sense…sort of. I probably should have driven. I lived here for years and know my way around."

"I don't mind, especially because you're doing me an enormous favor. What finally convinced you?"

Lucy thought for a minute before answering. "I want to support you, but as much as I like helping people, I seldom do things I really don't want to do. Honestly, I've always loved performing and really miss it."

"Wow, I didn't know that," said Denise.

Lucy sighed. "There was a time I would have jumped at an opportunity to sing with any big orchestra or opera company. The Met never actually fired me. They kept me on the roster of sopranos for years after I left, but I didn't get any parts. I tried to restart my singing career. I went to Europe. I took engagements in small cities in the US. I could have sung at the City Opera, but it was already having financial troubles, and the idea of appearing literally next door to the place where I'd once been a headline star was so demoralizing."

"I bet."

"I lived in New York, but it was the one place I couldn't sing. A powerful producer like Alex Dupuis had a wide reach. Once he started a whisper campaign against me, my career was effectively over."

Denise's lips had parted while she'd been listening. She was clearly shocked by what she'd heard. "That's terrible. What did Dupuis have against you?"

"He didn't have anything against me, at least, not in the beginning. It was what I had against him. My agent had been skimming my earnings and padding his own expense account. The worst part is, he wasn't paying my taxes. When Alex offered to help me find a good lawyer and a legitimate agent, I was grateful. I thought he was helping me out of friendship, but he had another agenda. He expected sex in return. When I resisted, he forced himself on me."

"Oh, my God! How horrible!"

"Emily is the result of the rape. She didn't know about it until recently. I'm surprised she hasn't told you."

Denise shook her head. "She hasn't said a word."

"She's probably still processing the information. That's how she works. She mulls over things and then asks questions. I told her months ago.

When I asked if she had any questions, she said no. At the thesis defense, I mentioned it and later, all the questions flooded out."

"I don't know why she didn't talk about something so big."

"Maybe she didn't tell you because she's embarrassed, or she thinks it reflects badly on her or me. I have no idea. I could make myself crazy second-guessing what Emily thinks. In many ways, she's still a mystery to me." Lucy glanced out the window so that Denise couldn't see her face.

"Emily is a mystery to herself. Like all of us, she's trying to figure out who she is and where she belongs."

"Yes, but I never want her to think I don't love her because of how she was conceived."

"Emily's much too smart to think that way."

"This isn't about intellectual understanding. It's about emotions and gut reactions, which we know Emily doesn't do well. But I'm surprised she hasn't told you. You're so close."

Denise glanced at Lucy cautiously. "We're not as close as we used to be. We broke up."

"Oh, no! I'm sorry."

Denise exhaled a long sigh. "Thank you, but you warned me that she's young, and she is. She didn't have a normal adolescence, which is when most people experiment with sex and relationships. I should have known better."

"How are you about the relationship ending?"

Denise thought for a moment. "I'm sad and disappointed, of course. I thought we had a special bond, and it was her idea to take it to the next level."

"You mean, sex?"

"Yes. And that's why we broke up. She doesn't like sex. She said it was disgusting." Denise looked suddenly flustered. "You're her mother. I shouldn't be telling you this."

"I'm glad you did. Emily doesn't share much about her personal life. Maybe she's afraid I'll judge her."

"Well, it can't be easy having a mother who's a priest, especially one who's just written a book on sex."

"You'd think it would make it easier, but she doesn't experience feelings like other people, so it's hard for her to talk about them. Are you sure it was the sex that scared her away?"

"Oh, I'm sure. She freaked out and told me she found the whole thing repulsive. I was very upset at first because I thought I was doing something wrong. I'm new to this too. I mean, in this body. I almost came to talk about it with you. But you're her mother."

"You could have talked to me as a therapist and a priest. I would have listened, but I probably would have sent you to Tom, who's less involved."

Denise shook her head. "I can't talk to a man about this."

"I understand, Denise, but Tom is a good listener."

"Still."

Lucy reflected for a moment. "For someone who doesn't like to be touched, it makes sense that Emily doesn't enjoy sex. In the abstract, sex goes against everything that we're taught about hygiene. Emily is fastidious, and sex can be messy. I can see why the idea of exchanging body fluids could repel her."

"Me too, but I assure you I did my best to prepare her. I was so careful and patient. You would have been proud of me."

"I'm always proud of you, Denise. You don't have to earn my approval."

"Thank you, Mother Lucy."

"When did this happen?"

"Not long after Christmas. She called when she got back to school to tell me the sexual relationship was over. She had approached the whole thing so clinically…like it was an experiment. Once she'd done it, she could check off that box. That's what hurt most of all. Making love seemed to mean nothing to her. Forgive me for saying this about your daughter, but I feel used."

"Oh, Denise, I understand why you would feel that way," said Lucy, reaching over to rub her shoulder. "Where did you leave things?"

"She wants us to remain friends but without the physical part. I'm not sure I can do that."

"I know she really cares for you. Your friendship means so much to her. She feels safe with you. She needs you to help her interpret parts of her experience that she doesn't understand."

"That's what I'm worried about. I'm not sure I can still be there for her in the same way. I care for her too much, but it really hurt to be rejected like that, especially because I'm still getting used to my new body. It felt like a double rejection. I know it's ridiculous to think that way, but you can understand why."

"This was Emily's first sexual experience. She can't compare you to a man or another woman. You know how she is. Don't take it personally. It's not about you." Lucy stroked Denise's shoulder affectionately. "I'm so sorry. Obviously, you appreciate how complicated the situation is, and you've been so supportive and sensitive."

"Please don't let on that you know anything about this," said Denise, turning to her shyly.

"I would never say a word."

"I know that it goes without saying. I trust you, Mother Lucy." Denise turned onto the bridge ramp. At the bottom, she eased into local traffic. "Not to change the subject, but I could really use your help finding my way around."

Lucy was more than happy to play navigator and leave the subject of her daughter in the rear-view mirror. She directed Denise through the annoying roundabouts, one-way streets, and high-traffic avenues until they finally pulled into the nearest parking garage.

"Have I told you how fabulous you look?" Denise asked as Lucy got of the car. "That dress is to die for. I love it when you wear your hair up like that. Your makeup and jewelry are absolute perfection. Mother Lucy, you are the very image of a diva."

Lucy looked down at the green couture dress. Along with its carefully coordinated accessories, it had once been her favorite outfit for meeting with people in the music business. Fortunately, its classic look had never gone out of style.

"Thank you, Denise," said Lucy, putting on her coat. "I don't feel like a diva…just some old has-been who dug some fancy clothes out of the back of my closet."

"Mother Lucy, I will *not* allow that kind of talk!" Denise ordered in a stern voice. "Remember you are Lucille Bartlett, star of the Metropolitan Opera!"

"Once upon a time."

"You are still one of the greats, and nothing will ever change that." Denise reached down and put her arm around Lucy's shoulders. Her embrace was powerful. Lucy imagined her spine being rearranged in the process.

"But I'm your coach. I should be giving *you* encouragement."

"A performer should encourage everyone in the ensemble. That's what my acting professor always said. It's one of the marks of a true professional." Denise released her. "Now, I won't hear any more negative talk. This audition will be a success."

Lucy wondered who Denise was trying to convince with the little pep talk, but it was surprisingly effective. Lucy felt more confident as they headed to Symphony Hall.

Denise showed the email inviting her to audition to the guard at the door. "And this is my teacher, Madame Bartlett." The heavy-set, black man looked Lucy up and down. He nodded indifferently and pointed them in the right direction. The scuff of their high heels echoed off the walls of the long corridor.

"What did you sing here last?" asked Denise.

"*The Verdi Requiem.*"

"One of my favorites and quite a workout. The *Mahler Two* is a piece of cake by comparison."

"It's probably better that the solo vocal parts aren't big showpieces," said Lucy. "It's good exposure without being too exposed, if you know what I mean."

"Yes, better to make a more modest debut and knock it out of the park than fail spectacularly."

"I don't think there's any danger of that, Denise. You are a professional. You're in great voice, and you know this piece cold."

As they approached the entrance to the auditorium, Denise put out her hand to slow Lucy's progress. "Remember you're not supposed to know that you're auditioning too. Please try to act surprised when they ask you to sing."

Lucy smiled. "I think I can manage that. The critics always praised my acting."

"I've seen you on video." With the back of her hand against her forehead, Denise struck a dramatic pose. "Desdemona," she explained, straightening.

Lucy rolled her eyes.

An aide met them in the hall and directed them to a room where they could warm up. Together, they sang scales and arpeggios designed to limber up the voice and then launched into the exercises Lucy's mother had taught her. An intercom interrupted to say that the audition would begin in five minutes and directed them to the backstage entrance.

Denise gripped Lucy's hand before opening the door of the practice room. "Ready?" she asked.

Lucy nodded decisively.

The theater was dark, but the stage was brightly lit as was usual for auditions. As soon as Lucy stepped out on the boards, her heart began to beat faster, but not from anxiety or fear. She was thrilled to be back in a real concert hall. Even the stale smell of the theater, shut up without ventilation, excited her. Her mind raced with memories of past auditions—at the Stuttgart Opera, where she'd honed her craft, and later for the Met's young artist program. She was so taken up with reminiscing, she didn't notice someone approaching from the side.

"Madame Bartlett?" inquired a voice with a strong Spanish accent. Lucy's ear placed it as South American. "You are the great soprano, Lucille Bartlett, are you not?" A tall man with a full head of long gray curls made a little bow. "You may not remember me, but I conducted you in *Tannhäuser* at the Metropolitan many years ago. It is truly an honor to see you again." Lucy scrutinized the sculptural features and lined forehead, finally connecting them to a smooth-faced young man, who had stood in the orchestra pit at the Met.

"Thank you, Maestro Morales," said Lucy as the man raised her hand to his lips. "I feel the same."

He looked charmed to be remembered. "I understand that you have been giving voice lessons." He nodded in Denise's direction.

"Not formally. Ms. Chantal needed help with register transitions. I remembered my own battles with that problem and could share some advice."

"But you are no longer singing."

"No," said Lucy. "I'm an Episcopal priest, the rector of a parish in Maine."

He folded his arms on his chest and regarded her skeptically. Lucy smiled, and his expression changed to surprise. "You're not joking."

"No, I'm not. It's true."

"Such a loss," he said with a sigh, "but let's see what you have accomplished with this young singer. You may sit behind the accompanist in case your pupil needs to consult with you." He gestured to the chairs behind the piano. "Please make yourself comfortable."

Lucy took off her coat and looked around for Denise. She found her chatting with a handsome young man. She guessed he was the friend who had arranged the audition. They were flirtatious with one another. Lucy had never considered whether Denise's previous relationships had been with men or women, but she hoped for the sake of Emily's health that she hadn't been promiscuous. *Stop it*, Lucy thought. *Don't judge.*

She sat down and took out her score of *Mahler's Second Symphony* and the sheet music for Denise's audition pieces. As she studied her notes, she felt the Maestro's eyes on her. She looked up and gave him a radiant smile. Instantly, he responded with a warm look. Lucy congratulated herself on still being able to charm her admirers. She relaxed in her chair, enjoying the sheer pleasure of being on a stage with other musicians. She'd only sung in Symphony Hall a few times, but she felt completely at home. Despite the constant travel, long rehearsals, and late nights, she realized how much she'd missed this life.

The Maestro clapped his hands to get everyone's attention. "Let us begin. Miss Chantal, what have you chosen to sing for us?" It was a rhetorical question because Denise had previously submitted her audition selections, so the accompanist would be prepared.

"First, I'm going to sing Mahler's fourth *Rückert Lied*," Denise said. "It seemed appropriate."

Morales descended the stairs to the auditorium and took a seat in the front row. "Proceed," he ordered with a wave of his hand.

Denise had practiced the audition selections under Lucy's direction. As usual, they'd used pre-recorded music that could be streamed to a speaker from a phone. Today, they had the luxury of live accompaniment. As might be expected from one of America's premiere orchestras, the pianist was exceptionally talented. While Denise sang *"Ich bin der Welt abhanden gekommen,"* Lucy followed along in her score. The accompanist's tempo was a little slower than they'd practiced, but Denise didn't allow her phrasing to drag. Lucy was pleased that Denise was showing off her newly learned ability to sound "sweeter" and "more feminine." After she finished the song, there was silence. Lucy studied the Maestro, trying to read his reaction, but his face was inscrutable. Finally, he said, "Madame Bartlett, your pupil has great promise. She has a rich and expressive voice that is perfect for Mahler. Will you favor us with another song, Ms. Chantal?"

For her next selection, Denise had chosen *"Der Einsame im Herbst"* from *Das Lied von der Erde* against Lucy's advice. In the end, she'd agreed that taking on a vocally challenging piece would count in Denise's favor. Lucy looked up from her score to watch the conductor's face while Denise sang. Despite Morales's attempt to appear impassive, he was impressed, as he should be. Denise had real talent, which was why Lucy had volunteered to coach her. Lucy began to wonder why Denise and her friend had involved her in this audition. Denise was clearly doing fine on her own.

"All right, Ms. Chantal, I don't need to hear more unrelated material," said Morales, interrupting her in mid-phrase. "Have you learned the part we are trying to cast?"

"Yes, I've been practicing it with Mother Lucy…I mean Madame Bartlett."

"Then perhaps you can convince her to sing with you," said Morales, sitting back and putting his feet on the chair in front of him.

Lucy experienced a flutter of panic. What if the plan backfired? What if she sang badly and wrecked Denise's chances instead of helping her? This was the moment when their little scheme turned serious. Lucy forced herself to get to her feet. Denise smiled warmly in her direction and waved to invite her to approach, but Lucy was rooted to where she stood.

"Madame Bartlett," said Morales, "I do not wish to put you under pressure, but I have been waiting many years to hear you sing again."

Denise, who had perceived what was happening, looked anxious that their plan would unravel. Her blue eyes pleaded with Lucy. Finally, she reached out her hand. The gesture broke Lucy's paralysis.

"Forgive my hesitation," said Lucy, heading to Denise's side. "It's been a long time since I've sung professionally. I hope you won't be disappointed."

"I have heard that you have kept up your voice, so I sincerely doubt it," said Morales. "But have no worry. We're all friends here." He smiled and raised his hands. "I shall conduct you. Let's take it from "O, *Glaube*."

As soon as she heard the familiar notes, Lucy knew that she could do it. She would let the music lift her up and carry her. She adjusted her posture and became once more a seasoned professional. At her cue, she opened her mouth and sang with pure joy.

❋❋❋

The desk chair complained with a squeal as Liz sat back. When she'd first opened Hobbs Family Practice, she might have put her feet up on the desk. The thoroughly unprofessional gesture was meant to announce that she had quit the medical establishment. Much of the early staff was left over from the days when the previous doctor had owned the practice.

Apparently, he'd been eccentric, so they didn't find Liz's behavior odd. One even said she was glad to see the informality. They'd all been worried about the hot-shot surgeon coming up from Yale. Now, with the beautifully renovated space looking so modern and pristine and Amy Hsu's unwavering professionalism, Liz didn't feel comfortable with her feet up.

She called Lucy again, but there was still no answer. Liz guessed she had turned off her ringer during the audition and had forgotten to turn it back on. She would have expected to hear from Lucy by now. She was a much better communicator than Liz, and she could be trusted to call when she could. Maybe she hadn't found an opportunity for a private call. Liz texted a few hearts to Lucy and put her phone on the desk. Almost instantly it began to buzz.

"About time I heard from you," said Liz. "How did it go?"

"It was a triumph. Denise got the part, and so did I."

"So, everything went according to plan. Please tell Denise congrats from me." Liz listened as Lucy conveyed the message.

"She says thank you."

"Where are you?"

"We're still in Boston. We're just leaving the parking garage now."

Liz glanced at her watch. "It took that long? I thought the audition was at ten."

"It was, and we started right on time. I remember that about Morales. He's a stickler for punctuality."

"But it went well?"

"Extremely well. Morales took us out to lunch, which is why we're so late leaving Boston."

"Well, I hope he took you to a nice place."

"He took us to the Capital Grille. He's Argentinian and really likes meat."

"They all do. That's why people die young in that country. Too many carnivores. All that red meat isn't good for the body. How was the food?"

"Delicious, but we have equally good restaurants in Portsmouth and Portland."

While Lucy had been talking, Liz had checked the Yelp reviews for the Capital Grille. "Wow! That place is pricey. He must have been impressed to wine and dine you like that."

"He said he wanted to talk business, but I think he just wanted to spend more time with us. After we sang the parts from the *Mahler Two*, he hired us on the spot. He asked me to indulge him by singing another selection, so I sang "*Frühling*" from the *Four Last Songs.*"

"Had to get a little Strauss in with your Mahler. Did the conductor like that?"

"He did. He made me sing the other three."

"Made you?" Liz barked a little laugh. "Yeah. Right."

"Okay. I sang them willingly. It just felt so good to sing in a real theater."

"What? My media room isn't good enough for you?" Liz could hear Denise snicker in the background. "Lucy, do you have me on speaker?"

"Yes," Lucy admitted in a guilty voice. "You'd better behave yourself."

"I always behave myself, except when I don't. But what kind of business did the conductor want to talk about? Don't the agents work out the fees?"

"They do. But he was so impressed by my *Vier Letzte Lieder*, he tried to convince me to sing the cycle in New York."

Liz felt a surge of pride at Lucy's success, but she'd expected nothing less. "You knew this might happen. What did you tell him?"

"That I'd think about it. I need to get through this first. And the rest of Lent and Holy Week…and get all my papers in on time…and get our wedding planned."

"You're going to be a busy girl."

"Yes, but now, Denise needs help navigating out of Bean Town. Love you."

The call ended, and Liz smiled. Lucy had picked up her habit of neglecting greetings and good-byes. From Liz's point of view, they were a silly waste of airtime. She doubted that Lucy neglected the amenities with other people, but she was intrigued by the idea that their quirks were rubbing off on one another. She got up to unlock the safe to get her purse, so she could head home.

"Liz, I hate to bother you, but…"

Liz turned around to see the nurse practitioner they'd hired when Cherie went part time. "Bobbie, I don't like the sound of that. My office hours are over. I wouldn't still be here if I hadn't been waiting for a call."

"Yes, I know, but there's a woman out there, insisting she needs to see you."

"One of my patients?"

"No, there's no record of her in our files. She says she's been having unexplained heart palpitations."

Liz's brows rose. "Then why is she here instead of going to the ER?"

"She says she has a high deductible for unjustified ER visits."

"It's always about money," Liz grumbled. "Did you listen to her chest?"

"I did. Her heart rate and BP are high, but not in the danger zone. It could be anxiety. She says she's been under a lot of stress. I didn't want to send her away without being seen. All the other docs are gone for the day, and she really wants to see you."

"Let that be a lesson to you, Bobbie. Never hang around when you're done for the day."

The pleasant-looking, heavy-set blonde laughed heartily. "I'll try to remember that advice. But what do I do with the patient?"

"Create a file in the system, take a history, and put her in an exam room. What else can we do?"

Liz locked up her purse in the safe again. *So much for getting work done on the boat today.* A moment later, the nurse buzzed her intercom from the exam room. "She's in three."

Liz knocked on the door and was surprised to hear a familiar voice reply. She opened the door to find Susan Gedney, sitting in the patients' chair. Liz's body instantly tensed at the sight of Lucy's former lover.

"Hello, Susan," Liz said cautiously, closing the door. She sat down on the doctors' stool and scanned Susan's history in the file Bobbie had created. "Tell me what you're experiencing."

"At night, when I turn on my left side, I can feel my heart pounding. Today, I felt it racing for no reason."

"Are you having chest pains?"

"No, but my chest feels really tight. My mother and sister died of heart disease."

"I'm sorry," said Liz. "Do you remember any details about their conditions?"

Susan shook her head. "Both died suddenly."

"With that family history, you have reason for concern. It's smart to be checked out. I can listen to your heart and do an ultrasound to make sure there's no imminent danger, but other than that, there's not much I can do for you today."

"Please help me. I'm scared." Her voice quavered, almost on the point of breaking. Liz felt sorry for her. She found a paper gown in the cabinet and put it on the exam table. "Put this on. Take your blouse and bra off. You can leave your pants and everything else on. I'll be back in a few minutes." Liz returned to her office. She hated being suckered into treating Susan, but if she wasn't diligent and something happened to her, Lucy would never forgive her. *Never mind Lucy. If something happened to her, I'd never forgive myself.*

Liz read the medical news headlines while she waited. After a few minutes passed, she glanced at the time at the top of her computer screen. She grabbed the stethoscope off her desk and headed down the hall.

She did a brief classical examination, checking for abdominal abnormalities. Common indigestion or acid reflux could cause chest discomfort. Everything seemed normal. She listened carefully to Susan's heart and lungs. Her heart rate was slightly elevated, but the blood flow sounded normal. There wasn't even a murmur. "Nothing serious so far, but I'm going to take a quick look at your heart with this nifty portable ultrasound," Liz said, picking up the device. "Okay?"

"Yes, of course."

Again, Liz found nothing unusual. "Your heart rate is slightly elevated, but not excessively so. I don't see anything else significant." She pulled closed the paper gown.

"That's a relief," said Susan with a sigh. She looked up into Liz's face. "You have such gentle hands."

Liz only nodded in response. "You can get dressed now. When you're finished, come down to my office. Make a left turn out of the room. It's at the end of the hall."

While she waited for Susan to return, Liz added notes to her file. A few minutes later, Susan stood in her doorway. Liz pointed to the visitors' chair.

"I've been so worried about a heart attack since my sister died. She passed out while she was driving to a hairdresser's appointment. Fortunately, the car stopped when it hit the curb, and she didn't hurt anyone."

"If you're so worried, why haven't you seen a doctor?"

"I've been taking baby aspirin religiously."

"Well, you can stop doing that. It's no longer recommended because the risk of bleeding outweighs the benefit…especially in patients who drink alcohol."

Susan's blue eyes turned steely. "I don't drink anymore," she said in an annoyed tone.

"Even so, the lining of your stomach may not have completely recovered. And your history means there could be vessel damage. Alcohol raises your blood pressure. Could you feel your heart racing when you drank?"

"Yes, often. But I tried to ignore it."

"When was the last time you saw a doctor?"

"Before I left Boston."

Liz did a quick mental calculation based on what Lucy had told her about Susan. "That's at least seven years ago," she concluded, barely hiding her surprise.

Susan nodded. "I had a high deductible. I couldn't afford to see the doctor unless I was seriously ill."

Money again, Liz thought, shaking her head. *Meanwhile, people die from treatable diseases.*

Susan's blue eyes gazed earnestly into hers. "You didn't have to see me. You're very kind."

Liz shrugged. "It's not kindness, Susan. I'm a doctor. It's what I do."

"The nurse said your office hours were over. You could have sent me elsewhere. You are kind. Lucy is very lucky to have you." Liz frowned, wondering where this was going. Susan took a deep breath. "Liz, we got off on the wrong foot. How can I make amends?"

"Is this part of your twelve-step program?"

"It is, but that's not why. I know you don't trust me after what happened last summer."

"Well, you did try to break up Lucy's relationship with me. Did you expect that would make me like you?"

Susan gazed at the floor. "No, of course not. But then I was a mess. I'm better now. I've been clean and sober since you got me into rehab last summer. I'm trying to make a fresh start."

"Here in Hobbs?"

"If possible, but that may not work out."

"It may not. St. Margaret's can't afford more staff."

"I put in an application to teach in the elementary school."

"Don't you want to be a priest?"

"Of course, I do. And I'll continue to apply for open clergy positions. Meanwhile, I'm hoping to get on the list of supply clergy." For some reason, that term always made Liz smile, but she stifled it because this was a serious conversation. "I don't have a lot of time to figure out where I'm going to land," Susan added. "My lease runs out in June."

Liz glanced at the clock on her desk. Getting work done on the boat was looking less likely by the minute. She could show Susan the door and be done with her, but she sensed the woman needed to talk. With a deep sigh, she took a seat on the wheeled doctors' stool.

"There are parishes south of here and nearby in New Hampshire," she suggested.

"I know. I've applied to every opening I could find. It takes a long time for people to get back to you. I'm trying to be patient." Susan raised her eyes and studied Liz's face. Liz frankly returned the inspection. She'd been so busy disliking Susan that she'd never really given her a hard look. She was an attractive woman, even though she was carrying a little extra weight. Facially, she vaguely resembled Erika. Susan was older, but her skin was smooth except for some permanent laugh lines and faint crowfeet around the eyes, which were a deep, compelling blue. Her expression as she returned Liz's gaze was gentle. She hardly seemed like the big threat Liz had once imagined her to be.

"Liz, I'd really like us to be friends. And I don't want you to worry about my friendship with Lucy."

"I'm not worried. I know Lucy loves me, but Susan, you can't flip a switch and make everything all right. It may take a long time for people to trust you again."

"I understand, but I just want a chance to show I've changed. Just a chance…"

Liz sighed. "I'm the kind of person who always gives people the benefit of the doubt, but don't expect instant acceptance in Hobbs. People have long memories. You might be better off starting over somewhere else."

"So, you don't forgive me." Susan's eyes became sad.

"Maybe I do, but I can't speak for everyone. As far as your friendship with Lucy goes, you'll have to work on that with her."

"But if she sees you accepting me, it might help her come around."

Liz recognized the manipulation for what it was. She decided it was better to end the consultation than confront her. "Susan, I was on my way out when you came. I need to get going. Because of your relationship with Lucy and our history, I feel uncomfortable taking you as a patient. I hope you understand. I'll send my notes to another doctor in the practice. Amy Hsu is a cardiologist, so she's the right person to see if you're concerned about your heart. My office will give you a call to set up an appointment." She rose to let Susan know it was time for her to leave.

Susan didn't get up. "Liz, will you please think about what I said?"

"I'll think about it. That's all I can promise."

"I understand." Susan finally rose from the chair.

"Down the hall to your left. Just tell the woman behind the glass I said there's no charge for today's visit."

"That's so kind," said Susan with surprise.

Liz shrugged. "I want you to look after your health. Come back and see Dr. Hsu."

"I will. I promise."

8

While the girls greedily consumed the freshly baked oatmeal cookies, Maggie checked her phone for messages. Three days had passed, and she still hadn't heard from Sam. By now, Maggie was beginning to worry that the rift was permanent. She hated to think she'd lost Sam as a friend after knowing her for years. Maybe getting involved sexually had been a mistake, but friendships with gay women could be complicated. Every other woman was a potential partner. The rules of the heterosexual world in which Maggie had lived most of her life seemed simple by comparison.

She watched her granddaughters happily munching their afternoon snack. The society in which they were growing up was so different. Now, there was an alphabet soup of letters representing gender identities and sexual preferences. Maggie had an uncomfortable history with labels. As college lovers, she and Liz never called themselves lesbians. They told themselves they were just two women who had fallen in love. Lesbians were those hard women who met in smoky bars and killed themselves once their identity was discovered.

Maggie had audited a film course at NYU on lesbians in cinema. In class, they'd watched Kurt Russell's *The Fox*, in which one of the partners is "saved" by running off with a man. *The Children's Hour*, *The Killing of Sister George*, and *The Bitter Tears of Petra von Kant* all ended with a suicide. The consistently tragic denouement was obviously intended as a strong moral lesson, one that Maggie took to heart.

She could have gotten credit for the course, but she didn't want anyone to know she was even remotely interested in the subject. If anyone had found out that she and Liz were lovers, they would have been kicked out of their Catholic college. Even when Maggie's marriage was ending, and she had an affair with an aging actress, they'd never used the L-word. Kathleen Gleason was in the closet herself, like so many actresses of her generation.

After her divorce from her cheating husband, Maggie went back to men. When she'd reconnected with Liz after forty years, Maggie had finally called herself gay, but the word lesbian still stuck in her throat.

"Can I have more milk, grandma?" asked Nicki, her dark eyes looking up expectantly. As Maggie poured the girl a glass of milk from the awkward gallon container, her phone pinged. Her hands shook in anticipation, but she carefully cleaned up the spill before checking her phone.

Sorry it's taken me so long. How are you?

Glad to hear from you. Are you okay?

I'm okay now. You hit a nerve.

Should I call you and we can talk?

No, I'm still at work. Meet for dinner?

Can't. Alina will be home late. I need to watch the kids.

Another night?

She'll be late all week. Want to come here for dinner?

There was a long pause. Maggie could see the virtual motion showing a reply was being composed. It started and stopped several times. Maggie sat down on one of the island stools while she waited.

Will we be able to talk there?

After the kids go to bed.

Okay.

Come when you're done with work.

Be there soon.

Maggie wasn't sure that a heart, even a purple one, would be welcomed, but she sent it anyway. She was relieved when a purple heart appeared in reply.

The alarm went off on her phone, startling her. She'd set it to remind her to call the kids to do their homework. There was the usual chorus of protest, but they dragged their backpacks to their rooms. In a few minutes, Maggie would check on them, but first she reviewed her dinner plans to see if there was enough food for a guest. When Sam was working on a job, she usually came home with a big appetite. Maggie took out another bag of shrimp to defrost under running water. She'd add more pasta to the pot and add to the salad.

As she ripped lettuce into the bowl, she tried to figure out how her Sunday conversation with Sam had gone so wrong. Obviously, Sam was sensitive about her appearance, but so were many women. Liz had also resisted Maggie's attempts to "dress" her. She'd rankle at Maggie's suggestions and bark, "mind your own business," but when Liz protested, it was a moment of annoyance, not a vehement, protracted silence. Sam had sat on her anger for days. *Because it's not anger*, Maggie suddenly realized. *Sam wasn't insulted. She was hurt. Why didn't I get that before?*

Maggie was still trying to understand why a simple suggestion could cause so much pain. This was one of those times when she wished she was on better terms with Liz. She could always be counted on to have a useful perspective. Maggie suddenly felt pangs of longing for the woman she'd known for almost half a century. Being Liz's wife had made Maggie's life feel secure and orderly. Now, she had to rely on herself to keep things under control, and not only her own life. She was also responsible for her fragile daughter, her two granddaughters, and the home they shared—not where she'd expected to be at this stage of her life.

Maybe Alina could check the kids' homework tonight, and Maggie could have a heart-to-heart with Sam. But Alina was usually exhausted at the end of the day. She'd been producing a series exposing the abuse of kids in foster care. The dark circles around her eyes signaled that the project had been keeping her awake at night.

Maggie had worried that the interviews with the victims might trigger Alina's bad memories of her early life in a Romanian orphanage. So far, Alina's medication had kept her PTSD and depression under control. Maggie would hate to see her relapse because she was under too much pressure from her job or worried about things at home. Distracted by her thoughts, Maggie nicked her finger with the sharp knife she was using to devein the shrimp. *Pay attention*, she told herself. *Liz isn't here to tend to your wounds.*

The old-fashioned front doorbell chimed. Maggie glanced at the time on the stove. Sam must have raced up to Scarborough. Maggie dried her hands on a paper towel and went downstairs to open the door. Sam stood there with a bottle of wine in one hand and a bouquet of spring flowers in the other. "I decided to call it a day after we texted," she explained. "Hope I'm not too early."

"No, I'm so glad to see you." Ordinarily, Maggie would have raised her face for a kiss, but she didn't know where things stood between them. "Come in. I'm still doing some prep, but you can keep me company in the kitchen."

Sam stepped cautiously into the house and looked around. "Where are the kids?"

"Doing their homework."

"That's right. It's a school night," Sam said, looking thoughtful. "Sorry. I didn't think of that."

"Yes, and that means I can't stay up too late because I have to get up in the morning to get the girls ready for school."

"I promise not to overstay my welcome," said Sam with a grin. Seeing her smile relieved some of Maggie's anxiety. She reached for the flowers, but she let Sam carry the wine.

"Come upstairs. I'll put you to work in the kitchen. Is that wine cold?"

"Yes."

"Good. You can open it, and we can have a glass."

Maggie took out a vase for the flowers. "These are beautiful. Thank you, but you didn't need to bring anything."

"My mother trained me never to arrive for dinner empty-handed." Maggie could feel Sam watching as she trimmed the flowers and arranged them. "You have a real knack for that," Sam observed. The compliment meant more because Sam had a trained eye for design.

"I took a class in floral arranging when I was a bored housewife. Barry encouraged me because he could see I was restless," Maggie explained. "My friends in the garden club all took it, so I went along for the ride."

"I'm sure that's a thing of the past now, like setting a formal table with china and crystal," said Sam, carefully winding the screw into the wine cork. "They still offer floral arranging classes at the trade school, but supermarkets are putting florists out of business, so I wonder where those kids will find jobs."

"Oh, I think some will. We can't throw out all formality. It shows respect."

Out of the corner of her eye, Maggie saw Sam stiffen. Maybe she expected a lecture about dressing up for church. Before she got the wrong idea, Maggie amended her statement. "Generally, it's a good thing that people are more casual now."

"I want you to know I wasn't being disrespectful to Lucy by not dressing up to go to church."

"I know, Sam. I just wonder why you reacted so strongly." Sam glanced at the door leading to the hall. "Don't worry," said Maggie. "The kids can't hear. Besides, they have no idea what we're talking about."

"I don't know about that," Sam muttered, focusing on withdrawing the cork from the bottle. She poured two perfectly measured glasses of wine. "My experience is that kids have big ears."

"They hear a lot of things they don't care about, but it would probably be a good idea to keep our voices down."

"Doesn't it bother you not having any privacy?" asked Sam, sliding a wine glass across the countertop.

"I do have privacy down in my little apartment, and when they're occupied. They don't hear a thing when they're watching TV."

Sam shook her head. "I don't know if I could live in such close quarters with other people."

Maggie studied Sam's face to see if there was an implied warning. "You do seem to like your privacy." Sam frequently talked about how her house at Jimson Pond was a retreat from other people.

"I've lived alone most of my life. You get used to it."

"Maybe, but I never did," Maggie said. "After Alina went to college,

I moved to New York. I never liked spending evenings alone, so I taught night classes and got involved in theater again. The only thing I did in my little apartment was sleep." After she'd said it, Maggie wondered if Sam might think their needs were at cross purposes. But it turned out Sam wasn't having deep thoughts at all.

"Maggie, I hate to ask, but do you have anything to eat? I'm starving."

"I'm sorry, Sam. I meant to put out snacks, but I didn't expect you so early."

Maggie opened a jar of spiced nuts she'd made the day before. "Here. Something healthy for you to munch on. It will be a while before we eat." She smiled listening to the pleasant crunching as Sam enjoyed the nuts. "You like them?"

"They're wonderful. How come you never made them for me?"

"Now that I know you like them, I will." Maggie patted Sam's shoulder. "Sam, we need to talk about why you were so upset last Sunday. I seem to have hurt you without meaning to. I hope you can forgive me."

"It's not you, Maggie. Well, yes, it is you." Sam reached for a handful of nuts. "I mean. You're the problem."

"I'm a problem?" Maggie asked incredulously. "How?"

"I don't know how to explain it, and I'm not sure I can talk to you about it."

"Why? Don't you think I'll give you a fair hearing?"

Sam scrunched her face in frustration. "No, that's not what I mean at all. Oh, crap! Here I go screwing up again."

Now, Maggie was truly baffled. "I'm sorry, Sam. If I'd known you were so sensitive about your appearance, I wouldn't have said anything."

"Grandma," said a small voice. They both turned to see Nicki in the doorway, holding up a paper. "Grandma, I don't know how to do this."

"Let me see, honey." Maggie's eyes swam looking at the jumble of symbols. No matter how she tried to understand the latest version of the new math, the logic behind it escaped her.

Sam gently took the paper out of her hand. "Maybe I can help."

Nicki studied Sam cautiously. "Grandma can't do math," she blurted out. "She doesn't know how!"

"Yes, she does," Sam explained. "She just learned math in a different time."

"But you're old like her."

Sam laughed. "Almost, but I've read about this new math, and I think I understand it. Want me to show you how to solve this?"

"Yes!" said Nicki and bolted from the kitchen.

"I think that's an invitation to her room. Consider it a compliment," Maggie said.

"Oh, I do," said Sam and followed Nicki down the hall.

***

When Alina came into the kitchen, she narrowed her eyes in a way that made Sam feel unwelcome. "Hello, Sam," she said in a cool voice. The tiny woman barely came to Sam's shoulder. She reached up to give her mother a kiss. "I didn't know we were having company tonight."

"I texted you," Maggie said, adding the pasta to the pot of boiling water. "Didn't you get it?"

"No, I was out in the field today. Way up in Maine, where I don't get good reception. It was a horror show. The foster kids kept being given back to a family where there was documented abuse. One of the girls got pregnant by the foster father."

"That's horrible!" said Maggie, her face registering her disgust.

"So many kids lost parents to the opioid crisis and then COVID. The system is overwhelmed. They're running out of places to put them." A look of panic flashed in Alina's eyes, and Sam realized she must be reliving a memory. When she sensed Sam looking at her, she turned away.

"Honey, get changed out of your work clothes," said her mother. "Dinner will be ready in five minutes."

"Okay. Where are the kids?"

"Watching TV. Their homework is done. Sam helped them."

"That's nice of you, Sam," said Alina, but she didn't look grateful.

What does she have against me? Sam wondered. *I plowed the driveway and shoveled her out while she was living in Erika's house. I got her heat started when Liz was in New Haven and couldn't help her.*

Maggie's daughter left the kitchen. After Sam heard the door close at the end of the hall, she said in a low voice, "Alina doesn't look happy to see me."

"She's just tired. She's been working so hard on this project. It's upsetting her because it hits too close to home."

"Liz says she still has nightmares."

Maggie grimaced slightly at the mention of her ex-wife, but maybe it was a reaction to bringing up Alina's nightmares. "The medication helps control them."

"Why would she want to work on a project that would trigger her?"

"Her therapist told her she needs to confront her fears, or they'll control her for her entire life."

"Sounds like tough love. Won't that make her condition worse?"

"Maybe. I don't think the therapist meant the advice as literally as Alina took it. She volunteered for this project. The news director, who knows a little about her history, wanted to assign it to someone else, but she insisted. Fortunately, the project ends next week. I just hope she gets through it without a crash." Maggie put the salad bowl in front of Sam. "Here. Make yourself useful. Toss the salad and then call the girls to dinner."

Sam briskly saluted.

"Never mind, Samantha McKinnon. Don't be a smart ass." The timer went off, and Maggie turned away to drain the pasta.

After Sam finished tossing the salad, she went into the living room to call the girls. "Suppertime," she announced. Neither of them moved. Sam stood between the girls and the TV. "Grandma says it's time for dinner."

Katrina rolled over and tried to look around Sam's legs. "It's almost over. Can't we wait?"

"I don't think so. Your mom's home, and she looks tired." That garnered a sympathetic nod from Nicki, who got up and found the remote. The girl's obedience impressed Sam. She wondered if the girls were unusually cooperative, or if they had learned to tiptoe around their mother the way Sam had to do when she was growing up. As she watched the girls march off to the kitchen, she felt a vague sense of anxiety.

Maggie was dishing out the pasta by the time Sam returned to the kitchen. "Would you mind bringing out the bowls as I serve them?" Maggie asked. "I don't usually have help, and I mean to take full advantage of it."

"I assume the smaller portions go to the children."

"That's one thing I really like about you, Sam. You're observant."

The steam from pasta water had frizzed the white hair that had escaped from Maggie's long braid. The departure from her usual, carefully groomed appearance was fetching, but Sam also saw how worn Maggie looked. How had this beautiful, successful woman suddenly become little more than a domestic servant? The obvious answer was she loved her daughter and her grandchildren, but her voluntary house arrest had clearly stolen some of her vitality. *You're reading into it*, Sam told herself. *Maggie chose this.*

And yet, when Maggie was married to Liz, Alina had lived alone. After she'd moved out of the beach house, where Erika had so generously allowed her to live rent-free, Alina bought a condominium closer to the TV station. Maggie had paid for childcare so Alina would be able to resume her career. She'd had lots of support from her mother, but she'd managed without her.

As Maggie sat down at the table with her own dish, she glanced at Sam. "You look deep in thought," she said.

"I'll tell you later," Sam replied. When Maggie's hazel eyes widened with concern, Sam smiled to reassure her.

Alina came to the table. She attempted a smile, but it came out as a grimace. "Looks delicious, Mom. Thank you. This is one of my favorites." She turned to Sam and explained, "Mom used to make this on special occasions when I was growing up."

"Is it a special occasion?" Sam asked curiously.

"Both girls made the honor roll this semester," Maggie replied. She smiled warmly at each girl in turn.

"They did? "Alina asked.

Katrina nodded enthusiastically. "I got an A in math. Even though the teacher said Grandma taught me wrong."

"Sam helped Nicki with her math homework today," said Maggie, grating cheese on her pasta. She handed the grater and the bowl containing the block of cheese to Sam. "I'm glad someone understands it. It's nothing like the math I learned when I was in school."

Sam looked up from her plate. "It doesn't make sense to me either, but I get what they're trying to do. I wonder what that says about me."

"That you have a big brain like Liz," Maggie replied, which stopped the conversation cold.

Alina tried to revive it by asking the girls about their day at school. She appeared engaged, but she was clearly distracted, which the girls seemed to sense. Their answers were often single words, despite Alina's persistent attempts to draw them out.

Sam wondered if all their family dinners were like this. Sam remembered mealtimes with Maggie's granddaughters at Liz's house. The conversation was always lively as they planned adventures. Liz was like a kid herself and made the girls conspirators in her mischief, usually at Maggie's expense. She always took it gracefully and seemed to enjoy the attention. Sam contrasted the warmth and silliness at Liz's table to this somber gathering.

"Grandma, can I be excused to watch *Young Sheldon*?" Katrina asked politely. Sam wondered why she hadn't asked her mother.

"Yes, you may, Katrina, but then it's bedtime."

"I'll do the dishes," Sam said, getting up.

"No, you don't," Maggie said. "You're a guest."

"You go out and watch the show with the kids, Mom. Sam and I will clean up."

Maggie looked both pleased and guilty. "I enjoy this show," she confessed. "It makes me think of all the geniuses in my life and wonder if you were like that when you were young." She smiled in Sam's direction before bringing her plate to the sink. After Maggie left with the children, Sam started clearing the table.

"I'm sorry I'm not better company tonight," Alina apologized.

"I know what it's like to come home after a hard day and have to socialize. It's not easy."

"No, but I have to show my kids I care about what goes on in their lives."

"I'm sure they know."

"I'm not so sure." Alina sighed. "But who knows what kids think?"

"Don't you remember what it was like to be a kid?"

"My childhood was so weird and scary I don't really like to remember it."

"I get it," Sam said, drying the stock pot Alina handed her.

"I'm sorry, Sam, but I don't think anyone can imagine it. That's why I want to make sure my kids never feel abandoned if I can help it. It's bad enough their father is such an asshole. After he took all the money and started drinking, he became abusive. We escaped with only our clothes. Liz had to come get us in a snowstorm because I didn't have enough money to pay for the airport bus. It was so humiliating."

"Why should you feel ashamed? It was his fault, not yours."

"It was my fault that I didn't see the warning signs and trusted him."

"It's not easy to be objective when you're involved with someone."

"But I'm an investigative journalist. I should have known better!"

"Hey," said Sam, putting a hand on Alina's shoulder. "Don't be so hard on yourself. You've had a hard day. You don't need this too."

Alina sniffed loudly, obviously holding back tears. "I'm sorry I was so crabby when I came home. I'm worried about Mom with the cancer, and the kids. They've been in and out of school for the last few years. It's so disruptive. Thank God, Mom was here to homeschool them."

"They seem to be doing well in school," said Sam, "so I guess she did a good job."

"They're lucky. You should see what I've been turning up in this investigation—parents becoming abusive because they were stuck at home with the kids. Women made homeless because they needed to choose between work and their kids. And now that fucker, Putin, is killing kids in Ukraine." Alina's voice was becoming progressively more agitated.

Sam carefully set down the big pasta bowl she'd been drying. "Alina, you can't carry the burden of the world on your shoulders. Sometimes, you need to unplug."

When Alina turned to Sam, her dark eyes were full of pain. "Sam, please don't make my mother choose between you and her family."

Before Sam could answer, Alina bolted from the room with tears streaming down her face. Sam, staring at the door through which Alina had disappeared, tried to figure out what to do. She didn't know the young woman well enough to offer comfort. Besides, it wasn't really her place. She slung the towel over her shoulder and put the skillet into the hot, soapy water. At least, she could finish doing the dishes. As she listened to the hum of the refrigerator, she wondered what she had gotten herself into. She turned off the light over the stove and sat down at the kitchen island to finish her wine.

Maggie came into the kitchen, looking to replenish her glass. "Nice job. Kitchen looks beautiful. Where's Alina?"

"She went to her room, I guess. She's not feeling well."

"I'm afraid that's pretty usual lately."

"You have your hands full."

"I do," Maggie agreed. She recorked the bottle and sighed. "This wasn't what I had in mind when I invited you to dinner. But I did want to talk to you. I was really worried I'd offended you on Sunday and wanted to clear the air."

"That's a big conversation for another time. You have enough to deal with at the moment."

Maggie put down her wine glass and gave Sam a kiss. "That's what I love about you, Sam. You don't say much, but you're so sensitive."

"Thank you." Sam gave Maggie a long, tender kiss. "I should probably go and let you deal with your family."

She was surprised by Maggie's sudden flirtatious look. "Don't rush off. I was really hoping you'd spend the night."

"With the kids here?"

"They go to bed, and I lock the door. Otherwise, they sneak into my bed. They know better now. Please. I've missed you." Maggie ran her hand suggestively along the inside of Sam's thigh. The tingling in response to the sexy touch made Sam open her legs wider.

"Are you sure?" she murmured.

"Yes, I'm sure."

"Grandma," called Nicki from the doorway. "Katrina keeps hogging the cushion!"

Maggie squeezed Sam's thigh. "Come out and sit with me while the kids finish watching the show. Then I'll put them to bed, and we can spend some time alone." Maggie gave her a sexy side-eye. "Okay?"

Sam was so aroused, she was barely able to speak, but she managed to choke out, "Okay."

PART II

RESURRECTION

9

Liz felt a pleasurable tug on her nipple and opened one eye. "Frisky this morning, aren't we?"

Smiling green eyes peered into hers. "Good morning," said Lucy and gave her a soft kiss. "It's Easter, and my fiancée is the reader at my service."

Liz groaned and rolled over. "And I thought you wanted some morning sex."

"Oh, I do, but we have a busy day, and Emily is coming later." Lucy reached under the duvet and outlined the perimeter of Liz's nipple with her fingertip. "You always carry on about my breasts, but yours are beautiful too."

"Glad you like them," Liz muttered, pulling up the duvet. She enjoyed a moment of peace before Lucy began enticingly caressing her from behind. The persistent motion was stimulating, but Liz played possum, hoping Lucy would let her go back to sleep. Then a sharp pinch made her jump. "Lucy!"

Lucy giggled. "Got your attention, didn't it?"

"You know, you can be a real shit sometimes!" Liz flung off the covers. As she headed to the bathroom, she could still hear Lucy's laughter. She swung the door closed, but it didn't shut, so she slammed it.

"I'm sorry," said a contrite voice on the other side. "You have such a sexy butt. I couldn't resist."

"Go away and let me urinate in peace," grumbled Liz.

"Okay. I'm going downstairs to make coffee. I'll heat up a cup for you."

Liz listened to the hangers rattling in the closet on the other side of the wall and guessed Lucy was looking for something to wear. The noise finally stopped, and Liz was relieved to be alone.

She had just begun to adjust to solo living when she'd acquired a full-time roommate. At least, the arrangement came with benefits, and her sex drive and Lucy's seemed well matched. Unfortunately, being involved with a priest meant leisurely Sunday mornings were a thing of the past. No more lounging in her pajamas to enjoy a second cup of coffee and read the Sunday papers.

Liz retrieved the T-shirt and boxers that had landed on the floor during the night. Still groggy from sleep, she considered taking the elevator from the third floor. She rejected the idea as laziness. As she plodded down the stairs, she wondered if she was going too far in trying to prove that she'd make a good pastor's wife. Until Lucy had appeared in her life, Liz had only shown up in church for weddings and funerals. Now, she was like unpaid staff at St. Margaret's. She accompanied Lucy on late night visitations and attended all church functions. Last Sunday, she'd sung hymns along with the congregation and waved a palm frond, while Lucy and the choir processed around the nave. Liz had never been a fan of audience participation and felt like a fool, but she was willing to do almost anything to show her support for St. Margaret's rector.

Lucy was spooning coffee into a pod when Liz came into the kitchen. Backlit by the bright sun from the window, the silhouette of her naked body showed through the sheer nightgown. Liz had to remind herself to breathe.

"Are you okay?" Lucy asked, looking up.

"Yes," Liz managed to say. "Enjoying the view."

Lucy glanced down. After realizing what Liz could see, she smiled flirtatiously. "Hope it made it worth getting out of bed. Sit down. I'll bring your coffee." She set it up and gazed out the window while it brewed. "There's a gorgeous cardinal at the feeder."

"Greedy creatures," grumbled Liz, slouching on the bench in the breakfast nook "Spring has been here for weeks. Time to cut off the animal welfare."

Lucy pouted. "But I love to watch the birds in the morning."

"If we keep feeding them, they won't learn to fend for themselves. And bird feeders attract bears."

"You're no fun."

"I'm just not awake yet. My fiancée woke me up too early."

The angle of the light had changed, so Liz could no longer see through Lucy's nightgown, but the silky fabric clung to every delicious curve. The sight of Lucy barely clothed, her red hair in disarray after a night of active sex, was far more interesting than the birds at the feeder.

Lucy placed the cup in front of her. She poured in a splash of cream and stirred it. "Drink your coffee. Maybe you'll be friendlier." Before she could get away, Liz reached around her hips, enjoying the warmth of her skin under the fine silk. Below the fragrance of the coffee, Liz caught a few notes of Lucy's unique scent. She tried to reach under her nightgown to caress its source, but Lucy squirmed out of her embrace. "None of that, or I'll want to go back to bed. Let me **go**. I want to make myself some coffee."

On her return, Lucy brought along a volume bound in well-worn red leather. Liz rolled her eyes. The intrusion of *The Book of Common Prayer* before she was fully awake wasn't fair. Lucy left the book near Liz's elbow. "I thought you'd like a chance to review the readings. I know how important it is for you to be prepared."

Liz sipped her coffee and opened to the pages Lucy had marked. She scanned the readings, closed the book, and slid it across the table.

"You can't have read it that fast," Lucy said, raising an auburn brow.

"Want to quiz me?"

"No, I believe you. It's just that Easter is a big feast, and I like to be prepared too."

"I know," said Liz, "which is why your services are like well-directed theater."

Lucy pouted.

"Oh, stop. That was a compliment. You don't just go through the motions. Ritual is more effective when there's some drama. And your sermons are inspiring, like the one you wrote for today…about the women bearing witness to the empty tomb."

"Women are important witnesses throughout Holy Week. Veronica wiping Jesus's face with her veil. The Marys at the foot of the cross…"

"But I thought the resurrection was the point," said Liz. She mimed the melodramatic narration of a horror movie trailer: "Easter…the day the zombie returned." She was enjoying her own wit until she looked up into Lucy's face. She was not amused, but before she could say anything, Liz added: "Oh, come on, Lucy. You can't really believe a body can rise from the dead."

"Why not?" asked Lucy in a cold voice.

"Well, for one thing, it's scientifically impossible."

"Don't people wake up in morgues and funeral homes?"

"Yes, but they weren't actually dead in the first place. Evidently, the Gospel writers thought people would ask the same question. They went out of their way to prove Jesus was dead, and the evidence is accurate. If someone deliberately breaks your leg, you'd scream in pain, but Jesus doesn't react. He doesn't bleed when he's pierced by a lance. When the heart stops, there's no pressure to pump the blood, so you don't bleed. Like any good fiction, the Gospels supply enough detail, so you'll suspend belief, but I'm always suspicious when people try too hard. I think the passion story is a setup."

Lucy stared at her. "Anything else you'd like to share, Dr. Encyclopedia-of-Useless-Information?"

Liz laughed at her own self-deprecating title being used against her. "No, I'll shut up now. I know Easter is a big deal in your world." She got up to make herself another cup of coffee. "I guess I can't understand how a smart woman like you could buy into this resurrection nonsense."

"Who said I do?"

Surprised, Liz put down the coffee pod she was filling and turned around. "What?"

"You heard me." Lucy said, staring into her coffee cup.

"Wow! I didn't see that one coming." Liz gazed out the window to let the information sink in.

"You're shocked," observed Lucy.

"No," said Liz. "Well, maybe a little. But you're one of the most unpredictable people I've ever met."

"Glad I'm keeping you on your toes, but now, you'll probably think I'm a hypocrite."

Liz shrugged. "Not necessarily. The Jesuits who taught at my college promoted healthy skepticism about religion. Based on them, I can understand how you can question your faith and still be a priest."

"Episcopalians don't believe in the literal interpretation of scripture. Reason is one of the pillars of our tradition."

"…and why I tolerate it…most of the time." Liz finished filling the pod and set up her coffee to brew. "How long has this been going on?" she asked.

"You mean the doubt? Erika encouraged me to think more critically when she'd critique my sermons."

"Leave it to a philosopher to upset a theologian."

"But Erika was a gentle agnostic. She always said it was better to take baby steps instead of a great leap into doubt. But when she died, I doubted everything, even my own sanity. I couldn't believe that God could take the life of such a kind, brilliant woman…but she was just snatched away while I napped on the sofa downstairs. I never even got to say good-bye." Tears formed in Lucy's eyes. Liz reached out to rub her shoulder.

"Erika loved you. She knew you loved her."

Lucy sniffled and wiped her tears with her wrists. "I know, but it's one of the many things I regret…and letting you kiss me on the boat. She didn't deserve that."

"Stop wallowing in old guilt. She forgave you. She was never monogamous before you came along, so I doubt it bothered her as much as you think."

Lucy yanked a paper napkin out of the holder on the table and blew her nose. "After she died, I looked for answers in my faith, but the old beliefs didn't work for me anymore. I've joined a deconstruction group," Lucy confessed shyly, "but it's full of refugees from fundamentalist denominations. I get that they've been hurt, but there's so much anger. I was hurt too by my Catholic upbringing, but I've let that go."

"That's good."

"Now, I just feel lost. For years, my faith was my anchor. Now, I feel like I'm drifting."

Liz put her arm around Lucy. "I bet it's even harder now that you've taken all those theology courses. But remember John's words, 'the truth shall set you free.'"

"I don't feel free, and when I read Bishop Spong's books for one of my courses, I felt like I'd been raped all over again. He took away all the comfort of my childhood faith and left me with nothing but vague metaphors."

"Welcome to being an adult. Spong eviscerates Christianity, but he still wants to justify having faith. Makes no sense, does it?"

"When did you read Spong?" asked Lucy with surprise.

"Years ago, when his books first came out. What a killjoy! Questioning Iron Age fairy tales is good, but do you have to kill Santa Claus, the Easter Bunny, and the Tooth Fairy all at once?"

"You read his books…even though you're an atheist?"

"Lucy, you know I'm not really an atheist. Atheists are too strident. Their rabid denial is as dogmatic as any religion. I don't believe any of the nonsense I was taught as a child, but I'm open to the idea of something greater than myself." Liz wagged a finger under Lucy's nose. "Swear to me you won't ever tell your fucking bishop I said that."

Lucy backed up from the wagging finger. "I promise."

"Little prick," Liz grumbled. She could hardly wait for the wedding to be over, so she would be free of Bishop Greene.

"You don't think I'm a hypocrite?" Lucy asked in a small voice.

"Not at all. You always tell me that you love the honest seekers most of all. Now, you're one of us." Liz pulled Lucy closer and gave her a little squeeze. "I'll try to be gentler about what I say on this subject…more like Erika. No need to be brutal like Spong, and no more zombie jokes."

"Thank you. I'm questioning church doctrine, but I believe in a gracious, loving God. I'm inspired by Jesus's radical message of love and social justice. I get comfort from prayer and worship and the music…especially the music."

"And there's nothing wrong with comfort. Sometimes, we need emotional security blankets, especially when everything is so uncertain. People are still dying of COVID. Russia is bombing the hell out of Ukraine. We all need a break from reality, like a feel-good movie that makes us cry."

Lucy sat up. "Not quite the same, but I get what you mean."

Liz gently kissed her freckled forehead. "We can talk more about this later, but right now, you need to rev yourself up to lead Easter worship—no pun intended, of course. And don't worry. I'll keep your secret." Lucy turned into her shoulder and began to cry. "Oh, baby, it's okay," soothed Liz, taking her in her arms. She enjoyed the warmth of Lucy's body against her and the light floral scent of her hair.

"It's so hard…" said Lucy between sniffles. "It's hard to pretend."

"But you are a brilliant actress. You can do it. I know you can."

"Thanks for listening," Lucy murmured, patting Liz's arm. "I love you."

"I love you too." She kissed the top of Lucy's head. "Are you hungry? I can make us some breakfast."

"Just hold me a few more minutes."

Liz strengthened her grip for a moment to confirm that she'd heard.

The ship's bell on the porch sounded. Liz glanced at the clock. "For fuck's sake! It's only six-fifteen. Who could that be?"

Lucy jumped up. "Whoever it is, I'm half naked. Let me run upstairs and put on some clothes."

"Get dressed. I'll see who's at the door." Liz took a sweatshirt from the hook in the hall closet and put it on over her T-shirt. She wasn't exactly presentable herself, but whoever would dare to ring the bell at that hour, had to be someone they knew. Liz guessed it might be Brenda, who sometimes stopped in for a cup of coffee on her way to duty. Liz pushed aside the sheer curtain on the front door and looked out. With her duffle bag at her feet and her backpack slung over her shoulder, Lucy's daughter looked like a lost waif. Liz hurried to open the locks.

"Hello, little girl. Are you looking for someone?" She opened the storm door wider so that Emily could enter.

Emily's mouth twitched, trying to figure out how to respond. Finally, she smirked. "Hah. Very funny, Aunt Liz." She pushed the duffle bag up to the threshold with her foot.

"What brings you so early?" Liz reached down for her bag.

"Couldn't sleep, so I figured I'd drive up from New Haven. Hope I didn't wake you."

"No, your mother already exercised that privilege. Easter is a big day for her, so she got me out of bed early."

"I guessed she'd be up. I was going to let myself into the beach house but there was all that stuff in the driveway, and it didn't look like anyone was home."

"Your mother has been living here. Sam is working on the garage project. That's why the driveway's full of construction materials. I'm glad you knew to come here. This is your home now."

"I know, Aunt Liz. But it's really early. Where's Mom?"

"Upstairs making herself decent. She'll be right down." Liz opened her arms. "Hug?"

"Yes," said Emily and collapsed into Liz's arms. It was hard to predict when Emily would welcome affection. Obviously, this was one of those times. "I almost fell asleep on the road," she said, releasing Liz. "I didn't consider that when I headed out at two this morning."

"It's a long drive, especially at night. Can I get you some coffee?"

"It will keep me awake. I think I should get some sleep before Mom's service this morning. I don't think she'd like me snoring during her sermon."

"Probably not." Liz picked up Emily's bag and headed down the hall with it. "Hungry? I can make you some breakfast. There are Easter eggs in the fridge. Your mother laughed at me for wanting to dye eggs, but I think she had fun."

"Thanks, but I'm not hungry. I'll just wait till Mom comes down. Then I'll head up to bed."

"Your mom has taken over the seashore room as her office. You can sleep downstairs or take one of the other bedrooms."

"I think I'll sleep in the North Woods room. I like the moose quilt."

"Emily!" Lucy called, hurrying down the stairs. "What are you doing here so early?" Lucy reached up for a hug.

As Emily stiffly embraced her mother, she explained again that she couldn't sleep. "I started thinking about the Russians bombing those poor Ukrainians. Did you know that Russia's nuclear arsenal is superior to ours? There's a lot of risk." Emily recited by heart the statistics of Russia's atomic weapons by class and range.

"Oh, Sweetie, you shouldn't think of things like that before bedtime," said Lucy. She cast a meaningful glance at Liz, who seldom slept through the night.

"I can't help it. It's all you see on the news." Emily picked up her bag. "Sorry to head straight to bed, Mom, but I won't make it to church if I don't get some sleep."

"Go ahead," Lucy encouraged. "Do you want us to wake you?"

"Thanks, Mom. I'll set my phone alarm." She turned and headed up the stairs.

Lucy sighed as they headed back to the kitchen. "Looks like everyone's stressed out."

"I've written more prescriptions for sleep aids in the last few weeks than during the whole pandemic. It's all this war talk. It's very unsettling."

"I keep praying. That's the one thing I keep doing, no matter what."

❋❋❋

Lucy peeked out the robing room door and scanned the congregation. The church was filling up quickly. Sitting in the pews were families Lucy hadn't seen since the pandemic began. As it dragged on, Lucy had wondered if they would ever come back. The church ladies had remained hopeful. Activity bags with children's books, coloring books with Gospel themes, and crayons hung on the back wall. A pew had been removed to provide a place where mothers could nurse their babies. The ulterior motive was keeping infants from howling during the service, but Lucy approved of her church being child friendly. Unfortunately, few of these things saw use during the pandemic. The kids' activity bags, hand stitched from colorful cloth, were emptied and run through the rectory washing machine to remove the accumulated dust. But now, the children were back, carefully dressed and scrupulously clean, standing beside their young parents.

"We're almost ready to line up for the procession," Denise whispered near Lucy's ear.

"I'll be right there." Lucy looked for Liz and found her sitting beside Olivia, who was the second reader that morning. Emily sat on Liz's other side. Sam, wearing an elegant tailored suit, was sitting in the row behind them. Lucy's eyes located Brenda and Cherie with Keith and Megan. Brenda bent toward Keith, who was pointing to the stained glass and talking her ear off. Two rows behind them were Melissa and Courtney and her daughter, Kaylee. The sight of so many children filled Lucy with joy.

"Doesn't Sam look sensational this morning?" asked Maggie.

Lucy turned around. "She sure does. Your influence?"

"No, I didn't say a word. She said she was dressing up because it's Easter. You're probably too young to remember when we all got a new outfit for Easter. The girls all got a new spring hat. We even wore white gloves."

"There was still some of that when I was a girl. The white gloves were mostly gone by then. And the hats."

"Denise said to come get you," Maggie said, tugging on Lucy's arm. "We're all lined up for the procession. We're just waiting for you."

"I'm coming." After Maggie left, Lucy bent her head and whispered a prayer of Thanksgiving for the full church. She added another word of thanks for the conversation with Liz. Admitting she had doubts to an avowed atheist had been a huge risk. Liz could have gloated and egged her on, but she hadn't. She had been kind, almost tender, when she listened to what was, essentially, a confession.

But Lucy couldn't dwell on the personal now. On Easter morning, she belonged to her congregation. She was their priest. She headed down the side aisle, hearing murmurs of "Happy Easter, Mother Lucy," along the way. When she reached the back, she took her place at the end of the procession.

As they walked toward the altar, Lucy could hear Maggie's strong voice shoring up the soprano section. It was good to have her back.

Lucy couldn't wait until the sermon to show her joy in the size of the congregation. "It's so good to be back in our church, to be together at worship. And while the pandemic isn't over yet, we can see a day when it will be. This is our community resurrected. Every one of you here this morning is proof that we are not defeated. We can come back to life." There was a murmur of applause.

Lucy's joy buoyed her up through the service. She enjoyed listening to Liz read in a careful, formal tone. Olivia read well too, but that would be expected from someone who'd paid for elocution lessons. Somehow, Olivia looked taller at the lectern. For a relatively small woman, she could convince people she was of greater stature.

Lucy's sermon got a few chuckles here and there. She always considered sermons that made people laugh a success. At communion time, they barely had enough hosts and had to dip into the supply that Tom had consecrated at the Easter Vigil the night before. The choir sang gloriously. Lucy was so happy that she sang louder than she ordinarily would until she caught herself. She never wanted people to think she was showing off because she was a professional. Most of all, she didn't want to drown out the choir, which she could easily do. Her mind fast-forwarded to the Mahler concert, now little more than a week away. Then she would have to make her voice heard over a large choir.

After the service, she was inundated with well-wishers. Starved by lack of physical contact during the pandemic, everyone wanted to shake hands or get a hug. Lucy felt the press of bodies one after the other in a seemingly endless line. Then Susan stood before her, hesitating as if expecting to be turned away. Lucy opened her arms wide.

"Happy Easter, Sister Priest," she whispered into Susan's ear.

"And to you, too. Alleluia! He is risen."

Ignoring the long line behind Susan, Lucy looked into her blue eyes. "I haven't seen much of you lately."

"I would have thought that would be a good thing." When Lucy made a sad face to refute the assumption, Susan glanced away. "I've been busy interviewing for clergy and teaching positions. The tricky thing is getting both in the same place or near enough to commute to my church."

"Any word on your priest's license?"

"Not yet, but I hope to hear soon."

Over Susan's shoulder, an obviously impatient man was making faces. "Let's make time for lunch, or at least a cup of coffee this week," Lucy said, giving Susan another warm hug.

Finally, Lucy reached the end of the line. She looked around for her family members. Emily was talking to Denise, standing close, which she reserved for people she really liked. Maybe there was hope for that relationship. Lucy caught Liz's eye, and she broke away from her conversation with Olivia to head in her direction. "Come with me to the robing room while I take off my vestments," Lucy said, taking her arm.

"That was quite a line today. I saw you talking to Susan."

"What are you? A spy?" said Lucy, laughing. "I'm not allowed to talk to my friends?"

"Of course, you are, but seeing her reminded me to ask you a question. That block of tickets I bought for your concert? I have one ticket left. Do you want me to give it to Susan?"

Lucy studied Liz's face. Liz had every reason to dislike Susan, so this gesture was unexpected, but as Lucy continued to think about it, she realized it made perfect sense. Liz was generous to a fault. "That's very kind of you, but are you sure that's what you want to do?"

"Well, if she's as pinched for money as you say, she wouldn't be able to afford it on her own. I know she's a big fan of yours and would probably really like to go. But if you don't think it's a good idea, I can give the ticket to Denise for one of her friends."

Lucy carefully lifted the chasuble over her upsweep to avoid dislodging the pins. "No, I think you should go with your instincts and give it to Susan."

"Good. Then I'll give you the ticket and you can give it to her."

"No, I think you should give it to her. After all, you paid for it, and it will mean more coming from you."

Emily appeared in the doorway. "Mom, can we leave soon? I'm sooo tired."

Lucy slipped on her jacket and hooked her arm in her daughter's. "Yes, honey, we're leaving. You can take a nap while Liz cooks dinner. Right, Liz?" She shot Liz a dazzling smile to make sure the answer was, "yes."

Lucy couldn't get through the parking lot without accepting more hugs and Easter greetings. She sighed in relief when she finally got into Liz's car and shut the door. The grueling Holy Week schedule was finally over. Now, her only agenda was enjoying the holiday with her family and recharging her physical and emotional batteries. For the first time in months, she allowed herself the luxury of feeling her exhaustion. She even dared to close her eyes and doze lightly as Liz headed home.

The chirp of her phone woke her. She pulled it out of her bag and looked at the screen.

"Gosh! It's my agent. I haven't heard from him in years."

"It's Easter," Liz said with a disapproving look. "Call him back tomorrow."

"I should take it. Roger worked his butt off for me, even though he wasn't making any money. He believed in me when no one else did and stuck with me until I finally called it quits." Lucy tapped open the call. "Hi, Roger. How nice to hear from you."

"Hello, Lucy. Happy Easter. Why didn't you tell me you were singing again?"

"Well, I'm not exactly. It's only one performance to help a friend. How did you find out?"

"Nothing happens in the singing world that I don't know." He chuckled softly. "I have you on a Google crawler, and an ad for the BSO just came across my screen. So, you're headlining the *Mahler Two*?"

"The alto is my music director."

"Denise Chantal, who used to be Denis Chantal, the rising counter-tenor superstar? She's singing as a woman now?"

"Yes, and this could be her big break."

"I get it, but clearly the world is not done with a real superstar, namely Lucille Bartlett. I hear you have a new book coming out, and the story of how you were blacklisted is in it."

"In broad strokes to make a point; the names changed to protect the guilty."

"Everyone should know that Alex Dupuis was scum, but the top guys at the Met protected their own in those days. Look at James Levine. I'm not sure what I think about Placido. I always thought he was an okay guy. Nilsson even awarded him the prize. Now, there was a lady who knew how to handle men."

Lucy didn't know what to make of that remark. Was the implication she didn't?

"Roger, it's great to hear from you, but I'm just getting home from church with my family, and I can't really talk now."

There was silence on the other end of the call as the man processed the information. "I'm sorry, Lucy. I didn't mean to interrupt your holiday. I was just so excited to see you were singing again, I couldn't wait to talk to you."

"That's fine."

"I want you to know that if you decide to get back in the game, I'm here for you. In my head, I'm already planning your comeback tour."

Lucy laughed. "Don't get ahead of yourself, Roger. This is just one event."

"Lucy, I know you. I can't see your face, but I can feel how itchy you are to get back on the stage."

The accuracy of the comment stung. Lucy tensed.

"I'll let you get back to your family and your Easter celebration," Roger said. "Nice talking to you, Lucy. I'll see you at the concert."

"You're coming?" Lucy asked with alarm.

"You kidding me? Nothing could keep me away from hearing you sing again. Besides, I like Bean Town. It's fun to get out of New York once in a while."

"Good idea. I look forward to seeing you. Thanks for calling."

Lucy hung up and threw her phone into her bag. She was aware of Liz watching out of the corner of her eye and regretted the obvious gesture of annoyance. To protect the privacy of her parishioners and clients, Lucy always kept her phone volume low. Even so, she'd been mindful of the fact that she had an audience in the confines of Liz's Audi, and tried not to say anything she didn't want overheard. She turned around to see if Emily had any reaction to the call, but she was looking out the window and seemed blissfully unaware.

"Do you have any legal obligation to this guy?" Liz asked, instantly zeroing in on the practical implications.

"No, once I was approved for ordination as a deacon, I formally terminated our contract."

"You mean, you were performing until then? Why didn't I know about it?"

"Because I was mostly singing overseas or in backwater venues."

"But you were still singing."

"I had to support myself and pay for my education," said Lucy, hoping Liz could see the justification.

"I guess you did. Sorry, I didn't know."

The luxurious interior of Liz's Audi suddenly felt smaller, as if the walls were closing in. Lucy opened the window for air. She realized she was still wearing her collar—a linen collar that Liz had pressed for her because it was Easter. Lucy carefully took it off, but she panicked trying to think of a secure place to put the gold collar studs. When Liz's hand reached out for them, Lucy gratefully handed them over to her care. Liz put them in a recess in the dashboard, where they reflected the brilliant morning sunlight.

"Mom, are you going back to singing?" asked a voice from the backseat.

"I don't know, Emily," said Lucy, flustered. "I don't know."

10

Leaning in the doorway of the hotel bathroom, Sam watched Maggie put on her makeup. She'd witnessed the process before but had never given it much attention because makeup didn't interest her. On the rare occasions she wore it, she could apply the basics—a little foundation, some blush, and mascara—in a matter of minutes. This minimalist approach had been a concession to working in a corporate architecture office. If she had a big meeting with clients, she might add some eyeliner and some neutral lipstick. Otherwise, she couldn't be bothered. For Maggie, putting on makeup was a full-blown production requiring a half hour or more.

"Do you go through this every day?" Sam asked, trying not to sound critical.

"Not quite, but tonight's a special occasion."

"It's a real procedure."

"When you're my age, looking good takes effort," said Maggie.

"You look great without makeup, and you're not that old."

Maggie's eyes engaged Sam's in the mirror. "Easy for you to say. You just turned sixty. I'm heading for the next big one."

"You have a whole year before you turn seventy. Besides, age is just a number. I don't even think about it."

"I do," said Maggie leaning closer to the mirror to brush on mascara. "I can see how much I've aged every time I look in the mirror." She thrust the brush into the silver tube and carefully screwed it closed. "So far, I've resisted getting a facelift. Liz talked me out of it."

Somehow, Liz always entered the conversation. Usually, Sam didn't mind. After all, Liz was what they both had in common, but recently, Sam had begun keeping track of how often Maggie mentioned her.

"You're still paying attention to what she thinks? You're divorced now. You don't have to follow what she says." Sam almost added that if Maggie wanted plastic surgery, she should go right ahead and get it. Then she realized it might sound like she thought Maggie needed a facelift, which was the wrong message.

"Liz always gave me good medical advice. That's why I went to her when my breast cancer came back. I trust her." Sam didn't like the look of regret in Maggie's eyes, so she glanced at her watch instead. They had plenty of time, but Sam was uncomfortable waiting around, especially so dressed up. She kicked off her pumps, which pinched a little, because she almost never wore them, and wiggled her toes to encourage the circulation.

"Come here," said Maggie.

"What?" asked Sam, looking up in surprise.

"You heard me. Come over here." Maggie loaded a brush with some dark beige powder and brought it close to Sam's cheek. Leading with the elbow, Sam's arm instantly rose to block it. Maggie eyed the raised arm with concern. "Sam, it's just a makeup brush, not a deadly weapon. I just thought your cheeks could use more definition. Those high cheekbones make you look so aristocratic. You should flaunt them."

"No thanks," said Sam, returning to the safety of the doorway.

"I've said something wrong again, haven't I?"

"How can you tell?"

"You're practically cowering. I'm sorry. I forgot you don't like me talking about how you look." Maggie closed the compact and tossed it in her makeup bag. "Offering suggestions is a habit. Actresses are always helping each other in the dressing room. I didn't mean any harm by it."

"Have you ever talked to Liz about why she hates to dress up?"

"Sure. We talked about it often. She associates dressing for success with corporate medicine, which she despises."

"Oh, I think it goes deeper than that."

"It does," said Maggie in casual voice. "She's still resisting her mother who tried to turn her into a lady."

"Well, doesn't that give you a hint about why it bothers me?"

"You're resisting your mother too?"

"Duh," said Sam, making a silly face.

"Sam, I might be older, but I'm not your mother. I care about you, and I want you to look your best. That's why I make suggestions." She crossed her arms on her chest, then uncrossed them, still self-conscious about the implants. "You and Liz and your weird mother dynamics."

"I'm sorry you think it's weird, but a lot of gay women have issues with their mothers."

"Sam, don't you think it's time you let that go?"

"Like it was that easy. My mother made it clear from the get-go that I wasn't the daughter she'd expected. She was a socialite and wanted me to make the right connections, but the other girls shunned me because I hated girlie things and played with the boys. My mother would sweet-talk the other mothers into inviting me to parties. I always ended up standing on the sidelines, feeling like an outcast. When you constantly hear that you're an embarrassment, it's hard not to believe it."

Maggie pulled Sam down into a hug. "Oh, Sam, I'm so sorry," she said, stroking Sam's back soothingly. "You're not an embarrassment. You're brilliant and beautiful and successful. Any mother would be proud to have a daughter like you."

"Not any mother. Not mine."

Maggie let her go and sighed. "What can I do to help you?"

"Just leave me alone."

Maggie shot her a flirtatious side eye. "Really?"

"No, not that way. I like sex."

"And you're very sexy," Maggie ran her hands down Sam's arms. "I like how you handle me." Maggie purred like a cat. "You do it very well."

Sam felt a sharp twinge of desire, which confused her because just a moment ago she wanted to run away and hide.

"Maggie, please don't try to fix me. I don't need fixing."

Maggie gave her a long sympathetic look. "No, you don't. And after this one last thing, I won't say another word about your appearance. You have more natural assets than I do. I'm a little jealous, but I want you to look your best because you are an attractive woman."

Sam felt herself squirming under the compliments. Her cheeks began to warm. "We should get going," she said to change the subject.

"Why? We have plenty of time. I thought we could go down to the lobby to have a drink."

Sam looked at her watch. "Yes, I guess we could."

"Put your shoes on. Let's go."

Sam slipped her shoes back on. She felt Maggie's eyes on her as she raked her fingers through her hair to neaten it. "Do I look okay?"

Maggie smiled. "I'm afraid to say a word, but since you asked, yes, you look more than okay. That suit is gorgeous, and you look spectacular." Sam blushed as she followed Maggie out the door.

"I'm glad we decided to stay in Boston for the night," Maggie said while they waited for the elevator to arrive. It's fun to have an excuse to get away. Almost like a mini vacation."

"Did Alina finally find someone to watch the kids?"

"There's a neighbor who had to quit her job to homeschool her children during the lockdown. The girls are friends with her children and already spend a lot of time there. I'm sure Alina could work out a financial arrangement with the woman. She could probably use the money, and I'm happy to pay a reasonable rate."

The wheels in Sam's mind began to turn. Maybe freedom from watching her grandchildren would make Maggie more available on weeknights. Sam never minded coming home to a gourmet dinner or sleeping next to Maggie, who fit neatly into the curve of her body. Sam found her presence much less intrusive than Olivia's, probably because Maggie didn't demand more than half the bed.

"Where did you go?" Maggie asked curiously.

Sam blushed, wondering what Maggie would think if she knew what she'd been planning. "Just thinking."

"I love my grandkids, but I really need to push Alina about childcare. I want to go back to work. I need to feel I can still contribute something."

Sam liked Maggie's new streak of independence. She'd always thought she'd retired too early. After she did, Liz had complained about her demands for attention and wrote it off to not having enough to do. "I think it's a great idea for you to go back to teaching…and acting too."

"I need the stimulation, Sam. My brain is turning to mush. I've already raised one family. I don't mind helping out, but not full-time."

Maggie abruptly released Sam's arm when the elevator door opened. Avoiding public displays of affection was reflexive in many women of their generation, so Sam took no offense. She ventured into the lobby, looking for signs to the main lounge. Behind her, she heard a familiar voice.

"Maggie Fitzgerald! Don't tell me you're staying here too!" Sam turned around and saw Olivia gliding in Maggie's direction. She looked elegant in a stylish dress and just the right amount of gold jewelry. Most people thought she came from old money. Sam knew her backstory—how she'd come from nothing, gotten scholarships to Ivy League colleges, met a blue-blooded stockbroker and married him for his WASP name and trust money. She'd become a stockbroker too and founded a wildly successful hedge fund. She was a brilliantly successful fraud, but Sam had always admired her skill in pulling off the deception.

Olivia air kissed Maggie on both cheeks. "It's so nice to see you," she oozed. "I wondered if you'd be here. Isn't this so exciting! Our own pastor and music director singing with the Boston Symphony Orchestra. Can you believe it?"

"It's a wonderful opportunity for Denise, and we know that Lucy was once a big star. This probably counts as a small venue for her."

Olivia's back was turned, so she hadn't noticed Sam yet, who scrutinized the scene from her vantage point. She was relieved that Maggie's face showed no sign of jealousy when she mentioned Lucy. Of course, Maggie was too good an actress to let her true feelings show, especially to a calculating woman like Olivia.

Maggie glanced in Sam's direction, unwittingly revealing her hiding place. When Olivia turned around and saw Sam, her smile instantly froze. "Samantha! Are you here with Maggie?"

"Yes," Sam mumbled, trying to make herself small as she approached. At her height, it was impossible. In the back of her mind, she heard her mother's admonition to stand up straight, so she did.

"How nice that you could both come," Olivia said. Her cold expression of disapproval made Sam feel like she was doing something, not just wrong, but illegal.

"It's so nice to see you, Olivia," said Sam, lying blatantly. Olivia offered her cheek, and Sam reluctantly bent to kiss it.

"You must join me for a drink," said Olivia, not missing a beat. "I was just heading to the bar to get something. Maggie, if you go into the lounge, you'll see Amy Hsu at my table. I'm sure she'll be glad to see you."

Sam uncomfortably cleared her throat. This situation was going from bad to worse. Amy's strongest memory of Maggie was probably the day she'd invaded her office after discovering her breast cancer had returned. The idea of sitting with two exes made Sam faintly nauseous, but she couldn't come up with an excuse to decline the invitation, and Maggie seemed eager to join them.

"I'll go with you to the bar, Olivia," Sam said quickly. "Maggie, what are you drinking?"

"Chardonnay would be fine." Maggie, evidently realizing the awkwardness of the situation, smiled sympathetically. She affectionately touched Sam's shoulder. "Thank you, Sam. Let me go find Amy." She turned and headed into the lounge.

When they stood at the bar awaiting their drinks, Olivia asked, "Are you seeing Maggie now?"

"I guess you would say so."

"Yes or no, Samantha?" Olivia demanded, which made Sam feel like she was back in grade school. She stood straight, trying to draw fortitude from her advantage in height.

"Yes."

Olivia's brows rose. "I do hope you know what you're doing. With her history of cancer, she might not be a very good investment."

The meanness of the remark made Sam want to slap Olivia, but she responded with a cold stare. "Unlike you, Olivia, not all of my relationships are transactional," she said in an icy tone.

"Ouch."

"I don't care about her medical history," Sam said, enunciating each word with precision. "I like Maggie and enjoy her company."

"But not mine."

"I did, but you kept pushing for more. I don't like to be pushed."

"So I've finally come to understand." Olivia's face became a mask.

"I know you can't help yourself, Olivia. You always say, if you want something, you never give up until you get it."

"In business, that's considered a good quality."

"I'm sure, but a relationship isn't business." Sam grasped Olivia's arm. "And please don't hurt Amy. She's a good person, and her ex-wife was a bitch." Sam wanted to bite her tongue for revealing that information. She hated giving Olivia anything she might use to manipulate Amy.

"Hmm," Olivia intoned with a frown. "She hasn't told me about that."

"Are you sharing a room?" Sam asked, surprised at being so direct.

"That's really none of your business, is it? But no, we can both afford our own rooms, even though this hotel is ridiculously expensive for what it is. The premier linen and absurd variety of pillows are nice, but certainly not worth the price they charge."

"I'm surprised that even matters to you, with all your money."

"Didn't your mother ever teach you that the rich only have money because they don't spend it?"

Sam had had enough talk about her mother for one day, but she said, "Yes, I remember her saying something like that."

Olivia had been watching her reactions carefully. "Don't get your hackles up, Samantha. I like Maggie. I feel bad for her. First, her wife wanders away, and then the cancer comes back. Poor woman."

Sam felt like saying, *Maggie doesn't need your sympathy, Olivia. You're pretty pathetic, yourself.*

"You may not think so," Olivia continued, "but I do care for you, Samantha, and don't want to see you get into trouble. I bet seeing Maggie hasn't done anything for your relationship with Liz."

"I'm not worried. Liz gave me the tickets for the concert."

"She *gave* them to you? Hmm. I paid for mine."

"You have a different relationship with Liz. I've known her for years."

"Of course. In fact, I insisted on paying for the tickets. She wanted to give them to me," Olivia said, not to be outdone. "She's so proud of Lucy, I'm surprised she didn't invite all of Hobbs!" said Olivia, reaching for the martinis she'd ordered.

"She did invite Brenda and Cherie, but they didn't want to leave the kids overnight."

The bartender finally brought the beer and the glass of white wine Sam had ordered, apologizing that he'd had to open a new bottle. She signed the check to her room tab.

As they headed to the lounge, Olivia said, "Let's pretend we get along for the sake of a pleasant evening."

"We do get along, Olivia. I just can't be in a relationship with you."

"A shame. I really miss the sex. Some of the best I ever had." Olivia shot Sam a smoldering look. Surprisingly, it instantly sent a signal to Sam's crotch. "I loved the way you fucked me," Olivia whispered as they approached the table where Amy and Maggie sat.

Sam pasted a smile on her face to cover her discomfort.

"I hope these martinis are as good as they look," Olivia said cheerfully.

"Enjoy it, Olivia," said Amy. "It's the only one you get tonight."

"My doctor is a tyrant, but I think I'll keep her," said Olivia, giving Amy an unmistakably seductive look.

***

Thanks to how the tickets were distributed, Maggie was sitting next to Tom instead of Liz. She was glad because she didn't want to see her ex-wife's face while Lucy was on the stage. Liz had always been a fanatical opera fan, but her adoration of Lucy bordered on disgusting.

"What great seats," Sam said into Maggie's ear. "Liz must have robbed a bank to pay for them. And she's having a buffet dinner in a private room after the performance. We're invited, of course."

"Of course," repeated Maggie. "Liz wants an opportunity to show off her trophy girlfriend."

Sam frowned. "Maggie, don't. I know you're better than that. And be happy for Denise. This could make her career. Lucy's just doing this to help her out."

"Really? I'm sure Lucy's enjoying all the attention."

"Wouldn't you?"

"Of course I would." Maggie sighed. Sam was right. She was better than this. Lucy had genuine talent, and it was a shame her career had been cut short. At least, Maggie had chosen to give up acting and go back to school for her doctorate. Lucy had been forced from the Met stage by the old-boys club.

Maggie looked down the row to see who else was there. Susan Gedney was sitting at the far end, talking to no one. She looked so lost and unwanted that Maggie felt sorry for her. While Susan was occupied with her program, Maggie scrutinized her. Her kind expression gave her almost a saintly look. Although her face was mostly unlined, her fading blond hair betrayed her age. Her dress was from an earlier era and a little too informal for the occasion.

Susan suddenly glanced down the aisle, apparently realizing she was being watched. Maggie instantly buried her nose in the program. She turned to the bios page. Lucy looked glamorous in her photo. Maggie wondered if Liz had taken the shot. She was good at portraiture, and Maggie had often asked her to take publicity photos when she'd appeared in shows at the playhouse or the state theater.

At the other end of the row was an empty seat. Liz was standing in the aisle anxiously watching the entrance to the auditorium. "Is Liz waiting for someone?" Maggie asked Sam.

"Emily."

"Oh, of course!"

"Liz told me she's taking the train up from New Haven," Sam explained, looking down the row. The house lights flashed on and off. Sam glanced at her watch. "Looks like they're going to begin. I hope Emily gets here soon."

A minute later, a tall, red-haired young woman raced down the aisle. Liz pointed to a seat, and Emily swung into it.

Maggie leaned forward and whispered loudly across Tom, "Hello, Emily."

Emily smiled what appeared to be an emotionally felt smile. Maggie had learned to interpret Emily's facial expressions when they'd all lived together during the lockdown. "Hey, Aunt Maggie. Good to see you. Mom will be pleased you're here for her." Maggie hoped that was true. On the surface, their relationship had gone back to normal, but who knew how Lucy really felt?

The overhead lights finally went out. There was an extended murmur of conversation before the audience broke into applause. Preceded by the two soloists, the conductor walked onto the stage. He bowed to acknowledge the applause and gestured to the soloists standing on either side. They all bowed together. The applause grew louder until it was nearly deafening.

Maggie wondered if the article in the *Boston Globe* about Lucy's return to the stage had drawn both fans and curiosity seekers. There were sharp whistles and shouts of "brava" from the back. Maggie looked over her shoulder to the balcony, where a group of young people were on their feet applauding enthusiastically. Maggie guessed they were Denise's friends. Liz was on her feet too, clapping loudly, as were Tom and Susan. Soon everyone in their row was standing, leaving only Maggie in her seat. Reluctantly, she rose to show solidarity. She felt forced, like when everyone was clapping at her daughters' soccer games, and she didn't know why.

The audience finally settled down. Maggie studied Lucy's dress and wondered if it was new or from the days when she was singing professionally. It was made of a gorgeous green lamé with darker threads of blue running through the fabric. The tight-fitting sleeves didn't look dated, nor the plunging neckline that strategically, but modestly, gave a peek at Lucy's perfect breasts. It was a daring outfit for a woman in her late fifties to be wearing, never mind a priest, but in it, Lucy looked glamorous and every bit a diva. Maggie glanced down the row at Liz. Of course, she was wearing that irritating look of abject adoration.

The concert began. Maggie recognized the music because *Mahler's Second Symphony* was one of Liz's favorites. She never tired of listening to it at an ear-splitting volume, which she usually reserved for working in her workshop. Maggie was not especially fond of classical music. She found it more tolerable as background music than in a live concert where the audience did nothing but stare at the orchestra.

Despite the symphony's constant changes of volume and tempo, Maggie's mind began to wander. She looked down the row. Everyone else seemed attentive. She didn't want anyone to think she lacked appreciation, so she faced forward. She tried to focus on the music, but her mind kept drifting back to the conversation with Sam.

She now knew that Sam's extreme reaction to her suggestions came from old wounds. Building up her self-esteem about her appearance would probably work better than making suggestions. Maggie had found that strategy effective with Liz. Of course, Liz had a surgeon's overdeveloped confidence, which helped.

Maggie returned to the concert with a sigh and continued her mindless attention. Finally, there was a brief intermission after the third movement for the orchestra to retune. It was long enough to get up and stretch, but not for a bathroom break.

"Are you finding it hard to stay focused on the music?" Maggie asked Sam, who was leaning against the vacant chair in front of her.

"A little. I like classical music, but we're all so used to multitasking, it's hard to sit and do only one thing. I feel myself itching to look at my phone."

"The singers don't seem to have much to do in this symphony. They're just sitting there."

"They will have more work to do soon," Tom interjected. "The alto solo is the centerpiece of the next movement. I'm sure Denise will execute it beautifully." He tapped his ear in response to Maggie's quizzical look. "I can hear Lucy rehearsing with her from my next-door office. They've worked incredibly hard for this moment."

"This performance doesn't seem like a big showpiece for either of them," said Maggie.

"They're soloists with the BSO with a superstar conductor. That counts for more than you might think. Lucy explained how it can open doors for Denise."

"Will she resign as music director at the church?" Maggie asked, smelling an opportunity.

Tom shrugged. "I haven't asked. And now that I've given up my role as associate pastor, I'm not in the loop the way I once was."

"Doesn't that bother you?"

"It's what I chose, Maggie," he replied in a philosophical tone. Then he winked. "But between you and me, I love juicy gossip. If you hear any, let me know."

Maggie patted his arm. "I will, Tom. I promise."

He chuckled and got up to stretch.

Finally, the house lights dimmed, and the murmur of the crowd grew softer. There was another round of applause as the conductor and soloists returned. Denise, who would be performing next, continued to stand. She looked sensational in a body-hugging red dress.

The conductor raised his baton. After the brief introduction, Denise began to sing in a warm, round tone that was richly feminine. In the recordings Maggie had heard of Denis Chantal singing, the voice was stunningly clear like a trumpet call. Maggie guessed that the change was partly due to Lucy's coaching, but also proof of Denise's hard work.

The English translation of the text projected on the sidewalls of the stage, combined with the achingly beautiful music, and Denise's sensitive interpretation created brilliant theater. Maggie was spellbound. The brief movement ended. Now came the finale they'd all been anticipating. It opened with a jarring burst of sound and continued with active and dissonant tones. All the brass and percussion was startling, but finally, things quieted down, and the chorus began to sing softly. The two soloists stood. Lucy's voice smoothly blended with the chorus and then powerfully rose above it in a thrilling moment of pure magic. Maggie had heard her friend sing light classics and Broadway tunes. She'd heard her sing at family gatherings or to entertain after dinner, but this was the first time she'd ever heard her sing in a real concert hall.

As Lucy's powerful voice soared above the mountain of sound, Maggie could understand why the conductor had been so eager for her to sing this part. The rising tension in the duet between Lucy and Denise made it seem almost erotic. The music continued to build in texture and volume, moving inexorably to a stirring climax.

As it wound down, Tom discreetly dabbed under his eyes with his fingertips. Liz, sitting forward in her seat, made no attempt to hide her emotions. Her cheeks were shining with tears. After the stunned silence in the theater, she shot to her feet and clapped furiously. Around her, the entire audience was standing. The applause was nearly deafening.

"Well, that was certainly moving," Tom said. "Well done. Well done indeed." He turned to Liz. "Thank you for the invitation. What a privilege to be here."

"My only regret is that Erika isn't here," Liz said, her voice thick with feeling.

Tom patted her shoulder. "I'm sure she is."

Liz glanced at her watch. "Our dinner should be available soon." She reached across Tom. "Maggie, I'm going backstage to collect our stars. Would you mind taking charge until I can get back to the hotel? Here's the key to the room I reserved for the party. There's an open bar. I ordered snacks before the buffet is served, but I should be back by then." Unnerved by Liz's request, Maggie hesitated before reaching out for the plastic card. "Thanks. I know you're a great hostess," Liz added.

After Liz left with Emily, Sam whispered into Maggie's ear. "Bet you didn't expect that to happen."

Maggie handed her the key. "Here. You're the one with pockets. Keep an eye on this." She stepped into the aisle and waited for the others to gather around. "As you know, Liz has invited us to a buffet dinner back at the hotel. If we stay together, we can share cabs."

Susan excused herself, saying she had to work the next morning and needed to get back to Maine. Maggie watched her plod up the aisle toward the exit, thinking, *Just another lonely, middle-aged woman living on the periphery of other people's lives.*

After the taxis dropped the invited guests at the hotel, Maggie led her little band to the second floor. As soon as she opened the door with the plastic key, a uniformed man swooped down on her. "This is a private party," he informed her with a threatening stare.

"Yes, we know, and we are the guests." Maggie held up the key that had opened the door.

"Are you Dr. Stolz?"

"No, I'm her wife." Out of the corner of her eye, Maggie saw Sam's sharp look. "Dr. Stolz will be here shortly."

He glanced at the people standing behind her. "The party is for a dozen guests. Will there be more?"

"No, I think that's a good estimate."

"Perfect," said the man. "The bar is open. We'll be serving appetizers shortly." He left to give instructions to another waiter.

Sam leaned down to whisper in Maggie's ear. "Why did you tell him you're Liz's wife?"

"Trust me, Sam. It's easier than making complicated explanations."

Sam frowned as she processed the information.

Maggie waved to the line of people waiting at the door. "Come in, everyone, and have a drink. The bar is open. Snacks will be served soon."

"I wonder how much they'll eat," Sam said, looking at her watch. "It's past ten."

"I'm sure Liz planned this because Lucy couldn't eat before a performance. I never could either. You can't really sing well on a full stomach."

"I didn't know that."

Maggie winked. "Stick with me, Sam. Who knows what you'll learn?"

They waited until the others got their drinks before they approached the bar. The bartender had just poured Maggie's wine when she heard applause. She turned around to see Lucy entering the room, followed by Denise, and several young people.

"Brava!" called Olivia, applauding enthusiastically.

Liz slipped in beside Maggie. "Thanks for handling this," she said with a little smile. "I owe you."

"No, you don't," said Maggie, nudging her with her hip. "Have I told you how wonderful you look tonight?"

"No, but I'm glad you think so. Thank you." Liz heard someone calling her name and excused herself, which left Maggie to compare how easily Liz accepted her compliment to Sam's incessant blushing. After Liz greeted the new guests, she returned to the bar for a drink.

Maggie tapped her arm. "You're the hostess. You should make a toast."

"Right. Thanks for reminding me." Liz raised her glass. Thank you all for coming. And a special thank you to Denise and Lucy for such a brilliant performance." There were murmurs of congratulations and "hear, hear!"

"And thanks to everyone for coming to hear us," said Lucy, raising her glass.

The waiter began to move through the gathering to offer hors d'oeuvres. People broke into small groups for conversation. The door opened and three men arrived. "Who are they?" Maggie asked Liz.

"Morales, the conductor, and the chorus master. They're both big fans of Lucy from the past. The other guy is Lucy's agent. Former agent, I should say. Morales asked her to sing the *Four Last Songs* in New York this fall, and the agent is trying to talk her into other bookings."

Maggie tried to banish the little flicker of jealousy. When she couldn't, she fell back on her skills as an actress. "Would Lucy really go back to singing?"

Liz shrugged. "She certainly proved tonight that she could."

"What about Denise? Do you think this has relaunched her career?"

"I guess we'll see," Liz said, taking a sip from her martini. She glanced around the room. "Everyone seems to be enjoying themselves," she said in a confidential voice. "I hope they don't expect free tickets and booze after every performance. This was a special occasion, but the stock markets have been dropping like a stone. I'm not feeling quite as flush as usual." Maggie looked at Liz sympathetically. She knew how anxious she could get in uncertain economic times.

"I'm sorry, Liz. Olivia keeps urging me to stay calm." She touched Liz's shoulder. "Thanks for trusting me to greet your guests."

Liz shrugged. "I know you're a wonderful hostess. We used to have the best parties. People always said how much they enjoyed them."

"Yes, they did," said Maggie wistfully.

Tom called Liz over to his group. "Excuse me a minute," said Liz.

Sam was busy talking to Amy, which left Maggie standing alone at the bar. Lucy quickly left her conversation with Denise's friends and headed in her direction.

"Oh, Maggie, thanks so much for coming," said Lucy, pulling her into a full-body hug.

"How could I miss it? You sang beautifully. I understand why the conductor had to have you for the part. You were perfect with Denise. Like you were made to sing together."

"Thank you. I hope it helps her. She's exceptionally talented and could go far. This concert was her first big test. I think she was totally convincing. Don't you?"

Maggie lowered her voice. "I could see how your coaching paid off. If I didn't know otherwise, I would have thought she was a woman."

Lucy gave her a sharp look. "She *is* a woman."

The adamance of Lucy's tone flustered Maggie. "Yes, of course, she is," she agreed and quickly changed the subject. "I hear your agent is after you to do more engagements."

Lucy frowned in the man's direction. "Yes, but that's the last thing I want to think about. I'm swamped with end-of-term papers due, and the wedding is coming up. The wedding planner keeps calling me to look at floral arrangements and go over menus. With everything else going on, when do I have time?" Lucy heaved out an exasperated sigh. Then she took some long, deep breaths. "One thing at a time, right?"

Maggie gazed fondly at the woman she used to call her best friend. "I'm sure it's overwhelming. You have a lot on your plate."

"I do…and so does Liz."

"Maybe I can help? If you're willing to trust me, I could look over the menus."

"Oh, my word! Would you really do that?"

Maggie realized the irony of helping to plan the wedding of her ex-wife, but she didn't regret the offer. She reached around Lucy and gave her a little squeeze. "Glad to help in any way I can."

11

"Thanks for agreeing to sleep down here during the kids' visit," said Liz, getting into bed.

"You gave me this beautiful room. It's wonderful to have my own space. It's sexy to have you visit me like the kings and queens of old." Lucy ran her hand over the profile of the bed post. "Thank you for bringing over the bed from the beach house. It's special to me because you built it for Erika. It fits this room, and I'm glad to have her desk too."

Liz clasped her hands behind her head as she lay down. "We'll have to figure out what to do with the rest of the furniture before Courtney and Melissa move in."

Lucy raised her head off the pillow. "Oh, Liz! Do you always need a problem to solve right before we go to sleep?"

"Well," said Liz, defensively, "we do need to find a place for your furniture."

"Stop thinking and relax." Lucy slipped her hand under Liz's T-shirt and gently stroked the soft skin of her belly.

"Is that an invitation?"

"I'm just petting you. The children are right next door. We probably shouldn't make love tonight."

"We can be quick," said Liz, excited by the possibility.

Lucy raised her head off the pillow. "Liz, it's only two nights. Can't we wait?"

Liz grunted in disappointment.

"I know it's hard, baby," said Lucy in a sympathetic voice and kissed her softly on the forehead, "but you'll survive."

"I worry that you'll lose interest in sex like Maggie did. She had an excuse, of course. The tamoxifen suppresses her libido, but is it inevitable?"

"I can't promise that in twenty years we'll still be having sex every night, but as you know, I really like sex."

"That's obvious. And in twenty years, I'll be pushing ninety, and you'll be close to eighty."

"I've read that many older women still have active sex lives, so there's hope for us." Lucy settled back against her pillow. "I'm sorry it's taken so long to find a weekend to have the kids."

"You've had a lot on your plate. I'm surprised you're still in one piece."

"Who says I am?"

"When we're married, and I have more say over how you spend your time, I won't let you wear yourself out like this."

"You think so? I hate to tell you, Dr. Stolz, but I don't take orders from anyone."

"You tell me when I'm overdoing it."

"Yes, but that's different. I make an observation. I don't order you to stop working so hard. I wouldn't dare, not because I'm afraid you'll bite my head off, which you probably would, but because I respect your agency as an adult."

Liz considered Lucy's message with a sigh. Training her in logic to help her write her dissertation had made her a more formidable opponent. Liz wondered if, by honing Lucy's already perceptive mind, she had created a monster.

Lucy continued the languorous stroking of Liz's belly. "You pet me like I'm a puppy," said Liz.

"Yes, I guess I do. Maybe that's because you're like a puppy—full of mischief and always affectionate."

"I'd be more affectionate if you'd let me." Liz glanced at the door. "It's quiet so far. I'm sure they're asleep."

"When you played that loud superhero movie right before bed, I was worried. Way too much stimulation for young children."

"Nah, Megan was completely unimpressed. She fell asleep in your lap."

"She seems to have a special attachment to me."

"She bonded with you the night her parents were shot." Liz reached into the bodice of Lucy's nightgown. "It's your gorgeous breasts. No one can resist them." Lucy's nipple instantly rose in response to the teasing fingers, so Liz gave it some appreciation with her mouth. Lucy moaned softly. "If we keep our clothes on and we're really quiet... Please?" begged Liz.

"Oh, you're impossible." Despite the protest, Lucy parted her lips for a kiss. As Liz explored her warm mouth with her tongue, she felt Lucy's desire in her passionate response. Her hand slipped into Liz's shorts. She was so excited she flinched a little when Lucy found the wetness between her legs. Liz raised Lucy's nightgown to touch her too, exactly mirroring the pace and motion. She shivered a little when Lucy moved inside her. The proximity of the children next door and the hurry to finish made Liz doubtful that they could achieve a mutual climax, which had become the usual end to their lovemaking. But the urgency was exciting. Liz could sense Lucy was close by the pulsing against her fingers. As her own orgasm began, Lucy withdrew to touch her outside and bring her along with her. Her timing was perfect.

"It usually takes me a long time to train others to come with me," Liz said, rolling on her back. "You're a quick study."

Lucy laughed. "Liz, I hate to tell you, but I've been training *you!*"

Liz wasn't sure she liked that idea. She tried to catch Lucy's eye to let her know, but her face was hidden, resting against her breast while she recovered.

"Aren't you glad I'm not a screamer?" asked Lucy after catching her breath.

"It's sexy to hear how much your lover appreciates your efforts. That's how you learn what she likes, but not necessarily with screaming. I'd say you're a moaner."

Lucy raised her hand and inspected her fingers. "My hands are so small compared to yours. I worry they're not big enough when I'm inside you."

"Don't worry. You do just fine."

"But I know you enjoy being stimulated inside."

"Why do I think you're about to introduce me to your dildo collection?"

"Don't get your hopes up," Lucy said, pulling herself up so she could rest her head on her pillow. "I got rid of them."

"Why?"

"I bought them for Erika. It didn't seem right to use them with someone else."

"So, you just threw them away?" Liz raised herself on her elbow.

"What was I supposed to do? Donate them to Goodwill?" Lucy gave her a quick, guilty look. "Don't tell anyone, but I threw them in the dumpster behind the diner. I was afraid to put them in the regular garbage in case I'd thrown away something with my name on it. I wrapped them in a paper grocery bag."

"You mean you disposed of them in a plain, brown wrapper."

Lucy giggled. "Hadn't thought of it that way, but you're right."

"Lucy, I'm sure that hardware was expensive. You threw away a lot of money."

"They can be replaced."

"Is that what this is leading up to?" asked Liz, sitting up.

Lucy sat up too. "Maybe, but I wanted it to be a surprise…a wedding present."

"Are you sure this gift is for me or for you?"

"For both of us of course," said Lucy with one of her sly looks. "You once told me you like them."

Liz thought back to that evening she'd encountered Lucy in the supermarket and impulsively invited her to dinner. They were both on their own that night. Erika's mother had died, and Maggie was in Connecticut, helping Erika pack up her father's apartment. As a doctor, Liz was shocked by very little, but a beautiful woman in a collar asking about sex toys had briefly rendered her speechless.

"I remember the conversation, but I also said I didn't have any recent experience. Maggie told me dildos are 'unnatural.' No Catholic influence there, of course," Liz added sarcastically. "I expected that reaction, which is why I didn't even bring it up until her interest in sex started to wane. I was willing to try anything to get her going again, but the idea of using a sex toy landed like a lead fishing weight."

"Well? What about you? Would you enjoy using one?" Lucy rolled over and leaned her chin on her hands. "Inquiring minds want to know."

"Well, maybe," said Liz cautiously. "Just don't get too ambitious right away. It's been a long time for me, and vaginas lose elasticity with age."

Watching Lucy's face, Liz could see her revising her plans. "Thank you for telling me. That's useful information."

"You're welcome, but what I don't understand is why you're blowing your wedding surprise."

"Because if you hated the idea, I wouldn't want to find out on our wedding night. I think it's important to talk about what we like in bed and get buy-in from the other."

"Lucy, you've been a shrink too long." By the time Liz remembered that Lucy had expressly asked her to stop using that word, it was too late. Lucy's frown grew deeper by the moment, so this seemed like a good time to change the subject. "I wonder how Brenda and Cherie are doing. I heard they were going to Nathan's for dinner."

"Oh, that's very romantic. Good choice, Brenda."

"It was Cherie's idea. They're staying for the concert, then going out for dessert and after dinner drinks. It's a full-bore date night."

"I hope they enjoy themselves and relax." Lucy sighed. "There's been so much strain on that marriage between Brenda's long COVID and adopting kids who have their own problems. They need a break."

"Has Cherie been talking to you?" Liz asked curiously.

"Liz, you know if she has, I can't talk about it." There was a soft knock at the door followed by a small voice calling Lucy's name. "Good thing we didn't wait to make love," said Lucy, arranging her nightgown to be more modest.

"I'll get the door," said Liz, sliding out of bed. "Looks like you're on duty, Mother Lucy." Liz opened the door to a small person sucking her thumb. Cherie had complained that her adopted daughter had reverted to behaviors usually seen in a younger child. Liz crouched to speak to her. "What's the matter, Megan? Can't you sleep?"

"L-u-u-u-cy," she crooned, trying to peek over Liz's shoulder.

Liz got to her feet. She stood aside and gestured toward the bed. "There she is."

"Yes!" declared the girl and bounded over to Lucy.

"Sweetie, why are you looking for me?" Lucy asked gently and pulled her close. Megan burrowed into the comfort of Lucy's breasts. Liz suddenly imagined Emily at Megan's age, but Lucy's autistic daughter might have been repulsed by being held so close, which would have broken her mother's heart.

"I'm scared!" Megan declared.

"Don't worry, sweetie," Lucy murmured into Megan's blond hair. "Aunt Liz and I won't let anything happen to you. Promise. You're safe here."

"I'm scared. Can I sleep with you?"

Liz chuckled. "Well, we knew that was coming."

Lucy kissed the top of the girl's head. "I'll bring her back to bed in a minute."

"Nooooo!" Megan protested, clinging to her. "I don't want to go back."

"Megan, when I was little, I always trusted my brother to protect me," said Liz. "Keith is sleeping in the next bed. I bet he'd defend you from anything."

"Is that true?" asked Lucy, looking up at Liz.

"About Keith? Or my brother? I was the oldest, and my brothers looked to me for protection."

"So, why are you training her to look to males to protect her? You should be teaching her how to defend herself." Liz rolled her eyes. She certainly didn't need a feminist lecture at that hour.

"Megan, did you know I have a brown belt in Jiu Jitsu?" Lucy asked.

"No, what's juju?"

Liz laughed aloud. Lucy shot her a warning look, then turned to Megan with a smile. "That's something different. Jiu Jitsu is a martial art. I may not look big and powerful, but I know how to defend myself!" Megan's eyes grew large. "Tomorrow, I can teach you. Would you like that?"

"Great," said Liz. "Now you're going to teach the kid to be a killer."

Lucy glared at her, so Liz sat down on the bed and shut up.

"Mamma B carries a gun," Megan said with a mix of fear and admiration. "She's the police chief."

"Yes, she is and very strong and brave." Lucy looked directly into the girl's eyes. "Now, Megan, I'm going to bring you back to bed, and you will be safe. I will stay with you until you fall asleep. Okay?"

"Nooo! I want to sleep with you."

Liz sighed. "Trust me, Lucy. You're not going to win this argument."

"Liz, stay out of this." Lucy's green eyes transmitted a stiff warning. "Megan, have I ever told you anything that wasn't true?"

"No," Megan admitted.

"Now, you're using logic?" Liz asked. "That doesn't usually work with kids."

"You watch," said Lucy. She reached out her hand to the girl. "Come with me, sweetie. I'll sing to you until you fall asleep. Would you like that?"

"Can I come too?" asked Liz, grinning suggestively.

Lucy rolled her eyes at the lewd pun. "You already came, Liz, but if you're good, I might sing to you when I get back." She took Megan's hand, and out they went. Fully expecting to sleep alone, Liz got back into bed. She opened her tablet to read the medical news while she waited. When Lucy returned, Liz had barely gotten through the front-page.

"It worked?" asked Liz in surprise.

"Sound asleep," said Lucy and closed the door. She got into bed.

"How do you do that?"

"Lullabies have been putting children to sleep for millennia. They even work on big kids, like you. Now, turn out the light, and I'll sing to you."

"Can I make love to you first?"

Liz felt Lucy smile against her cheek.

"Sure."

✳✳✳

Sipping her coffee, Lucy watched Liz make pancakes with the kids. Each child had been assigned a job, measuring in the blueberries and stirring the batter. The griddle insert was imprinted with fanciful animal shapes, from dinosaurs to cats. The kids couldn't get enough of them. Their fingers were sticky with warm syrup as they demolished the treats. The cook seemed to be having just as much fun as the children.

Lucy loved her soon-to-be wife's childlike enthusiasm. When Liz wasn't playing doctor or grumpily fending off affection or compliments, her innocent joy was infectious. It was a shame that she usually reserved it for children.

"Lucy, how many pancakes would you like?" Liz asked, leaning her elbows on the countertop.

"I'm sure your pancakes are delicious, but I think I'll have strawberries and yogurt. I want to fit into my wedding dress."

Liz dramatically clapped her hand to chest. "Lucy, I am crushed!" Out of the corner of her eye, Lucy caught Keith with his hand over his heart, imitating Liz.

"You have to have pancakes," Megan said, tugging on Lucy's skirt. "The ones with the cats are best." She nodded several times for emphasis.

Lucy slipped off the stool and bent so she was at the girl's eye level. "Megan, what makes them better than the others?"

"I like cats."

"Me too." Lucy stood up and sighed. "Okay, Liz, make me some pancakes."

"Coming right up!" Liz said, pouring batter onto the griddle.

Lucy stood beside Liz by the stove, so she could deliver her message privately. "You conspired with children to shame me into eating something I didn't want. That's not fair."

"You won't be sorry. My blueberry pancakes are good."

"I know they are, but that's not the point," said Lucy, folding her arms on her chest. "What do you plan to do with the children today?"

"After breakfast, we're going crabbing. That's why the chicken legs are defrosting on the counter. Tie a string around the drumstick. The crabs latch on and you haul them up. Low-tech but effective."

Lucy wrinkled her nose at the thought of the crabs devouring the raw chicken. "Do you mind if I skip that activity? That emergency therapy session on Wednesday kept me from finishing my sermon."

"I invited the kids, so they're my responsibility. But I'm thinking of taking the boat out this afternoon. I hope you'll join us."

"Let me see how far I get on my sermon. Can I tell you at lunchtime?"

"Sure." Liz flipped the pancakes out of the molds and turned them over to brown on the other side. "It might be fun to invite some people to come out with us. Forget Brenda and Cherie. They're on their date weekend. I'm not sure I want to encourage Olivia and Amy. And Sam is involved with my ex. Throwing that bunch together could be a disaster."

Lucy had been listening to Liz dismiss her friends one after the other, and it made her sad. She knew Liz missed them, especially Sam. "Things change, honey," said Lucy, affectionately rubbing the small of Liz's back.

"We had so much fun at 'Thirsty Thursdays.' I liked how well we used to play together. Since Erika died, nothing is the same." Lucy knew how much Liz missed Erika—the woman she'd once described as the sister she never had. Only Lucy's training kept her from reacting when Liz talked about her deceased wife. Every mention brought fresh pain. She was a little jealous that Liz could talk about her loss so openly. While she could bear listening to others, Lucy still found it difficult to speak about Erika without dissolving into tears.

Liz scooped Lucy's pancakes onto a plate and moved the pitcher of warmed syrup within her reach.

"Why don't you invite Maggie and Sam?" suggested Lucy, picking up her fork. "We had such a nice time with them at the concert. And Olivia needs company too. Invite Amy."

"Won't it look like I condone the match?"

"Not necessarily. You're inviting some friends for a boat ride. That's all."

Liz's face brightened. "So, that means you're coming along?"

"I only need a few hours to finish this sermon. I have most of the ideas in place."

"Honey, if you need some down time, I understand. You've been so busy, but eat your pancakes before they get cold. Meanwhile, I'll make sure these kids get dressed. Baths can wait until after crabbing. That's a messy activity." Liz corralled her charges and directed them upstairs to dress.

Lucy looked down at her plate. She smiled and set aside the pancake with the cat for last. When Megan asked about it, Lucy would tell her how wonderful it tasted. Children, like adults, liked hearing that someone appreciated their suggestions.

The sweetness of the syrup on Lucy's tongue made her smile. She was trying to avoid added sugar, but the tender cakes were delicious. She hadn't objected because the food Liz cooked wasn't healthy. She'd made the pancakes from buckwheat flour and only served real maple syrup. Lucy's problem was that she liked sugar too much.

She'd gained a few pounds since moving in with Liz, more from having regular, nutritious meals than from eating forbidden foods. She wasn't exaggerating when she said she was worried about fitting into her wedding dress, which had been exactly the right size when she'd found it on clearance in a boutique in New York. The strapless white dress had a form-fitting white bodice that revealed dots of color beneath. Fortunately, the top was elasticized, so it would be somewhat forgiving. One of the reasons Lucy had bought it was the secret pockets hidden in the folds of the full skirt. She loved pockets.

She was glad that they had decided on a casual wedding. Wearing a formal bridal gown would remind her too much of her wedding to Erika. Never expecting to need their dresses again, they had donated them to an charity organization that provided bridal gowns to women who couldn't afford one.

Lucy had learned about the option after her mother died. Hidden in the back of a basement closet, she'd discovered an exquisite lace dress, professionally preserved in a showcase box with a cellophane window. The dry cleaner's phone number on the address label lacked an area code, giving a clue to the age of the contents. It had been over half a century since its owner had worn it. Because the gown had been so painstakingly preserved, Lucy didn't have the heart to discard it. That's when someone told her about the wedding gown charity. It seemed a perfect solution, but when time came, Lucy had found it difficult to hand over the box. While the dress had remained in Lucy's possession, it was a link to her mother, tangible evidence that she too had once been a young bride.

"I hope it's not too old or out of date," Lucy had said when the smiling volunteer won the undeclared tug of war over the box.

"Don't worry, Ms. Bartlett. These vintage gowns are very popular—the fancier, the better."

While she'd been remembering the scene in the charity's warehouse, Lucy had finished all the pancakes except the one with the smiling cat. She finally ate it, making a special effort to remember the taste. She smiled because it did taste different, at least in her imagination.

With a bustle of noise and activity, Liz came into the kitchen with the children. "I hope you get lots of work done," she said, bending to offer Lucy a kiss.

"What do you do with the crabs?" Lucy asked.

"We put them in a pail and watch them fight. We let them run races on the dock. Then we throw them back. They're too small to eat, although some fancy restaurants have been trying to make them a menu item."

Megan was suddenly at Lucy's side. "Did you like the cat pancake?"

"It was delicious, the best one of all." Lucy winked conspiratorially and Megan grinned.

The sound of excited conversation became muffled once Liz shut the door to the garage, and there was blessed peace. Lucy made another cup of coffee and brought it upstairs to her room. She pulled the bed together and sat down at her desk, once Erika's. Before she began work, she rested her elbows on the surface, imagining her wife once doing the same. The desk, the handmade bed, and Erika's books were the only things Lucy really wanted from the beach house. The rest could be moved into the garage apartment, and anything that didn't fit could be left for Melissa and Courtney. Neither of them had much furniture of their own.

Lucy opened her laptop. She didn't feel like working. From the window over her desk, she had a partial view of the ocean. The weather was perfect, and she would much rather be spending it outside with Liz and the kids. But tomorrow, she would be the celebrant at the ten-thirty Eucharist and needed to be prepared.

She scanned all the readings again. In the lectionary, they were in cycle C. This was "Good Shepherd Sunday," because the famous psalm was one of the readings and John's Gospel referenced sheep. Lucy had decided not to preach on sheep, but on doubt. In the Gospel, the disciples had demanded to know if Jesus was the Messiah, and he'd given the perfect answer—have faith. When all the theological complexity was teased apart, and the debates all ended in a draw, the only thing left was faith.

Only Liz and Professor Spangler knew about her doubts. She hadn't even told Tom, whom she considered her spiritual advisor. When she'd told Spangler, he'd gazed at her for a long time with a little frown. She was afraid he might be wondering if a faithless woman like her was worthy of a theology degree. Of course, he wasn't thinking any such thing, and she wasn't faithless. She still believed in God with her whole heart. It was the dogma she doubted.

"Show me a member of the clergy who hasn't doubted doctrine or scripture," Spangler finally said, "and I'll show you a minister with no curiosity. I'll tell you a little secret, Lucy. For years, I performed my duties as a priest and taught theology while being plagued by doubts. I still doubt, but it doesn't torture me as much as it once did. I've learned to live with the uncertainty. Ironically, it's made my faith stronger." It was the most personal thing her professor had ever shared, and Lucy was moved by the intimacy of the moment.

She reread what she'd written. She added a few more paragraphs, but she couldn't figure out how to wrap it up because she didn't have the answer. *Because it's the question that matters*, said a voice in her head as clearly as if someone were sitting beside her. Lucy instantly identified Erika's wise and gentle voice. It was imaginary, of course. Lucy hadn't lost her mind, at least not yet. *Remember what Kierkegaard says, "Leap of faith, yes, but only after reflection."* Yes! Lucy felt Erika near as she quickly pulled together the loose ends into something that made sense. She edited the homily for clarity as Liz had taught her. Finally, she committed the whole thing to memory. One of the benefits of musical training was learning to memorize things quickly.

Liz and her charges returned before lunchtime with the bustle of activity and noise that usually accompanies small children. Liz's cheeks were pink from the sun, which made her eyes exceptionally blue. Even the silver in her hair looked brighter. She looked very inviting, except she smelled like the tide had just come in. Unconsciously, Lucy made a little face when she bent to kiss her.

"That bad?" Liz asked. "Will you keep an eye on the kids while I run up and take a quick shower? I'll supervise their baths before I make lunch."

While Liz showered, the children regaled Lucy with tales of their crabbing adventure. "And they chewed up the raw chicken until the bones showed," said Keith, his blue eyes wide.

"It was disgusting," Megan chimed in. "Ewwww!"

Liz returned in a matter of minutes, having obviously rushed through her shower. Her hair was still wet and water droplets bled through her T-shirt.

"You could have taken your time, Liz. You can trust me with them. I've looked after children before."

"I trust you, but I'm starving. I want to get them cleaned up, so we can have some lunch. I'm grilling some red snappers."

"They'll eat fish?"

"Well, they're Mainers, so maybe, but no, I'm making the bright pink hot dogs and baked beans."

"You're a doctor, and you're feeding children stuff that isn't supposed to be good for people?"

"I'm feeding them what I know they'll eat. Besides these hot dogs are made locally. At least, I know what's in them. I can't say that for the national brand. You'll have some, won't you?"

"Do I have a choice?"

Liz laughed. "Of course, you do. There's leftover chicken from last night."

"No, I'll have hot dogs with you and the kids, but I'll skip the roll. I don't want to put on any more weight."

Liz bent to kiss her. At least, she smelled better now. "You look fine, Lucy. Stop worrying." Liz left to run a bath for Megan in the downstairs bathroom. When she returned, she was scrolling through her phone.

"So far, Sam and Maggie are coming. Oh, and Olivia and Amy too! We'll need snacks. I'll order a tray of cold appetizers from Dockside. Of course, I'll have to hear about it from Maggie that I didn't take the time to make my own snacks, but too F'ing bad."

"You still care about what Maggie thinks?" asked Lucy, surprised.

"I know she judges people who rely on prepared foods. Ms. Fancy Chef can cook a seven-course meal while supervising children planting a formal rose garden."

Lucy laughed. "So, you're in competition with her?"

"No, I'm not," replied Liz in a prickly tone. "Let me check on Megan to make sure she hasn't drowned. Cherie and Brenda would kill me if anything happened to one of their kids."

By the time they were on their way to the boat dock, Lucy could see that Liz's patience for the children was wearing thin. They were slow to obey orders and liked to test boundaries. No wonder Brenda and Cherie had needed a break from them.

The parking lot at Dockside was packed, which meant they had to wait for their order. Stuck in the warm car, the kids began to get restless. Lucy encouraged them to sing with her. Denise had been training them in the children's choir, and it had paid off. They could follow a tune and stay on key. People coming out of the restaurant stared at them, but Lucy smiled and waved, and they returned the wave and smiled too.

Finally, Liz came out of the restaurant with several large shopping bags. "We have enough food to cover us for dinner. Hopefully, the kids will like the snacks I picked for them."

Olivia had a compulsion for punctuality, so it was not surprising to find her BMW already in the harbor parking lot. "How can I help?" she asked, approaching.

"Can you manage this?" asked Liz, handing her one of the bags. Amy's SUV pulled into the lot, which instantly diverted Olivia's attention.

"Did you invite your colleague for my benefit?"

"Not exactly. Amy works hard. I thought she could use an afternoon out on the water."

"So, you're not opposed to my dating her?"

"Olivia, I'm her employer. What she does on her own time is none of my business."

"You're not fooling anyone, Dr. Stolz. Of course, you care what she does."

While they were squabbling, Sam and Maggie had arrived in Sam's truck. After greetings and hugs, Liz distributed the remaining bags and containers from the back of her car.

"I'm glad the sea is calm today," Sam said to Lucy as they handed up the food and drinks to the crew already on board. "Maggie really gets seasick."

The children were excited, so Liz took them with her into the pilot house while she warmed up the engine. Lucy went back to help with the cast-off, but she saw that Olivia had already appointed herself Sam's assistant. She steadied herself because the wake from passing boats was causing The Wet Lady to rock. She noticed Maggie looking queasy and sat down beside her.

"Are you all right?" she asked.

"I hope so. I took some Dramamine before we left. Sam really wanted to accept Liz's invitation, and I couldn't disappoint her."

Lucy was glad Maggie was prepared, but she wondered why she never took seasickness medicine when she was married to Liz, who'd begged her to come out on the boat.

Sam and Olivia had the castoff under control, and Liz was occupied in the pilot house. Lucy had no excuse to leave Maggie's side. Fortunately, they were soon underway, and the others came to sit with them. It was an awkward mix—Sam sitting between her two exes; Lucy beside her fiancée's former wife. The conversation was stiff until Olivia started complaining about town politics.

"The select board is resisting my recommendation to appoint rather than elect the town clerk. They know I'm doing it because they keep pushing through questionable building permits for their friends."

"The town clerk also oversees the elections," said Sam. "Maybe they're worried about partisan control. Of course, they're all Republicans now, so why would they care?"

Olivia gave Sam an overtly hostile look, and her face turned bright red. "I'm a Republican, and when did you become so interested in politics?"

"Calm down, Olivia," Amy said. "There's no need to get so excited. You're among friends."

"Am I?" said Olivia, meeting Sam's hostile stare.

Lucy reached over and patted her knee. "Yes, you are. And we came out today to enjoy the ocean, not argue."

"You don't want Liz to put you on restriction again, do you?" Amy said. "You love being town manager, but you can't fight the select board while confined to bed rest."

Olivia shot Amy a filthy look. "Whose side are you on?"

"Your side," said Amy in a quiet voice. "Take some deep breaths. Relax." Surprisingly, Olivia took the suggestion without further argument. Her face returned to its normal color.

Liz came out of the pilothouse. "I'm going to drop anchor here. Sam, the kids would like to troll for flounder. Would you mind supervising?"

"Sure, Liz," said Sam jumping up, obviously glad for an excuse to escape the tense atmosphere. "Where's the bait?"

Liz pointed to a closed bucket and handed Sam some short rods. In the brief diversion, Lucy saw the opportunity for a much-needed bathroom break. She'd been putting it off because "the head" was so tiny. She didn't usually experience claustrophobia, but the rocking of the boat could make the simple act of peeing uncomfortable, not unlike being in an airplane bathroom during a sudden drop in altitude. She'd just sat down when she heard someone rummaging around in a cabinet nearby.

"I thought I'd find you here," said a female voice that Lucy recognized as Maggie's.

"Do you need something?" Liz asked with barely contained hostility.

"Only a minute to talk to you alone."

"So, talk," replied Liz brusquely. "Don't mind me. I'm looking for a bottle opener."

"Liz, look at me." There was a moment of silence. "Please don't punish Sam because she's seeing me. Ignoring her really makes her feel bad. She's your friend, and she loves you. Don't hurt her because of me."

"Has she told you this?"

"No, but I can see it."

In the bathroom, Lucy dared not move or even breathe. If she opened the door now, they would know she'd been eavesdropping.

"Maybe I don't want everything that goes on in my life getting back to you," Liz said.

"You know Sam's not like that. She would never say anything about you behind your back. Please don't push her away because of me."

"I invited her today, didn't I?"

"That was Lucy's idea, I bet."

Lucy noticed that Liz didn't deny Maggie's statement. Apparently, Liz had resumed her search for the bottle opener because a drawer opened, and the contents rattled around.

"Liz," Maggie said in a gentle voice, "you're better than this. Sam misses you. You should spend more time with her."

"I didn't want to disturb your little love nest."

"We're only together on weekends. What's your excuse the rest of the week?"

"I'm busy."

"When we were married, you were never too busy to have a beer with your friends. I lived with you for seven years. Don't talk to me like you don't remember."

"Maggie, are you looking for a fight? Because I'm not."

"Please, Liz," Maggie pleaded. "Don't hurt Sam because of me." There was another extended silence. "Are you ever going to forgive me?"

"Are you?" Liz instantly countered.

"Yes, I'm trying. Despite how we ended, I still love you. I want us to be friends. I miss you, and I miss Lucy. I miss being in Hobbs with my friends." Maggie's voice was on the verge of breaking. Lucy imagined that during the moment of quiet that followed Liz was taking Maggie in her arms.

"You should go back upstairs and keep an eye on Olivia and Amy," Liz said with feigned gruffness. "Everyone will be wondering where you are."

"Okay. But think about what I said."

"I will."

Lucy heard the sound of someone climbing up the ladder to the deck. Finally, she could open the door and escape her tiny prison.

Liz stared wide-eyed when Lucy emerged from the cramped bathroom. "For fuck's sake, Lucy. Were you in there the entire time?"

"Yes," Lucy admitted sheepishly. "Once your conversation turned serious, I didn't want to interrupt. Maggie's right, you know. You shouldn't punish Sam. I know you miss her. She's been your confidant since Erika died. Everyone needs someone to talk to."

"I have you."

"Besides me."

Frustrated, Liz impatiently threw the things she'd removed from the drawer back into it. "I hate dyke drama. We're so fucking incestuous. When someone breaks up, it's always a mess."

"We're a small community within a small community. We have to learn to adjust."

"You adjust. I don't have time for this shit," replied Liz in a surly voice. She stared at the shelf in front of her. "Look. The fucking thing was here all along." She snatched the bottle opener and headed to the ladder. "Are you coming up?"

12

Maggie allowed the smooth, intense chocolate to slide over her tongue and closed her eyes in pleasure. She took another bite and sighed. "Oh, my God. That is the best fudge truffle I've tasted outside of France."

The young woman blushed slightly but looked pleased. "Thank you. That's quite a compliment."

"Where did you train, Tiffany?" Maggie bit into another fancifully decorated pastry. The cream inside it was as rich and silken as the ganache in the truffle.

"CIA, Hyde Park. People always laugh when I say that. They think I'm a secret agent."

"Doesn't matter what they think. The Culinary Institute is a wonderful place for any chef to learn."

"You mentioned France. Did you study there?" asked Tiffany.

"At La Varenne. My husband's company transferred us to France. I was bored, so I took a cooking class."

"Like Julia Child."

"Before my time," snapped Maggie, "but I can remember my mother watching *The French Chef.* Unfortunately, it didn't improve her cooking."

Tiffany chewed on her lower lip. Maggie guessed she'd figured out that she might have given offense, and it could cost her business. Now, she was probably trying to decide whether to apologize. Maggie realized that the inability to judge age went both ways. At some point, her college students had begun to look like children.

"Well," said Maggie, indicating a change of topic. "I think I've found our pastry chef, but I don't have the last word. Could you pack a few samples for me to take to the bride? I should say, 'brides' because there are two of them."

A smile spread across the young woman's face. "A gay wedding. Even better!"

"Yes, and let's hope there will be many more of them. This leaked decision on abortion from the Supreme Court could also put same-sex marriage in danger."

"What do you mean?" asked Tiffany, looking puzzled.

Maggie was annoyed that she needed to explain that had been all over the news. "From what I've read, many civil rights decided by the court are based on the privacy principle used to justify Roe v. Wade. That means gay marriage, interracial marriage, even birth control decisions could be overturned."

"Wow! I never thought abortion rights could be overturned in this country. That right has always been there."

"For you, yes, but I'm old enough to remember a time when abortion was illegal. I had trouble getting pregnant, so I had fertility treatments. I met a woman at the clinic who'd had an illegal abortion. It damaged her uterus. When she later married and wanted to have children, she couldn't." The poor woman's tale fit the Catholic propaganda about women who'd had abortions. Supposedly, they were tortured with guilt and always regretted the decision. Yet, Maggie had known women in the theater world and academia who had taken their choice to terminate their pregnancies in stride.

"I want to do something, but I feel so helpless," Tiffany said. "If the Supreme Court has already decided, what can we do?"

"Vote," Maggie said bluntly. "Vote for politicians who support the right to choose. Urge your friends to vote. Help drive people to the polls. Contribute to Planned Parenthood and pro-choice organizations. March in protest. I was raised Catholic, but I support a woman's right to control her own body. I just can't believe I have to fight for rights women won fifty years ago!"

While Maggie had been talking, she saw the expression in Tiffany's eyes change. It had gone from polite interest to respect. Maybe young women weren't as apathetic as she'd come to believe. Erika, who'd taught philosophy and specialized in political discourse, had always vacillated between despair and hope for the future. "I don't know why we must go through these cycles of enlightenment followed by fundamentalism, but apparently, we do," she used to say. "Meanwhile, we need to teach history, and hope the young pay attention, which is doubtful."

Other customers entered the shop, so the political discussion and Maggie's private pastry tasting needed to end. "I'll pack up a selection for you to take to your brides," said the young woman. "It would be an honor to do their wedding. I do cakes too."

"I'll let them know," said Maggie, "but they seem sold on the idea of finger pastries rather than a formal wedding cake. It's a second marriage for both." Maggie wondered what Tiffany would say if she knew she was speaking to one of the first wives.

Tiffany eyed the newcomers anxiously. "Let me help these customers. If you can wait a minute, I'll pack up some free samples."

"I'm happy to pay for them."

"No need. If this wedding is as big as you say, the publicity alone is worth it."

"We'll be sure to spread the word about where we found this delicious and beautiful work."

While she waited, Maggie decided to see if Lucy was available to taste her new find. Wednesdays were reserved for preparing her sermon and catching up on paperwork, so she might be free. The phone rang and rang. Maggie was about to hang up when Lucy finally answered.

"Maggie!" Lucy said brightly. "How nice to hear from you."

"Lucy, I think I've found your wedding desserts. The new pâtisserie in town is wonderful. If you have a minute, I'll bring over some finger pastries to try."

There was a muffled sound for a few seconds before Lucy returned to the call. "Sorry, Maggie, I needed to say goodbye to the person in my office."

"I'm sorry. I didn't think you'd answer if I were interrupting something important."

"We were just wrapping up. Are you coming now?"

"As soon as the proprietor bundles up the samples. Is that all right?"

"Absolutely! I'd love to see you."

Sometimes, Maggie had to force herself to sound cheerful, but with Lucy, it never seemed like pretense. How did she do it?

After the customers left, Tiffany delivered a beautifully wrapped box to Maggie's table. "It's all in the presentation," she said.

"The box is spectacular and makes a nice impression, but in this case, it's what's inside that counts. Thanks for the samples. I'll let you know as soon as they decide." Maggie waved on her way out.

St. Margaret's rectory was literally down the street from the bakery. Lucy's SUV was the only car in the parking lot, which meant the church admin had gone for the day. Coming in from the bright sunshine, Maggie's eyes needed a moment to adjust to the darkness of the rectory. She found her way to Lucy's office and knocked on the open door.

"Maggie!" Lucy got up from her desk and gave Maggie a warm hug. "I didn't know you were in town today. We could have had lunch!"

"It's been a busy day. I had a meeting at the community college about the courses I'm teaching this fall. Between that and the university, I'll have a full schedule." Maggie set the pastries on Lucy's desk. "Just look at the box first. Is it not a feast for the eyes?"

"It's gorgeous."

"This girl knows what she's doing. Wait till you taste the chocolate truffles. Like a mouth orgasm!"

Lucy laughed at the hyperbole. "I don't want to cut the ribbon and spoil her beautiful work."

"Go ahead. Otherwise, you'll never get to the good part."

Maggie watched Lucy's face as she opened the box. "Oh, my word! How beautiful."

"She uses confectionery gold sparingly but in just the right places. Now, imagine these beauties on trays carried by waiters. The perfect finale to a wonderful day." Maggie picked up the fluted paper cup holding the truffle. "Open up, but don't eat it too fast. You need to savor the smoothness of the filling."

Lucy closed her eyes as she chewed. She covered her mouth with her hand to say, "That's divine!"

Maggie chuckled. "From a priest, I'll take that as high praise. Look, she gave me two of everything, so you can have Liz sample them too."

"She'll love them, I'm sure, but she's pretty much turned all the decisions about this wedding over to me."

That came as no surprise to Maggie. Liz had done the same for their wedding. For a person who loved to entertain, her lack of interest made no sense. Finally, Maggie had figured out that wedding planning just wasn't butch.

"Liz probably won't be much help," Maggie said, "but she will be interested in the food because she likes to eat. Want to try another one?"

Lucy shook her head. "No, I can wait until I get home and see what the wedding Grinch has to say about them."

Maggie studied Lucy's face. The little permanent furrow between her brows had become deeper and she looked exhausted. "Are you okay, Lucy? You look completely wiped out."

Lucy forced a smile. "I'll admit I'm tired. I haven't recovered from all those services during Lent and Easter. I was busy writing my papers at the same time, and then the preparation for the concert on top of it."

"I don't know where you find the energy for all that you do."

"I don't either, but Reshma is a big help. Now, there's an inexhaustible font of energy. Tom and I are hoping for an ordination at St. Margaret's in the not-too-distant future."

"That's so exciting."

"Have you talked to Reshma? She's amazing. Brilliant as well as empathetic."

"Now that I'm part of the St. Margaret's community again, I hope to spend more time with her."

Lucy studied Maggie's face. "That's a lot of back and forth for you. Teaching at the community college, singing in our choir."

Maggie perceived the hidden question below Lucy's observation. "I don't mind the drive. I used to go up to Biddeford almost every day when I was teaching full-time at UNE. And the state theater in Portland isn't exactly next door. But no, I'm not moving in with Sam. She hasn't offered, and I wouldn't dare impose on her hospitality. Sam likes her own space."

"Sit down, Maggie," said Lucy, gesturing to one of the visitors' chairs. Maggie sat and Lucy took the chair next to hers. She gave Maggie a long evaluating look. "I'm so glad we've been able to find common ground after all that's happened, but I'm worried about Liz and Sam."

"Me too. They've been friends for so long, and I'd hate to come between them."

"I've asked Liz to reach out to Sam, but you know how stubborn she is." Lucy sighed. "The more you talk about something, the more she resists it."

"Sam's the same, and she's so quiet. She never complains. Sometimes I feel like I do all the talking, and yet when she says something, it's always important and meaningful." Maggie gazed at her hands in lap. "I'm afraid she's taken sides. I don't want her to take sides. I want the anger and division to end."

Lucy sighed. "Liz is keeping it going too. She says she's forgiven you, but she doesn't always act like it. You know what they say, the opposite of love is not hate, but indifference. She's certainly not indifferent where you're concerned. I think part of her still loves you."

"And I'll always love her, but she belongs to you now. I won't say I'll settle for her friendship, because it's not the booby prize. I'm grateful she could get past her anger to help me through my last bout with cancer. She could have referred me to another doctor. She knows all the best people in the field."

"Liz is a professional. She can put her feelings aside when necessary."

"Yes, I've watched her do that many times. Or stoically do her duty because that's how she was raised. Whatever her motives, she was there for me, and I will never forget it. And you. You never faltered in your kindness to me. You welcomed me back to your church, into your life. You kept reaching out to me."

"People would say it was easy for me to be kind. I was the 'other woman.'"

"Lucy, I know you didn't go after my wife. I even know that she tried to resist her attraction to you. Yes, you were both emotionally cheating on your wives, but I was the one who blew up my marriage by sleeping with that guy. I just wanted to get back at Liz for falling in love with you. I'm so tired of people cheating on me!"

The sympathy in Lucy's green eyes forced Maggie to look away. "You feel sorry for me."

"No," said Lucy, shaking her head. "I was thinking that this is a long-standing pattern. Maybe you should figure out why, before it happens again."

"You mean go back into therapy?"

Lucy shrugged. "I heard Gloria Parrish got bored in retirement. She's taking on a few select patients. If she's not available, I could make a referral."

"Thank you, but I thought you were seeing her. Wouldn't that be a problem?"

"No, I'm not in therapy now. I got as far as I could with my grief over Erika's death. Besides, I didn't have time for it between work and school. It was too much."

"How do you cope? You listen to everyone, but who listens to you?"

"Oh, I have my rabbi," said Lucy with a mysterious little smile. Maggie knew that some people used that expression to describe a go-to person for career advice, but she wouldn't put it past Lucy to have an actual rabbi. "In fact, our talk made me think of getting in touch with her. Thanks."

"Glad to be useful for something," Maggie said, getting up. "I should go. I have some shopping to do for dinner tonight."

"Thank you for doing the footwork for the wedding desserts."

"I have an appointment with two caterers for next week, and anything else you need me to do, Lucy, just let me know."

"You're too good," Lucy said, reaching for Maggie's hands.

"Don't tell anyone, but I'm enjoying it." She glanced at the beautifully decorated box. "You might want to refrigerate those pastries until you're ready to go home."

∗∗∗

Sam thought she heard someone calling her name, so she pulled the cup of the hearing protector away from her ear to listen.

"Sam!" Liz's insistent voice. "Sam, you up there?"

Sam got up and looked down the two flights of stairs. "Yeah, I'm fixing the case molding that kid screwed up."

"Mind if I come up?"

"It's your house."

"Not until I'm married." Liz started up the stairs. She was wearing her blazer and chinos, so she had come from work. She reached the floor where Sam had been working and looked around. Sam tensed. It wasn't easy doing work for someone who knew as much about finish carpentry as she did. "Looking good," Liz concluded with a nod.

"I hate redoing other people's work, but I know you're a perfectionist."

"Like you're not," said Liz.

Sam grunted out a chuckle. "Guilty as charged." She followed Liz's line of vision to the view from the third story balcony. "Nice. Isn't it?"

"It is. Now, we just have to hope the neighbors across the street don't get the idea to build another story."

"A lot of people are doing it. Everyone is clawing for a view of the ocean. The only way to get it is to build up," said Sam. "What are you doing down here?"

"Unannounced inspection." Liz's face was perfectly serious, but Sam recognized the glint of mischief in her eyes.

"You're shitting me."

Liz grinned. "Of course, I am. I came down to see if you have time for a beer."

"At your boat?" asked Sam, straightening. The compressor went off and she ran over to flip the switch. Fortunately, the racket stopped instantly.

"No, Dockside. They got in some new brews I'd like to try." Liz turned to look out the window. "The weather's nice. We could sit on the deck."

Sam glanced down at the sawdust that covered her jeans and shoes. "But I'm filthy, and you're all dressed up."

"If I remember correctly, you always keep a change of clothes in your truck. But if you're busy, we can do it another time."

"No, I'm done here. Mind if I use your new shower?"

"Go right ahead. I won't tell the owner."

Sam unplugged the compressor and emptied the nailer. When she worked alone, she wasn't as fussy, but Liz was a stickler for safety and Sam wasn't in the mood for a lecture. "I'll be quick. Have a look around while you're here."

Liz slid her hands into her pockets. "Don't mind if I do."

While the deliciously hot water beat on Sam's back, she tried to figure out why Liz was there. She never did anything without a reason. In fact, Sam liked that her friend was so purposeful. It made predicting her behavior much easier. Sam guessed she'd come to make peace. With the wedding coming up, it didn't look good for best friends to be at odds.

As much as she was enjoying the hot shower, Sam remembered that she'd promised Liz she'd be quick and turned off the faucet. She'd passed on washing her hair and would just brush out any sawdust. She dried off quickly, pulled on her underwear and jeans. She was still damp, so it was hard to get on her sports bra, but she finally managed to stretch and wiggle it in place. She yanked a sweatshirt over her head and brushed her hair.

Liz was out on the cantilevered balcony when Sam came upstairs. "How's your vertigo handling that height?"

"It makes me a little queasy, but if there's something to hold onto, I'm okay. I like the way you built the railing."

"I semi-enclosed it for privacy from the street below and your neighbors, especially if they do build up. I thought it might help with your fear of heights too."

"It does. Looking down makes it worse." Liz stepped inside and closed the sliding door. "You did an amazing job on this project. Lucy will be pleased."

"She's been down here a couple of times. She says she likes what I'm doing," Sam said. "Ready?"

Before Liz got into her car, she stood at the open door to look back at the new house created from the garage. "You really do nice work, Sam."

"You said that already. Did you think I didn't hear you?"

"No, I just think I don't tell you often enough how much I value you."

"Oh, Liz, please don't get sloppy on me. That's not your style."

Liz laughed. "No worries. Not going there."

"I'll meet you at Dockside," Sam said, climbing into her truck. Liz zipped off in her fancy car. Sam had no doubt she would arrive at the restaurant before she did, but she wasn't in the mood to be pushed. Instead, she headed down Ocean Avenue at a leisurely pace.

She found Liz out on the deck overlooking the harbor. Sam took the Adirondack chair next to her.

"I took the liberty of ordering you a beer," Liz said. "The new IPA. It's called Swiftly."

"I've heard it's good. Thanks." Sam studied Liz's profile as she intently gazed into the harbor. Obviously, she was gathering her thoughts. Liz liked to be prepared when she had something important to share. The beer arrived, frothing over the sides of the glasses. Sam took a sip. "Citrusy," she pronounced, "and resinous. Nice amber color."

Liz took a sip from her glass. "Yes, it's not bad."

Sam slouched a little to make herself more comfortable. "Thanks for asking me out for a drink. Were you being sociable, or did you have something on your mind?"

"Both. I haven't seen enough of you lately. But I know how it is when you're in a new relationship. Your friends come second."

Sam tamped down the little spark of anger that glowed at the projection. Unless Lucy was busy with schoolwork or her job, no one ever saw Liz. She'd heard Liz had resigned from some of the civic organizations and clubs she used to lead. She told people she was stepping back as she came closer to retirement, but Sam knew the real reason was Lucy.

Sam took a swallow of beer. "Maggie's not around that much, so don't worry about intruding. Alina needs her to watch the kids."

"Well, Maggie should work something out, so she can get out more. Alina has turned her mother into a babysitter, and it's not fair to her."

Sam bristled. Maggie's life was none of her business. Then Sam realized Liz was interested in what Maggie did because she still cared and calmed down.

"I've encouraged her to go back to work. She's teaching at UNE next year and the community college. I think it will be good for her."

"I always told her she retired too early," said Liz.

"I remember." Sam put her feet up on the rail in front of her. "So, what's really on your mind, Liz?"

Liz sat up straight and studied Sam's face. "I'd like you to be my witness at my wedding."

"Me?"

"Yes, you. You're my best friend. Who else would I ask?"

"What about Brenda?"

"I love Brenda, but you've known me for years. You were there for me when Jenny and I decided to split."

"Erika was too."

"Erika was up in Maine by then. You were the one who mopped up the mess."

"That's what friends do." Sam gazed out at the water. She remembered when Liz decided to end the relationship with Jenny. She'd decided to move Maine and was already in final negotiations to take over Hobbs Family Practice. She'd invited Sam to look at the old house she was thinking about buying and the building that housed the practice.

At first, Jenny seemed fine with the separation. After nearly two decades, the relationship had lost its sizzle, and neither of them had been monogamous for a while. Then Jenny abruptly changed her mind, or maybe it was more accurate to say, she lost her mind. The screaming matches in the Guilford house were loud. Liz later admitted that she was glad most of their neighbors were summer people and couldn't hear the arguments next door. Things got so bad that Liz crashed at Sam's townhouse in New Haven. Eventually, Jenny calmed down. Liz agreed not to force Jenny to sell their showplace house on Long Island Sound, and they remained friends.

"That mess with Jenny was pretty ugly," said Sam.

Liz grunted. "What a clusterfuck. But you were there for me, Sam. And I'm grateful."

"You're welcome."

"So, will you be my witness?"

"I'm thinking about it." Sam studied Liz's familiar profile. "Tell the truth. Did Lucy put you up to this?"

"She's been encouraging me to spend more time with you, but I came up with this idea on my own."

"I'm honored, Liz, but who is Lucy choosing?"

"Emily, of course."

"Of course," Sam repeated. "Make sense."

"The ceremony will be informal, so you won't have to get too dressed up. We've decided not to have wedding parties and all that nonsense. Fuck! I hate weddings. I even hate going to them when they're not mine. I tried to get Maggie to marry me at the town hall. I asked Lucy to elope."

"Weddings are for the people getting married, but they're for the guests too. People love an excuse to drink a lot and dance." Sam took a few swallows of beer while she thought about what to say. "Yes," she said, gazing out at the harbor.

"Yes, you'll be my witness?"

"Of course, I will."

To Sam's surprise, Liz's eyes got misty. "Thank you, Sam."

"Don't mention it."

"And would you like to go out fishing with me on Saturday afternoon? Cherie's giving Brenda the afternoon off."

"Sure," said Sam. "Sounds like fun. I'll bring the beer."

"I'll buy the lobster rolls."

"What will Brenda bring?" asked Sam.

"Herself. She hasn't had a moment's rest since those kids came into her life."

"Her choice," said Sam with a shrug.

Liz looked at her with a raised brow. "Good point. On second thought, I'll ask her to bring the bait."

Sam's phone began to vibrate in her pocket. She pulled it out to look at the screen. "It's Maggie."

"Go ahead and answer it. Ask her if she wants to come down and have a drink with us. Invite her to dinner. My treat."

"Are you sure?" asked Sam, finger poised to tap open the call.

"Yes. I'll call Lucy." Liz took out her phone and walked a few paces away for privacy.

Sam tapped open the call with Maggie. "Hi. Liz and I are down at Dockside. She wants us to eat here," Sam said into the phone. "She's calling Lucy to join us."

"I was just heading to the supermarket to get dinner makings. I called to ask if you need anything. Are you sure about this, Sam?"

"Yes, it feels okay. Strangely, it's more comfortable than having drinks with Olivia and Amy in Boston."

Lucy arrived first because she was closer. She'd taken off her collar and was wearing an open-necked pink blouse. After she greeted Sam, she bent to kiss Liz. The smoldering look that passed between them made Sam wonder if they might burst into flames. In all the years Sam had known Liz, she had never seen her look at a woman like that.

"Well, this is a nice treat!" Lucy declared, settling into the seat next to Liz. She put the box of fancy pastries on the little table in front of them. "I didn't want to leave these in the car. It's a little too warm."

"What's in there?" asked Liz.

Lucy smiled slyly. "You'll find out soon. Be patient."

"I'll get you a drink," Liz offered, but Lucy put a hand on her arm to stop her from getting up.

"Relax. I can wait until Maggie gets here." Lucy leaned forward to see Sam's face. "Liz says you've agreed to be her witness. Thank you. Someone needs to make sure she shows up."

"Oh, I think she's serious this time. Of course, I thought she was serious the last time. But you never know with Liz." Sam grinned to soften the gentle criticism.

"I always look for the best in people," said Lucy, nodding. "Think I'm missing something, Sam?"

"No, absolutely not. Liz always keeps her word, even when it hurts."

"Hello, everyone," Maggie said, approaching. "Don't you all look comfortable?"

"I'll get the drinks," said Liz jumping up. "Chardonnay for you, Maggie?"

Maggie turned to Lucy. "What are you having?"

"Hmm. It feels like summer today. Maybe a Margarita."

"Sounds good. I'll have one too."

Liz left to get the drinks.

Maggie gestured to the box on the table. "Glad you brought the pastries. It's a little too warm today to leave them in car."

"Let's try them on Sam!" said Lucy in an excited voice.

"All right, but we need to save the truffle for Liz," said Maggie, opening the box. "She's addicted to chocolate." Sam felt uncomfortable, and she saw that Lucy did too. Maggie smoothly moved into actress mode. "We all have our guilty pleasures," she said, blithely excusing her remark. She chose a colorful petit four from the box. "Open your mouth, Sam." She offered the tasty morsel, then snatched her hand back. "Don't bite me," she teased before putting the pastry into Sam's mouth. As she chewed, Maggie's hazel eyes peered seductively into Sam's. "Well? What do you think?"

Sam swallowed. "Oh, my God. That's amazing."

Maggie turned to Lucy, who smiled in agreement.

Liz returned with the Margaritas. "What's this? Dessert before dinner?"

"We're deciding on the pastries for your wedding," Maggie explained.

Liz pouted. "Don't I get a vote?" She set down the drinks and handed a glass to Lucy.

"Of course, you do," said Maggie, selecting the chocolate truffle. "Open up."

Sam watched Lucy's face as Maggie fed the pastry to Liz. Lucy's smile never faltered, but an unidentifiable emotion passed in her eyes. Sam could guess what she was thinking. Everything had been rearranged, but they were all trying to pretend that nothing had changed. It would take time for them to get used to their revised roles…if they ever could.

13

The faculty of Union Theological Seminary in their colorful academic attire sat on one side of the stage. The scarlet-robed graduates sat on the other side, with the doctoral graduates in the front row. They were arranged in alphabetical order. When the time came to award their degrees, the Rev. Dr. Lucille Bartlett would come first.

Liz swallowed hard to clear the lump in her throat. She secretly loved pomp and circumstance. During the Vietnam era, when patriotism was out of fashion, Liz reverently covered her heart whenever "The Star-Spangled Banner" was played. A stirring march at a parade could reduce her to tears. Erika wrote off Liz's sentimental response to her Teutonic heritage. "Military music is like a second heartbeat for Germans of a certain era," Erika used to say. As a specialist in political discourse, she could explain why public rituals were important to bring people together and mark important transitions. But Erika's rational explanations never kept Liz from overflowing with emotion at times like this.

How Erika would have loved to see this graduation! She'd put Lucy up to getting her doctorate. While she was alive, she'd steadily, but subtly encouraged her. Erika had been a model of how to handle a spouse's ambitions. Liz always tried to be supportive of Maggie's professional goals, but she couldn't help being critical. She considered coaching the high school drama club a waste of time and a drain on her energies. Maggie had rightly responded that Liz shouldn't judge how others spent their time or what made them happy. With Lucy, Liz tried to comment only when her advice was asked but keeping her opinions to herself wasn't easy.

Rebecca Morgenstern, sitting beside Liz, tapped her arm and smiled. "I'm *verklempt*," she whispered, fanning her face as if to banish the tears.

"Me too," Liz admitted. She took her phone out of her pocket and set up the camera to preserve the exact moment Lucy received her degree. Getting photos before the ceremony had been difficult. Rain had forced the graduation, which had been planned for a local park, indoors. The auditorium and the surrounding halls of the seminary were packed.

The dean of the graduate school approached the lectern. "It is now time to award the doctoral degrees. This year's class of PhDs have brilliantly shown that progressive theology is alive and well and thriving at Union. Individually, each of these scholars has made an outstanding contribution to understanding faith in the twenty-first century. Now, we will reward their labors by granting their degrees." He smiled in the direction of the graduates. "Our first doctoral graduate is the Rev. Lucille Bartlett." Lucy stood. "Rev. Bartlett is awarded the degree of Doctor of Philosophy in Theology with distinction. Her dissertation *Divine Eros: Rediscovering Human Sexuality as a Mirror of God's Love* will be published by High Roads Press this fall. It's quite a stimulating read, so you won't want to miss it. Forgive the shameless publicity plug." There was a brief murmur of laughter. He nodded to Lucy, and she approached the lectern. "Congratulations, Rev. Dr. Bartlett," he said. Lucy removed her velvet hat, and the dean passed the elaborate hood over her head. Another faculty member, standing by, helped arrange it on her shoulders. Liz enthusiastically joined the applause as the dean finally handed Lucy the presentation folder containing her diploma.

The rest of the ceremony was a blur. The other doctoral graduates received their degrees. Liz was vaguely aware of the president of the seminary rising to close the ceremony, and the school chaplain giving a blessing. The choir rose to sing "Be Thou My Vision" as the graduates marched down the center aisle. Lucy shot them a joyous smile as she passed their row. Emily, who was sitting on the aisle, reached out to pat her mother's shoulder and give her the thumbs up sign.

The crowd in the auditorium began to break up and file out of the exits. Making headway in the crowded aisle required mincing steps. Progress was extremely slow. Liz was glad to see that most people were masked, or this graduation could have the potential to be a super spreader event.

"I'm so glad you had to come to New York and could join us," Liz said to Rebecca. "Are you staying the night?"

"There will be more conference events tomorrow, so I'm staying over in Queens with my aunt. I've hardly seen her since I moved to Maine, and we're having a nice visit. Honestly, I don't mind the break from the kids."

"What about your congregation?"

"A retired rabbi is taking tomorrow's service. He said he misses leading services, so it's a mitzvah and more."

"Lucy shouldn't be long. She doesn't have to wait in line to return her robes because she bought them. She wanted the hood to wear with a cassock and surplice for low church events."

"So glad Jewish religious garb is simpler," said Rebecca. "I would never be able to keep straight what to wear and when."

"They're not all so fancy and complicated," Emily said matter-of-factly. "Some Protestant denominations frown on fancy vestments, but Episcopalians seem to love them."

"All those gay men in the church love a fancy dress-up occasion."

"Liz!" scolded Rebecca. "Don't be so cynical and keep your voice down. Remember you're standing in a crowd of religious people."

Liz glanced around. No one was listening, as if they could hear over the din of conversation. "After Lucy gets here, we'll head straight to lunch, so that Emily can catch the train back to New Haven."

"Lucy might be a while," said Rebecca. "I'm sure she wants to say goodbye to her teachers and friends. I doubt she'll be back here soon."

"She will," Emily corrected. "Mom said the seminary scheduled a lecture right after her book comes out."

"I'm sure she's going to have plenty of calls for public appearances," said Rebecca. "I hope it doesn't demand too much of her time."

Liz worried about that too. Lucy was finally done with school, but she had the book release ahead of her and now, the potential revival of her singing career. Liz dreaded another crash like the one following Erika's death. Despite her grief, Lucy had tried to prove she could continue her pastoral duties. Her stubbornness and hubris ended with her collapse in the churchyard on Christmas Eve. Liz had learned from the early days of her medical training that dedication was a good thing, but exhaustion helped no one. She wondered how to help Lucy learn to pace herself.

The new graduate finally appeared, carrying a garment bag high to avoid dragging it. Liz took it and slung it over her shoulder. The sidewalks around the seminary were mobbed while the graduation crowd dispersed. It was difficult to leave the parking garage, and once they made it to the street, the traffic was constantly stopping to let pedestrians cross. Liz inched ahead but ducked off into a side street at the first opportunity. She skillfully squeezed past the double-parked cars.

"You drive pretty well in Manhattan traffic," Rebecca said, leaning forward in the back seat.

"Oh, I was a cabby one summer. When my parents found out, they put a stop to it. I used my hack license to get a job chauffeuring air crew to and from flights. Nice money for a college kid, and I really learned how to drive."

They headed downtown to Lucy's favorite Szechuan restaurant. There was a line to get in, but the food was worth the wait. The conversation was animated. Even Emily had a lot to say, but Liz was glad when Rebecca headed downtown on the subway, and they had dropped off Emily at Penn Station.

As they rode up from the hotel parking garage, they were alone in the elevator. Lucy leaned her head against Liz's shoulder. "I need a nap."

"That sounds like a great idea!"

Lucy stared at her. "Liz! I meant sleep, not sex! You have a one-track mind. We have that dinner with Roger tonight, and I need to be wide awake for that conversation. I love the man to pieces, but after what my first agent did to me, I don't trust any of them."

They hung up their clothes in the closet and climbed into bed in their underwear. "It always feels so decadent to take a nap during the day," said Liz.

"It can't be a long one. I need to sleep tonight because I'm getting up early. I told Rebecca when we were in the ladies room that I'd meet her for breakfast."

"I don't know if I like the idea of you making dates with women in the bathroom."

Lucy punched her playfully. "You don't need to worry about me, but what about you? Women crawling into your bed when you're supposedly on a mission of mercy."

It took Liz a moment to figure out what Lucy was talking about. "Oh, you mean Maggie trying to seduce me when we were at Jenny's? That was a moment of temporary insanity."

"Right. Just remember. I'm the only woman who sleeps with you."

"Oh, I remember all right," said Liz sliding down to spoon Lucy. Liz trailed her fingers up and down her bare thighs, lightly teasing. Lucy turned around. "You know what? I changed my mind about making love. Right now I need to feel as close to you as I can be."

When the phone alarm started beeping an hour later, Liz didn't know where she was. She'd often experienced such disorientation when she'd awoken in a hotel room during medical conferences. It had taken days to familiarize herself with a new place, and by then, it was time to go home. Fortunately, she no longer traveled the way she had when she was running the surgery department at Yale.

"I wish we didn't have to go out again tonight," said Lucy, sitting up. "Wouldn't it be fun to order room service and watch a movie instead?"

"Honey, it was your idea to meet your agent for dinner."

"I know." Lucy brushed back her hair with her fingers. "I'm trying to make the best use of our time here. We won't be back until our honeymoon."

"Do you really need an agent? I thought you were only going to do that New York Philharmonic concert in the fall."

"Roger says he has a list of engagements he thinks I should do. And he's willing to represent Denise, so I kind of owe him a hearing."

Liz pulled a T-shirt over her head. "Lucy, tell the truth. Are you only helping Denise, or are you seriously thinking of going back to singing?"

Lucy got out of bed and put on a negligee. "That would be hard, considering I already have a day job."

"And a very demanding job at that. Wouldn't you have to give up being rector of St. Margaret's?"

"I don't know. I love being a pastor. My therapy clients really need me."

"At your age, your career would be short," said Liz, continuing to play devil's advocate.

"Maybe not," said Lucy with a shrug. "Renee Fleming is still singing. She's older than I am."

Liz stared at her. "You're serious!"

"Don't get so excited. There's a lot to consider." Lucy bent to kiss her. "You smell like sex!" She raised her hand to her nose. "Me too! I need a shower before we go out."

Liz feigned insult. "I showered this morning. You're exaggerating."

Lucy smiled. "Of course, I am. You smell good, but if I have even a whiff of your scent on me, I'll be thinking of sex, not business. Come on, gorgeous, up and at 'em."

But Liz didn't get up. While the water beat against the bathroom wall, she reflected on the unsettling conversation they'd had. It hadn't occurred to her that Lucy might consider reviving her singing career. Unless specifically asked, she rarely even spoke about it. She'd used the constant travel as an excuse when Liz suggested an overseas trip. Liz understood, knowing what a burden business travel could be, but as an international opera star, Lucy had practically commuted across the Atlantic. Her schedule included weekly, even daily, trips during the season, and to music festivals all summer. Just the thought of hassling with the security and connections in all those airports made Liz tired. She sank back on her pillow with a groan.

Lucy came out of the shower with a towel wrapped around her. "Sweetheart, you can't go back to sleep. You need to get dressed. The bathroom's free." Lucy had already put up her hair and retouched her eye makeup to create a glamorous, smoky eye evening look. Her dark lipstick made her mouth inviting and lush. Liz had the impulse to get up and kiss her, but when Lucy dropped her towel, being a voyeur was even more appealing.

Liz was disappointed when the soft, white buttocks disappeared into a pair of black lace panties. She turned her attention to Lucy's perfect breasts before a matching lace bra covered them. The low neckline of Lucy's elegant green dress offered a flirtatious peek, but nothing more. Lucy added a classy rhinestone necklace and stepped into a pair of spike-heeled shoes. In a matter of minutes, she had transformed from Lovely Lucy, her fiancée, into Lucille Bartlett, world-famous soprano. Liz felt her heart rate increase.

"Come on, Liz," Lucy urged, fastening on glittering drop earrings. "Stop ogling me and get into the shower."

"We have plenty of time," protested Liz, unwilling to miss the final act of the stimulating private show.

"Liz, it's rush hour, and there will be traffic. I don't want to be late." Lucy sounded frustrated and impatient. Liz didn't want to add to her anxiety, so she reluctantly got up.

After she showered, she put on the same suit she'd worn to the graduation that morning. She'd chosen it because it could easily be dressed up with a shimmering blouse and some showy jewelry, but she didn't want to overdo it. Tonight, Lucy was the star, and Liz was merely the supporting cast.

Even though the restaurant was within walking distance, they decided to take a cab. Through the taxi window, Liz watched the familiar sights pass and felt a nostalgia for the New York of her youth. Some of the famous restaurants where she'd dined with her parents had become parodies of themselves, tourist attractions rather than serious places to dine. Restaurant Daniel, where they were meeting Lucy's agent, had maintained its reputation for culinary excellence.

"I've been trying to get a reservation to this place for years, but it's always booked when we're in town."

"I'm sure Roger has connections. He knows everyone."

"I'm glad he's paying. This meal will cost more than our room at the Plaza. He must really want you back, Lucy."

"Don't be jealous, but I think he's always had a little crush on me."

"Everyone falls in love with you, Lucy. I'm sure men were hitting on you all the time."

"They were, but I thought I knew how to handle them until Alex stopped playing by the rules."

Liz looked at the window to hide her disgust for the man. "I can't say that I'm sad that bastard is dead."

"I don't miss him either, but I prayed for him when he was alive, especially when he was dying from cancer."

"You don't pray for him now?"

"The dead don't need our prayers," said Lucy but didn't explain further, leaving Liz to ponder this new theological twist.

When they arrived at the restaurant, they were asked to show their vaccination cards at the door and had their temperature checked. The interior looked every bit as up-scale as the internet photos had suggested. While they were waiting to be seated, they were handed a sheet with the day's menu. "I'm salivating already," said Liz, scanning it.

"Liz, I know you're a foodie, and I want you to enjoy yourself, but I really need you to pay attention to what Roger is saying. I don't want to forget anything. Plus, I'll want your business advice afterwards."

"Don't worry. I'm used to multitasking. Hey, look! They have Maine Peekytoe crabs on the menu. Those are the crabs I was catching with the kids. Our fishermen consider them trash, but here they're a delicacy. People are so gullible!"

Liz looked up and saw Lucy wasn't paying attention. She was scanning the dining room for their host. She followed her line of vision and saw a short, balding man stand up from a table and wave. The waiter led them into the dining room.

"Madame Bartlett, you look glorious as always!" Lucy's agent took her hand and raised it to his lips. "How nice to see you again."

"Thanks, Roger." Lucy stepped aside. "You remember my fiancée, Dr. Stolz?"

"Liz," she corrected gently and offered the man her hand. He shook it warmly.

"I hear you're a doctor now too," Roger said, turning to Lucy.

"As of this morning. But Liz treats patients. I just write sex books."

Roger laughed heartily. "Sit down and let's have a glass of wine. Forgive me for passing on the wine pairings, but at my age, I can't drink that much. I've ordered a bottle to start."

Lucy leaned down to read the label. "You remembered! Thank you!" she said with a delighted smile.

"Anything for our Lucy."

While Liz took a seat, Roger gallantly helped Lucy to hers.

"Should we eat first and talk business later?" he asked, sitting down.

"Why don't we get the business out of the way?" said Lucy, taking charge. "Then we can relax and enjoy our meal."

"Fine with me, and I have so much to tell you. You won't believe this, but I've already gotten four bookings for your young alto. The video clip of the *Mahler Two* is popular on YouTube. That's helping you too, Lucy. I've gotten the contract with the New York Philharmonic for the *Four Last Songs*. The Aix Festival would like you to sing the *Mahler Two* in July with Denise. And hold on to your seat. The Met wants you to sing two performances as Elsa in their new *Lohengrin* next spring."

Liz had been watching Lucy's face while Roger spoke. She'd seen Lucy's neutral, professional look when she was in her therapy role, but with Roger she revealed none of her feelings. "That's very exciting, and I'm flattered, but I'm not sure I want to sing opera again."

"Lucy, this is the Met. Your return to their stage will be a sensational event and get huge coverage. As you probably guessed, there's politics involved. The management wants to make amends now that the real story has come out. Take the olive branch."

"I'll consider it," said Lucy. Under the table, she reached for Liz's hand.

"There's more, but that's the big news," said Roger, opening the black linen napkin and dropping it in his lap. "The rest can wait till later."

The first course arrived on beautifully presented plates. Liz was usually a fast eater. She slowed down to savor every delicious bite but also paid close attention to the business conversation.

Roger asked Lucy how she'd kept her voice in shape during her long absence from performing. Lucy described her daily schedule of vocal exercises in detail. Most people would be bored silly by the technical talk. Liz was glad that her opera addiction had taught her something about vocal technique and training. She paused her enjoyment of a perfectly prepared single scallop when Roger told Lucy she needed to expand her daily practice. As if Lucy needed to add more to her busy daily schedule!

Roger had saved the engagements in smaller venues until dessert. The dish Liz had chosen featured a chile-infused Crémeux with a deep cacao flavor to satisfy any chocoholic. Lucy, apparently still worried about fitting into her wedding dress, chose fresh fruit dusted with vanilla sugar.

After sending back the check with his credit card, Roger took an envelope out of his pocket. "The contract," he explained, handing it to Lucy. "You can read it over and send it back in the mail." Lucy frowned at the envelope, then carefully put it into her purse.

In the brief cab ride back to the hotel, Lucy rested against Liz's shoulder. "Did you enjoy the dinner?"

"It was delicious. Everything I expected. Now, I can cross Restaurant Daniel off my bucket list."

Lucy took Liz's hand. "If I go back to singing, I'll have to travel…a lot. Will you go with me?"

Liz couldn't see Lucy's face, so she spoke to her red hair. "I'd have to make arrangements at the practice. Now that Amy's on board, I feel more confident. We could afford to hire another full-time PA. Or maybe, I'll finally retire."

Lucy sat up to look at Liz. "You wouldn't retire when Maggie asked."

"That was different. She just wanted a playmate, and I still had work to do. Do you think I'll need to retire, so I can travel with you?"

"No, and you wouldn't have to go everywhere with me. I traveled alone for years."

"Lucy, I love you, and I'll support you in whatever you choose to do."

"I would never ask you to give up practicing medicine." Lucy sighed and moved closer. "Oh, Liz! I hope you know what you're getting yourself into."

"I know that I'm exhausted, and I'm sure you must be too. It's been a long day—a busy and exciting day. Let's sleep on it and talk about it tomorrow on the way home."

"Good idea," said Lucy, snuggling closer. She seemed relaxed, but Liz could picture the synapses firing in her active brain.

❊❊❊

Rebecca opened her mouth wide to bite into the enormous bagel. She smiled as she chewed. "Nothing like a real New York bagel," she said, covering her mouth to talk with her mouth full.

"I agree," said Lucy, "but I can't believe we live less than an hour apart in Maine and have to come to New York to meet for breakfast."

"Crazy, isn't it?" Rebecca reached for her coffee. "It gets so busy at home with two teens. Mostly they're in the same activities because they're twins, but now that they're older, they've developed separate interests. Chauffeuring them around is a challenge. I can't wait until they're old enough to drive." When Rebecca bit into her bagel, the "everything" toppings rained down on her plate. While she chewed, Rebecca focused on Lucy's face. "You're very quiet, Lucy," she said. "What's going on with you?"

"I'm tired. It's been a whirlwind. Finishing school. The BSO concert. Graduation."

"I'm sorry I missed your concert. I just couldn't get away."

"There will be others," Lucy said casually.

"Really? I thought you were only going to do this one, a mitzvah for your music director."

"That was the plan."

Rebecca's gaze became more intense. "Lucy, what aren't you telling me?"

Lucy took a deep breath and let it out in a long sigh. "I never expected to have so many secret admirers. I thought everyone had forgotten me. Now, the man who conducted the BSO concert wants me every time he needs a lyric soprano. And the Met suddenly wants to make amends for banning me on Alex's say-so."

"You're going back to singing?" Rebecca was obviously trying to control her surprise, but her eyes grew wide.

"I haven't had time to give it much thought. It all happened so fast. I thought I was done with singing. For fun, I've sung in some amateur opera productions. I've done benefit concerts for our local summer theater. Otherwise, the only public singing I do is in Church. And that's another thing. My bishop got it in his head that I should do concerts of sacred music to benefit the cathedral. Now that the BSO concert has put me back in the public eye, he's even more anxious to get going on that project."

Rebecca put down her bagel and leaned on her elbows. "Singing was your first vocation."

"But when it fell apart for me, I thought God had other plans for me."

"Lucy, you are one of the most naturally talented ministers I've ever met. You have a gift for pastoral counseling. Your sermons are always down-to-earth yet uplifting. I'm not Christian, but I'm always moved by your services. Your faith is so true and authentic."

Lucy swallowed hard before she spoke. "Well, that's my other problem," she said, staring at her plate.

Rebecca leaned forward and spoke quietly, as if sharing an unspeakable secret. "You mean, the dark night of the soul?"

When Lucy realized her friend knew exactly what she was about to confess, she nearly wept with gratitude. "Oh, Becca. I'm questioning everything. I even joined a Facebook deconstruction group."

Across the table, Rebecca made a face. "That's all the rage now, isn't it? Doubt faith. Doubt God. Doubt the tradition in which you were raised. Hell! As if they discovered skepticism. Don't get me wrong. I'm glad some fundamentalists are refusing to accept institutional hatred. I'm especially glad that people are fighting back against the emotional and physical abuse."

"I'm furious about the pedophilia scandal in the Catholic Church, and now the Southern Baptists have been caught with their pants down. I hate the bigotry of right-wing evangelicals, but I'm not as angry as some. The Episcopal Church is progressive and inclusive, but sometimes I struggle with being a part of such a patriarchal tradition. God is still a He."

"Yes, I find that hard too." Rebecca picked up her bagel and opened wide for another bite. She munched thoughtfully. Finally, she said, "Lucy, it sounds like the shine is coming off your faith. That's not unusual for people who rediscover religion as adults, especially when they find it under difficult circumstances. For people in twelve-step programs, the concept of a higher power can be the new drug of choice."

"It's not that simple, Rebecca," said Lucy, shaking her head.

"Of course, it's not. I know you think God saved you from your depression when your career crashed, but you were never simplistic about your faith. Does this have anything to do with your newly minted doctorate?"

"When I was studying for my divinity degree, there was more emphasis on preparing for ministry. My doctoral courses showed me aspects of doctrine and scripture I'd never questioned. My eyes were opened. Suddenly, I found myself left with more questions than answers."

"Education will do that. Why do you think conservatives and religious fundamentalists are so against it?"

"You know that's why my daughter left her adoptive parents. Witnesses of Jehovah don't believe in higher education, especially not for women. They wanted Emily to quit high school and join her mother's cleaning business. I'm so glad she found me. Depriving a brilliant woman of an education is just criminal."

"Unfortunately, that's what the Taliban is doing right now in Afghanistan…again. Who knows how many brilliant women are being stifled by those bastards?"

Lucy smiled. "That's what I love about you, Becca. You never mince words."

Rebecca shrugged. "I'm talking to a friend. I behave myself when I'm on duty…mostly. I'm a reform rabbi. Most of my congregation believes as I do."

"Sometimes, I wonder how you do it. At least, I have the loving message of the Gospels. I struggle with the misogyny in the Old Testament."

"Yes, but there are female heroes and prophets too. Our tradition has many examples of powerful women. We encourage women to become educated and enter the professions."

"True," Lucy conceded.

"I hear you, Lucy. It's not easy. For all our progress, men maintain their grip on religious denominations. You're lucky. Women seem to be taking over the Episcopal Church, including women of our persuasion."

"Yes, but the people who sit in the pews are aging, and there aren't enough young people to replace them."

"We have that problem too. Although, the pandemic has brought some people back." Rebecca gazed thoughtfully at Lucy's face. "You're marrying an atheist. Is that contributing to the problem?"

Lucy shook her head "Liz is extremely well-read on religious topics, which is why she was such a big help when I was writing my dissertation. But I'll admit, her questions challenge me."

"Having your faith challenged is not a bad thing." Rebecca started on the other half of her bagel. It was enormous. Lucy was glad she'd had the lox platter without the bagel.

"When I told Liz about my doubts, she was gentle and sympathetic. She didn't gloat or say, 'I told you so.'"

"I'm surprised. Usually, she comes on like a Mack truck."

Lucy laughed at Rebecca's blunt assessment. "I can see where you might get that impression. It's her hard shell. Inside, she's a marshmallow."

"I'll take your word for it, Lucy." Rebecca took a sip of coffee. "Have you tried praying?"

"Yes, and I find it a comfort."

"I'm glad it helps. Some people can't pray when the doubt hits. Of course, prayer won't take away all the pain and confusion. You might just have to squirm for a while and sit with the uncertainty. I've been there many times since I was ordained. I pray. I read. I talk to other people of faith. Realizing I'm not alone helps."

"That's why I wanted to talk to you."

"Well, you know where I am. Like you said, we shouldn't need to come all the way to New York to see one another." Rebecca finished the bagel and wiped the cream cheese off her fingers on a napkin. "I don't know what to say about your other problem. If the Met wanted me back, I don't know what I'd say."

"At another time, I would have killed for this chance. God gave me the gift of a beautiful voice. My mother trained me to become an opera star since I was a little girl. Few ever succeed as classical singers. A tiny fraction ever make it to the top. I was a principal soprano of the Metropolitan Opera. Is it selfish to want to do what I was trained to do?"

"Unlike many people, you had the chance to realize your dreams. You had a successful career."

"But it was cut short because I stood up for myself. Here is an opportunity to go back and pick up where I left off."

Rebecca shook her head. "That's what you think, but it won't be the same. It will never be the same."

"No, it won't. And there's so much to consider. I love my parish. I love being a priest. The woman I'm going to marry is very much a part of that community. Being a world-class singer means traveling all over the world. Sometimes, the schedule is brutal. That's one reason I never settled down long enough to have a relationship. I didn't think it was fair to a partner. Liz says she will support me in whatever I decide, but I don't think she has any idea what she's getting into."

"Obviously, you're going to have to lay it out in detail, so she understands."

"Obviously."

"You're not having second thoughts about this marriage?"

"No, but she might, once she finds out what being married to me could entail."

Rebecca's eyes grew wide. "Lucy, your wedding is only a few weeks away."

"I know." Lucy stared at her plate, feeling guilty about the wasted food, but the conversation had stolen her appetite.

14

"Stop squirming and stand up straight!" Maggie ordered sharply. She carefully adjusted the shoulders of the blouse under the jacket of the moss-colored linen suit. "Hold still! Sam, I swear, looking for clothes with you is like shopping with a child!"

Sam didn't know whether to laugh or be insulted. "I still don't understand why I can't wear one of the suits I have. They were unbelievably expensive!"

"I'm sure they were, but they're too tailored. You'll look like you're going to a business meeting, not a wedding. Liz and Lucy want a more casual look, a kind of beach vibe."

"They're being married by a bishop. Isn't that formal?"

"He'll wear his vestments. They can wear what they want." Maggie took a step back for a different perspective. She exhaled an exasperated sigh. "It would be so much easier to find you a dress."

"Never!" declared Sam. "The last time I wore a dress was over forty years ago!"

"But you wear suits with skirts," said Maggie.

"That's different."

Maggie gave the outfit another critical look. "It's the blouse. Maybe something without a collar, or a deep neckline to show some cleavage."

"I can do without the collar, but I'm not showing my boobs at my friend's wedding!" Sam protested adamantly.

"But, Sam, you have gorgeous breasts. You *should* flaunt them." Sam wondered if Maggie was thinking of what the mastectomy had taken from her. Now that the scars had fully healed, they were almost undetectable. The sensation had completely returned in one nipple and about seventy-five percent in the other. Maggie wasn't convinced that the implants looked natural, but to Sam, they looked fine. Actually, she didn't care what they looked like as long as she could give Maggie pleasure.

"Your breasts are beautiful too," Sam said in a whisper. "I love them."

Maggie looked up and smiled. "You're prejudiced."

"So what? I'm your lover, and I'm happy. I understand you're self-conscious, but I have no complaints."

Maggie sighed and glanced toward the rack of blouses. "Let's see if we can find something without a collar."

"I like this blouse. It goes with the suit, and I'm tired of shopping."

Maggie rolled her eyes. "Why do I always find partners who hate shopping?"

"Because you're attracted to butch women. And Liz loves to shop when she knows exactly what she's looking for. I've seen her hunt for a part for a repair project like a terrier. She'll even drive to another state to find it. I've spent hours in lumber yards with her, picking through boards. It made the yard workers crazy because they'd have to restack everything, but she was such a good customer they never complained."

"But she hates shopping for clothes."

"Not when she needs something specific. Once she decided she wasn't going to wear a white dress for your wedding, the hunt was on for an alternative."

"I'm not sure I've forgiven her for that, but the marriage didn't last, so what difference did it make?"

Sam eyed Maggie with a frown. "It made a difference. You know you talk about Liz a lot."

"I do?"

"Yes, you do."

"Have you been keeping track?"

"Not exactly. I don't keep a list of dates and times, if that's what you're asking."

Maggie glanced away. "I still care for her. I thought we had a good partnership."

"As someone looking in from outside, it looked that way. I've always known that Liz is a horndog, but I thought when she married you, that was in the past."

"So did I. Then we went to that carol service. As soon as Lucy began to sing, Liz's eyes were on springs."

"I look at beautiful women all the time, sometimes with my tongue hanging out. Is that going to be a problem?" asked Sam with a frown.

"You can look, but don't touch."

"It's not like we're in a committed relationship."

"No, we're not. And if you have someone else in mind, maybe you should tell me now. I'm done with cheaters."

In the privacy of the dressing room, Sam would have put her arm around Maggie to reassure her, but doing it in the open would only upset her. "Maggie, I have no intention of sleeping with another woman, and I don't play the field. That's why I ended my relationship with Olivia before I got involved with you."

"That's very honorable," said Maggie. "But if you think you might want to leave, just give me some advance warning. I'm still raw from the divorce." Maggie rearranged the collar of the blouse over the lapels of the suit. "That gives it kind of a retro look. Maybe that will work. While you're changing, I'll look for another blouse."

"Don't bother. This one is fine. I just want to pay and get out of here."

"You're no fun, Sam, but I am getting hungry, and my feet are starting to hurt."

"There's a clam shack up the road. I'll buy you some chowder and a lobster roll for your trouble."

"Oh, you owe me more than that, Sam," Maggie said, raising a brow. "I'll take a foot rub later." She patted Sam's behind. "Go on. Change your clothes. I'll browse. Maybe I'll find another blouse."

Maggie's search didn't turn up what she was looking for. When they left the store, Sam caught her scanning the retailers on the opposite side of the parking lot. "We could try Talbots," Maggie suggested.

Sam made a face. Her mother used to shop in Talbots for what she called "sportswear." To Sam, sportswear was an anorak or hiking shorts. "No thanks," said Sam. "I'm hungry. Let's go eat." Sam hung the bag holding the new suit and blouse on the backseat hook. "Can your sore feet handle a short distance? I'd rather walk than move the car."

"No, I can manage," said Maggie, taking Sam's arm. "I can use some air, and I don't want you thinking I'm an old woman."

"Maggie, why do you worry about your age so much?"

"Well, I am older than you."

Sam stopped to engage her attention. "Maggie, what's going on with you today? You seem insecure about everything…your boobs…your looks…your age…me."

Maggie tugged on Sam's arm to urge her forward. "All this wedding business, I guess. Reminds me of my own wedding. Weddings, I should say. I wasn't sure the first time, but I went through with it because I couldn't bear to disappoint anyone. Mom nearly killed herself planning that wedding. She collapsed at the rehearsal dinner, and we had to bring her home to rest. She was getting radiation for her breast cancer, so we were all worried. Fortunately, my big sister jumped in to manage things."

"Maggie, that was a long time ago."

"Yes, but you know how events can trigger old memories."

"Were you certain when you married Liz?" asked Sam.

"More certain than when I married Barry. I thought reconnecting after forty years was a sure sign that we were meant to be together. But I suspected Liz only married me because of the cancer. She was together with Jenny for all those years, but they never married."

"That was a different situation," Sam said after a moment of thought. "They were young when they got together. I think they thought they had all the time in the world. By the time gay marriage was legal in Connecticut, the relationship had already worn thin."

They reached the restaurant. The hinges on the screen door on the old clam hut squealed as Sam opened it. She stepped back to let Maggie go in first. They had to wait in line to get a seat.

"Did Liz talk to you about marrying me?" Maggie asked.

Sam shrugged. "Not really. By the time she told me, she'd already decided. Why does it matter? It's in the past. You can't change it."

"No, but I can learn from it."

A table near the window became available, and Sam nudged Maggie in that direction. The debris from the previous diners still littered the table as they sat down. Sam watched Maggie neatly stacking the paper dishes and empty cups before moving them to the end of the table.

"I've never been married," said Sam, "but I imagine everyone has doubts before the big day. Maybe Liz did marry you out of a sense of responsibility. That's not an evil reason. She meant well, and even you admit things were good for years. I think Liz really loved you, but I could see your relationship changing. It got worse after you retired."

"I agree. We had a much more equitable partnership when I was still working."

"I think you were happier too. I'm glad you'll be teaching again. It will be good for you."

"Yes, but I don't want to take on too much all at once. I've decided not to coach the high school drama club again. I still want to spend time with my grandchildren. They grow up so fast."

The waitress came to clear the table, and Sam ordered two lobster roll specials. After their server walked away, Sam said under her breath. "The food is twice as expensive here because of all the tourists, and not half as good."

"I'll pay," said Maggie.

"No, you won't. I invited you."

"I'll pay, Sam," said Maggie with stern emphasis. "I don't want us to start off our relationship playing roles."

Sam grinned. "You like it in bed."

"That's different."

"I like it in bed too. And you do it very well. You really turn me on."

"I'm an actress. Remember?"

Sam pouted. "It's all acting?"

"No, of course not, but I enjoy watching your face when you're playing the big, strong aggressor." Maggie lowered her voice and gazed directly into

Sam's eyes. "And when you move inside me forcefully, I like how you fill me with your fingers."

Sam felt her crotch begin to tingle. The very thought of being inside Maggie made her wet. "We'll go right home after we eat," she said, raising a suggestive brow.

"Down, tiger. Let's enjoy our meal. We have the rest of the day…and all night."

❄❄❄

Maggie smiled when Sam began to snore lightly. She had fallen asleep between Maggie's legs with her head on her belly, her favorite way to catch a quick nap after sex and the only way she would rest her weight on Maggie's body. She was still afraid of damaging the implants, despite Maggie's reassurances.

The sex had relaxed Maggie, but she was too keyed up to sleep. She gazed at the suit hanging on the back of the bedroom door and decided it was an acceptable choice. At least, it wasn't stiff like Sam's business suits, and the pale olive color would complement her graying chestnut hair.

Sam startled awake. "Oh, I didn't mean to fall asleep on you."

"You did most of the work. Sorry it takes me so long to come."

"I don't mind," said Sam, sitting up with a grin. "I was enjoying myself. It's not work for me."

Maggie admired her sturdy shoulders. Construction work kept her body strong and toned.

"You're so sexy," Maggie said, running her fingers along Sam's muscled forearm. "I want to thank you for trusting me to go shopping with you today."

Sam shrugged. "Who else could I ask? I can't ask Liz. It's her wedding. Brenda is so busy with those kids."

"Yes, I know, but you don't always like my suggestions about what to wear."

"Not when you say I should wear a dress. For God's sake, Maggie, I thought you'd know better."

"Of course, I do. I knew you wouldn't like that idea, but you have such a nice figure and gorgeous long legs. But you don't like dresses, and that's okay."

Sam's brow was slightly puckered as she studied Maggie's face. "I over-react sometimes when you make suggestions. Like I told you, it goes back to my mother and her snooty friends criticizing how I dressed. They never actually said anything, but their cold stares made me want to sink into the floor."

Maggie continued to stroke Sam's arm, enjoying how the blond hairs rose to her touch. "But you're attracted to feminine women. What's that about?"

"I like women who look like women. I find them really sexy, but when they're really feminine, like you, they scare me."

"The danger is exciting."

"Yes," agreed Sam, looking delighted that Maggie understood. "You're so different from me—how you look, the way you dress and act."

"We're mysterious—'the other.' It scares you, but attracts you."

"Exactly!" agreed Sam enthusiastically.

"I'm beginning to understand, but Sam, I don't want to change you. I like you the way you are."

"That's good," said Sam, getting up. "Because this is who I am." She headed to the bathroom.

Maggie got up and put on her underwear. It was a warm day. She found a pair of shorts in her bag and put them on. Sam returned wearing shorts too.

"Let's sit out on the dock and get some sun." Maggie gave her a sharp look. Had Sam forgotten how careful she needed to be about the sun? As if Sam had read her mind, she said, "Don't worry. There's a shady patch. I'll pull a chair over there for you."

"What about you?"

"I thought I'd sit on the dock and cast a line to see what's biting. If it's anything worth keeping, maybe we can have it for dinner. If not, I have a steak to throw on the grill."

"I wouldn't mind eating your catch. I loved it when Liz brought home fresh fish." Maggie gave Sam a quick guilty look. "I know. I'm talking about her again."

Sam sighed. "She was a big part of your life. A big part of mine too."

"Please understand. I still need to work through some stuff. I made plenty of mistakes in that relationship. I don't want to repeat them. Lucy suggested I go back into therapy."

"I'm not a big believer in therapy, but if it works for you, hey, go for it." Sam reached out her hand, and Maggie took it. "Come on. Let's not waste this beautiful day."

Sam pulled an Adirondack chair under some big oak trees before heading to the barn for her fishing gear. Maggie saw her digging near the compost pile and realized she was looking for worms to use as bait.

"My dad used to say fishing isn't about catching fish," Maggie said, watching Sam set up her pole.

"Which every real fisherman knows. It's about the peace and quiet and being near the water. It's hard to catch the big ones off the dock, but since you're here, I won't take out the boat."

"You can, you know. I can keep myself company. I'm kind of used to that since I moved out of Liz's house. Alina's never home. The kids talk nonstop, but you can't really have a conversation with them. When you're with kids, you talk about kid stuff."

The yellow and orange bobber landed with a plop. "Does Alina mind that you spend time down here with me?"

Maggie studied Sam's back wondering whether to tell her the truth. "She was used to having me as a babysitter on weekends. So yes, I guess you could say she minds."

"Maggie, you have a right to a life. Now that you'll be teaching nearby, maybe you'll consider staying more often."

Maggie tamped down the little flash of excitement at the idea. "Are you sure, Sam? You always say you don't like to be crowded."

"You're not crowding me. I like having you around. I enjoy our conversations. I *really* enjoy your cooking. Don't worry. If I need more space, I'll let you know."

"I'll hold you to that, but I don't want to overstay my welcome. You don't always speak up when something's bothering you."

"I've lived alone most of my life. I'm not used to explaining myself to other people. I suppose with you around, I'll have to get better at it."

"Communication is important in a relationship."

Sam looked over her shoulder. "Is that what we have? A relationship?"

Maggie hoped her moment of panic wouldn't be obvious, but her face was partially hidden by her big hat and sunglasses. Her thoughts were racing. Maybe she'd presumed too much, or it was too soon to have this conversation. "Even a friendship is a relationship," she said, hedging her bets.

"It is," Sam conceded, reeling in her line. She cast out again and landed in another spot. "But I don't think that's what you meant. We've been friends for years. Now, we're having sex. Does that mean we're in a relationship?"

"What do you think?" Maggie asked cautiously.

Sam reeled in again and recast before answering. "I think we are."

"How do you feel about it?"

There was a long silence. The only sound was the whirring of the reel. "It feels okay," Sam finally said.

"I sensed that. But you need to tell me if it doesn't."

"I will. I don't mind having people around, but sometimes, I need time alone to think."

"Creative people often do."

Sam turned around, looking a little surprised that Maggie understood. "I'm glad you get it. I haven't shown anyone my new designs yet. Would you like to see them?"

Maggie felt flattered, but she didn't want to scare Sam away by re-sponding with too much enthusiasm. "Sure. I'd love to see them…when you're done fishing."

"I'll come back later when the sun is off this side of the pond." Sam finished reeling in the line and pulled up the hook. "Fish got my bait anyway. Come with me. I'll show you what I've been working on."

Maggie stowed her tablet in her bag and followed Sam into the barn. It took a moment for her eyes to adjust to the darkness inside, but the cool temperature was welcome. Sam gave her a quick tour of her woodworking shop and seemed impressed that she could identify most of the machinery.

They went upstairs to her design studio, where windows and skylights let in huge swaths of natural light. She led Maggie to a drawing board. "I work in CAD like most architects, but I like to make rough sketches by hand. Keeps the right side of my brain working," Sam said, tapping her temple.

One by one, she flipped down the pages of an enormous sketch pad. The drawings showed different iterations of a large building, but each exhibited the clean, strong lines considered to be the hallmark of Sam's architecture. "These are the preliminary designs are for a museum of women's history in California," she explained. "I keep working on it, but I'm still trying to work up the courage to submit the entry. It's been a long-time since I've played in the world of full-scale architecture."

"I'm no expert, but it looks impressive to me," said Maggie. She noticed a group of miniature buildings on the table near the window. "Do you build models of everything you design?"

"Most of the time. You can never get a true idea from a two-dimensional drawing, and computer modeling, for all its amazing capacity, is still flat."

Maggie examined the perfectly detailed miniature buildings. "Katrina would love these. She likes to build models."

"Maybe you could bring the girls some weekend. Liz told me they like to fish."

"I'm sure they would enjoy that. I bet they'd really love it here."

"We could camp on the little island in the pond," said Sam with growing enthusiasm. "I put a fire ring out there, and I have a tent big enough for all of us. What do you think?"

Maggie imagined the little expedition. The girls had always enjoyed doing outdoor things with Liz. "Let's plan it," she said.

Sam flipped back the pages of the sketch pad to the last drawing, which was clearly incomplete. "Have you had enough architecture for now?"

"Yes, but another time, I would like you to explain it to me, so I know what I'm looking at."

"Okay," Sam said, looking pleased. "Thanks for your interest."

Her shy gratitude made Maggie's eyes fill. "Oh, Sam, don't thank me. Your work is beautiful, and I care about what you do." Maggie pulled her into a gentle kiss. "Thank *you!*"

15

In the anteroom to the bishop's office, Lucy fidgeted. She'd rehearsed her excuse for Liz's absence on the way up in the car. At least, it had the virtue of being the truth. Amy Hsu had taken a vacation for the first time since she'd joined the practice, and Liz was doing double duty. Technically, the marital counseling had ended with their last session, but Lucy knew the bishop took a dim view of Liz missing any of their meetings.

Once Liz had discovered that the purpose of this meeting was to plan the ceremony, she had instantly decided she wouldn't attend. "Church rituals are your department, Lucy, and I'm swamped. Sorry, but you're on your own."

Her fiancée's lack of interest in this wedding was frustrating. Lucy was grateful that she could get her attention for the big decisions. They'd chosen Cliff Manor, even though it had been the reception venue for Lucy's wedding to Erika. At first, Lucy felt uncomfortable with the idea, but none of the locations they'd scouted could compare to the unencumbered view of the ocean from high on a cliff. Liz had accompanied Lucy to sign the contract and hand over a big check. Everything else she'd left up to Lucy. When Lucy had complained, as far as her murmured acknowledgements of fatigue could be called complaints, Liz had shrugged and said, "I told you we should elope."

"Gee thanks," Lucy murmured aloud at the memory.

The bishop's door finally opened. "Welcome back, Reverend *Doctor* Bartlett," he said, dramatically emphasizing her new title. "We're all so proud of the new theologian in our diocese! And with distinction, no less!" He opened his arms for a hug. "Congratulations!" After he released her, he looked around the waiting room. "No Dr. Stolz today?"

"One of her partners is on vacation, and she's filling in for her."

"A shame, but we'll soldier on without her. Come in. Come in," the bishop urged, guiding her by the shoulder. "We have happy work to do today. I *adore* planning weddings," he said with a dramatic gesture that startled Lucy. She had never seen him act so flagrantly gay.

She took the visitors' chair she'd come to identify as hers. She glanced with regret at the empty seat beside her. That's where Liz should be sitting this afternoon, but she wasn't.

"Let's get the details of the wedding out of the way first. Then I have a few other items to discuss," the bishop said briskly.

Lucy had learned from her first meeting with Bishop Greene never to get in the way of his agenda. He was an extremely efficient and ambitious man, which probably accounted for why he'd become a bishop at such a young age.

"Jim, I hope you're not disappointed, but my fiancée wants a simple, traditional wedding. She had only one request. She wants us to use the old-form Anglican ring vows.'"

He sat back and studied Lucy with a frown. "There's nothing wrong with tradition, Lucy. I've always thought the old formula was charming. But will she accept the substitution of 'Holy Spirit' for 'Holy Ghost?'"

"I doubt she'd object to that. We both grew up with it as Catholics."

"Did she give a reason why she wants the Cranmer wording?" asked the bishop, looking curious.

"Not exactly, but Liz is a traditionalist. She cringes when operas are performed in modern dress."

He laughed. "Sometimes, directors take the idea of relevance a little too far. But I'm fine with using the old text if you are." He typed some notes into his computer. "May I suggest something to acknowledge your role as a priest?"

Lucy was curious but leery of running afoul of Liz's request for a by-the-book ceremony. "Please," she said to be respectful.

"David and I were both ordained when we married. He came up with the idea of giving one another communion. You know, like the ritual of the bridal couple feeding each other the first piece of wedding cake. At communion time, I could give you communion and then hand you the Ciborium."

"That's a wonderful idea," said Lucy.

"What about your wedding party? Will they have a role in the ceremony?"

"We're not having a wedding party, but each of us has chosen a witness. My daughter, Emily, will stand for me. Liz has chosen her friend, Samantha McKinnon. My former father-in-law is 'giving us away,'" said Lucy, setting off the phrase with air quotes. "It's more like we're bringing him up the aisle. He's well into his nineties and needs our assistance."

"The past supporting the future, and the future supporting the past. I like that idea," said the bishop with a nod. "And the music?"

"I've given our music director free rein. She'll also be singing."

"I'll make sure to have the Cranmer version of the ring vows on hand. Tom is giving the homily, so I don't have to worry about that. I think that covers it all," he said with a curt nod. "That was easy."

"Oh, one more thing," said Lucy quickly. "I would like my friend, Rabbi Morgenstern, to give a Hebrew benediction before the dismissal. You don't mind?"

"Not at all. Any opportunity for an ecumenical service is welcome. The press usually shows up when I'm officiating. This time, my office requested it because you're a high-profile lesbian couple." Lucy sighed, watching their plans for a quiet, simple wedding vanish. "I want to promote inclusiveness and our support for same-sex marriage, especially because our rights may soon be in danger." Bishop Greene shook his head. "If the Supreme Court overturns Obergefell, there will be chaos."

"Liz follows politics very closely. She's worried, but she doubts they can overturn existing marriages."

"Probably not, but it's terrifying thought." He stared out the window with concern. Finally, he turned and smiled. "So! Let's move on to other business. Otherwise, you'll wonder why I dragged you up here for a five-minute meeting."

"It's always good to see you, Jim," said Lucy diplomatically.

He tapped his steepled hands to his chin as he considered how to begin. "Remember when I mentioned singing some fundraising concerts at the Cathedral? Have you given the suggestion any more thought?" Lucy was reluctant to admit that she hadn't. Fortunately, he didn't wait for her to answer. "I read the reviews of your Boston Symphony concert. What a triumph! I want to capitalize on the publicity as soon as possible. People have short memories."

Lucy wondered if this was the time to bring up the prospect of performing more regularly. After a moment of internal debate, she decided she should tell him. "I'll be singing a few more concerts. My former agent has arranged for one in France next month and another in New York in September."

Bishop Greene looked surprised. "Will we need to deal with your agent if you sing at the cathedral?"

Lucy laughed. "No, of course not."

"So, maybe something in late summer before Tom disappears to Key West?"

"That sounds good. August?"

"I will let our music director know, or you can be in touch directly."

"I'll call him," said Lucy, writing a note in her phone.

"I want to get you on our calendar before you become famous again and disappear." Lucy tensed. How had he guessed her dilemma? "You just finished your doctorate, and now you're singing professionally again. Your book is releasing in the fall. I'm sure your publisher will expect some publicity appearances. And you're in a new relationship. How do you do it?" He smiled, but Lucy was wary, wondering where this was leading. "I didn't intend to ambush you, Lucy, but I am concerned." He peered intently into her eyes. Lucy instantly dropped hers, which she hoped he would interpret as modesty, when she was really trying to hide her panic.

"I don't want you getting in over your head again. Tom is going to be away half the year, and eventually, he'll retire."

"Reshma is really coming along. She should be ready to be ordained soon."

The bishop shook his head. "You may think she's ready, but she doesn't."

"Why not?" asked Lucy, unable to hide her surprise quickly enough.

"Yes, I was surprised too, but she feels she needs more experience. She loves working with you, Lucy. You've become her hero."

"Me? But I haven't been a priest that long myself."

"Doesn't matter. You're older and more experienced. You're charismatic. Now, you're officially a theologian. She lost her mother early to cancer. Maybe she sees you as a mother figure."

Lucy wondered why Reshma hadn't come to her before going to the bishop. "Did she say why she's hesitant?"

Bishop Greene frowned. "Vaguely. Honestly, I don't think she knows herself. She told me she had some experiences that have unsettled her, but she wouldn't tell me what they were. She said she wanted to talk to you but needs to think about it first."

"All right. I'll wait until she approaches me, and I won't say anything about our conversation."

The bishop gazed directly into Lucy's eyes. "The point is, we can't count on Reshma to solve your staffing problem—at least not in the short term—and I can't have you running yourself ragged again. How much time will this sideline career take up?"

"You mean the singing? I'm holding off my agent until I can figure out how much performing I want to do and how much I can manage. I'm no longer a young, ambitious singer willing to go anywhere for exposure. International travel is hard on the body and the voice."

"But you're thinking about more commitments beyond those you mentioned."

Lucy took a deep breath. "Honestly, I haven't decided. The offer that's most enticing is from the Met. Morales is conducting two performances of *Lohengrin,* which is especially significant because it was my debut role. He's demanding they hire me to sing the soprano lead, and the Met is trying to make amends for blacklisting me. I'm tempted, but I don't want to let them off so easily. Before I sign on, I want them to issue a statement explaining why I haven't been performing."

"Will they agree to that?"

Lucy shrugged. "If they want me to sing, they will. This is my 'me too' moment. We can't let people forget how women have been abused by men in power. But before I make any demands, I need to get my voice back in shape. I haven't sung a full-length opera in years, never mind in a house as large as the Met."

"Many performers make a successful comeback late in their careers," he said, obviously playing devil's advocate.

"They're not opera singers, which requires incredible stamina and a faultless memory."

"I wouldn't know about that, but I do know how determined you are when you set your mind to something."

Lucy sensed he meant well, which made her more inclined to share her concerns. "There have been other offers," she finally admitted.

The bishop's brows rose. "Would you leave the priesthood to resume your singing career?"

Lucy had feared this question would arise. Fortunately, she had an answer ready. "Not unless there is no other option."

"I'm going to leave that up to you to decide, Lucy. As long as you can perform your duties as rector and your vestry agrees, I won't interfere."

"As I said, I haven't decided, and it will take work to get my voice back in shape."

"What can I do to help?" he asked in a kind tone.

"Please just let me sit with my uncertainty until I figure out what I want to do."

"Of course, and I know you'll make a good decision, but meanwhile, I may have a solution for your staffing problem."

"I don't think that will be an issue. In the winter months, Hobbs is practically a ghost town. Tom promised to be back by the time the tourists return."

"But winter is also the classical music season, so you may need to be away from St. Margaret's more often. I have a proposal." Lucy knew she wouldn't like it when he raised his hands and showed his palms. "Before you object, please hear me out."

Lucy stifled a sigh because she didn't want to seem impatient. "I'm listening," she said, sitting back in her chair.

"After you expressed your concerns about Susan Gedney, I was almost certain I'd deny her application for a priest's license. Then I realized I shouldn't judge her on hearsay, so I invited her here to see for myself. We had a long talk…a good talk, and I'm glad I gave her the opportunity to tell me her side of the story."

Lucy's skin prickled. She wondered what details Susan had selected to share. After last summer's deceit, Lucy didn't trust a word she said. "How kind of you to invite her to a meeting," she said.

He apparently heard the faint sarcasm. "It's not that I didn't trust your perspective, Lucy. I was only trying to be fair."

"And I was only trying to give you some context. Her attempts to interfere in my relationship made me very uncomfortable. Lying about why she'd left South Dakota was even more disturbing."

"I understand, and you have every right to be suspicious and cautious, but after I spoke to Rev. Gedney, I understood why her bishop allowed her to keep her license."

Lucy relaxed her defensive stance and folded her hands in her lap. She hoped the bishop would interpret her body language as willingness to listen, when she really wanted to jump up and set him straight.

"When Rev. Gedney was here, she made a full confession. She talked openly of the damage her drinking caused others, including the woman injured in the hit-and-run accident. Did you know that she's been paying off the woman's medical bills to make amends?"

"That's noble of her."

The sarcasm drew a sharp look. "She's been attending AA meetings in the Methodist Church because she feels unwelcome in yours. She tells me she's been deliberately avoiding you, because she doesn't want to offend you."

"I'm sorry she feels that way. Liz gave her a free ticket to my concert. I saw Susan at Easter and invited her to lunch, but I haven't heard from her."

"Did you follow up with her?"

Lucy squirmed. "No, as you've heard, my life has been pretty busy."

"Then let me fill you in," he said firmly. "She got a teaching job at the elementary school in your town. It doesn't start until the fall, so she's been working at McDonald's. I'm surprised you didn't know."

"I never eat at McDonald's," Lucy murmured.

"She told me you were appalled when she applied for a job there. She thinks you're ashamed of her."

Lucy prayed for patience. "I'm not ashamed of her. I only said that a woman with two master's degrees could do better than flipping burgers."

"Lucy, that smacks of privilege. She says the experience has taught her humility. She's discovered new compassion for minimum wage workers because she can see how they struggle to survive. Listening to her, I heard a story of redemption. I've prayed for discernment and decided to give her a priest's license. She's been added to the roster of supply clergy until she finds something more permanent."

"That's a good idea, but what does this have to do with me?"

"I think you could use her help at St. Margaret's."

Lucy compressed her lips. "Some in the community know her story," she said with forced calm.

"You said you kept it to yourself."

"Yes, I did, but the police chief was the one who discovered the hit-and-run in South Dakota. I'm sure she's told her wife. Liz knows, but of course, she's bound by professional confidence. Others may know the basic elements of the story."

The bishop gazed out the window, evidently considering the information. "Are they capable of keeping it to themselves? We don't want a scandal."

"Yes, of course, but even if the story gets out, most people in our community are forgiving."

"Except their pastor."

Lucy lowered her gaze so the bishop wouldn't see the rage in her eyes, but she was shaking. She had forgiven Susan, but this looked like another instance of the Church giving clergy a pass.

"I can see you don't approve, Lucy, but can you agree that your friend deserves a chance to get on with her life?"

"I sincerely hope she does, but I'm not sure I want her serving in my parish."

The bishop sat back and gave her a firm look. "I'm surprised at you, Lucy. We both know substance abuse is a disease, not a moral failing. Especially you, a licensed therapist. And it's not like you to be so unforgiving."

Lucy clenched her teeth to avoid telling him what she thought, namely that he was being naïve to assume a few months of rehab and AA meetings had solved Susan's problems. "Giving her a job and pretending nothing has changed is enablement. I gave her a chance. Before she lied to me about why she'd come to Maine, I tried to help her."

The bishop sighed. "I'm sure the deceit was more painful because you were in an intimate relationship, but don't let your anger color your perceptions."

Now, he's reducing my objections to personal grievances! thought Lucy, screaming in her mind.

He must have sensed her anger because he studied her carefully before he spoke. "Why don't you think about it, Lucy? Please. As a personal favor to me."

Lucy let her breath out in a long stream. "All right. I'll think about it. As you know, it's not up to me. The vestry must approve this plan."

"Yes, they do, but you manage them very skillfully. You convinced them to accept a trans woman as music director, which was quite a feat. Lucy, I can't force you to hire Rev. Gedney in your parish. All I ask is that you think about it."

Lucy nodded because she was too furious to speak. She couldn't wait to get out of there. When they parted, she drew heavily on her therapy training and acting skills to appear calm and pleasant.

On the way back to Hobbs, she gave Tom a call from the car. Before she shared the difficult part of the meeting, she summarized the plans for the wedding ceremony.

"I'm glad he's okay with me giving the homily," said Tom, "but it really annoys me that he's trying to turn your wedding into a photo op."

"I don't think that's really his intention, but he doesn't mind the publicity either."

"I hope you didn't say anything about my plans to get married in Connecticut."

"Not a word."

"Good. I'll tell him at the last minute out of courtesy. After it's too late for him to interfere."

"Tom, what I really wanted to talk to you about is Susan Gedney. Greene is trying to push her on me." She quickly recapped the conversation with the bishop. When she finished, there was a long silence on the other end.

"Lucy, I think you're reading it wrong," Tom finally said. "You're missing the strategy here. For some reason, he feels obligated to give her a chance. But he's not sure about her, so he wants someone to keep an eye on her. Be flattered that he trusts you to do it."

Lucy hadn't even considered that possibility. "So, he adds to my list of duties in the guise of helping me."

"Something like that, but he'd never admit it."

"This is why I needed an agent when I was singing. Dealing with politics isn't my forte. Tom, what am I going to do when you're down in Florida?"

"The same thing you're doing now. Call me. I'm always happy to listen."

❊❊❊

From the moment that Lucy walked into the kitchen, it was obvious that something was wrong. Her kiss was perfunctory. She made a bee line to the refrigerator for the bottle of pino grigio. Most telling of all, she was still wearing her collar.

"How did your meeting with the bishop go?" Liz asked cautiously.

"Fine. He agreed to all our plans. He expects a big crowd…and the press."

"That wouldn't surprise me. He gets press coverage wherever he goes. The problem is there's not enough real news in Maine."

"Thank you, but I can do without the murders and scandals," replied Lucy briskly.

From the impatient tone, Liz realized that Lucy needed to vent about whatever had put her in such a bad mood. Dinner could wait. She wrapped up the ingredients and put them into the refrigerator.

"Come on, almost-wife. Take off the collar. Let's sit out on the deck. I'll listen to what's bothering you, and I'll throw in a foot massage at no extra charge."

Lucy succeeded in offering a little smile. She unpinned her collar and was going to toss it with her jacket, but Liz reached out her hand.

"No, you don't. That's one of your fancy linen collars. Give it to me. I'll put it in a safe place. The studs too." Liz put them in a whiskey glass and hung the linen collar on the bannister to go upstairs. She opened a beer for herself.

When she came out to the deck and found that Lucy had already finished her wine, she was glad that she'd thought to bring along the bottle.

"Thank you," Lucy murmured as she refilled her glass.

"I'm listening," said Liz, sitting back in her chair.

"The bishop wants me to consider taking Susan as a part time priest now that Tom is going to be a snowbird."

Liz wondered what to say. She'd gotten past actively disliking Susan, but she'd been hoping that she'd find an assignment far from Hobbs and leave them in peace. "That's a church decision," she replied neutrally.

"But if Susan officially becomes part of the church staff, she'll play a bigger role in our lives."

"She tried to get you back, and I can't blame her for trying. You're a real prize. But you set her straight, and so far, she hasn't been a problem for us. Obviously, the idea of working with her bothers you."

"She lied to me. How can I trust her?"

"Lucy, you know how common lying is among alcoholics." Liz put her beer aside and patted her lap. "Here. Give me your foot." When Lucy slipped off her shoe, Liz admired her bright red toenail polish. She gently worked the muscles and tendons in her foot. "What are you going to do?"

"I only promised the bishop to think about it. I'll decide after we get back from our honeymoon."

"Doesn't Susan's lease run out soon?" Liz asked.

"Yes, it does, but I've barely seen her lately, so I have no idea what she's planning."

"Tom's been talking about moving in with Jeff. Maybe…"

"Liz! Whose side are you on?" said Lucy, sitting up straight.

Liz grasped her foot and held it tight. "Yours, Lucy. Always yours. I am the warrior at your back."

Lucy reached out to pat Liz's arm. "Of course, you are. I'm sorry."

"It's okay. You've had a rough day."

"That's no excuse. What about your day? I haven't even asked."

Liz shrugged. "It's easier when Amy's in the office, but she'll be back in a couple of days. She'd better be! We're going on our honeymoon." Liz resumed massaging Lucy's foot. "How about we relax and enjoy our drinks? We're always taking care of other people. We should take care of ourselves too." She gestured to Lucy to give her the other foot.

Lucy closed her eyes and settled back in her chair. "Where self-care is concerned, your foot massages are on the top of my list."

"I'm glad they help."

Lucy sighed. "You have no idea."

Liz's phone vibrated in her pocket. "Let it ring," she said. "I'm not on call tonight."

"At least, see who's calling," Lucy urged, taking back her foot.

Liz pulled out her phone. When she saw Brenda's face on the screen, she immediately tapped open the call.

"Liz, there's a five-alarm fire at Cliff Manor. Started in the kitchen, but now the whole place is up in flames. It's spread to the guest rooms. The place was full. There's a call out for medical responders. I'm heading down to help. Can you come too?"

The prospect of racing to the fire scene gave Liz an instant adrenaline rush. It had been a long time since Brenda had called her to respond to an emergency, not since the town had upgraded the ambulance service and hired more EMTs.

"I'll be right there." Liz ended the call and jumped up from her seat. "I need to go."

"Go where?" Lucy's green eyes were wide with concern. "What happened?"

"Big fire at Cliff Manor. There's a call out for medical personnel."

Liz didn't wait for more questions. She raced down the hall to her office and found her medical bag. If the fire was as large as Brenda described, they might be short on medical supplies. Liz grabbed the workshop key from the hall closet. In the machine room she yanked the industrial-sized first-aid kit off the wall with a sharp tug. She left the truck engine idling while she emptied the contents of the first-aid kit on the garage wall into her medical bag.

When she returned to the truck, she found Lucy, wearing her collar, already seated in the passenger seat.

"I'm going too."

"Are you sure? You had a hard day."

"It doesn't matter. Maybe I can help."

"Buckle up," Liz warned. "I'm not stopping until we get there."

Once they were on the main road, Liz put on her flashers. She used the turn lane to pass cars, weaving through traffic and cutting off other drivers. She ran a couple of red lights. She slowed down at stop signs, but she never stopped.

Lucy, hanging on to the hand grip above the door, closed her eyes. "I can't watch." Her lips moved silently. Liz wondered if she was praying for the safety of the fire victims or her own.

"Don't worry," Liz said, "I've done this before. We'll get there."

As they approached Webhanet, the scent of smoke seeped through the vents on the dash. Liz pressed the button to recirculate the cabin air. "We're almost a mile away. If we can smell it already, that's some big fire!"

Liz could see the orange glow in the sky through a break in the trees. Flames leapt above it, shooting bright sparks into the sky and plumes of black smoke. Although the restaurant and inn were set on a cliff above the ocean, there was a rise between it and the main road. For the fire to be visible from that distance, it had to be enormous.

Liz's phone rang and she put it through the dashboard Bluetooth. "You coming?" Brenda's voice demanded to know.

"I'll be there momentarily. Lucy wanted to come. She's with me."

"Good. We'll put her to work too."

Liz pulled into the street leading to Cliff Manor and found it blocked by emergency and volunteer first responders' vehicles. She pulled the truck onto the front lawn of a private home where other cars and trucks were already parked. With all the rain they'd been having, the lawn would be full of tire ruts. Liz hoped the homeowner had good insurance. She got out of the truck and grabbed her bag and the first-aid kit out of the back seat.

"Let me carry something," Lucy offered.

"Never mind. I've got it. Just watch your step in those girlie shoes." Liz noticed that Lucy was struggling to keep up with her long strides and moderated her pace.

"Thank you," Lucy murmured. "When you walk fast, it's hard to keep up with you."

"I forget you're so short. You always seem taller in my mind," Liz said, which made Lucy smile.

They hurried down the street, already flooded with water from the fire hoses. They stepped carefully because it was littered with floating debris. Ahead, huge flames leapt above the trees. The shower of cinders glowed as they descended like dying fireworks.

Liz whipped two KN90 masks out of her pocket and handed one to Lucy. "Put this on. It will help with the smoke as well as COVID spread."

The Hobbs fire chief saw Liz approaching and headed in her direction. "Thanks for coming, Liz." Rivulets of sooty sweat ran down his face. He was a seasoned fireman, but Liz could see the undisguised worry in his eyes. "This is the biggest fire we've had in years. Glad you're here."

"Hey, Paul. What I can I do?"

He pointed to a spot where a fire-rescue truck was parked. "They've set up triage over there. Maybe you can help them. Lots of burn victims from the kitchen. The staff tried to put it out themselves, but it spread too fast. We called in the hospital ambulances and the rigs from the paid services. We're waiting on Medevacs from Portland and Boston for transport to their burn units." He looked over Liz's shoulder to Lucy. "Glad to see you, Rev. The guests are being relocated to area hotels. Maybe you could help keep it orderly. Over there." He pointed in the opposite direction of where he was sending Liz.

Lucy reached out her hands to Liz. "Please be safe!"

"You too," said Liz. She clutched Lucy to her in a fierce hug. "I love you," she whispered into her ear.

16

WEBHANET LANDMARK DESTROYED BY FIRE read the shocking headline. Maggie scanned the brief account on the front page, then turned to page eight for the continuation of the story. The chef and kitchen staff had been transported to Boston with severe burns, some in critical condition. Fortunately, there had been no fatalities. The historic inn and surrounding buildings were in ruins. The printed photos of the fire damage were devastating.

Stunned, Maggie put down the newspaper. Her first thought was of the many meals she'd shared at Cliff House with friends and colleagues from the playhouse or the community college. Her mind flashed back to Erika's and Lucy's wedding reception on the patio overlooking the ocean. The sea was rough that day, crashing against the cliffs below, but it was perfect High-October weather with blue, cloudless skies. The brides in their lace wedding dresses were beautiful, and so in love.

Maggie stifled a thought about karma being a bitch when she remembered that Lucy and Liz had reserved Cliff Manor for their reception. Schadenfreude always mad her feel guilty. She pushed aside the paper editions of *The New York Times* and the *Portland Press Herald* and opened her tablet to see if there were updates on the fire.

The famous restaurant and hotel had been declared a total loss and would be closed indefinitely. When the final toll was taken, there had been more human damage than had been previously reported. Many guests had been taken to local hospitals for smoke inhalation and injuries. A policeman had suffered multiple lacerations from broken glass while trying to rescue a trapped child. He had been treated by an unnamed, retired surgeon at the scene, who Maggie guessed had been Liz. She'd always said she liked to respond to emergencies it because it reminded her of her early training in the days before specialized trauma surgeons and ER docs.

In the online news report, there was an embedded recording of an interview with the Webhanet town manager, praising the first responders and volunteers. Maggie was listening to it when her phone rang.

"Good morning, Maggie," said Olivia Enright in a cordial tone. "I hope I didn't wake you."

"No, I get up early to see my grandchildren off to school. It's nice to hear from you, Olivia."

"I assume you've heard about the fire."

"Yes, what a terrible loss."

"I won't keep you." Olivia was using her efficient business voice, so it was clear she was on a mission. "I've been up most of the night trying to relocate guests from Cliff Manor in Hobbs motels. Before I head to bed for some rest, I wanted to talk to you." She paused for a breath. "As you probably know, Lucy and Liz were planning to hold their wedding reception at Cliff Manor. While I was calling around to properties looking for rooms for the victims of the fire, I tried to find another venue for the reception. So far, I've come up empty handed. When I get up, I'll make some more calls."

"That's kind of you, Olivia. But why are you calling me? Do you want me to make some calls?"

"No, I'd have to send you the list of the places I've already called, and I'm too exhausted. I'm guessing the answer will be the same everywhere. It's wedding season, and everything has been booked for months."

"So, what can we do?"

"I'm going to offer my house for their reception. My son built it to hold big parties, so it has a professional kitchen, two freezers and two large capacity refrigerators. You're a professionally trained chef, which is why I thought of you." Maggie felt her shoulders tense when she realized what Olivia was about to suggest. "I know it's a big ask, especially considering the circumstances. But you were involved in helping Lucy choose the menu, so I'm asking for your help."

"Are you sure about this, Olivia? It's a big project."

"I love a challenge, Maggie. How do you think I was able to build the Enright fund into something that got Wall Street's attention? If you don't want to help me, I completely understand, but I really wish you would."

"I have the menu they chose. I'm not sure we could recreate it."

"We can't. There is no way we can make a sit-down meal for over a hundred people. Instead, we should focus on finger food and small plates. After I get up from my nap, I'll call Martha for some suggestions."

"Martha…?"

"Martha Stewart. I've known her since her Wall Street days. The chef at Cliff Manor ran her test kitchen for years. Most of his recipes are derived from hers. Of course, she would say he stole them, but the fact is, he created them."

"Sounds like you know her well," said Maggie.

"Yes, and unfortunately, her reputation is deserved." Olivia's sigh was audible through the phone. "It's unlikely we can replicate the dishes they chose for the wedding, but I'm sure we can do even better. Can we meet this afternoon to discuss it?"

"Yes, but I need to call our neighbor and my daughter. They need to know I won't be here for my grandkids after school."

"But you can make arrangements. Good. Come around two and bring your favorite party cookbooks. And one last thing…I'm sure Samantha would like to help. She has a truck, which would be useful to pick up liquor and food. Could you…?" In the long moment of hesitation, Maggie could imagine Olivia's face as she struggled to get out the question. For such a proud woman asking for help couldn't be easy. "Could you call her?"

"Okay, but I'm sure she wouldn't mind if you did."

"Maggie, I despise triangulation, although I was forced to use it in business, especially to leak information to the right people. I would really appreciate it if you'd call Samantha."

"Okay, I'll do it."

Maggie quickly reviewed what they'd discussed to see if she had any questions. The magnitude of what Olivia wanted to attempt finally penetrated her mind.

"Olivia, are you sure your heart is well enough to do this? I'll help you every way I can, but…"

"Maggie, I assure you I'm fine. We'll start today and pace ourselves. We're not going to do this all by ourselves. I'll see if I can hire some of the restaurant staff who lost their jobs because of the fire. I'll ask people I know on the town council and the church vestry to help. We can pull this off. I know it!"

Maggie was encouraged by the determination and optimism in Olivia's voice. "I'll see you at two. Meanwhile, I'll make arrangements for my granddaughters and look through my cookbooks."

"And call Samantha."

"Yes, that too."

❃❃❃

Sam rubbed the small of her back and stood straight. For days, she'd been helping people move. Yesterday, she'd pulled a muscle hauling a chest of drawers up three flights of stairs to Lucy's new apartment. Liz had examined the sore spot and confirmed that it was nothing serious. When they returned to Liz's house for another load, she'd given Sam some cream that made the pain go away like magic. "Don't tell anyone your doctor dabbles in herbalism, but some of the old remedies really work."

Now that everything Lucy had wanted from the beach house had been moved, they were transporting the things Courtney had stored in Liz's barn. The staging area in the beach house was already full. Sam was waltzing around, looking for a place to put down a box when her phone rang. "Shit! Never fails." She perched the box on top of a precariously stacked pile and watched it cautiously as she answered the phone.

"Sorry to bother you," said Maggie's voice.

"You're not bothering me," said Sam with a slightly surly tone. She hated when Maggie apologized for doing nothing wrong. "What's up?"

"You heard about the fire last night?"

"I heard the whole story from Liz. She was there most of the night. Must have been something. The news said it's a complete loss. It may be years before it's rebuilt."

"Are you home yet?"

"No, I'm still helping Courtney and Melissa move."

"How much longer will you be there?" Maggie asked.

"We're almost done. This is the last load." Liz called to her from the second floor. "Hold on," said Sam and muted the call. "I'm on the phone!" she shouted back. Liz came downstairs and gave her a dirty look before she went outside to get another box. "Sorry, Maggie. What were you saying?"

"Obviously, Lucy and Liz won't be able to have their reception at Cliff Manor. Olivia is working on an alternative plan."

Leave it to Olivia to come up with an alternative plan, thought Sam. *That woman is always plotting something.* Then she mentally slapped her wrist. Olivia's schemes often had good intentions—like when she refused to accept Brenda's resignation after long COVID had left her heart weakened.

"All right, I'll bite. What's the plan?" asked Sam.

"To hold the reception at her house."

"What! That's insane," Sam exclaimed but as she thought about it, she realized it was a brilliant idea. The first floor of Olivia's enormous pseudo-Victorian had an open floor plan that made it ideal for entertaining. She had a professional kitchen, a huge wraparound deck, a wet bar in the basement, and direct access to the beach. "But what about her heart condition?"

"I asked about that. She blew off the question as you might expect. I'm on my way to her house now."

"Maybe I should come over and make sure you two don't get into trouble."

Maggie laughed. "You're kidding, right?"

"Not completely. You like big challenges. Look how you and Tony got the money together to renovate the playhouse."

Sam heard Maggie sigh. "The good old days."

"Never mind. Your best days are still ahead!"

"Keep sweet-talking me, Sam McKinnon. I love it, and I'm glad you're coming to Olivia's. You saved me the trouble of asking if you'd like to help. Finish unloading and meet me there."

"Okay. I only have a few more boxes to bring in."

"Thank you. You're wonderful."

Sam smiled. "Say that again. It sounds good."

"What sounds good?" Liz asked, adding another box to the pile.

Sam spoke into the phone. "Gotta go, Maggie. The slave driver is back."

"What's going on?" asked Liz, stretching backwards. Obviously, her back was hurting too.

"Maggie and Olivia are plotting to save your wedding reception."

Liz waved dismissively. "Forget about it! We'll postpone the party till the fall. By then, restaurants and hotels will be less crowded, and we can find another place."

"Olivia wants to hold it at her house."

"What! Is she fucking crazy? With her coronary issues? No way!" Liz must have realized she'd said too much. Her face instantly assumed her neutral doctor expression.

"I thought you said she's okay."

"She is okay, but throwing a wedding reception for a hundred people on short notice is a huge undertaking. Nobody's heart needs that kind of stress."

"Try telling Olivia that."

"You can be sure I will."

"She put Maggie up to asking for my help. I'm going over there after we finish this load."

"I'll go with you to see what they're up to. It's my wedding, after all."

They finished unloading the two trucks. By that time, Courtney had arrived with her daughter and more boxes to unpack. Sam and Liz helped her bring them inside before heading to Gull Island.

When Sam rang the bell, Olivia spoke to her via intercom. "We're on the deck. Come in." The door clicked open.

They found Olivia and Maggie sitting at the patio table with an open bottle of wine, piles of cookbooks, and open laptops. "Have a seat. I'll get some more glasses. Liz, I don't have any beer in the house since Sam left, but I can make you a martini."

"It's too early in the day for a martini," said Liz, giving Olivia a half hug.

"But you love my martinis."

"Yes, I do, but if I pass out, put me in a place where I won't hurt myself. I didn't get much sleep last night."

"Neither did I," said Olivia. "Fortunately, there are two comfortable couches in the living room. They can lay us out side-by-side. Have a seat while I make your martini."

"Lucy is coming in a few minutes. I called her from the road. It's her wedding too. She should probably be here for this."

"Good. The more the merrier," said Olivia, heading to the kitchen.

"Hey, Maggie," said Liz, eyeing her cautiously. "Thanks for doing this."

Maggie reached out her hand. "It's important for Hobbs. People in this town adore Lucy…You too, Liz."

Olivia returned with a shaker and a martini glass, three olives on a bamboo spear and more in a bowl. "A woman after my own heart," said Liz. She got up to kiss Olivia on the cheek. "Thank you for remembering."

Olivia patted the air. "Sit down, all of you, and let's begin." Her phone rang. "That's Lucy. Samantha, can you get the door and see what she wants to drink?"

Sam jumped up to obey the order as if she were still a permanent guest in Olivia's house. She felt Maggie's eyes on her as she left to answer the door. They stopped in the kitchen to get Lucy a glass of wine before heading out to the deck to join the others.

"Thank you all for coming," Olivia said in a formal voice as if she were addressing a board meeting. "As you all know Cliff Manor burned to the ground last night. We can't let our friends go without a celebration on their big day." She nodded toward Liz and Lucy. "If you agree, I would like to offer my home as a venue for your reception. Maggie and I can create a small-plates menu to replace a sit-down dinner. I've called a party supply company to price a tent as well as tables and chairs and the florist. We'll have jobs for everyone from prepping food to setting out floral displays. Samantha, I hope you'll be able to pick up the food and alcohol once we get the menu together."

"Of course," said Sam, miming a body builder pose. "After all, I'm the best woman."

"You are the best," said Liz, smacking Sam lightly on the shoulder. "I'll go with you."

"It's your wedding, Liz," Sam protested.

"Yes, I know, and that's why I'm going to help. Besides, someone needs to pay for this stuff."

"I'm paying for it," Olivia said. "It's my party."

Liz's eyes grew wide. "Olivia, I'm grateful, but…"

"But nothing. You paid a lot of money to Cliff House, and it will be a long time before you get it back…if ever."

Sam could tell from how Liz's shoulders rose that she was prickly about the offer. "We'll discuss it later," she said, engaging Olivia with a challenging stare.

"I'm sure Cherie can help," said Lucy, jumping in to diffuse the tension. "Do you mind if we have the kids here while we work on the food preparation?"

Olivia smiled. "It might be nice to have some children around, but someone will need to keep an eye on them."

"I'm no use in the kitchen," Lucy said, "so I'll help with babysitting, and I'm sure Brenda will come along."

"Perfect." Olivia raised her glass. "Here's to our intrepid team of wedding planners!" She sounded almost silly. Sam wondered how many glasses of wine she'd had before they'd arrived.

❋❋❋

Maggie rubbed her arms briskly, hoping the friction would warm them against the evening chill.

"Are you cold? We could go inside," Sam offered.

"No, I'm all right. It's a beautiful night. Look at all the stars!" Maggie hugged herself closer. Sam got up. A moment later, Maggie felt a sweatshirt, still warm from Sam's body, being draped around her shoulders. "Oh, Sam, you don't need to give up your shirt. You'll be cold."

"I'm fine," muttered Sam, sitting down beside her in the double Adirondack chair.

Maggie hugged the shirt closer. She inhaled the faint scent of Sam's clean perspiration and smiled. "Where did you learn to be so gallant?"

Sam gazed up at the stars. "From watching my dad, I guess. My mother always became more affectionate when he did something she liked."

"Those little caring gestures are important. Don't you like them too?"

"Sure. I like when people bring me coffee in the morning. Or make my favorite dinner. Or put a throw over me when I fall asleep on the couch… like you do."

"I'm glad you notice."

"Of course, I do." Sam raised her arm, and Maggie ducked under it to snuggle closer. "Being close like this will keep us both warm," Sam explained.

Maggie smiled because it relieved some of her guilt about wearing Sam's shirt.

"Have I told you how proud I am that you're helping with the wedding?" asked Sam. "Everyone would have understood why if you didn't. We all know the story."

"I know, but I love to cook, and I was touched that Olivia thought of me." Maggie knew that Olivia had chosen her for practical reasons, not affection. Her keen business instincts had identified the most qualified person to collaborate in her scheme. She'd scared almost everyone into thinking that she was tough and mean, so when she acted any other way, people felt privileged. "Olivia is not the worst person."

"She just wants to be liked and accepted like anyone else," said Sam. "She just goes about it the wrong way. She often said that you and Lucy were the only ones to reach out to her."

"Well, it was really Liz. I didn't like Olivia at first. No one did. But Liz and Olivia worked together on the chamber of commerce. When it comes to business, Liz can shove down a lot of dislike. But I was shocked when you got involved with Olivia. Maybe I shouldn't have been. You've always liked feisty women."

Sam drew back to look at Maggie's face. "You mean, like you?"

Maggie pulled Sam back, welcoming the return of her warmth. "I'm not feisty," said Maggie and sighed. "I was raised to be a good girl. That's been my problem my entire life. Here I am, almost seventy, and it's taken me this long to ask for what I want instead of trying to please everyone."

"Better late than never."

Maggie smacked Sam's thigh. "Don't be a smart ass." She sighed. "Yes, I would have been happier if I learned to speak up a long time ago. I should have read Liz the riot act when she started ogling Lucy."

"Too late for that, and it probably wouldn't have made any difference."

"I don't know. Lucy seems to have her well trained."

Sam laughed. "That she does."

Maggie's phone rang in her bag. "Oh, for God's sake. Who's calling me now? I hope it's not Alina. I don't feel like driving home tonight." But the number on the screen wasn't recognizable. "I don't know who this is."

"Then don't answer it," said Sam with a shrug.

Maggie was tempted to follow Sam's advice, but a gut feeling told her to answer this call. "Could be important. I'm Alina's emergency contact. Maybe something's happened at home."

Sam took back her arm from around Maggie's shoulders. The chill was instantly perceptible as Sam moved away. "I'm going in to get another beer and a sweatshirt. Be right back." Maggie watched Sam walk away as she greeted the caller.

"Ms. Fitzgerald, I'm so glad I caught you," said a slightly familiar voice. "It's Tiffany Marsh." Maggie had already connected the voice with the baker at the new pâtisserie, but she was glad to be reminded of her name. She could guess why the young woman was calling.

"Are you worried that the wedding might be canceled because of the fire? According to the contract, they need to give you a week's notice."

"I know, but unfortunately, that doesn't stop people. I've already made most of the pastry shells. The truffles are all done. Ms. Fitzgerald, do you know if they'll still need them?"

"Yes, the wedding is still on, but plans for the reception are being rearranged by the moment. And Tiffany, please call me Maggie."

"Sorry. I forgot."

"It's okay. Yes, we'll still need your beautiful pastries. The reception has been moved to a private home on Gull Island."

"Are they having it catered?"

"Actually, Olivia Enright and I are going to supervise some local women in preparing an apps and small-plates meal in place of a sit-down dinner."

"Oh! What a great idea!"

"It is, but I'm the only one with professional training. I've given large dinner parties, but never for a hundred people!"

"I can help. The CIA required us to take classes in the basics before we could specialize. When are you doing the cooking?"

"I'm waiting for Olivia to pull together a schedule. We'll be getting the food from the wholesale club tomorrow morning. We can probably begin the prep tomorrow afternoon. Fortunately, we have professional refrigerators and freezers available for storage."

"I have room in my bakery if you need it."

Maggie paused to consider the offer, which made her wonder why the young woman was being so generous. "We're grateful for the help, Tiffany, but won't this interfere with your business?"

"I'm ahead for a change, and I really would like to help Rev. Bartlett. She was so kind to my mother when my grandmother was dying. Dr. Stolz was there too. What do they say? 'One good turn deserves another?'"

"I'm sure they will both appreciate your kindness and expertise. It could mean the difference between us making this work and a disaster. Ms. Enright promised to put a schedule together by tomorrow morning. Can I call you then?"

"Please. I really do want to help."

As Maggie was ending the call, Sam returned wearing a faded Princeton hoodie. She brought along the open bottle of white wine and a beer for herself.

"Thanks for bringing me more wine," said Maggie as Sam sat down. "I could use a drink."

"Yes, it's going to be a busy couple of days." Sam sat down and took a sip of beer. "I guess Brenda and I will have to ditch our plans for a bachelor party for Liz."

"You can still do something for her. Maybe skip the mischief. I'm sure Lucy doesn't want to have to claim Liz from the police station like when she and Erika got married.

Sam shrugged. "Well, Liz was stupid to carry her gun into Boston, where her permit isn't honored. She deserved to be detained. And what were they doing in that strip club? They were supposed to be going to a concert."

"They did go to the concert. The strip club was an afterthought, a sudden inspiration on Liz's part. Of course, they had no reason to think it would be raided. How would they know most of the performers were illegal aliens? If Liz hadn't protested their arrest, she probably wouldn't have been taken into custody."

"Good thing she and the CEO of Dana Farber were buds, and he knew the judge."

"Thank God. Liz could have lost her medical license."

"Is that my name I hear being taken in vain?" asked a familiar voice. Liz came around the corner. "Hey, Maggie," she said with a nod. "Hope you don't mind me barging in unannounced. I was looking for a place to have a beer."

"Liar," said Sam, sitting up straight. "You came to see what we're up to."

Liz narrowed her eyes. "I really don't want to know, to be honest."

Sam jumped up from her seat. "I'll get you a beer."

"Thanks, Sam." Liz's eyes followed her as she headed into the house. Maggie pointed to a chair opposite her, and Liz sat down. "Do you often just drop by at Sam's house?" asked Maggie.

"Less than I used to…now that you're here. I guess I'll have to get into the habit of calling first."

"That would be nice."

"I didn't expect you to be here tonight. You're usually only here on weekends."

"So, you keep tabs on me."

Liz glanced away. "Don't flatter yourself. I'm not that interested."

"Liz, please. Let's not have an argument. We've been getting along so well, and I'm only here because I'm doing you and Lucy a favor. Alina was beside herself when I told her I wasn't going to be home for most of the week."

"Sorry to disrupt your household," said Liz in a belligerent tone.

Maggie sat forward. "Liz, stop. I don't want a fight."

Sam, returning from the house, quickened her pace. "Hey, hey. I leave you two alone for five minutes and you start arguing. Quit it. Right now." She handed Liz a beer bottle. "Why are you such a crab ass?"

"I didn't get much sleep last night," said Liz, slouching in the Adirondack chair. "Makes me irritable."

"So why aren't you home in bed?"

"I'm too wired to sleep."

"Does Lucy know you're here?"

"Yes, I told her I was coming over. She went to bed early. She was up half the night too." Liz took a long pull on her beer and smacked her lips. "That's good. Nice and hoppy. Thanks, Sam." She took a deep breath. "Maggie, I'm sorry I was crabby. And I need to thank you for pitching in with this wedding. That is truly above and beyond the call of duty."

"I'm having fun, and it's a challenge to see if we can pull it off, but you're welcome."

Liz nodded. "Whatever your reasons, it's appreciated. I know Lucy feels the same."

"Olivia's supposed to have that list of what we need by ten or so," said Maggie. "When are you two heading to the wholesale club?"

"We can be on the road as soon as we get the list," Liz replied, stretching out her legs in front of her. "Olivia is very organized. If we have a good list, it shouldn't take long."

"Don't rush," said Maggie. "Olivia, Lucy, and I have a date at the salon tomorrow for a mani-pedi."

"A what?" asked Sam.

Maggie wiggled her painted toenails. "It's part of our girls' party with Lucy. We planned this before the fire, and it was hard to get an appointment for all of us at the same time, so we're not canceling." She watched Sam and Liz exchange a look. "Never mind looking at Liz."

"I didn't say a word," Sam protested.

"You don't need to," said Maggie with a frown. "If you can go out drinking with Liz and Brenda, we can have our nails done."

17

Liz awoke and reached across the bed for Lucy only to remember that she wasn't there. Sleeping downstairs in her own room had been Lucy's idea. They were both were stressed over the wedding and not sleeping well, but the real reason for sleeping apart was abstinence.

"It will make our wedding night more special if we sleep apart for a few days," Lucy had suggested.

"You mean no sex?"

"Yes. A little break will make it more exciting and special, not just something we do every day."

Liz had rolled her eyes and complained every night before she went to bed, but she'd gone upstairs to sleep alone. She was exhausted from the feverish preparations and, if she were honest, lacked the energy for sex.

Her eagerly anticipated bachelor party had turned into a few beers on her boat with her equally tired friends. Liz had returned from The Wet Lady before midnight to Lucy's smile of approval. "I'm glad Sam and Brenda didn't have to carry you home."

"They almost did, but not because I drank too much. I'm so tired I was stuttering. I'm afraid I wasn't very good company."

That was a night when Liz wanted to sleep next to Lucy for simple animal comfort. The rhythm of her breathing always calmed her enough to fall asleep. But sometimes, Lucy slept so quietly that the rise of her chest was almost imperceptible. Panicked, Liz would anxiously reach out to touch her to make her body was still warm, and thankfully, it always was. At those moments, Liz remembered the lesson learned from Erika's sudden death from a brain aneurysm. *Life is short, and there is no time to lose.*

Liz rolled over and stared at the ceiling. Contemplating her own mortality had left her wide awake. She'd given up reminding Lucy about their age difference, but she still worried about it. Lucy had just turned fifty-eight, her birthday celebration muted because they were doing food preparation at Olivia's that night. Liz was almost nine years older. She'd watched her parents, fourteen years apart, grow old and knew how age-gap romances really end.

With a long sigh, Liz finally conceded she couldn't go back to sleep. She got out of bed and quietly made her way down the stairs. The door to Lucy's room was ajar. Liz nudged it open wider so she could contemplate her sleeping lover. According to the clock it was still early, but because Maine was out of synch with the time zone, the sun was already coming up. It flooded into the room and illuminated Lucy's red hair, making it seem to glow from within. The sight of her beauty took Liz's breath away.

Quietly, she crept into the room and slipped into bed. Lucy rolled over to avoid the bright light in her face. She pulled her legs up to her chest, and Liz molded her body around her. Lucy insinuated her backside more deeply into Liz's lap. "Mmm. You're nice and warm," she murmured. Then her head popped up. "Liz! What are you doing here?"

"I was lonely upstairs. It doesn't feel right without you in the bed."

Lucy gave her a playful smack on the hip. "Okay, but no mischief. And you should go back to sleep. We have a busy day ahead, and your family will be arriving this afternoon."

Liz found the feel of the soft buttocks against her thighs arousing, but now that she had Lucy in her arms, she quickly fell asleep.

When she awoke, she heard water draining from the upstairs bathroom. *Lucy must be taking a shower*, she thought and turned to see the clock. "Fuck!" she exclaimed, flinging off the covers. She ran up the stairs, taking them by twos, and hurried into the bathroom, where Lucy was arranging her hair in an upsweep.

"Good morning, sleepy head."

"Why didn't you wake me? We have so much to do."

Lucy turned to her and smiled. "You were sleeping so soundly, and you needed the rest. Feeling better?"

"Yes, much."

"Good. Then maybe you won't bite everyone's head off today. You've been a real grouch." Lucy's smile softened the remark, but Liz got the point. "I have some good news for you." Lucy finished pinning up her hair and reached out her arms. "Come here and give me a kiss."

Liz enjoyed the sweetness of Lucy's soft lips against hers, but she hadn't brushed her teeth yet, so she decided not to linger.

"What's the big news?" asked Liz, picking up her toothbrush. She engaged Lucy's eyes in the mirror.

"Turn around. I want to look at you when I tell you."

"Okay," said Liz, drawing out the word. She put down the toothbrush and turned around.

"Bishop Greene called this morning. He tested positive for COVID and won't be able to officiate at our wedding."

Liz raised her eyes to the ceiling. "Yes! Yes! There is a God! Thank you!"

"Liz, that's terrible. You know the dangers of COVID better than most people."

"Oh, I'm sure he had all his shots, and he's younger than both of us. He'll be fine." Liz went back to brushing her teeth. Lucy continued to talk to her reflection in the mirror.

"Are you saying that as a doctor or someone who's relieved to have him out of the picture?"

"Both," mumbled Liz with the toothbrush in her mouth.

Lucy put her hands on her hips. "What am I going to do with you?" she asked, shaking her head. "I'm going to call Tom and ask when he can come over and discuss the ceremony."

"Tell him I'll make him breakfast. That will get his ass over here."

"His job as a priest will get him over here, but I'm sure the promise of a good meal won't hurt. Make yourself decent, gorgeous." Before she left, Lucy gave Liz a playful pinch on the buttock.

Liz began to hum. Hearing that the bishop couldn't officiate at the wedding had made her day. By the time she was dressed, she was singing in full voice. She came downstairs to meet a wall of disapproval.

"All right, Liz. I'm glad you're in a better mood," said Lucy with a stony face. "But do you have to be so happy about the bishop catching COVID? The poor man sounded really sick."

Liz put her hand over her heart to demonstrate her sincerity. "I hope he gets well soon, but I never liked the little prick, and I'm not a hypocrite. I'm glad he won't officiate at our wedding." After delivering that message, Liz turned to the cabinet to take out the ingredients for making blueberry pancakes. She tried to ignore Lucy's eyes boring into her back, while she measured buckwheat flour into a bowl.

"Tom said he'll be over right away. He was at Jeff's place in Webhanet, so it will take a little longer."

"He should just move in with Jeff and vacate that apartment. Then Susan could move in there."

"I'm not sure the vestry would approve unless Susan is working for the parish."

"I thought you were thinking about hiring her for a halftime position."

"I still haven't decided what to do about Susan."

Liz measured off the remaining dry ingredients. She took out a bottle of buttermilk and an egg and cracked it into the bowl. She'd wait until Tom showed up to add the frozen blueberries, so they didn't bleed into the batter.

The doorbell rang, and Lucy went to open the door. Liz could hear her talking to Tom in the hall and the sound of his hearty laughter.

"Good morning, Liz," he said, giving her a hug as he came into the kitchen. "Lucky you. You escaped being married by the bishop." His blue eyes twinkled. "Of course, I wish the man a speedy return to good health, and I will certainly pray for him." He sat down next to Lucy at the island and took a little leather-bound notebook and a pen out of his pocket. "I'll take some quick notes on your wishes for the ceremony."

Liz flicked cold water off her fingers to test the heat of the oil in the pan. "Why don't you wait until we finish eating breakfast?" She suggested, pouring batter into the skillet.

"Liz, I thought you weren't interested in the ceremony," Lucy said. "Tom and I can work this out later."

"I'm cooking, so I'm a captive audience. Carry on. I'll just listen."

"Liz wants to use the ring pledge from the old Anglican rite," Lucy explained. "You know, 'With this ring I thee wed, with my body I thee worship, and with all my worldly goods I thee endow…'"

Tom wrote some notes in his book. "It's surprising how popular the Cranmer wording is. But you know, Liz, that vow is only meant for the groom to say in the traditional service. Do you intend that both of you should say it?"

"Yes, both of us. Right, Lucy?" Liz put a pitcher of syrup into the microwave to heat.

"If that's what you want, Liz, but you never explained why it's so important to you."

"Because I adore you, and when I make love to you, I worship you with my body. And in merging our finances, something I didn't do when I married Maggie, I'm showing the trust I have in you and my faith in our marriage." Liz turned around. Tom was staring at her. Lucy's eyes were glistening. "What's the matter? Did I say something wrong?"

Lucy wiped under her eyes with her fingertips. Tom got up to pat Liz's shoulder. "You understand the vow perfectly."

"Sit down," ordered Liz. She took two heated plates from the oven with mitts and flipped pancakes onto them. She set them in front of Lucy and Tom. "Eat up while I make another batch. Tom, would you like some eggs too?"

"Thanks. This is more than fine. I have to keep my girlish figure for my own wedding." He chuckled at his own joke.

Lucy described the plans for the rest of the ceremony. "The bishop suggested that after he gives me communion, he would hand me the Ciborium, and I give Liz communion. A little nod to my priesthood."

"I like that idea. Maybe I'll incorporate it into my wedding service." Tom wrote himself a note. "Good thing I had the homily all prepared, but I had plenty of anecdotes to share about both of you. I could have gone on extemporaneously for hours."

"Be glad you don't have to," said Liz, sitting down with a plate of pancakes for herself. "Someone must be looking out for me. I wanted you to do our wedding right from the beginning."

"Watch what you wish for, Liz," said Tom, wiggling his brows. "You have no idea what I'll say in my sermon."

***

When Lucy arrived at her office, the first thing she did was compose an extended email to the bishop to wish him a speedy recovery. She diplomatically expressed her disappointment that he couldn't be the celebrant at the wedding but played it lightly. Although she sincerely regretted the wasted effort Bishop Greene had put into her wedding, she shared Liz's joy that he couldn't officiate. Her anger over the meeting had cooled, but his interference had profoundly undermined her respect for him.

Her main purpose in coming to the rectory that morning was to make sure church business was in order before she left on her honeymoon. She shut the door and murmured a prayer of thanksgiving for the quiet time, especially after the frenzy of preparations for the wedding.

Although she wasn't much use in the kitchen, she'd shown up at Olivia's to provide moral support and watch the Harrison children while the cooks worked. Ellie, the house cleaner, led a crew of local women, who cleaned the house to a high polish. A local florist strategically placed arrangements in all the common areas. When they finished, Olivia's oceanfront home looked as if it had been built to host weddings.

Lucy forced herself to look over the parish accounts, still one of her least-favorite duties as rector, but she didn't cringe the way she had when she'd first come to St. Margaret's. Olivia's endowment kept the coffers full. The chief warden and the vestry managed church resources prudently. They'd even been able to make some much needed repairs to the roof and renovate the kitchen in the church hall. Lucy had many reasons to be grateful. The restoration of her crumbling church was well underway. She'd turned around the flight from the pews, and her congregation was growing. With Tom's help, she'd learned to become a more effective leader. Although she hadn't been eager to take on a deacon, Reshma had certainly eased her burden by visiting the shut-ins and leading prayer services. Everything had fallen into place for Lucy's continued clerical success, but why wasn't she content?

She sighed as she thought of Roger Weinstein's long list of requests for singing engagements. She'd invited him to the wedding in a fit of generosity, knowing he'd expect an answer to his proposal, even a vague one. Lucy still hadn't decided what to do, but maybe he'd have the courtesy not to discuss business on her wedding day.

"Lucy?" said a familiar voice. Lucy looked up to see Susan Gedney standing in the doorway.

"Hello, Susan," said Lucy warmly, but her body instantly tensed. Here was another decision she'd been putting off.

"I saw your car parked outside, so I thought I'd stop by and see if you have a few minutes." Susan glanced down the hall as if she were expecting someone. "If it's not a good time, I can come back later. I'm sure you're busy with the wedding tomorrow."

"I am busy, but life doesn't stop just because I'm getting married. Come in, Susan," said Lucy, pointing to a visitors' chair. "I can talk for a few minutes."

Susan smiled sweetly and took a seat. "I got a job," she said. "At Hobbs Elementary."

"I heard," said Lucy with exaggerated enthusiasm.

"They hired me as a full-time teacher. The salary is good, but the job doesn't start until the fall. For now, I'm still on the morning shift at McDonald's."

"Did you find a place to live?"

"No, and my landlord wants me out by the end of the month. Maybe you can keep your ears open for a short-term rental."

In fact, Lucy already knew of several options. With Courtney moving out, Liz's garage apartment would soon be vacant. Tom was living with Jeff most of the time and had already offered to move out of the rector's apartment. And no one was using the new apartment in the garage. Lucy felt mean not mentioning any of those possibilities, especially because Susan had been there for her when she was down. If not for Susan, Lucy wouldn't be a priest or rector of St. Margaret's. If not for Susan, she might not even be alive.

"I'll ask around to see if anything is opening up," Lucy finally said out of guilt. "Are you still looking for clergy positions?"

Susan nodded. "I've applied to at least half a dozen parishes within driving distance. The bishop added me to the supply clergy list, and that will have to be enough for now."

Lucy drummed her fingers on the desktop as she considered her words. "The bishop suggested we hire you as a half-time priest."

"He did?" asked Susan, brightening. Her enthusiasm faded, replaced by a cautious look. "And…?"

"I'm thinking about it. There's no open position right now, but after Tom gets married, he'll only be in Hobbs during the summer months."

"What will you do while he's gone?" asked Susan, looking concerned.

"I have my deacon to help me."

"Oh, Lucy, we both know that a transitional deacon is more work than help. Remember when we were deacons in Boston? I'm surprised our rector survived. But I think we made a good team, don't you?"

"I always thought so, but after last summer, I feel like I don't even know you."

Susan stared at the floor. "I'm so sorry. My behavior was shameful."

"You deliberately deceived me. How do I know I can trust you?"

Susan raised her eyes. "How can I prove I'm trustworthy if you won't even give me a chance?"

Frustrated, Lucy glanced away. "I'm angry your bishop let you off so easily. There were no consequences for your actions."

"That's what you think. Yes, I got my driver's license back, but I lost my teaching job. I wasn't defrocked, but people in the parish never treated me the same again. How can I minister to people who despise me? That's why

I came back East. Worst of all, I've lost your friendship…and your trust. I know I caused a lot of damage to our relationship. I've sensed your disapproval. That's why I've been staying away."

"So, instead, you've isolated yourself."

"Not completely. I've made a new friend."

That was an encouraging sign. Lucy dared to inquire gently. "Someone in the parish?"

"She's not religious, but I don't hold that against her."

"That's kind of you," said Lucy, then wanted to bite her tongue for the sarcasm.

"She needs kindness," said Susan with a sigh. "Her partner is older. She has Alzheimer's, and dealing with it has been a real struggle for both of them."

"You're good at supporting people in difficult situations. I hope your new friend appreciates it. I know I did and still do."

Susan smiled. "I'm glad to hear it. Maybe there's hope for us."

Lucy instantly tensed. "As long as you realize our romance is a thing of the past."

A shadow of pain passed over Susan's face. "I have no choice. You're marrying Dr. Stolz tomorrow. I have to face facts."

For an extended moment, they studied one another. "Susan, I'm truly happy that you're trying to turn your life around. I'm proud of you for staying sober. I can see that you're trying to make amends. There's no reason why I shouldn't give you a chance, but I still have doubts."

"None of us can ever be completely sure of anything," said Susan. "We have to have faith and hope for the best. Please give me a chance."

Lucy sighed with exasperation. "It's against my better judgment, but out of compassion, I will suggest that the vestry hire you on an interim basis…six months at a time. If Tom agrees to vacate the rector's apartment, you can live there temporarily. Meanwhile, you should keep looking for another place to live."

"Thank you, Lucy. That's very generous."

"I care for you, Susan. Don't make a fool of me, or that's the end. I'm not kidding."

Susan studied Lucy's stern face. "I won't let you down. I promise you won't regret it. I don't want to lose you again."

***

Lucy studied her daughter's image in the wall-to-ceiling mirror that ran the length of the salon. She wondered what Emily thought of sharing the intimacy of getting their hair done for the wedding. Lucy had hoped it would create a special bond between mother and daughter. She tried to interpret the look on Emily's face. There was some curiosity about the process, but otherwise not much else to see. Sentiment seemed to mean little to her.

She was so tall that the hairdresser had needed to let down the chair to the lowest setting to reach the top of her head. Other than her height, blue eyes, and clear skin completely devoid of age lines, Emily could be Lucy's younger sister.

"Mom, do I have to do anything as your witness?"

"All you do is sign the marriage certificate after the wedding. Otherwise, you just stand there and look beautiful."

"You're beautiful too, Mom. But how come Aunt Liz isn't here getting her hair done?"

"You're not serious." Lucy could see the glint of mischief in Emily's eyes. Her daughter's subtle humor was a new development. She had grown so much since she'd gone off to Yale.

The stylist arrived with the flowers that would be woven into Lucy's hair. They were white and red rosebuds from Erika's Garden. Emily watched with keen interest. "Why did you decide not to have a veil?"

"Because when I married Erika, we had a big wedding, and I wore a traditional gown. Liz and I wanted something different because this is a different relationship."

"How is being with Aunt Liz different?"

"Erika was almost ethereal. Her head was so far up in the clouds, it was a wonder she didn't just float away. I mean, she was practical, like all Germans, but she lived in the world of abstraction. Liz is more down to earth. Like Erika, she's incredibly kind and loyal, but she's also direct. Some would say blunt. I can always count on her honesty."

Emily looked thoughtful. "Denise says I'm so honest I'm brutal."

"The truth can hurt. It's important to express yourself, but it's equally important to speak kindly, if you can." Lucy regarded her daughter curiously. "Are you seeing Denise again?"

"Yes. I guess so. I wanted to break up, but she didn't, so we've stayed friends. She says she'll be patient. She even invited me to come to Aix next month."

Lucy listened carefully, trying to hear the subtext. Denise was certainly persistent. Lucy only hoped she wouldn't wait in vain. She studied Emily's placid face as the hairdresser placed the pins that strategically held her upsweep in place. "Are you going to Aix?"

"Yes, I'm going to show my support. When I told Grandpa, he said it was a wonderful opportunity. He's paying for the trip."

Lucy blessed Stefan for his generosity, but she didn't want Emily taking the old man's money. "I can pay for you to go to Aix, Emily."

"Too late, Mom. I already got my ticket. I wasn't going to tell you. I wanted it to be a surprise."

"That's fine, sweetheart, but now that I know, I'll give you spending money."

"Grandpa already gave me money."

Lucy was surprised to feel both out of the loop and replaced. She decided she needed to have a little talk with Stefan, but she could already guess his response. He'd tried to give Lucy money when the repair after a minor car accident turned out to be expensive. She'd gently refused, reminding him that Erika had left her well off. He'd insisted, saying, "Lovely Lucy, at my age, it gives me great pleasure to give away my money while I'm still alive. That way I can see the happy faces. When I'm in the ground, I can't."

The stylist had been listening intently to the discussion about money. When Lucy caught her eye in the mirror, she responded with a furtive, guilty expression.

"Do I really need that many pins in my hair?" Lucy asked.

"I made this style a little tight, so it holds together. Try not to move your head suddenly. When you're ready to let your hair down, just take out the pins here and here, behind your ears, and at the base of your neck."

"Thank you," said Lucy, but her hair was pulled so tight that her scalp itched. She dared not even touch it. Fortunately, the elaborate style only had to last for a few hours.

✽✽✽

When Sam showed up, Liz left her niece in charge of clearing away the lunch dishes. Every guest room in the house was filled. Some of Liz's family had planned to stay at Cliff Manor, and it had been a scramble to find room for everyone. Liz had even opened the pullout in her office.

"Before I forget," said Liz as they headed out to her car. "Here are the rings." She handed Sam a velvet-covered box.

"I thought the ring bearer brings up the rings."

Liz laughed. "He does, but those are just dummies sewn into the pillow. I learned my lesson when my brother dropped the rings at my aunt's wedding. They landed in the leaves, and the ceremony was delayed for twenty minutes while we all looked for them."

Sam opened the velvet covered box. "Obviously, the smaller one is for Lucy."

"Obviously," said Liz, starting the engine. "Where's Maggie this morning?"

"She's at Olivia's, putting the finishing touches on the appetizers. She promised to be on time."

Before they headed out, Liz looked over her friend. "You look terrific in that outfit. Where did you get it?"

"Maggie helped me find it at the outlets."

"She's good at dressing people. I didn't always like her suggestions, but she has a good eye for fashion. I appreciate all her help with this wedding. I just hope she doesn't freak out when we exchange our vows."

"You know Maggie. She's the consummate actress. No matter how she feels, she'll put in the right performance." Liz hoped so, but she could remember some loud scenes during the divorce that she'd rather forget.

"When we get there, I'm going to put you in charge of getting Stefan's walker to the front of the chapel. His place in the front pew is marked with masking tape. After the service, Emily will help him."

"You've thought of everything, haven't you?"

"Comes from doing my old day job. In surgery, you plan for every eventuality, and even then, you get surprised."

Liz pulled up to the main entrance to Ocean Terrace. "I'll bring him down," she said, turning off the engine. "COVID deaths among the elderly, even the vaccinated, are still high. They don't want more people coming in and out of the building than necessary." She grabbed a mask off the dashboard. "Be right back."

The receptionist knew Liz and waved her in without requiring her to sign the guest register. Liz sighed, savoring the solitude in the elevator, the first time she'd been entirely alone for days.

She waited patiently at Stefan's door. Finally, she heard shuffling on the other side and the barrels in the lock turn. The old man's smile was nearly beatific. "And here's one of my beautiful brides," he said, reaching up to grasp both of her cheeks. He pulled her down into a hug and kissed each cheek. "You look so elegant, my dear. And I can't wait to see our Lovely Lucy."

"Where's your walker?" Liz asked, glancing over his shoulder.

"In the living room. I don't need it unless I must walk a long distance. I can hold onto your arm to get downstairs." She went into the apartment and found the tricycle walker carefully folded and leaning against a bookcase. She offered her free arm to Stefan, and they made their way to the elevator. "I have your boutonnière in the car with mine. The roses are from Erika's garden."

Stefan's smile was tinged with sadness. "Yes, she would be glad to have a presence here today. She loved you both."

"Lucy's sure she'll be watching from wherever she is."

"How nice to have faith in the afterlife and think such thoughts," replied Stefan with a sigh.

"I know you're an atheist, but doesn't it comfort you to imagine we might survive death?"

"Maybe we do, but I'm not counting on it." He looked sad and nodded. "Although I would dearly like to see my Helga and my little Erika again."

Liz swallowed a lump in her throat. She fought back the tears, so they wouldn't ruin her makeup. Her anxiety built as she drove the coastal road to St. Mary's by the Sea. The pale blue, red, and white Episcopal flag fluttered at the entrance to the drive. Beneath it flew the rainbow flag because it was Pride month. She noticed that the sign had been repainted. Now it read: Rev. Dr. Lucille Bartlett, Rector. Since Tom had resigned as associate rector, his name had been removed, which saddened Liz. In the few short years since Lucy had come to Hobbs so much had changed.

Don't be sad, said a voice with a distinctive German-inflected British accent. *I asked you to look after her if anything happened to me. I'm glad to see you performing your duty. And of course, I approve.*

"That's good," replied Liz aloud.

Sam turned to stare at her. "What's good?" she asked.

"It's good that most of the guests have already arrived," Liz ad libbed. "That means we won't have a tie-up in the parking lot." She glanced at Sam to make sure her explanation had satisfied her. Sam nodded.

Liz found a space in the reserved area and pulled into it. After helping Sam get Stefan out of the car, she watched them slowly make their way down the path. She felt her heart rate increase and suddenly wished she had thought to bring a tranquilizer. She glanced at her watch. *Six minutes to zero.* She was too antsy to sit any longer, so she got out of the car and began to pace. A moment later, Denise drove up in Lucy's car with Emily and Lucy.

"I thought you might stand me up at the altar," said Liz, offering her hand to help Lucy out of the car.

"Not a chance. You look wonderful. I'd give you a kiss but I'm afraid to move too much with this bonnet they've made of my hair."

Liz looked over the pile of red waves dotted with rosebuds. "That stack is impressive, but better than a veil, I suppose."

"If this were a traditional wedding, you wouldn't even see me before I walked down the aisle."

"Even if I were a groom, I don't like surprises, and we both need to help Stefan make it to the front of the chapel." Liz cocked her elbow, and Lucy took her arm. "Denise, can you help Emily find her place? Lucy will be on the right as you face the altar."

After Emily and Denise left, Lucy turned up her face to Liz. "Liz, are you ready for this?"

"I think so. Are you?"

"Yes!" said Lucy enthusiastically.

Tom, fully vested, saw them approaching and hurried in their direction. "Are we almost ready to begin?"

Liz scanned the crowd. The overflow from the chapel pews had taken over the lawn. People had brought sling chairs and beach chairs as seating. "There's space for latecomers on the lawn. Sure, Tom. You can begin whenever you're ready."

He smiled and put a hand on each of their arms. "Blessings on you both. You look absolutely beautiful." On his way to the altar, Tom signaled to Tony Roselli, who led a chamber orchestra of musicians from the Webhanet Playhouse.

Stefan struggled to get up from his seat. Liz worried that they might have to get to the altar without him, but he put on a brave face, leaned heavily on Liz's arm and stood. Lucy took his other arm. He beamed at her. "Lovely Lucy, you are a vision," he whispered.

Denise began to sing "*Ombra mai fù*" from Handel's *Xerxes*. The stately pace was perfect for Stefan, who held his head high and proudly nodded to the guests as they passed as if to say, "Yes, they're mine." After he delivered them to the altar step, Brenda got up to help him to his seat.

Taking her position in front of Tom, Liz felt herself begin to tremble. Her head shook, and no matter how she tried to steady it, she couldn't keep it still. Tom leaned forward to ask, "Liz, are you all right? I've never seen you like this."

"Yes. I don't know why I'm shaking."

"Why don't you and Lucy sit down?" Tom suggested gently. "While you get yourself together, I'll make some opening remarks. Go on." He watched anxiously as Lucy led her to their seats.

Lucy took her hand and began to stroke it gently. "Relax. I'm here with you," she whispered, continuing to pet her hand as if it were a creature with a life of its own. She smiled and her green eyes never left Liz's face. Mesmerized by her gentle gaze, Liz could feel the tension draining away. As suddenly as the mysterious, trembling had begun, it stopped.

"Good morning, everyone," Tom said in a hearty voice. "I know you were expecting the bishop this morning. Unfortunately, he's fallen ill from COVID and has remained away for our safety. Please join me in praying for his swift recovery." Tom bowed his head for a brief moment of silence.

"For those who don't know me, I'm Tom Simmons. I've been proud to serve with Mother Lucy as her second in command, but even more proud to call her my friend. Liz Stolz and I have known one another for over four decades. In fact, she knew me even before I was ordained, when she was training at Yale and I was a graduate student. Our mutual friend, Erika Bultmann, Lucy's first wife, introduced us.

'Both Liz and Erika loved opera. When they heard Lucille Bartlett sing at the Met that night many years ago, little did they know they would both fall in love with her. But that is how life is, a series of intersecting circles, a spiral dance of sorrows and joys. Today, we are here to celebrate one of life's happy moments. We've been invited to witness the commitment of Elizabeth Stolz and Lucille Bartlett, a new beginning and another step in the dance." He nodded in their direction. "Lucy and Liz, if you will step forward, we can begin."

Liz wanted to get up, but she was frozen to her chair. With perfect calm, Lucy offered her hand. Liz took it but still couldn't rise. Lucy gave her hand a little tug, and Liz finally got to her feet.

Tom gestured to where they should each stand. Once the service began, Liz looked into Lucy's eyes and could see nothing else. She repeated the words after Tom. She sat, stood, and knelt as directed. Finally, she had the opportunity to say the ancient pledge as she slipped the gold band on Lucy's finger. "… with my body, I thee worship…"

The wedding ceremony was followed by a Eucharist service. At communion, Tom passed Lucy the Ciborium. She offered Liz the host with that look of ineffable love. Liz was so overcome that she forgot to reach out her hands. Instead, she opened her mouth the way she was taught at First Communion. Lucy smiled knowingly and put the host on her tongue.

Liz was vaguely aware that Lucy's friend, Rabbi Morgenstern, was blessing them in Hebrew, followed by Tom's benediction. Then everyone was hugging her and clapping her on the back. Liz anxiously scanned the crowd for red hair. She saw the green eyes gazing at her from across the aisle. She gently nudged people aside and took Lucy into her arms.

"We're married," Liz said with amazement.

"Yes, we are. Now, kiss me."

❋❋❋

Lucy's feet hurt from dancing. She took off her heels and went barefoot. She'd already let down her hair. When the pins were pulled, Emily had collected the roses that rained down to preserve them as a keepsake.

Lucy looked around the deck and decided she'd already danced with the people that mattered and deserved a break. Everyone seemed to be having a good time, so it seemed like a perfect opportunity to sneak away from the crowd and sit down for a moment. She found a chair and rubbed her feet. She looked around, hoping her new wife could perform this service, but Liz was deeply engrossed in conversation with Brenda.

"Hah, I caught you," said Maggie, sitting down beside her. "The band is great. I recognize most of them from the playhouse."

"Yes, they're good." Lucy smiled. "Having fun? I saw you out there shaking your bootie."

Maggie arched a perfectly tweezed brow. "You're a married woman, Lucy. You shouldn't be looking at my behind, big as it is." She laughed. "Yes, I'm having fun. I dreaded this day, but now that it's finally come, I feel almost peaceful—as if order has been restored to Hobbs after a big storm."

Lucy nodded, understanding what she was trying to say. "Thank you for all your hard work in making this party happen. The food was delicious, much better than we would have eaten in a restaurant."

"We had lots of fun. I enjoyed working with Olivia. We tried some new recipes, got lots of raves from the crowd. We got to prove what two old ladies can accomplish when they set their minds to it. In all, a good day."

"I appreciate it, and I know Liz does too."

"For a moment there, I thought she was going to faint. She did the same thing at our wedding. The surgeon whose hands are as steady as a rock shook like a leaf. I think she's allergic to weddings."

"Maybe so. But she's the one who wanted to get married."

"I know. She's a paradox, that one." Maggie patted Lucy's thigh. "Congratulations. Enjoy your time in New York. I'm so jealous. I miss the place. Maybe I can convince Sam to go down this fall. Maybe we can all go together."

"That sounds like fun," said Lucy.

Maggie got up and headed back to the party. Not a second after she got up, Roger Weinstein took her place.

"You were a beautiful bride, Lucy. What a moving service. I especially liked the Hebrew blessing at the end."

"Rebecca is a friend of mine." Lucy leaned closer to speak confidently. "I tell everyone she's my rabbi."

Roger laughed, instantly getting the joke. "Well, maybe she can give you some good advice about this." He tapped open his phone, and handed it to Lucy. "I sent it to your email too."

"What's this?" she asked.

"Those are all the requests for bookings. Scroll down."

Lucy scrolled and scrolled but still didn't get to the end. "Roger, I can't do all these. Not even half of them. Not even a tenth!"

"I know. It's not humanly possible, but everyone wants you, Lucy. Morales has been spreading the word."

Lucy handed back his phone. "Roger, I appreciate what you're doing. Maybe I'll do the Met performances."

"They called. They want you for *Otello* too." His smile was kind, but his expectation was palpable.

"Roger, as you can see, I have a day job, one that I love very much."

"You also love to sing. And people love to hear you sing."

"I'll think about it, Roger, but this isn't what I expected. I was only doing a favor for a friend."

He leaned forward. "You worked your butt off trying to make a comeback after Alex screwed you. Here's your chance." He lowered his voice. "Don't blow it."

Lucy was shaken by the warning. Roger could be pushy, but she'd never heard him speak so bluntly. "Excuse me. I need to use the ladies' room."

He jumped up when she rose from her chair. "Of course, Lucy. I'm sorry I brought up business on your big day. We'll talk later."

Lucy fled to the bathroom. She fished the pins she'd missed out of her hair and flung them into the trash. A small pink rosebud was still wound into a lock. She yanked it out, pulling out a few red hairs in the process. The unexpected pain brought tears to her eyes. She stared at the rose, wondering what Erika would have said about this opportunity.

Use your reason, Lucy, said a distinctive voice in her head. *Use what Liz has been trying to teach you. Don't let the situation overwhelm you. Think clearly.*

Someone knocked on the door. The problem with holding a wedding in a private home was the limited number of bathrooms. Lucy hurried to avoid holding up the line. She stuffed the rosebud into the pocket hidden in the folds of the dress and felt her phone with Roger's overwhelming list. She yanked her hand away from the phone like it was on fire.

The knock on the door became more insistent. Lucy opened it to find Cherie waiting outside with her young daughter.

"I'm sorry, Lucy, if I had known it was you. I wouldn't have been so persistent," she apologized. "You were so beautiful today. Congratulations."

Lucy tried to smile and look grateful, but she desperately needed to escape. "See you later," she whispered, hurrying away.

She remembered that Olivia's house had a door in the basement that opened directly onto the beach. She went downstairs and found a throng of guests gathered around the wet bar. Not stopping to acknowledge their greetings, she wound her way through them. Finally, she pushed open the heavy door. A gust of wind greeted her. She gratefully inhaled the fresh air and took in the vast expanse of ocean in front of her.

One of the guests sitting on the sand noticed her and got up to approach. Lucy waved to him but quickly walked in the opposite direction. She'd been crowded all day and couldn't talk to anyone right now. She headed toward the jetty, enjoying the spring of the damp sand under her feet. When she got to the huge rocks, she thought of sitting down, but she didn't want to stain her white dress. Part of the reason she'd chosen it was that it was informal enough to wear on other occasions.

Contemplating the restless ocean, she just wanted to cry, but the sight of children playing in the surf held back the tears. Lucy watched them, envying their easy laughter. She wished she could jump into the water with them and shriek with joy over the simple pleasure of being doused by a wave. How wonderful not to care what others thought, to be free of adult responsibilities and tough decisions.

She would have stayed longer, but she knew the wedding guests were probably wondering where she'd gone. Reluctantly, she turned to head back to the Olivia's house. In the distance, she could see a tall figure walking at a rapid pace in her direction. Her long strides quickly ate the distance between them.

When Liz reached Lucy, she fell into step beside her. "I was looking all over for you! First, you were there dancing, and then you were gone! Is everything all right?"

"I'm sorry. I just needed to get away for a little while."

"Do you want to leave?" Liz asked. "We can."

"No, we can't. People have come a long way for us. Look how hard our friends worked to make our wedding day special. We can't just abandon them."

"Sure, we can. They expect us to escape and get down to business." Liz grinned.

"No, they don't. Everyone knows we've been living together for months."

"Did something upset you?" asked Liz, anxiously searching her face. "You looked like you were having a good time. When I last saw you, you were dancing up a storm."

Lucy glanced back at the noisy children playing in the surf. "I needed some time to think."

"Can't change your mind now, Lucy. We're married."

"Not about that!" said Lucy. She reached into her pocket for her phone and opened Roger's email. "Look at this."

Liz stopped to focus on the screen. She whistled softly through her teeth as she scrolled down. "Holy shit, Lucy. You can't do all this. It would kill you."

"It would kill any singer. I can't even do a fraction of it."

"Well, at least you know you're wanted." Liz returned Lucy's phone. "What will you do?"

Lucy heaved out an exasperated sigh. "I don't know! Part of me wants to do some of these engagements."

"So? Do them."

"But it's so much traveling. How can I do my job as rector?"

"Now that you're hiring Susan, she can help out. Tom will be here except in the winter. You have Reshma."

"But we're married, Liz. I don't want to leave you at home while I chase singing engagements."

"Then I'll go with you. Lucy, I love you with all my heart. I'll go anywhere to be with you."

Tears sprang to Lucy's eyes. She no longer cared about ruining her makeup, so she let them run down her cheeks. "Oh, Liz, I love you too, but what about your practice? You can't give it up now. You always say you haven't retired because of the shortage of doctors in Maine. People need you."

"But if you ask me to retire to follow you around the world, I will, because I love you."

"I love you too, Liz, but I would never ask you to quit being a doctor. It's who you are."

"Lucy, take it easy. We don't have to figure out everything today. Tomorrow, we'll sit down for dinner in a nice restaurant. We'll look at the list, and you can pick the events you most want to do. If I need to take time off, I will. We'll decide *together*. That's what married people do, isn't it?"

By now, they had reached Olivia's beach. The people who'd been outside were gone, but a crowd had gathered at the railing of Olivia's deck.

"We have an audience," Lucy said, nodding towards the house.

Liz turned around and looked up. "They probably think we're having a fight." Her mouth twitched into that crooked grin Lucy had come to both treasure and dread. "Let's give them something to talk about." Liz scooped Lucy up, lifting her off her feet. When she let her down, Lucy relaxed against the strong arms supporting her. She allowed Liz to kiss her deeply and intimately to the sound of cheers and clapping from above. Then Liz broke the kiss to say, "Ignore them."

When the warm mouth returned, Lucy had only one thought—how right it felt against hers.

Also by Elena Graf

Ebooks are available on Amazon Kindle and Kindle Unlimited. Paperbacks are available at major book retailers and from Bella Books.

THE HOBBS SERIES

HIGH OCTOBER

Liz Stolz and Maggie Fitzgerald were college roommates until Maggie confessed to her parents that she'd fallen in love with a woman. Maggie gave up her dream of becoming an actress and married her high school boyfriend. Liz became a famous breast surgeon. Maggie is performing in a summer stock production near the Maine town where Liz is now a general practitioner. When Maggie breaks her leg in a stage accident, she lands in Dr. Stolz's office. Is forty years too long to wait for the one you love?

THE MORE THE MERRIER

A HOBBS CHRISTMAS STORY

Maggie and Liz have been dreaming of a quiet Christmas since they got back together after being separated for forty years. This year they are determined to celebrate a romantic holiday alone. Their plans of sitting by the fire, drinking mulled wine and watching old Christmas movies get scuttled by surprise visits from friends and family. The Christmas chaos provides some holiday cheer and a touching lesson in the real meaning of Christmas.

THIS IS MY BODY

The new rector of St. Margaret's by the Sea Episcopal Church has a secret. Lucille Bartlett was a rising star at the Metropolitan Opera, but she disappeared from the stage, and no one knows why. Philosophy Professor Erika Bultmann is a confirmed agnostic who doesn't have much use for religion, but she is fascinated by Mother Lucy. When Erika returns to her summer cottage in Hobbs to finish her last book before she retires, Lucy is drawn to the enigmatic professor, but she wants much more than a casual affair. When Lucy's secret is revealed, she needs Erika's support more than ever. Can they put aside their differences and find common ground?

LOVE IN THE TIME OF CORONA

It's midwinter in Maine, and the biggest problem is a snowstorm. Only Liz Stolz, the senior doctor of Hobbs Family Practice, is paying attention to the strange virus in China that's roiling the financial markets. She tries to alert the town leaders to the potential danger, but police chief Brenda Harrison is distracted by Liz's new physician's assistant, Cherie Bois. The friends are pushed together during the lockdown. Friendships and relationships are strained as they act selflessly and selfishly out of love, faith, and duty. Can they find new strength and forge deeper connections through helping one another and the town survive?

THIRSTY THURSDAYS

Hobbs, Maine, is gradually reopening after the lockdown. Liz has begun a new tradition—Thirsty Thursdays, a weekly cocktail party on her deck, designed for her friends to socialize safely. An impulsive kiss shakes up friendships and relationships. Pretentious, overbearing Olivia is pursuing Sam and trying to find her way into the tight-knit group. Will the down-to-earth, independent women of Hobbs accept an outsider who's so different?

THE DARK WINTER

The residents of Hobbs are relieved to have gotten through the summer relatively unscathed. Liz agrees to help architect Sam McKinnon build a soundproof practice room for Erika Bultmann's wife, former opera singer Rev. Lucy Bartlett. Fortunately, the early Christmas gift is ready before tragedy strikes. In the process of keeping a promise to a friend, Liz causes stress in her marriage, which has been rocky since an impulsive kiss. As the women of Hobbs pull together to help a beloved friend deal with her loss, the dark winter brings tension and realignment in their small community.

SUMMER PEOPLE

After a dark winter of loss and isolation, the summer people are returning to Hobbs, including forty-something Melissa Morgenstern, a trust lawyer from Boston. Liz introduces her to the new assistant principal of the elementary school, Courtney Barnes. Courtney has a daughter and considers herself bisexual, which raises red flags for Melissa. Liz and Rev. Lucy Bartlett seem headed for a relationship when their courtship is interrupted by the arrival of Lucy's ex, the woman who inspired her to become a priest. Susan secretly wants to rekindle the relationship, but that's not the only secret she's keeping.

STRANDS

Lucy and Liz have finally announced their engagement. They get pushback from surprising places, even from friends they've counted on for support. Unresolved issues from Liz's first marriage cloud the prospect even more, especially when her ex-wife returns, desperately needing help. Across town, Police chief Brenda Harrison and her wife are settling into a new relationship, but Cherie hears her biological clock ticking. When a shocking tragedy creates an opportunity for them to become parents, all their friends need to step in to help. Couples rearrange in surprising ways, and the women of Hobbs find their lives intertwined like the strands of a rope.

THE PASSING RITES SERIES

THE IMPERATIVE OF DESIRE

A coming-of-age story that takes a young woman from La Belle Époque, through a world war, a revolution that outlawed the German nobility, the Roaring Twenties, to the decadent demimonde of Weimar Berlin. A quirk of inheritance law allows Margarethe von Stahle to inherit her family's titles. Margarethe reluctantly marries, but that doesn't prevent her from finding solace in the arms of women. She trains under the best surgeons in Germany and England and rises to prominence as London's infamous "Lady Doctor." Finally, duty requires her to return to her homeland and take the reins of the family fortunes.

OCCASIONS OF SIN

For seven centuries, the German convent of Obberoth has been hiding the nuns' secrets—forbidden passions, scandalous manuscripts locked away, a ruined medical career, perhaps even a murder. In 1931, aristocratic physician, Margarethe von Stahle, is determined to lift the veil of secrecy surrounding her head nurse, Sister Augustine, only to find herself embroiled in multiple conflicts that threaten to unravel her orderly life.

LIES OF OMISSION

In 1938, the Nazis are imposing their doctrine of "racial hygiene" on hospitals and universities, forcing professors to teach false science and doctors to collaborate in a program to eliminate the mentally ill and handicapped. Margarethe von Stahle is desperately trying to find a way to practice ethical medicine. She has always avoided politics, but now she must decide whether to remain on the sidelines or act on her convictions.

ACTS OF CONTRITION

World War II has finally come to an end and Berlin has fallen. Nearly everything Margarethe von Stahle has sworn to protect has been lost. After being brutally abused by occupying Russian soldiers, Margarethe must rely on the kindness of her friends to survive. Fortunately, the American Army has brought her former protégée, Sarah Weber, back to Berlin. As Margarethe confronts painful events that occurred during the war, she must learn both to forgive and be forgiven.

About the Author

In addition to the books in the Hobbs series, Elena Graf has published four historical novels set in Europe in the early 20th century. *Lies of Omission*, the third volume in the Passing Rites Series, won a Golden Crown Literary Society award for best historical fiction and a Rainbow Award. The fourth volume, *Acts of Contrition* also won a Goldie and a Rainbow Award.

The author pursued a Ph.D. in philosophy but ended up in the "accidental profession" of publishing, where she worked for almost four decades. She lives with her wife in coastal Maine.

If you liked this book and would like more stories about the people of Hobbs, Maine, write to Elena at elena.m.graf@gmail.com.

Elena Graf is a member of iReadIndies, a collective of self-published independent authors of Sapphic literature. Please visit our website at iReadIndies.com for more information and to find links to the books published by our authors.

9 781953 195166